Stolen

J M Johnson

This is a work of fiction. Names, characters, places, and incidents either are the product of the author's imagination or are used fictitiously. Any resemblance to actual persons, living or dead, events, or locales is entirely coincidental.

Copyright © 2024 by J. M. Johnson

All rights reserved. No part of this book may be reproduced or used in any manner without the written permission of the copyright owner except for the use of quotations in a book review. For more information, address:

jmjohnson.author@gmail.com

First paperback edition August2024

Book design created using Canva.

Custom page edges created by Painted Wings Publishing

J. M. Johnson

jmjohnson.author@gmail.com

ISBN: 9798326046369

Author's note

Please note! This is written in British English as opposed to American English. If you see a letter "u" in places you don't recognise, don't worry! It's meant to be there!

Without giving any spoilers: This book is part one of a trilogy and ends on a cliffhanger.

Before going into this book, I want to say this it is heavy with trigger warnings. If you would prefer to go into this blind- which is my preference when reading, then you can skip this and know that I've written characters that I would never condone in the real world, but that I love writing about and love reading about.

If you do want to be aware in advance of the trigger warnings, the list is extensive, but I'll do my best to cover most of them below:

Abuse, violence, physical harm, kidnap psychological torture, knife play, dubious consent, sexual harassment, guns, cheating, death, murder - you name it, this book has got it.

However, this is a work of fiction. I do not condone the actions of these characters; I do not support this. If this was real life, I'd be horrified. I wouldn't be lapping up the drama, I'd be ringing the police. But we've all got that hidden desire within us. The characters exist to provide entertainment, not a guideline on how to live life.

If this book isn't for you, if you don't like the trigger warnings, then that's okay. You can put it down now and read something else. Reading is always a choice.

Dedication

Becky
You might send your ghosts to haunt me, and quite frankly, I live in terror every single day at the thought of your nanan sat on my sofa casually waving at me. You might also try to manipulate me into doing spooky tarot cards and also spook me senseless with the thought of demons and mimics coming for me. You might also laugh like a lunatic every time you remember that psycho who tried running me over because he thought I was his neighbour. Silly bastard chasing me down the street with his car, making me hop on a wall to avoid being squashed alive, when all it was, was a mistaken identity crisis due to owning the same coat!

However, you are an angel, and I'll always be grateful for you and your friendship. I might be a pain in the ass sometimes, but at least I brought the joy of Turkey teeth into your life!

P.S. sorry I haven't watched any of the movies on your stupid list. I'll start it tomorrow, I promise.

Maybe.

Also, thank you to Gabriella. You never knew, but the day you messaged me, I was ready to quit. I was overwhelmed, stressed, and fed up. You allowed me to read through your eyes, and were so enthusiastic and lovely, and just so amazing with your feedback and review. Thank you.

Not dedicated to you, Claire. You can fuck off.

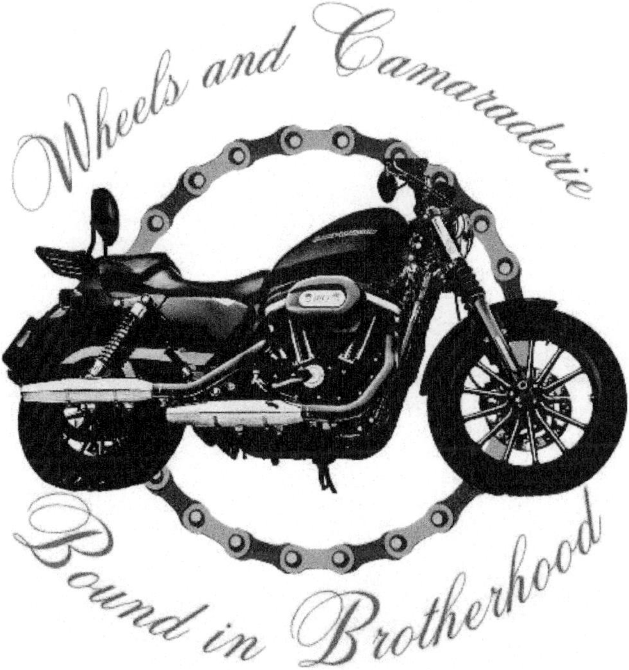
Wheels and Camaraderie
Bound in Brotherhood

Prologue

Rachel

Dante had changed my life. The day we met in that God awful diner, I never could have predicted what was about to happen to me.

In a matter of weeks, he had become the very air I breathed, and I was about ready to cut off my oxygen supply.

As I stood in my bathroom, looking at my bust lip, the blood colouring my teeth as I ran my tongue over them, checking for cracks, one might think I was full of regret at the choices I had made.

My body was bruised, but my mind was even worse.

The life of an old lady wasn't for everyone, and it wasn't something I had made by choice.

I was thrust into this role, and as God is my witness, I fulfilled it more than anyone before me.

It's not the life for the weak, the criers, or those that needed guiding through it with a gentle hand.

Only the strongest survived, and Dante had taken me to the edge of the cliff, and only my strength had stopped me from tumbling into the abyss.

I could feel his cum leaking out of me, evidence of our latest argument. If I closed my eyes, I could still feel the chilling cool of the gun pressed against my temples as he fucked me harder, daring me to open my smart mouth one more time. Warning me without saying a word.

Anyone else might have stayed silent whilst playing Russian roulette with their lives.

But not me.

I loved it.

I met the challenge in his gaze with one of my own. I toyed with him. I angered him. I thrilled him like no one else could.

I told him he wasn't shit. I told him his dick game was weak. I told him he couldn't get a puppy to submit, never mind a full-blooded woman. I let him know in no uncertain terms that he was out of his depth with me. He had more chance of finally finding my clit than he did of getting me to bow down and accept my role as "old lady" with a gracious smile.

I looked him straight in the eye and let him know that his ego had got the better of him, and this time he had bitten off more than he could chew.

That's when he bit my lip until it bled. And then he fucked me harder when he didn't get the whimper of pain he was looking for. His hands came round my throat, choking away anything else I could have said.

If he couldn't silence me with sex, he'd silence me with violence.

That was Dante's way. He was a walking contradiction. He wanted me to submit to him, but was angry when I did.

He wanted me to be silent and dutiful, and yet his dick was never harder than when I was hurling insults at him and fighting back. The day I first slapped him, he fucked me for hours, getting off on having me beneath him begging him for more, screaming his name, finally giving him the response he wanted as he inflicted pain and pleasure on any part of my body he could reach.

Maybe you'd be concerned at how often violence appears in our sex life, and maybe you have a right to be. But what two consenting adults choose to do is no one else's business.

I had no regrets.

I didn't choose this life, but this life damn sure chose me, and sooner or later, we all must accept our roles on this earth. We can't all be Stepford wife material – missionary three times a week, making sure the lights are off and not so much as a toe escapes the confines of the bedcovers. Barely working up a sweat as our bodies slap against each other.

"Did you cum, darling?"

"Doesn't matter to me, sweetness, so long as you're happy."

Couldn't be me, wouldn't be me.

Some of us needed the thrill of danger. The sweet release as we toed the line between sex and murder. To be fucked as though we were hated.

And make no mistake about it. I was hated.

Loathed.

In fact, I think he may have hated me more than I hated him, and that was really saying something.

I could make an endless list of the things he hated.

He hated that he wanted me. He hated that he couldn't get enough of me. He hated that he couldn't stay away from me, that I consumed every waking thought and every sleepless dream. He hated that he sought me out, craving my company. And the more his body craved me, the more he hated me. It was a vicious circle, and my very being was slap bang in the middle of it, the root of all the problems.

I can accept my portion of the blame. When he first saw me, he thought he was getting the Stepford wife. The one who would cook, clean, and silently raise his children. The one who would suck his dick in silence whilst he washed the blood off his hands. Never questioning, always accepting, and supporting.

Well, jokes on him.

He might be the vice president of this club, but that didn't come with a side of intelligence.

Dante should have known better than to assume appearances were all that mattered. He had met his match with me, and it would be a cold day in hell before I let him get the better of me in any way other than sex. And that's what truly bothered him. He could get my body to submit by pressing the right buttons, but when the deed was done, and the reality crept back in, I was back to being the stubborn, hardheaded, spiteful woman he had come to hate.

Maybe he had thought that when he took me – fuck it, let's call a spade a spade, he kidnapped me more like – that he could model me into his perfect woman. If that didn't work, he'd cast me aside and move on to the next one.

Fat chance of that happening, and we both know it. We just won't admit it out loud.

The dirty little secret, the reason Dante hates me the *most*, is that there will be no other woman after me. Whether we like it or not, both of us know deep down that we are perfect for each other. A match made in hell. Two fucked up souls completing the other.

I've left my mark on him. I know I'm in there, under his skin, the itch that can't be itched. The plaguing scratch that reminds him he can't get rid of me, can't forget me, can't stop thinking about me. I know I'm on his mind. No matter where he is, or who he's with, I'm there, tormenting him.

Consuming him.

And I'll make it my mission to be a cunt, every step of the way.

Was this healthy? Absolutely fucking not. But I can assure you, when you've got a man, built of nothing but solid muscle, heads and shoulders taller than you, screwing your brains out, both of you almost fighting more than fucking… there's nothing quite like it.

This man could kill me six ways to Sunday, with minimal effort. I feel the power in his body every time he picks me up and slams my back against the wall. His huge arms remind me he could snap me in two without breaking a sweat. And yet he uses that powerful body to slam into mine, fucking me until it hurts, keeping me begging for more.

Yet despite how much I beg, he's the one under my control, bound by his desire for me. My pussy owns him, and it's what brings him back for more.

I know some people might be looking at me right now and thinking I was a mess. That I was full of regrets that my own life choices were responsible for the position I was currently in. They'd be thanking God it was me and not them.

Those people were not me.

I looked in the mirror, seeing the blood once more, and I grinned.

I regretted nothing.

And this? This was only the beginning.

Chapter 1

Rachel

One, then two, then three. Three, then one, then two.

The counting of the trees was the only thing keeping me sane. I noticed they came alone, or sometimes in clusters, the thick branches fighting to get their leaves to the top, eager for the sunlight.

The trees made me feel calmer. Despite the passage of time, they were a constant, remaining the same, reminding me that we were insignificant. The trees would outlive everything. Any problem I had, no matter how immediate and pressing it seemed, the trees in their age-old wisdom had seen it all before, and those problems had passed, just like I would. Time would erase the memory of me and all that I had done.

Time was a healer of all wounds. And time would bring the gift of forgiveness and forgetfulness. The trees proved this to me, and it remained a fact, no matter what else seemed to be going off around me. The trees would outlive it, and all problems would pass.

Some people had an issue with their own impending death. They didn't want to face their morality.

But not me.

I welcomed the day I would leave this world behind, and in turn, leave behind all the problems I had caused.

Time would erase that, as surely as it would erase me. I couldn't for the life of me find a problem with that. The sooner that happened, the better.

There were a select few members of this world affected by my actions, and those too would soon be a distant memory. The trees were looking down on us, watching the soap opera that was our lives, but they would soon have a new generation to entertain them, to draw them into a new set of problems and dramas. They stood the test of time.

Stolen

I took great comfort in the fact that thousands, millions even, had passed before me, looking at the same clusters of trees. From people speeding past in their cars, to the horses and carriages, the penny farthings and those on foot. So I stared, and I counted, and I reminded myself that this was a problem that plagued me right now, but I would get past it. I would be back in my safe haven soon, and, just like the trees, I'll move on.

One, then two, then two, then five. Then three, then two...

I had only been back in England a handful of times since it happened. There was nothing for me here, but it kept drawing me back. I'd only ever bumped into *them* the once. But it was enough to spook me into not returning. At least until now.

The odds were in my favour, but that hadn't stopped me from living in perpetual sweat and anxiety since the moment the plane touched down.

Still... I would feel better once I had American soil back under my feet. I could feed myself all the soundbites in the world about being safe, but nothing was safer than distance.

And I'd be back on American soil just as soon as Mrs "Call me Elizabeth" Geller ordered her food. She was taking her sweet ass time, as usual, and with every passing minute, the trees became less comforting and more sinister.

Mocking.

Reminding me that they had seen it all, and in their wisdom, they could predict the outcome.

I couldn't stop the uneasy feeling from creeping over me, causing me to shiver and hunch my shoulders.

This time felt different. There was something in the air. A chilling forewarning that could not be denied, nor ignored.

Mrs Geller's voice filtered through my thoughts, her nasal twinge penetrating through the cloud of anxiety as she whinged at the waitress. I cringed, feeling my face flame as she drew unnecessary attention to our party of four.

Another fact of life was that people talked. You could hold water easier than people could hold their tongues. And what I did was juicier than any steak on the menu. One person ate it up, and fed that gossip to another, regurgitating it like a mother bird would to feed her chicks, and before you knew it, the world, its brother, and its great uncle Frank knew about it.

I was a sitting duck, waiting to be noticed. Waiting to be exposed. They would know I was here, and they would come looking for me.

But all Mrs Geller cared about was that her fork was polished to perfection, and she had precisely three cubes of ice in her water – let's not even mention the bitch fit over it being *tap* water. You'd think a summer trip around Europe would have opened her eyes to the fact that not everyone in the world uses bottles. But no, here we were, listening to her scream at an undeserved waitress, whilst I waited for the inevitable pang of recognition to flicker in the surrounding people's eyes.

My entire family had been on the news. They all knew who took the blame, but everyone also knew who really deserved to be punished.

Me.

It was bad enough to do what I did. It was even worse to remain unpunished.

Time might heal everything, but vengeance was time's biggest enemy. Vengeance did not like to forget. It did not like to forgive, and vengeance certainly had not forgiven nor forgotten me.

I should never have come. It was stupid. But it was my job. It was this, or hit the streets, reputation in tatters.

I played with my blonde hair, reminding myself that I wasn't the same girl. Gone was the hair as dark as a raven's wing. In its place were perfectly styled, perfectly cut, perfectly coloured blonde waves. The heavy gothic makeup had been replaced with a natural look, applied with an expert hand. All thanks to a training course Mrs Geller had insisted I enrol in. I represented them, and image was *everything.*

I had been with the Geller's last year, on the exact same holiday, and everything had been fine. There was absolutely no reason why this year should be any different. But something was screaming at me to get out. To escape. To free myself before they found me.

But there was another part of me, a dark, evil, disturbing side that screamed at me to stay. To relish in seeing the pain on their face when they cast their eyes upon me, knowing I was the one that was responsible for extinguishing the flame in someone else's eyes.

I could never quite tell which side of me I agreed with.

I scanned Mrs Geller as she stood with a huff, following the waitress to the bar so she could inspect the food as it came out of the kitchen. That woman needed a reality check. We were in a greasy spoon cafe at a shitty service station on the way to the airport. Aptly named; Greasy Spoon. Gordon Ramsay wasn't about to pop out and suddenly give this place a much-needed makeover and provide her with Michelin star level food. She knew what to expect, and she still complained.

"Rachel!" Joseph cried from my left. "You're not even listening!"

I slapped a quick smile as Mr James "I'd love to fuck you, but I'm too much of a bitch" Geller looked our way. I could hear his thoughts clear as day: *Keep him busy, Rachel. Keep him from bothering us. Don't allow him to talk to us, Rachel. We're very busy and important people, you know. We haven't got time for his endless questions and demands.*

They were such sacks of shits. As far as I was concerned, they could eat a bag of dicks. But despite myself, I had grown fond of Joseph. He deserved better than parents like these. Parents who had only had him so they could brag about getting him into the *right* schools, with the *right* people.

Who knew children were such status symbols? But they were in this world. Joseph opened up a whole new door to them. He had the best of everything. You bought your crib from IKEA? Joseph had his custom made by a team of top designers. Your child had a dummy – or pacifier, as they would say. Joseph had a custom made one dipped in a sacred river. Your clothes were from Gucci? Joseph's were handwoven by dying, blind nuns, whose last wish was to create bespoke, custom, one-of-a-kind pieces for the special little guy.

Okay, not really, but you see my point. Joseph was the ultimate possession. The list of brags never ended. He was walking by nine months. His first words were "stock market". He was potty trained by seven months.

It was such bullshit.

I happened to know his first word was "no", and he still sometimes had nighttime accidents. There was nothing to be ashamed of – if you were a regular parent. The Gellers were not regular parents.

"Sorry, little man! I was miles away! You know this is my home city, right?" He nodded his response. "Lots of memories here. I got lost in them. But I wasn't ignoring you. What were you saying?"

Joseph rambled on about some nonsense or other, and I played my part well. I smiled when he smiled and enthusiastically nodded my head. If he looked shocked, I gasped. If he frowned, I frowned with him. I could be nailed to the cross, only able to save myself by repeating this conversation, and I still wouldn't be able to recall a single word. But that was the beauty of children. They were easily pleased, especially one like Joseph, who thrived on attention, yet was born to parents who didn't even know his favourite colour.

I saw the irony in my words. I was guilty of doing the exact same thing to him. But I couldn't help it. My mind was elsewhere.

Maybe I was tired.

Maybe that's the reason I was on the bridge of a panic attack.

We had spent the summer travelling around Europe, the same as the Gellers did every year. The same as I had last year. And, once again, England was our last stop before returning to America. Back to home. Back to my job. Back to where it was safe.

Where *they* couldn't find me.

You're not returning to America!

I shook my head, forcing out the mocking tone that I could have sworn came from the trees. But, regardless of where it came from, it was back. The nagging feeling that something was wrong.

I had been with the Gellers for three years now, working as an au pair as they went about their business. They basically left me to raise their son, only hauling him out when needed to play their part as the hard-working parents. I didn't mind the work, and Lord knew it kept me busy, kept me away from those I should never have entertained going near. I still missed home, though. No matter how many hours I worked, as I climbed into bed at night, thoughts of home always came to me.

I lived and breathed for England. I wanted so desperately to be able to return here, to finally be able to call this place my home again.

It was a fool's wish. There were people rotting in jail cells because of me, and another cold in the ground, as a direct consequence of my actions. I could never stay here. Too many people had been hurt, including myself. Too many people with a grudge to grind. Not that I cared much who was rotting in the ground. As far as I was concerned, he deserved it and so much more. Fuck him and fuck his entire family. I'd do it again in a heartbeat, and I'd do it with the same smile on my face.

The only thing that kept me going, that convinced me my life was worth living and to not keep fucking it up, was the other people. People I *did* care for. They were the ones that made me stop wishing for time to erase me, and to keep going, because they had made sacrifices for me. They had given their life away to a jail cell so that I could be free. I owed it to them to keep on going, to make something of myself, or else it all would have been for nothing.

Mrs Geller returned to the table with a sneer on her face. She slapped the plates of food down, grumbling about how she had been forced to bring it over herself. I accepted mine with a grateful smile and did my best to placate her before she embarrassed us any further.

"Thank you, Mrs Geller. It really does look lovely."

"Elizabeth, please! I've told you a million times! We'll drill it into you eventually, won't we, James?"

His eyes flicked over my face. "I'm sure she'll be a willing pupil when she's ready."

I bet you'd like to do some drilling with me – willing pupil indeed! Vile fucking maggot.

"Maybe one day," I said politely, turning to Joseph so I could help him cut his meat and make sure he wasn't sprinkling too much salt on his food. It was his new obsession. He had recently learned about seasoning, and as far as he was concerned, the more the better. We made toast before we started our holiday, and one bite in, my mouth puckered like a baboon's asshole, and all the water left my body.

Our plane was due to depart this evening, and though we could have easily eaten in the airport, Joseph had begged to stop off earlier, saying he desperately needed the toilet, that he would die if he didn't go immediately. I think he was just reluctant for the holiday to end. This was the only time he spent with his parents all year. I knew he loved me, but he was desperate for their attention, whereas I gave it willingly.

Mrs Geller had given into his demands and told her husband to stop at the nearest facilities – not because she cared about her son, more the fact that she wanted him to stop talking. And since we were already here, didn't it make sense to eat here rather than at the airport?

I knew logically it made sense.

It did. Of course it did. But it also meant I was stuck here that little longer. At the airport, I would have felt the same as Joseph. He would have been sad to see the end, but I would have been elated. The airport signifies the holiday is over. It makes it all feel that bit more final. I would have been getting the fuck out of here. Leeds Airport was safe, but it was also far too close to my hometown. Where people knew me.

I was a sitting target, waiting to be found, and I knew it.

One, then two, then two, then three. Look at the trees, Rachel. Time will erase all of this. The memory fades further and further every day. You only have a few more hours to go.

I knew better than most that the entire world could change in a few hours. A few hours were all it took to completely alter the course of my life and the lives of all those around me.

I vaguely heard the ding of a bell as someone entered the cafe, but I focused on Joseph and the trees. The person didn't immediately shout my name and start kicking ten bells of shit out of me, so they didn't know me. I didn't care who else it was. I remained with the trees. I would be out of here soon. I had to believe that.

I had to.

Dante

Every fucking day, something new to worry about.

The Rough Riders were giving us nothing but shit, trying to patch in an old member of ours, and then pissing about on the edge of our borders, peddling their fucking shite. They were determined to turn our streets into herds of zombies that could barely remember their name as they were that doped up.

Stolen

Sometimes a man just wants to chill out, you know? But the minute I kicked my boots off, and cracked open a cold one, my Mam decides she needs me to collect payment from the shops, and my daughter needs help with her homework.

Easy decision. The boots came right back on, and I went to collect payments. No fucking thank you to homework.

I'm too old to be learning that nonsense. When I went to school, we learned ABC. It was simple. Now, it's "ah", "beh", "keh," only to then relearn the capitals at a later date "when they were old enough". It's confusing. I taught Bee ABC; we had it mastered. I was actually pretty fucking proud of the two of us. Only for that idiot of a teacher to tell me it was wrong, and Bee had until the end of term to catch up with the class and learn the alphabet. She knew the fucking alphabet! I refuse to argue with that woman one more time. They want to teach her the soft letters, they can damn well do it themselves.

Which is why I was now pulling into the Greasy Spoon, my bike roaring beneath me, letting everyone inside know exactly who had arrived.

The Greasy Spoon had been on our books for a few years now. It was only a ride away from our community, and pretty much every member of the club stopped by here more than a few times a week. When they started asking questions about the scary guys in leather, we knew it was time to step in and explain who we were before they heard it from anyone else.

Fast forward to a few years later, and they were now paying us for protection, and go out of their way to make us feel welcome. It's become a sort of mini club house for us, and we stayed loyal to them. We never sold on their property, we kept to ourselves, and only ended trouble that someone else started. The Greasy Spoon was located at a service station on the way to the airport, and they had a lot of issues with drunk holiday makers stopping off here before getting on their flight.

But as with anything in this world, our loyalty came at a price, and they knew they'd be fools if they crossed us and saw how quickly we can turn on them.

I pulled into the zone reserved specifically for the Devil's Disciples, and my eyebrows raised at the fancy car parked out front.

"Afternoon, Dante," the co-owner, Beth, grinned at me. "Is it that time of the month already?" She breathed, leaning against the bar so her tits pushed upwards.

"Comes around quick, don't it? Who's the car belong to?" I asked, gesturing behind me with my thumb.

"Don't ask," she said with a roll of her eyes. She leaned further forward and lowered her voice. "What's it to be this time? Payment as usual?"

"We'll see," I said back, probably curter than needed. I had been fucking Beth on a semi-regular basis in lieu of payment. Not because I particularly wanted to. She wasn't much to look at. It was mainly because I could. It wasn't as though we needed the money, either. The Devil's Disciples had their hands in many different businesses, and we were booming at the minute. Beth just happened to be a willing partner. She never said no, and it was a quick-fix stress relief when I couldn't be bothered working for it and going anywhere more challenging.

"I'd make it worth your while," she replied, running her hand down my arm. I pulled away before I even realised what I was doing, and the smile fell from her lips. "Can I fix you anything to eat?"

"Just a coffee and make it quick. I've got..." my voice trailed off as I spotted her.

She was staring out of the window, her long blonde hair pulled over one of her shoulders. Her chin was resting on her clenched fist, her elbow on the table, and she had a haunted look on her face. Every couple of seconds, she would remember and straighten her features. But it would creep back in moments later. The young boy at her side got her attention, and she smiled at him, making him laugh as she screwed her nose up at whatever he said. Then her eyes drifted back to the trees on the other side of the road.

"They're the ones with the car," Beth said in a low voice as she slid the coffee over to me. "Fucking nightmares."

"Posh wankers?" I responded, bringing the cup to my lips.

Beth scoffed and rolled her eyes. "Posh isn't the word for it. Americans. Absolute pricks."

"Say no more."

I raked over the blonde again. She didn't look like an asshole. She seemed quite sweet as she sat there in her smart grey dress resting modestly against her knees. It fitted her perfectly; the arms cutting off at her elbow; the neckline showing the faintest hint of skin. I could see from a mile away that her tits looked phenomenal in it, even though she was doing her best to hide them. I caught the way the man opposite her looked at her. Now *he* looked like a prick in his fancy, expensive suit, his eyes lingering on her, almost devouring her. Every time he took a bite of his burger, his gaze darted to her chest.

She didn't notice, though. She didn't seem to notice much of anything but the boy next to her.

Son? Nephew? I was going to find out.

She gave him a small smile once more, and I was drawn to the soft, gentle air that hung around her. She screamed of innocent and sweetness. Almost motherly. She had a kind and gentle way of soothing the boy's excitement without even trying, her patience infinite as he pulled on the sleeve of her dress to get her attention.

I heard the boy say "sorry, Dad," as the man shot him a firm look. He let go of the girl's sleeves and cast his eyes down towards the table. She looked at him and discreetly nudged him with her elbow until he smiled. It was then I knew. She wasn't his mother, because it was damn obvious she had never fucked the older guy. No-one looked at a woman with that much longing and want if they had tasted her previously. Especially as he kept trying to hide it from her. It was unrequited. But despite the boy not being hers, she still had a maternal instinct towards him. The need to protect children even if they weren't hers. It was exactly what I had been looking for. Now *that* would be a woman who knew the difference between abc and ABC.

Sometimes you can tell a lot about a person just by looking at them – especially when they don't realise anyone is watching them. The fact that the little boy seemed at ease with her, but cringed whenever his dad looked at him, told me everything I needed to know.

"They been here long?" I said to Beth, leaning over the bar to bring my upper body closer to hers.

"Too long for my liking. They appeared, demanded food pronto, and then haven't stopped complaining since."

I grinned at her. "I think we might be too rough for their liking."

"The fucking Ritz would be too rough for her liking," she snapped, bobbing her head towards the older of the two women. "Only wants bottled water, only wants Royal Doulton plates. Do I look like the type of woman with Royal Doulton plates?"

"I hope you gave her one of the cracked ones," I laughed back.

"I'd like to give her a crack. I'd pull out the stick she's got stuck up her own crack."

"Charming."

"You haven't dealt with them, Dante," she sighed in exasperation. "She's a real piece of work."

"Did you tell them we don't take too kindly to strangers around here?"

"I doubt she'd listen to be fair. She couldn't get back to her little family fast enough. They're all uptight fuckers."

"Case in point," I said, my lips twisting as I noticed the older woman pull out a bottle of hand sanitiser and thoroughly douse her hands before she even contemplated picking up her fork.

"They reek of money, too."

"Yeah, the car sort of gave that away."

"Apart from that one," Beth nodded at the blonde. "The younger one. She hasn't had much to say for herself at all. She's practically been kissing that window, she's been staring out of it so much. She only moves when the young lad talks to her, otherwise she's like a little haunted doll."

"They her parents?"

"Employers, apparently," she replied with a shrug. "One of those fancy nannies is my guess. Money always buys nannies. Pretty blonde ones for the daddies."

"She'd do for me if my wife brought her home," I laughed as Beth slapped at my arm.

"I'm sure they'll be off soon. I heard the boy ask when they were going on the plane. No doubt off to Leeds airport going home."

That got my attention. She wouldn't be going to the airport, that much was certain.

"They say when?"

"Nope. Didn't ask, don't care."

"Waiter," the older woman hissed, clicking her fingers in the air.

"You see what I mean? I'll rip those fingers straight off her fucking hand—" I grabbed her arm as she went to push past me.

"I'll deal with it, Beth. It's fine." I pushed myself off the bar before she could argue and made my way over to them. Not one of them had the decency to even look up at my arrival, and that irked me. Money didn't buy manners, apparently.

But that wasn't the way we did things here. We were a friendly bunch, so long as you were friendly back. We didn't take kindly to strangers, that much was true. Although, that was simply because they came in here, saw the biker décor, and immediately judged us based on some idiotic TV programme they had seen. They automatically decide we're less than them because we chose a different lifestyle.

"Everything okay, folks? Beth tells me there's been a problem or two." I smiled at the older couple, my hand resting casually on the table. Then my eyes went back to her.

She looked my way for all of a split second, her eyes quickly raking me up and down, before she turned away, disinterested.

I'm not an egotistical man, but I also don't like being dismissed with such ease. My fingers drummed on the table, but that was the only sign I gave that I was growing annoyed.

She definitely wasn't going to any fucking airport, I thought to myself, stifling a growl.

"Yeah, listen, if you could just bring the bill. We're not looking for small town diner chit-chat, thanks." The man waved me off, a protective look coming over his face as he noticed me looking at her.

"What was that?" I said pleasantly enough, but already planning on which window I was going to smash his head through.

"Bill. This isn't Gilmore Girls. We're on the clock here, pal." He even had the audacity to click his fucking fingers at me.

If I hadn't been decided before, I certainly fucking was now. I could tell by the way he was looking at her that he wanted to fuck her – but he hadn't. And now he never would. Even if I had no plans to have her myself, I'd take her just for the satisfaction of him knowing I had her and he didn't.

"I'll get right on that for you, *pal*," I said with gritted teeth and pushed off the table.

"See what I mean?" Beth asked with a smirk as I made my way back to her.

"Watch them," I hissed as I stormed around the counter and into the kitchen, pulling out my phone.

"Everything okay?" My dad answered on the first ring. "Anyone causing a fuss?"

"Nothing I can't handle. That's not why I'm calling. I want you to tell mum to make up the guest room. I'm bringing someone home."

That family would soon learn that I'm not fucking staff. I own the place, and soon enough I'll own her too.

Chapter 2

Rachel

"Are you ready, Rachel? You've barely touched any of your burger," Mr Geller said, pulling my attention away from the trees. I was clinging to them, hoping for a wisdom they would never whisper to me. I thought the dinging of the bell earlier had meant I was safe, that they didn't know who I was. But ever since then, there was a sinister atmosphere in the air, almost choking me with how thick it was. And that sinister presence only wanted me. I had felt eyes on me ever since.

It was intense. Uncomfortable even.

"Rachel?" Mr Geller pressed me, and I forced myself to get it together.

"What? Oh, don't worry about me. I'm not hungry."

"It's a long flight, and you know how vile aeroplane food is. Are you sure you're okay?"

"Absolutely." I beamed a huge smile at him. "I was just lost in thought. You know I'm a nervous flyer," I reminded him. I had used this excuse every time we had boarded a plane, so that I didn't have to sit next to him. I sat next to Joseph, who took the window seat, and Mr and Mrs Geller took their seats in the row in front of us. He had tried to convince me that a boy needed his mother during the flights, and I should sit next to him to keep him company. I had almost laughed out loud. Mrs Geller had looked horrified at the mere thought of having to sit next to her child, of the prospect of keeping him occupied for so many hours. "Besides," I added. "It looks as though the main man has had his fill. So long as he's nice and full up, I'm good to go," I grinned at Joseph, making him laugh as I bopped him on the nose with a wipe whilst cleaning the sauce off his face.

"He's still not brought the bill, James," Mrs Geller reminded him as he hurried to gather up all our belongings.

"The man looked as though he couldn't string two sentences together, never mind the basic math needed to calculate a bill.

He's probably jamming his fingers into the calculator as we speak and grunting in frustration." He winked at me, as though we were in on this cruel joke together. I didn't smile back. I had seen the man in question, and I wasn't about to fuck around and get on his bad side. James would do well to remember he wasn't at home right now, and though he might prance around as lord of the manor in America, he wasn't the lord here in someone else's establishment. Especially not when that someone was well over 6ft, built like a God and riddled with tattoos.

Not that I had been looking. He was just hard to fucking miss.

You were looking, that annoying inner voice whispered at me. I ignored it, just like I had ignored the man's piercing gaze. He was trouble, and I didn't need any more trouble in my life.

"Oh, get it together, Liz!" James hissed as she wrung her hands in worry. "Chuck some money on the table and have done with it. What are they going to do? Chase us down the freeway?"

"Motorway," I corrected before I could stop myself. James' lips tightened, and fury flashed in his eyes. "Motorway. Thank you. Get him sorted," he jerked his head at his son. "Meet me in the car." He got up and left, letting us know in no uncertain terms that he was done with the conversation. As far as he was concerned, his word was law, and we should follow if we knew what was good for us.

Mrs Geller huffed and shot me a dirty look, blaming me for her husband's temper. But she did as she was told, hurrying to pack up the rest of our stuff and clicked her fingers at me and Joseph to usher us out from the booth.

I fucking hated it when she clicked her fingers at me as though I was a dog, but I had long since learnt to put my pride aside and obey. I wouldn't be with this family forever; they were just my safety net right now. I couldn't afford to piss them off and leave before I was ready.

Mr Geller blasted the horn, causing Mrs Geller to jump and click her fingers even faster. "Come, come," she snapped, grabbing Joseph's arm, and pulling him around to her. "Thanks to someone," she said pointedly. "Your father is in a terrible mood. So, best behaviour. We wouldn't want to anger him any further. Understood?" I rolled my eyes. She couldn't have made that any more obvious if she tried. Joseph nodded his head, and when she looked my way, I did the same, forcing myself to have an apologetic expression on my face. There was no point arguing.

James was like this all the time. He hated to be questioned, and he hated to be corrected even more. Especially in front of his wife. He had a powerful position in his workplace, and he thought that power extended everywhere else as well. He was the boss at home; he was the boss of his family, and since his family was here, the location didn't matter. He was simply the boss. He ruled as far as he was concerned. It was ridiculous, really, as I had never seen a man look less powerful. His money bought fear, and fear bought power. He was as manipulative as he was cunning, and the working world back in America knew this. They knew not to cross him, because James had *connections.* Connections only money could buy. He used his means to get what he wanted, and that, in turn made him a very powerful man.

But he wasn't a powerful *looking* man. And sometimes he seemed to forget that not everybody played by the rules of the business world.

The server, on the other hand – *he* had looked like a powerful man. I didn't usually turn around to address people who approached the family. It wasn't my place. I was the au pair, not the main party. My job was to blend into the background and keep Joseph in line. The two of us were invisible. But something about that man had shifted the air around me, and I could no more keep myself from looking at him than the sun could keep itself from rising. One look was all I needed. He was a powerful man, and he didn't need to flash the cash or rely on his associates to prove it.

James was laughable in comparison.

The man was fucking huge. It was actually overwhelming how huge he was. He seemed to take up every inch of space, sucking all the oxygen out of the air. He made the room close in, until it was just us, boxed into this tiny corner. It shocked me to realise that it wasn't an entirely unpleasant feeling.

His arms were the size of my legs, and huge arms were always my downfall. My porn history was filled with me searching for men with arms that could snap me in half.

Concerning? Maybe.

I was more concerned about my porn fantasy coming to life. I could see through his jacket that he was built like a house. He had the smallest hint of a beard coming through, a scar above his eyebrow, tattoos on his fingers, and the air around him screamed wild sex and a shitload of trouble.

I hadn't allowed myself anything more than the briefest of glances. I knew straight away that the more I looked, the more I was going to be drawn to him.

But my God. Play dangerous games, win dangerous prizes, and I wanted a piece of that prize. You can't throw a man like that in front of a sex starved woman – whose only other option was James fucking Geller – and expect her not to have some sort of reaction. The rebellious teenager in me reared her ugly head and reminded me I had once chased after men like that as though I was a bitch in heat.

"Wait!" the woman, who I assumed was the owner, shouted over to us as we headed towards the door. "Where are you going?"

"We're done," Elizabeth sniffed, her nose in the air. "Is this a prison, or are we free to leave at will? Money is on the table. And you, young lady," she said, pointing her finger at the poor woman. "Should be grateful we come from a place where tipping is customary. Lord knows you haven't earned it. Come, Joseph. Let's get in the car." She ushered her son outside, and that was my cue to follow. She tried not to address me when we were near strangers. It wouldn't do to converse with the *staff*, heaven forbid.

"But if you could just wait a moment. Dante – the man who came to your table – he wants... well, he's only in the back. He'll be a few more minutes if you could just—"

"Whatever he wants, we won't be interested." I bit my cheek to stop myself from scoffing. Now that James had left, Elizabeth was in charge, and she was going to let this woman know that one way or another. She had already decided she was better than her, and she was going to put her in her place. She would never have dared speak to a man like that, and she was only throwing her weight around because she was embarrassed at the way her husband had spoken to her – something she knew this woman had overheard. Pride made Elizabeth particularly vicious. Had the man actually come back out, she would have been cowering at his feet. She knew it, I knew it, and the woman probably had a pretty good idea of it too. It's why she wanted us out of here as quick as possible. Elizabeth was a bully, and she was picking on someone she thought was beneath her. She sensed weakness in the poor lady behind the bar, and she had no problem exploiting it.

She had yet to sense the same weakness in me, which is why her bullying never worked on me. It was also why she always, always reminded me that I was beneath her in *rank*. I was a mere employee; she was the boss.

I felt her grab hold of me and haul me out of the diner, cutting off any further thoughts.

Café, I corrected myself. I was getting as bad as James for making everything Americanised. Although, café didn't feel quite right for a place like this. When I thought café, I thought tea and scones. This place was definitely not tea and scones! It was a truck-stop through and through, and would more likely serve afternoon AA meetings rather than afternoon tea.

"Awful place," she said, brushing off imaginary crumbs from her clothes.

"I liked it!" Joseph piped up.

"You would," she said, wrinkling her nose. "You think McDonald's is the height of luxury."

"Mrs Geller…" I began, seeing Joseph's face fall. "He's just a child." I whispered to her.

"So?" she replied, looking at me as though I were mad. "He's old enough to know decent food." A roar of motorbikes cut off any further conversation as Joseph let out a squeal of excitement, his sadness forgotten.

"Did you hear that?" He breathed, tugging on my hand as his eyes grew wide. "Can't we stay for a few more moments? They sound like they're coming this way!"

"In the car, Joseph," Elizabeth said, opening her side of the door.

"Please, Rachel! I want to see the bikes!"

I looked down at him, and then at Mrs Geller, who was drumming her fingers on the top of the car door.

"Maybe next year," I told him.

"Why wait a year when they're here now? Please let me see the bikes, Rachel, please!" He tried to dig his heels into the ground as I gently pushed him towards the car.

"When you're old enough, I'll buy you your own bike," James shouted from the window, his anger long since forgotten since he was getting his own way. He shot me another wink – that was two today – as though we were both the best of buddies, always joking and laughing. I made a mental note to be curter and more formal with him going forward. That shit needed to be shut down.

I couldn't give a flying fuck if he bought Joseph a bike. The only reason he winked was because bikes were beneath someone of his calibre. They were driven around in fancy cars, not flying down the freeway like hooligans. Bikes were uncouth. Not at all suitable for the Princeton life Joseph was destined for.

"Come on, buddy," I gave him a firmer push. "I'll find a story about a young biker boy on my phone, and we'll read it together on the drive. How does that sound?" I extended my hand to him.

"What if you can't find one?" He eyed me suspiciously, but he stopped his fighting.

"Well, in that case, I'll make one up. In fact, I think the biker boy might just be called Joseph, and he might just be the biggest, baddest biker in town. He wins all the competitions, *and* he gets to eat at all the McDonalds for free, since he's just that much of a superstar celebrity racer."

"I want to hear that story!" He squealed, jumping into the car. I climbed in behind him, closing the door with a soft slam, and shook my head at Joseph as he looked up at me with huge, expectant eyes. "You want to start now?" I laughed, and he nodded his head frantically.

He threw his arms around me and hugged me tight. "Rachel?"

"Mm?"

"You're the best," he whispered, and I stroked his soft hair as I began telling him the story of Joseph the Biker, King of the Racetrack.

Stolen

Dante

"Beth, where the fuck have they gone?" I all but shouted at her as I came back to the dining room to find her gone.

"There was no stopping them, Dante. I'm sorry! I tried but—"

"How long?" I interrupted, ripping my phone back out of my back pocket. If my mother had just fucking accepted that I was bringing her back, instead of asking a million fucking questions, I wouldn't have been so long. Sometimes she forgot that she was just an old lady, and she didn't actually have any input on what any member of the club did. She also forgets I'm a grown man, and who and when I decide to fuck someone is none of her business.

I told her I was bringing back someone who would be a mother for Bee, and that should have been the end of it. The child needed a mother. Isn't that what she was always saying to me whenever word got back to her that I had been with one of the club whores?

There would be absolute hell to pay if she fucked this up for me. She had been perfect.

"Maybe five minutes? Dante, I really am sorry I—"

"It's fine!" I barked at her, cutting her off with a wave. I'd deal with her failures later. I dialled my dad back, mentally calculating how long it took to get to the airport. "Yeah, Pops, listen," I said as soon as he answered the phone, cutting off any chit chat. "Get that useless brother of mine and the rest of the lads together. Meet me at Greasy."

"When?"

"Five minutes ago."

"Right. Get away from you, did she, son?"

"A little cat-and-mouse chase never hurt anyone."

"Apart from the mouse."

"The mouse shouldn't have been stupid enough to run away."

"Dante... You sure about this? If this gets reported—"

"I'll worry about that later. I'm not going to harm her."

Yet.

I heard him sigh down the phone. "I'll get the lads together. We'll be there in a few minutes."

"Things might get messy. The man she's with… he's got his eye on her. He's not letting her go without a fight."

"Messy is the club's motto. Don't worry about it. See you in a minute."

He hung up without saying goodbye, and I made my way outside the Greasy Spoon, heading straight for my bike. I threw my leg over it and started the engine. The rest of the lads wouldn't stop, they would follow my lead, and the quicker I was ready, the quicker we could get going.

I was about to catch my mouse. Let the fun begin.

Chapter 3

Rachel

"Can we play a car game, Rachel? Please." I looked down at Joseph and smiled. He grinned back up at me when I turned the smile into a mock stern frown.

"Are we not finishing this story, then? I'll let you choose the ending."

"We can save it for the plane instead. I'll think of the best ending, I promise. I hate planes, they're so boring, there's nothing to see—"

"Well now," I interrupted. "There are people who aren't lucky enough to fly on a plane at all, never mind as often as you get to." I reminded him. "The views from the window seat are unlike anything else."

"I don't care about a stupid view," he huffed, and I bit my cheek to keep from smiling.

"Of course you don't. What game do you want to play, buddy?"

"The quiet game sounds good," James chuckled from the front seat. I clenched my fist to stop myself from flipping him the bird, and brushed the hair out of my eyes to disguise the fact I was rolling them so hard, I was surprised I didn't go blind.

"Not much chance of playing the quiet game with this one." I gave Joseph a playful tickle. "He was just about to tell me his top ten favourite sights, weren't you?"

"I was not!" He squealed, his little body shaking with laughter as I continued my tickles.

"What do you mean? You promised!" I laughed back, only to be met with the stern, angry face of Mrs Geller as she whipped around in her seat.

"Rachel, please! We don't pay you to frolic around," Mr Geller raised his eyebrows at that and gave me a subtle smirk in the mirror.

Pig.

"Keep him quiet, please. I've got a terrible headache after that awful place."

"Sorry, Mrs Geller."

"Sorry, mum," Joseph and I said in unison.

"How about we play the counting game?" I asked him in a quiet voice. "There's not much to see, but you could count how many red cars you can see, and I'll count the blue ones."

"I want the blue cars!" He said, his nose already pressed against the glass.

"You take the blue ones then. Mrs Geller, would you like to play?"

"No. Just keep the noise down. Please." The way she said please was more of a command than a request.

Stuck-up bitch.

"Of course we will." I turned to look out of the window on my side and quickly noticed the first red car. "That's one for me," I said, nudging the side of Joseph's leg.

"No fair!" Joseph yelped, and I quickly hushed him as I heard Mrs Geller sigh in response.

"It'll never be fair if you don't look," I pointed at *his* window as he pouted in the seat. "Keep looking, or you'll miss all the cars, not just the blue ones. Maybe a bike will even go past." That got his attention. He scooted back over to the window and pressed himself as close as possible.

"Blue car! I see a blue car!" He yelled, earning us both a nasty look from his mum. "And another!" He said, but this time much quieter.

"Another red for me!" I whispered, beaming with excitement. Though that quickly turned to a frown as I noticed the red car brake hard, and pull in behind us, leaving the fast lane wide open. Two scary looking bikes flew past us in a blur, the roar of their engines rattling my ears.

I grinned as I remembered my dad raging against bikes all those years ago. He always said they were death traps with the way they flew down the motorway. He raged even harder when his little girl blossomed into a teenager and loved nothing more than the dangerous motorbikes – well, maybe she loved the men on the bikes a little more.

I relaxed slightly, easily explaining away why the red car had pulled away and tucked in safely behind us. It was just easier to get out of their way sometimes.

"Bikes!" Joseph hissed, his little face turning red as he did his best to contain his excitement. I turned my head to his side with a scowl, noticing four more bikes pull up next to our car on the opposite side from the ones I had seen. Two of them rode ahead to join the others, but the remaining two stayed by our side. One of the bikers waved at Joseph, and he practically fainted in elation.

I was just about to open my mouth when there was a knock on the glass beside me, almost making me jump out of my skin. I smothered a yelp of fright and shot around. There was a huge man at my window, riding an absolute monster of a machine. I couldn't see his face underneath the jet-black helmet he wore, but he still cut an intimidating figure – probably even more so, since what he looked like was left up to the imagination. He signalled at us to pull over, showing me hands that were covered by leather gloves. Alarm bells rang, and instinct told me that underneath those leather gloves would be the same tattoos belonging to a certain man we had seen only a few minutes earlier.

I looked at James as he swore, swerving to the side to avoid the motorbikes. Those that had travelled in front of us had slowed down, almost making us crash into the back of them. My gaze flickered to the rearview mirror, and just as I knew there would be, there was a whole stream of motorbikes waiting for us behind.

"James...?" Elizabeth began, her voice sounding strained.

"I see them. They're just idiots messing around – probably from that diner back there."

"I guess them chasing us down wasn't out of the realm of possibility after all, huh, Mr Geller?" I questioned, my voice as sweet as honey.

"I told you not to throw the money on the table, James!" Mrs Geller hissed, and I had to force myself not to let out a barking laugh.

"Ignore them. This is how they have their fun. They're looking for a reaction, and we're not going to give them one.

We'll be back on the free… Motorway," he corrected himself, throwing daggers at me through the rear-view mirror. "We'll be able to speed past them again in no time."

"Are there any cameras around these parts?" Mrs Geller questioned, turning her head to direct her question at me. She quickly turned back around when she noticed the beast at my window that I was still doing my best to ignore.

"Not as far as I'm aware. It's pretty rural around here. Not much cop activity. And any cops that do patrol out here will more than likely have heavily lined pockets, if you get my drift? The only cameras people have will be to protect their own property. They're not going to use it to assist the police."

"What?" She sounded so appalled it was almost comical. All I could do was give an apologetic shrug of my shoulders.

"It's just the way it is."

"Brilliant," she muttered sarcastically. Another knock at my window had us both tensing, but once again I refused to turn around and acknowledge it. I wasn't about to give them the satisfaction of playing the part of the damsel in distress in whatever sick game they were in the middle of.

"Shit!" James hissed as the bike that had been riding at Joseph's window took a sharp turn, forcing him to pull to the left to avoid him. James wasn't overly comfortable driving on this side of the road at the best of times, never mind having to perform tricky manoeuvres to stop us from ending up in a head on collision.

I ignored one more knock at my window – this one pissing me off more than it did scare me, even if it was fiercer than any that came before it. The windows rattled under his fist, but I kept my eyes on the window ahead of me. I watched as six bikers came together to line up in front of our car, two at the front windows, one on either side, and four just ahead of us. The roar of their engines was deafening as they revved the engines, and that's when Joseph spoke up.

"Rachel?" His voice was nervous as he shuffled closer to me. Shadows fell over his face just as two bikers pulled up to his window, and another two pulled up to mine. I flicked my eyes to the mirror, and saw two more on our rear, their front wheels almost touching the car.

They had well and truly surrounded us.

Stolen

"James! Do something!" Elizabeth hissed as the bikes ahead of us slowed down even further.

"What the fuck am I supposed to do?" He growled, sweat beading on his forehead.

"Look," I said calmly, knowing it was down to me to get control of the situation. "If they wanted to hurt us, they could have made us crash at any moment. Notice them two have been slowly dropping their speed? They want us to slow down safely. They could have easily run us off the road, and yet they haven't. I say we follow their lead. We're practically at a standstill now, anyway. Let us just do as they're clearly wanting us to do and stop the car. We can see what they want, and we'll be back on the road before we know it." James looked as though he wanted to argue the matter, and so I spoke up before he could get a word out. "There's no point letting egos get the better of us. We're surrounded. There's no out-driving them, and there's no getting out of this circle they've created. I've had this twat knocking on my window—"

"Swear!" Joseph interrupted.

"Now's not the time, buddy. I'll give you a dollar when we get home. Anyway, as I was saying, this *idiot* has been knocking at my window trying to get attention for the past few minutes. Just slow down," James growled low in his throat and revved the engine in return. "James!" I all but snapped. "This is a situation that could quickly spiral out of control. Slow down before it escalates any further and someone ends up getting hurt. Your son is in the backseat," I reminded him, giving him a jolt of reality. I wouldn't have put it past him to think he was the next breakout star of "Fast and Furious 204."

James put on his hazard lights and slowed the car down. I had to admire the biker's skill, as they all slowed down in unison, never once breaking their formation, and never once putting themselves – or us, I begrudgingly had to admit – in any danger. James swung the car to the left and sharply pulled up at the side of the dirt road.

"Now, everyone, listen up," he said, his voice low as his head dipped to his chest as he fought to contain his anger. His fingers gripped the steering wheel, turning his knuckles white before he raised his head to look back and forth between me and his wife. "Let me do the talking here, okay? Whatever they want, they can deal with me. Man to man. Elizabeth, you're to come with me."

Ahh. Yes. Man to man-with-the-wife. Intimidating.

"Rachel, you stay in the car with Joseph. Do not get out. Are you listening?" I nodded my head, but there was no fight in me whatsoever.

You don't need to tell me twice, pal.

James "The Man" took a deep breath and opened his door just as all the bikers pulled to a stop. Some came off their bikes, but others stayed on theirs, only turning their engines off.

The guy who had been knocking at my window kicked his stand into place and came towards the car.

I was even more reassured by the fact that all the bikers kept a fairly respectable distance between us, and none of them came immediately charging over. The man was taking a leisurely stroll over, as though we had all the time in the world.

"What can I do for you, fellas?" James asked, and I got a sick kick out of hearing the wobble in his voice.

Man to man, my arse! I'm more of a man than he is.

"Do you think Dad's gonna fight?" Joseph whispered, not sounding the least bit nervous about his dad taking on a bunch of bikers. If anything, he sounded excited.

"Let's just listen," I whispered back, my breath catching in my throat as the man removed his helmet and my suspicions were confirmed.

It was him.

You're not returning to America. You're not going home.

The trees mocked me louder than ever.

I almost choked on the breath I had been holding, and my heart started pounding in my ears. I vaguely heard Joseph say something along the lines of, "that's you!" in shock and awe, but I didn't pay much attention to it. It didn't register. Nothing was registering, other than the deafening roar of my blood pounding through my body.

Immediately my mind went back to the diner, trying to replay the image of him, trying to place if I knew him and where I knew him from. I couldn't for the life of me ever recall seeing him – and I'm pretty fucking certain I'd have remembered. Which means he either knew me, or he knew what I had done.

"What girl?" James demanded.

"Is this really the way we're going to do things?" The biker laughed. He didn't give James the chance to respond. I heard the crack as his fist connected with James' jaw, knocking him clean to the ground.

Elizabeth's ridiculous shrieks pierced my ears as she demanded her husband get up. "That's for clicking your fingers at me like I'm a fucking dog. I'm not here to play games, so we'll try this one more time. We've come for the girl. The sooner you hand her over, the sooner you can be on your way." He raised his voice slightly, and I knew, I just knew, he was doing it to make sure I could hear him.

"She's not going anywhere," James mumbled as he pushed himself into a sitting position. "She belongs to us. She works for us. She's *staying* with us."

Fair play. I didn't think you had it in you. Amazing what a bit of unfulfilled sexual desire can do for a man.

The biker sighed again. "If you make me hit you again, it won't be for clicking your fingers at me. It will be for the way you ate her up with your eyes. The way you stared at her when you thought no one else was looking. For the way you dared to lust over what belongs to me. For the way you just tried to declare what is mine as your own. What do you think a punch like that will feel like? Because make no mistake about it, she belongs to me, and I'm taking her with me. With or without your blessing."

"James?" Mrs Geller barked. "What is he talking about?" Her voice was almost hysterical. James gritted his jaw and threw daggers at the man.

"I've no time for dramatics. Your husband wants to fuck the nanny. Now, last try, and I mean it." He addressed his next words to Mrs Geller. "I mean no harm to you or your family, lady. But rest assured, if she isn't out of the car in the next ten seconds, I won't hesitate to set the entire thing alight with her and your son in it. So what's it to be?"

I didn't wait for an answer. Joseph's murmur of terror was enough to have me unclipping my seat belt and climbing out of the car before anyone could say any more. I leaned over to give him a kiss on the head before I opened the door and whispered against his hair to be a good boy, and that I'd see him again soon.

He let out a small, pitiful "Rachel" as I pulled away, but I ignored him. There was no doubt in my mind that this man would do exactly as he said. I grabbed my purse, giving it a squeeze to make sure I had my supplies in there, and once satisfied, I pushed open the door and stepped out.

"Ahh, there she is," he grinned as he saw me emerge from the car.

"Here I am. The loser of the world's shittiest game of hide and seek." I responded dryly. "How can I help?"

"Jump on," he said, heading to his bike.

"I'll do nothing of the sort," I replied, staying exactly where I was. The only movement I made was to allow the car door to shut behind me, keeping Joseph safe from his view.

"I already told you, she works for us, and she'll be staying with us," James said triumphantly, getting back to his feet now that he knew I had a clear view of him. "It's where she wants to be."

How heroic of you. I saw you on your ass after one punch. Even I've taken harder punches than that.

"Employments are terminated every day. She's coming with me. That's the end of it. You're welcome to come with her if you can't stand a day not being able to look at her – but I can't promise your stay will be as pleasant as hers."

"James," Elizabeth whispered. "Just leave it. Come on. We're going home."

"Thanks for that," I muttered sarcastically, ignoring the ridiculous small pang of hurt. "What's three years of living together, anyway?"

"Ahh, she doesn't want you near her husband now the truth is out, lass!" One of the bikers shouted over.

"Rachel, please," Mrs Geller said, looking at me as though I was a moron. It pissed me off that she used my name. I had been planning on giving these reprobates a fake one.

Stupid bitch.

"We can't get caught up in this… whatever this is," she waved her hands towards the bikers, and pulled back with a grimace as though she was going to catch something. She almost threw up on the spot when the biker with the huge beard blew her a kiss. "You know James can't afford to mess up this promotion. We can get another au pair, but he can't get another job."

"Well, that's a fine way to treat somebody."

"Lovely employee you've got there, lass."

"Eat the rich!"

The bikers began to yell, each laughing and slapping each other. The man looked at me, but I kept my face blank.

"They're right, you know. Did you say you had worked with them for three years? And they're casting you off like this?" He looked at me for confirmation, but I still didn't respond.

This man was not getting the satisfaction of getting a response from me. I'd live in stubborn silence before I let him get his kicks out of toying with me. "You don't even know what I'm planning. I could have a murder scene set up back home, with Rachel here in the starring role." Nice. Letting me know, he heard Mrs Geller give my name.

Nice one.

"If you wanted her dead, you could have run us off the road and have done with it," James said with a scoff, his bravado coming in the form of my earlier words.

"Tell yourself what you want, mate. So long as you keep your job, and the rich get richer, fuck what poor little peasant bitch must die, right?"

I knew what he was doing. He wanted me uneasy and nervous. It wasn't going to happen.

"I'm not planning on murdering you, by the way," he grinned down at me, as though he was doing me a favour offering me reassurance. I deepened my scowl and turned my head away with a sigh, showing him I was bored with the conversation.

"Right, I'm beginning to get impatient now."

My little act of defiance must have pissed him off, because before any of us could register what was happening, he grabbed hold of James in one swift movement and pulled a knife from the back of his jeans. "Are you coming with us willingly, or after we've killed your little loyal family here? And the boy you so carefully tried to hide from me is included in that threat, Rachel. It makes no difference to me."

"If you don't care about our jobs, then think of Joseph for fuck's sake, Rachel!" Elizabeth wailed as James struggled to get free. The man didn't move a muscle, keeping James held as easily as he would a puppy.

"I was already out of the fucking car!" I hissed at Mrs Geller, making her head jerk back in shock as I swore at her for the very first time. "It was your idiot husband trying to play the hero that got him in this mess. *I* was ready to leave. Let him go," I said, raising my voice to the man. "I'll come with you."

"Was that so hard?" He dropped James like a sack of potatoes and came towards me, grabbing hold of my arm with far more force than was necessary. He pulled me with him, taking long, quick strides towards his bike.

"Where should we send her things?" James asked as Elizabeth climbed back in the car to calm down a hysterical Joseph.

Poor kid.

His life was about to get a whole lot worse.

I couldn't help but let out a scoff as James quickly adapted to the situation. So much for "she's not going anywhere."

"Macbeth," the man barked. "Give them the details. We're out of here." He threw me onto his bike. Not that he needed to have bothered. I'd have climbed on, regardless.

I realise others in my situation might have attempted to put up a fight, but I wasn't fucking stupid. Twenty-plus angry bikers verse me. It was a death sentence to even try. Escape would have to come later.

"Here." He thrust a helmet at me before he rammed it over my head, taking time to make sure it was safely secured in place.

I looked down at my arm, noticing that it was red with his fingerprints. "Safety first, eh?" I muttered sarcastically, but he just hit the helmet, knocking my head against the inside.

He took time to make sure I was on the bike properly before he climbed on in front of me and twisted the key. Just as I thought we were about to head off, he paused, looking back at me.

"Hey, Rachel? I'm Dante. Welcome to the rest of your life."

"Can't wait," I muttered, and then vowed to myself that those would be some of the last words I ever uttered to Dante.

Fuck him and his games. He'll soon grow bored with a mute.

I didn't bother looking at the Gellers as we passed them. The roar of Dante's engine drowned out anything they were saying, anyway.

Instead, I silently wished them away to hell and paid attention to my surroundings.

The trees swayed in the breeze, waving their goodbyes. But I'd see them again. I wasn't done with them just yet, and I had more twists up my sleeve.

But for now, I knew I was beat. It is what it is, and if I had any hope of getting out of this fucked up situation, I first had to know exactly where I was, and where the fuck he was taking me.

Chapter 4

Rachel

We rode for about twenty minutes, but nothing I saw enlightened me to where we were. When I lived in England, I was too young to take proper note of my surroundings. As I got older, my teenage self always had an escort, and we stuck to the same club scene. We were never near the motorways or the back roads. We stuck to the places they knew, where they were confident they could get away with whatever they wanted. Dante, of course, knew these back roads like the back of his hand. They were his stomping grounds.

Unless I wanted to memorise different blades of grass, or leave breadcrumbs like Hansel and Gretel, my surroundings were absolutely useless. Especially because it was hard to concentrate when Dante had all but forced me to wrap my arms around his waist, so my chest was currently pressed against his back, and every vibration from the bike rattled through me in the most delicious, unexpected way. I was positive he knew it, too, because there was no need for a bike to rev this much, yet it did. At one point, I swear I heard him chuckle when I tensed behind him, thanks to a particularly strong wave of vibration. I ignored it, just as I had ignored everything else from him since the minute I got on this bike. It wasn't fucking easy though when my hands were clinging to him, and his smell invaded my senses, surrounding me. Intoxicating me. I was at war with myself. One half of me was pleading to bury my nose in his leather jacket and take the deepest breath of my life. The other half was threatening to throw us off the bike and slam my head into the road over and over if I even dared lower myself in such a way.

It was fucking tempting, though.

I vaguely recognised the diner at one point, but we weren't at the front like I had been with the Gellers. So that alone told me that Dante had deliberately taken a different route to his home, as the bikers had arrived from the front of the diner in order to follow us down the motorway.

Dante took a particularly sharp turn, and I followed my instincts, holding on that little bit tighter as I followed his lead, leaning with him, keeping my legs as close to the bike as possible. The heat radiated off him, and, not for the first time, it registered just how huge he was. My hands were clutching at his jacket, because he was too big for my arms to meet in the middle.

The more time passed, the more I was able to reassure myself that this man didn't know a fucking thing about me. If he did, he wouldn't have been encouraging me to lean into him. He wouldn't have been looking at me with undisguised desire in his eyes, and he wouldn't have been laughing at the stupid vibrations hitting the right spot. No, he wasn't involved, or knew anyone from those days. He was just another psychopath that had taken me from my life and tried to implant me in another.

I had dealt with those before, and I could deal with him.

If he knew me, I'd know about it. Everyone was still angry about what I did. And whilst Dante was angry, he was angry at the entire world.

So since my surroundings were useless, and I had to do something to distract myself from the man I clung to like he was precious gold, I was left with nothing else but to think of what it was he wanted for me. And that did nothing but cause a slow burn of anxiety to tingle through my body.

We quite clearly had nothing in common, and he was hardly going to be asking me for advice on fashion. The man would keep me in no clothes at all if he had his way. I knew that as surely as I knew the sky was blue.

So what could he want? Sex? More than likely. But looking like he did, I highly doubted he had trouble getting women, and he would hardly need to go to such lengths to get one either. I'd imagine women were throwing themselves at his feet. Some of them would probably envy me for being in this position. Good-looking men were dangerous because they removed the ability for women to possess a moral compass. All the red flags looked green when you were colour blind with desire.

In fact, that many red flags became a red blanket, and what wasn't comforting about a nice, warm blanket?

I tensed as we slowed down, and Dante pulled into what looked like a pub. There were bikes everywhere I looked, covering the muddy grass in front of the building. There was some sort of animal skull above the door – I assume a stag – with a cowboy hat perched on its antlers, which made me give a small chuckle.

A small chuckle I quickly turned into a cough lest Dante thought I approved.

Dante pulled to a stop in one of the spaces closest to the door and jumped off the bike. I noticed he didn't pull into the first spot and having seen the Vice President patch on his leather jacket, I figured they lined up in order of rank.

"I'm not carrying you in," Dante called over his shoulder, interrupting my thoughts. "I suggest you follow me. Don't make me come back out for you." I rolled my eyes beneath my helmet and made a very immature face that I'm not proud of, but I did all the same.

He closed the door behind him, and I climbed off the bike, leaning against it as I pulled the helmet off and rested it over the handles. I looked around me and breathed a deep puff of air.

I could see plenty of houses, but no people. No cars, but plenty of bikes. This was definitely a biker community, and if Dante was the vice president, I had no chance of making any "friends" that wouldn't betray me at a moment's notice in favour of him.

"Now!" Dante barked as he pulled the door back open. I was half tempted to see how far I could push him, but that was only going to draw more attention to me.

Romance is alive and well! I thought to myself, taking another deep breath, and closing my eyes for a moment before I followed Dante's footprints inside, smoothing my dress over my hips and thighs as I did so.

I could hear the noise of the bar before I even had the door open. But the minute I stepped inside, you could have heard a pin drop. Everyone froze at the same time. Some still had their drinks halfway to their mouths. The bartender stopped pulling pints; the girls stopped their ridiculous dancing and giggling. Every pair of eyes turned their hungry gaze to me.

It was obvious I was wildly out of place here in my modest grey dress and neat blonde hair. All I could see was leather, skin, and tattoos.

"Rachel," Dante called from behind the bar, nodding his head towards the door that led to the back.

If I wanted to make my way to him, I had to pass through the entire club, giving them all a good look at me. He was leading me through the lion's den, and I had a feeling this was my first test. There was obviously a back entrance he could have taken us through, but he made a deliberate decision to come in this way, letting everyone know I was with him. Something told me that he was half expecting me to fail this test. That he believed he was going to have to come and drag me through this bar, that I'd be too nervous to do it myself.

I'd be right behind him if he didn't have such gigantic fucking legs!

But that wasn't true.

Even if I had jumped off the bike at exactly the same time as him and followed him the minute he started walking, he still would have left me in the dust. I was tiny compared to him, and I was always going to have to walk this alone.

And well he knew it, the smug bastard.

I noticed some of the girls sneering at me, and some of the men looking at me with a hunger that made the hair on the back of my neck stand up.

I grew angry at being stared at like a zoo animal, and a sudden burst of pride had me straightening my spine, throwing my head back, and glaring at them all as they were glaring at me. I flicked my hair over my shoulders with a small shake of my head, and crossed the floor, my heals making the only noise as they click-clacked across the wood. These people would not intimidate me. I met the gazes of those closest to me, but not once did I smile, nor did I murmur any sort of greeting. I kept a deliberate blank expression, refusing to give them the satisfaction of even a flicker of fear.

"Sometime today would be nice," Dante called out, and I flicked my eyes over to him. He looked mildly surprised that I had got this far on my own, as though I was a baby in need of guidance.

Say nothing, Rachel. Say nothing. Don't rise to it. Don't play the game.

I didn't pick up the pace. In fact, if anything, I slowed down to a sultry strut. I shifted my bag higher up on my shoulder and walked with more determination, letting my hips swing as I did

40

so, knowing the men I passed were watching me greedily. May as well toy with the devil if he was going to up heave my entire life.

I said don't play the fucking game!

But when have I ever listened to myself?

I stifled a grin as Dante's jaw tightened as he came around the bar to grab hold of me and pulled me to his side.

I won though. I didn't need rescuing, and he couldn't stand it.

"Everyone," he called out. "This is Rachel. And before any of you even have the fucking stupidity to ask, yes, she's off limits to every single one of you."

"How long is she staying?" One of the girls called out, with a look of hatred aimed straight at me.

"None of your fucking business. Any other questions?"

"A week?" She persisted. "A month? Longer? I don't want to have to look at her any longer than necessary. What is she wearing? She looks like a fucking lawyer. You fucking the law, Dante?"

Dante dropped my arm as he strode towards her and grabbed her by the face. "How about you fuck off and look at your own bloke instead of eyeing up my woman? How's that for a compromise," he hissed, pushing her away from him with such force she had to grab the bar to steady herself.

At the same time, we both jolted at the words of *"my woman"*. I recovered quicker than she did and watched in amusement as her mouth fell open and closed again.

"Your woman, huh? So you're not just fucking the law, you're *really* fucking the law. When did you decide this? And more importantly, does Beth know?" She said eventually.

"Put a fucking sock in it, Spunky. You love your sister, we get it. But Beth is a big girl. She can defend herself. She knew what she was getting into with Dante," the guy I recognised as Macbeth called out as he came through the door, slapping the girl on her ass as he came up to her. "As for you, you'll end up getting yourself shot before I've had my chance." He squeezed her ass tight and pulled her body close to his.

"In your dreams, Macbeth," she giggled.

"Make it a beautiful nightmare, and you got yourself a deal," he kissed her lips before he grabbed her drink off the bar and raised it in the air. "Glasses up everyone. Dante's brought back his old lady."

Dante

Rachel, so far, hadn't said more than a few words to me.

In fact, ever since she had climbed on my bike, she had maintained a radio silence. Even when I revved the engine – knowing from previous women exactly what the vibrations did to them – she kept her silence. I toyed with her, revving far more than was necessary, hoping for a gasp, a pant, anything. Other than the odd stiffening of her body, which could easily have been from the speed, there was no response from her.

I couldn't tell if that annoyed me or pleased me. I knew just from looking at her that she was going to be quiet and submissive. Maybe the odd snarky remark like I had heard earlier. More to reassure herself she was more than a walking sex doll than any real defiance. But the complete and utter silence? It was weird. I had always believed that was exactly what I wanted in an old lady and yet… it was fucking annoying getting no response from her at all.

I even began wondering if she was all there, if I'm being honest.

She wasn't showing any signs of being nervous, intimidated, nothing.

Was it even registering with her that I had essentially just kidnapped her, got her fired, and made her homeless? Where would she go if I decided enough was enough and discarded her? Was a flicker of emotion out of the realm of possibility? I had prepared myself for a day or two of hysterics before she settled down into her new life. It unnerved me to see her so silent, her huge green eyes taking everything in, but never showing a shred of what she was thinking.

She hadn't even reacted when I told the entire club she belonged to me. I thought I had seen the smallest of jumps out of the corner of my eye, but I was too preoccupied with the loud-mouth piece of gash to pay attention. Then, when she hadn't responded to my brother calling her my old lady, I knew I had been mistaken.

Did she even know what that term meant?

Ahh, fuck it.

I wasn't looking for a proper partner, anyway. So long as she knew how to suck a dick and was a good mother to Amy, I really didn't give much of a fuck that she had nothing to say for herself. She was nice to look at, and that would do me.

But that fucking blank stare, man. It was bugging me more than I cared to admit.

I grabbed her arm again and dragged her out of the bar and up the stairs leading to my room. We lived at the bar, with an entire house behind it. We had a house in the middle of the village, too, but none of us spent much time there. In fact, I think the only time Macbeth and I visited was when we had a woman with us, and we wanted a bit of privacy. Otherwise, we spent all our time here since the bar was open early until late and it's where most of the club spent their time.

With more force than was needed, I pulled Rachel up the stairs and dragged her down the hallway. She followed willingly. There was no need for me to be treating her this way. She didn't so much as drag her feet. She was half my size and kept up with my stride, even if it meant doing a little jog now and then. Once again, she showed no emotion, made no noise, and it barely even looked as though she was breathing. It annoyed me to death. How could she be so blasé about all of this?

As I continued down the hallway to the room my mum had made up for her, I noticed her fiddling around in her handbag, but didn't pay it much attention. At least I knew she had the use of her arms. So far, I'd only seen her move her arms to wrap them around me – holding on just as much as necessity demanded, before letting go of me again as though I was poison. The only other time she had moved was when she was acting as though she was on the fucking catwalk, walking through the pub like a hooker in the red-light district, giving everyone a view of the sexy way her hips moved back and forth.

What annoyed me the most was it didn't even look as though she was *trying* to be sexy. She looked as though she'd had a rare burst of defiance, but sexy wasn't her goal. Lord alone knew what she would look like if she were trying. She ought to pray to whatever deity she believes in that she never let my buddies find out. There would be hell to pay, and she would be the one paying the ransom.

Not that any of them would touch her now that they knew she was my old lady and not another club whore I had recruited. But that didn't stop Rachel from trying, as though one of them would be her saviour from me. The members of this club were loyal to me, and would tell me in an instant, and she'd be the one on the receiving end of the consequences.

I pushed her through the door to her room and followed after her, pushing my way past her frozen body. I sat on the edge of the bed, noticing that she stayed by the door, her hand still in her bag.

"Do you want to sit?" I asked her, patting the space next to me. She just looked at me with that blank look that was fast becoming the most annoying thing in my life.

I scanned her face, praying there was some sign of emotion, but it was empty. How the fuck could it be empty? Was she in shock? It was the only thing I could think of. Most other women would be kicking and screaming at being kidnapped. They'd be on the verge of fainting if they were locked in a bedroom with their kidnapper. She had no idea what I had planned for her, and yet she was as calm as she would be if we were taking a romantic stroll on the beach. In fact, that probably would elicit more emotion from her.

I softened my voice, which annoyed me even more, because I didn't need to play nice with her, but I also didn't want to start off on completely the wrong foot.

"So, let me just line things out for you. I'm Dante, as you know. I live here with my brother and parents. You've met my brother, that was Macbeth back there – his real name is Cole, but he was such a spiteful, jealous bastard growing up, we all called him Macbeth. It became his club name – you'll find most everyone here has a club name. It comes naturally. My dad is Crash - real name, by the way. My mum is Big Mama. Old ladies don't usually have club names, but hers was sort of given to her in honour by the rest of the lads. My dad's the president, she's his old lady, and when I take over, they'll go and live in the main house in the village. That won't happen anytime soon, though. My mam likes being the loudmouth behind the bar, knocking heads together when things get too rowdy. She enjoys it far too much to allow my dad a decent retirement." I smiled at her, but there was no response. "You'll notice all the men have the club patch on their vest, and if they have a rank, it'll be there too. You only really need to know the main men – everyone else you'll learn with time. I'll introduce you to them all tomorrow, rather than overwhelm you with names right now."

Nothing

"We're the main branch of the Devil's Disciples – you may have heard of us. Most of it is bad, I'm sure. But we're loyal to those we call our own, and we'll never do you wrong, so long as you give us the same courtesy."

Still nothing. Nothing other than that ridiculous fiddling in her bastard bag. "I have a daughter. She's five. Her mother died when she was a baby – no, I'm not going into details, so don't bother asking." Unnecessary, as she wasn't going to ask. I swear, the bitch wasn't even blinking. "She's called Amy. Thanks for asking," I muttered the last part under my breath, hating myself for showing my annoyance. "We all call her Little B – little biker. Or Bee, for short. I don't think she'd even respond to Amy anymore."

Fiddle, fiddle, fiddle.

I watched her for a moment, letting her process what I had just said, to see if there was any flicker of recognition as to where this conversation was going.

"Amy needs a mum. And that's where you come in. I'll introduce the two of you in the morning, but all you need to know right now is that, as my old lady, your job will be to raise her. I don't believe in nannies or babysitters. She should be raised by family. And whilst you're a stranger to her right now, as my old lady, you'll be a constant in her life from now on. You *do* know what an old lady is, don't you?"

Nothing.

"Old lady," I began, getting off the bed and making my way towards her. She still didn't move, other than to flick her eyes upwards so she could keep making eye contact with me. "Means you belong to me. You will cook for me, clean for me, manage the bar, and anything else I deem essential. When I want something, you will be there. I say jump, you say how high. Your life from now on will be making sure mine runs smoothly and keeping your nose out of club business. If I ask for advice, you can give it, otherwise you will be looking after Amy and any other children we have together. Do that well, and we'll have no issues. As for the rest of the men – well, respect around here is earned, so you'll get none from the people down there. They'll respect you as mine, but they won't respect you as a person. You'll need to prove yourself first. You'll do that by keeping me happy. And I mean happy in every sense of the word, Rachel." I warned her, stopping inches away from her.

Still, nothing.

Alright, this was fucking bugging me now. I gritted my jaw as I spoke next, going for the shock factor. "That means you'll speak when you're spoken to. You'll do as I told. If I tell you to go on your knees and suck me in front of the entire club, you'll do it. If I tell you to bend over and spread your ass cheeks, you'll do it without hesitation. I own all of you, and you'll give it to me willingly. If you feel like putting up a fight, by all means, go for it. I'll win in the end. You belong to me now... Jesus fucking Christ, are you ever going to fucking say anything?" I roared at her, losing my patience. My angry breath hit her face, brushing the hair out of her eyes, and the crazy bitch didn't so much as flinch. "Rachel," I grabbed hold of her jaw and dug my fingers in, lifting her face to mine. "So help me God, if you don't fucking say something soon."

"What's the matter? Didn't you want a submissive little girl at your side?"

"Submissive is one thing. I didn't sign up for a mute."

She let out a barked laugh. "Yeah? Well, I didn't sign up for this at all, so you can go fuck yourself as far as I'm concerned." She went on her tiptoes and pushed her face as close to mine as possible. "I'd sooner bite your dick off than suck it anywhere, least of all in front of the bitches you call your *biker buddies*," she said the last words with such derision and spite that it took all I had not to punch her straight in the face.

"Don't test me," I warned her.

"Or else what?" She shot right back. My fingers tightened on her jaw, and I took great pleasure in waiting for the yelp of pain, but it never came. Not even when her lips puckered with the force of my grip. She just looked at me with that same blank, irritating expression, with just a flicker of defiance in her eyes.

I felt a movement to my side as she fiddled in her bag again. "What the fuck are you doing in there? Messing about with stress balls or something?" I used my other hand to try to grab hold of it, but she was quicker than me, her hand shooting out of the bag.

I barely had a moment to register the sound of the click, the flash of the metal under the light before she shoved the blade into my thigh with all the strength she had.

Shock more than pain had me letting go of her, and she ran for the door. Just as she twisted the handle, my brain caught up with what was happening and I grabbed her by the back of the hair, slamming her head into the wood, closing the door again. I spun her around, noticing that there was already blood on her lips. Before she had a chance to recover, I backhanded her, sending her head flinging to the side. She attempted to bring her knee up to catch me off guard, but I had been in this game too long. I knew all the defence tactics. I twisted my body to avoid her movements and tightened my grip on her hair, pulling her head back to stare at me. "That," I hissed at her. "Was a mistake." I yanked her hair with such force, her head snapped back at a painful angle. When she didn't so much as whimper, I threw her to the floor, staring down at her with all the hate I could muster.

She recovered quickly, scrambling to her back and edged her way away from me. She still didn't look scared. If anything, she looked pissed. As though any moment she would get up and come back for round two.

Not what I had been expecting.

I grabbed her bag that she had dropped and tipped its contents on the bed before spreading them out with my hand so I could see exactly what she had with her. Tightening my lips, I grabbed her again by the hair and dragged her over to the desk by the window, pulling out the chair and pushed her into it. The entire time she scratched and kicked at me, pulling her head back with such force, I'm surprised she didn't rip her hair out. I let go of her hair, and as quick as a flash, gathered her wrists behind her back and secured them tight with the strap of her handbag.

"You're a fucking idiot," I sneered at her, bringing my face close to hers. She threw her head forward, trying to headbutt me, and I just laughed.

"Has your fight or flight finally kicked in? It's not often I'm surprised, but you got me, I'll give you that. I'd have been less surprised had a goblin walked in here and taken my child to the Goblin King," I told her as I straightened up. "I wouldn't have pegged you as fight, though. You scream flight." She stopped her struggling and just stared at me, breathing hard, blood dripping from her nose and lips.

As the adrenaline wore off, the pain in my leg kicked in, and I looked down, noticing the knife was still in there. It was a small thing, and as I pulled it out, I smirked as I saw it was a self-defence knife hidden inside a key. That's why she had been fiddling. She was pulling the blade out.

"What's a sweet thing like you doing with this?" I asked, coming close to her, and bringing the knife up over my head before I slammed it into the wood mere inches away from her thigh.

She had no reaction. She didn't cower, didn't flinch. She just kept looking at me and, despite myself, I found a flicker of respect growing for her. She blinked slowly at me, almost looking bored, despite the fact that I now had her bag of goodies at my disposal.

"What else do you have?" I asked, turning away from her, and making my way back to the bed where I had tipped her belongings out. I whistled quietly as I picked up a variety of self-defence tools.

She had this black keyring, with a bunch of things added to it. There was a small knuckle duster, a mini taser, which I tested, and it let off a powerful blast. There was an emergency power bank, a mini pepper spray, an alarm and flashlight, a door opener, a sharp metal rod, which I assumed would be for breaking windows or delivering a sharp stab, a belt/rope cutter, and a cute little pompom to tie it all together nicely.

I whistled again, turning around with the keychain dangling from my fingers. "I'm impressed. A woman who knows how to defend herself. I didn't think a little princess like you would even be aware of the dangers of the world, never mind defending yourself against them. You know these are illegal, right?"

"Yeah, well, so is rape and murder, but they happen every day and the perpetrators get away with it. If I get sent to prison for self-defence, so be it. But it won't be me lying on the side of the road, left for dead."

"It's one thing to have the tools. It's a completely different thing altogether to actually use them," I said, crouching down in front of her and met her eyes with my own. "You think you're capable of stabbing a man? And not that pathetic attempt you just gave me. I mean, truly stab him, to watch his life drain before your eyes." I grabbed her chin and brought my face close to hers. "You think you're capable of that, Rachel? Do you think you can take another man's life? Even if he was about to commit the most horrific crime a woman can suffer through, do you really think you have it in you to take his life from him? To feel a knife cut through flesh under your own hand?" I brought my lips close to hers and whispered my next words against them. "Somehow, I don't think you do. Look at you now. Silent and still as a doll. I don't think you're capable of much at all." I pecked her roughly on the lips before pushing myself up away from her and headed back towards the bed.

She made a noise that had me freezing and spinning back around to face her.

She looked up at me through her lashes and let out a laugh that succeeded in sending a chill down my spine. She licked the blood from her lips and gave me an evil smile. "You have *no* idea what I'm capable of, Dante. And the funniest thing is, you haven't got the faintest fucking idea of what you've just invited into your life."

Chapter 5

Rachel

Dante continued looking at me as though I had grown an extra head, but I couldn't help myself. Once the laughter started, there was no stopping it.

He honestly thought he would intimidate me. I had cigarette burn marks on my ass from bigger and better men than him; he was a complete fucking walk in the park. I used to get tied up on a daily basis. So much so I learnt to eat without the use of my hands.

It was laughable for him to even think I was this sweet, demure little woman because I didn't fight him and walked through a fucking pub where a few men were. He had no fucking idea.

"Look at you now. Silent and still as a doll. I don't think you're capable of much at all."

What a fucking *ass*. I had put an end to a man like him. I had watched the life drain from his eyes, and I felt zero remorse for it. The only thing I regretted was not doing it sooner. What had Dante called me? Quiet? Submissive?

Good grief, amazing what a dye job and a smart dress can do to people's perception. Which had been my exact plan. Present a respectable figure, and people believe you're respectable. Peel away the mask, and you might just find that buried beneath the expensive haircut and the tailored clothes lies a woman with a soul as black as death.

"Take a good look, Dante," I said finally, grinning at him, feeling the blood on my tongue. "That quiet woman who followed you in here? She's gone. You want to unleash the beast, then on your fucking head, be it. You'll never regret anything in your entire life more than you will the day you decided I was a suitable woman to have around." I gave one final tug at the straps that were keeping my arms behind my back and then took mercy on him. "If you have any common sense, you'll let me go. You'll put me back on your shit bike and drive me far, far away from here. I won't say a word, and I'll pick up the pieces of my life that you've already shattered. But..." I paused as he moved towards me and once again crouched down in front of me to listen. "But, if you decide to keep me, if you decide to go ahead with whatever plans you have, then Lord help you, because I will slice you open and laugh in your face as you bleed out in front of me. I will destroy everything you hold near and dear. And that's not me putting on a bravado. I can promise you that."

His head cocked to the side as I spoke, nodding along with the words I said – who knew such a small gesture could seem so mocking?

"Are you finished?" He asked me.

"I've not even started."

"Okay," he nodded again. Then, before I had a chance to react, his hand shot out, his fingers grabbing hold of my cheeks in a death grip. He dragged my face towards his and forced his lips down on mine. I clamped my mouth shut, refusing to allow him access, but his other hand crept around my head and fisted into my hair, pulling hard enough to have tears wanting to spring into my eyes.

His lips were cruel against mine, pushing my lips against my teeth, causing one of them to split as he forced them open. More blood spilled into my mouth, landing on his tongue as he pushed it into my mouth, demanding entrance. I tried to bite down, but the grip he had on my cheeks tightened, so my lips were pursed open for him.

Just as his lips were beginning to soften, he had a second thought and pulled back, also pulling my hair back at the same time, putting distance between us. His lips were still close enough to mine that I could feel his breath against them.

"Let the games begin, darlin'" he grinned, grabbing my lower lip between his teeth, and biting down hard enough to make me wince. He allowed me to pull back enough that my lip escaped his grip. He surveyed me, his gaze scanning my face, his fingers still keeping a tight hold on my cheek. He seemed to come to some sort of conclusion in his mind because he nodded once more.

"I had intended on your first night here being much more comfortable – hell, we both could have gone to bed satisfied had you played your cards right. But if this is the way you want to be, you can stay in this chair until sunrise. Maybe a bit of starvation and humiliation will humble you."

"I don't eat much." I scoffed.

"Maybe so, but everybody's gotta piss, Rachel. Can you hold out another twelve hours or so?"

"Is this the best you've got? So I'll piss myself. Do I look like I'd give a fuck? It's hardly the end of the world. *Oh no,*" I mocked. "*Rachel pissed herself!* I'm not in fucking high school, Dante. I don't care what the mean girls are going to be whispering about me. Like you said, everybody's gotta piss. It doesn't matter to me where I do it. You can lap it up like the little dog you are."

"We'll see," he laughed back. He pulled me close again, delivering a sharp, quick peck to my lips before he squeezed my cheeks again and spat the blood from our earlier kiss back into my own mouth. My fingernails dug into the palm of my hand, and I forced myself not to react.

There was something fucking wrong with me, because the second I felt the spit on my tongue, my thighs clenched together as a jolt of pleasure shot through me.

What sort of woman likes being spat on?

A damaged one, I thought to myself.

Is that what I was? Damaged?

He let me pull away from him, but I didn't give him the satisfaction of recoiling in disgust. I made a big show of swallowing dramatically, and opened my mouth wide, my tongue hanging out to show him I had swallowed the lot. Another jolt shot through me, as I imagined being in the same position, but swallowing something a hell of a lot more pleasurable. Of Dante rewarding me with a "good girl," as he saw my tongue hang out for him to inspect. I hated myself at that moment, but I couldn't stop the fantasy playing in my mind. My one fucking weakness was having a praise kink. However, what I also possessed was the ability to be an exceptional brat before I liked being praised.

"That's the last thing of yours I'll be swallowing," I glared at him. "Now fuck off. I'm bored with you."

I closed my eyes and leant back with a sigh, as though I was the most comfortable person in the world, about to fall into a relaxed sleep.

I heard the door open and click close a few seconds later, but I still didn't open my eyes. I wouldn't be able to stand it if I opened them and he was standing there with a smug fucking smirk on his lips.

Instead, I sat and thought about all the things I'd do to him once I got out of these goddamn restraints.

Dante

As much as I hadn't wanted to leave, I did so because, despite myself, I felt a seed of respect growing for her.

I had half expected her to burst into tears, to plead with me to let her go. It had almost seemed like it was going that way when she said she wouldn't tell anyone, but then she had fired back with even more threats, and once again, I was mistaken.

I was fast beginning to realise that I had already made a lot of mistaken assumptions when it came to her.

And as fucked up as I was, I actually felt myself growing aroused. The blank look had been replaced by one of fire, and it ignited something in me. She was a knockout, even with blood on her chin and a bust lip. She had thrown her head back in defiance and challenged me, almost mocking me, daring me to take things further. And as much as I had been wrong about her before, I would have sworn I wasn't wrong about the brief flash of arousal that had flared in her eyes before she shut her lids, closing me off from what she was thinking. So I left, because if I had taken things further, I would have challenged her to see just how much pain she was capable of taking. Which wasn't what we needed for our first night together. As fucked up as I was, I knew things like that needed a conversation first.

I gave a small chuckle as I replayed her swallowing our spit and shook my head in amusement. She was wilder than I expected. Who knew if it would last, but I liked the taste I had got.

"How'd it go?" Macbeth asked as he came up the stairs and spotted me.

"Fine," I said simply.

"Hers or yours?" He nodded at the dried blood on my lips.

"You think I ate her or something? I don't mind eating a woman, but cannibalism isn't high on my to do list."

He gave a dry laugh. "There's not much I'd put past you."

"Fuck off, Macbeth," I said with a scoff, pulling away from him.

"Ahh, she's got to you, hasn't she? Was it really that easy? A tight dress and a nice pair of tits, and you're lost. Does she know the power she has over you already?"

"Put her out of your mind, Mac. She's no concern of yours." I brushed past him, heading to my own room. He always was an annoying little fuck. Even when we were kids, he'd do anything to get under someone's skin. I was usually good at ignoring him, knowing attention was exactly what he was seeking, but after dealing with Rachel and her little dramatics back there, I wasn't on usual form.

"Maybe I'll do the exact opposite," Macbeth called after me with a smug tone in his voice.. "Maybe I'll go pay her a visit an—" He didn't get to finish. The rage that crept over me in such a fierce wave had me turning around and charging him, slamming him against the wall of Rachel's room with such force the door rattled to the left of us.

"You'll do no such thing," came a voice from me that I didn't even recognise.

"Has she got under your skin that deep already, brother?" Macbeth asked, but the quivering of his voice betrayed his words.

"Dante," a warning voice came from behind us. "Leave him."

"Listen to your mummy," Macbeth mocked. My fist came up and connected with his jaw before he had time to move and before my mother had a chance to stop me.

Second punch of the day, and I hadn't even been trying.

"Get him out of my sight," I spat at my mother, who was shaking her head at the both of us. "I've enough to be dealing with without him pulling his usual bullshit."

I stepped over him and walked away, without so much as a backwards glance. I heard my mother help him up and ask if he was okay. The two of them would sit and talk for hours about what a bad bastard I was. Macbeth was good at that. He always knew how to play our mam like she was a fiddle.

Macbeth was my older brother, but he had always been an irresponsible thorn in my side. I spent more time cleaning up his messes than I did anything else. He was next in line to be the club leader up until a few years ago. After Bee's mother died, my dad had said Macbeth simply wasn't up to the job, and had passed the reins on to me, telling me it would get my mind off the grief.

Macbeth had been worse since then.

Everything he did was to get a rise out of me, and usually I let it slide, not letting the slime ball have the pleasure of a reaction. I hadn't been in grief over Bee's mother, and we both knew it. My dad was looking for an excuse not to give Macbeth the club, and Laura's death had been the perfect tragedy. I really hadn't cared for her one way or another. I had married her because it's what was expected. My mother loved her, she knew the club lifestyle, and she was easy to deal with.

I hadn't needed to protect her from anything. She kept herself to herself and made the perfect housewife. There was no fire there. No passion. We had the same sex every day, and she thought she was doing me a service by swallowing and not spitting.

I'd heard plenty of club members say things about her. Not out of spite, but out of concern. Which is why I had never bothered to lash out at them for it.

Yet the mere sound of Rachel's name on that dickhead's mouth had provoked a reaction from me that neither of us had been expecting.

I hated that.

I hated that I was impressed by her.

I hated that she had enough fight in her to stand up to me.

I hated that she knew how to push buttons I didn't even know I had.

I hated that she was here, yet I hated the thought of her not being here. Less than half a day, and that blank expression was becoming my favourite thing in the world, even though it angered me to distraction.

I hated that I was beginning to realise I might have made a huge fucking mistake.

But I'd see it through to the end, and Rachel was about to realise what it really meant to anger a biker.

Chapter 6

Dante

"Is everyone here?" Crash asked, as he took his place at the head of the table. We were all waiting for church to begin, which we did at least once a week.

"Almost, Pres," Zach answered, taking his place at the right of Crash. Zach was my dad's childhood friend, and they had been raised in the club together. He was the current Sergeant at Arms, and was responsible for keeping order amongst the members, and was the most senior member after myself and the president.

I took my place at Crash's right-hand side and waited for the other men to take their seats. "We're just waiting for Doc," I told him, lighting up a cigarette.

"It's always fucking Doc," Crash scowled, eyeing the door.

"It's the dogs," Hacksaw – the club's secretary laughed, earning a smirk from me.

Monster was in charge of the dogs. And he was fucking useless at it. They were always biting him or refusing to listen to any of his commands. Still, he decided to stick at it, chasing them around the yard like a toddler would a butterfly. It made for some funny watches, but also made for a lot of trips to the doc.

"Those dogs will be the death of me," Crash shook his head, but there was a smile on his face. He always had a fondness for dogs, and he was the main reason the club had so many, too. He was also the only one the dogs really listened to, but we weren't allowed to say that out loud lest Monster lose his shit.

"So why did you bring that rabid looking one to bed with you, then?" I asked.

"Your mother. Need I say more? If there's anywhere that needs a guard dog, it's the bloody bedroom. You all need to stop pissing her off, because it's always my fault."

My eyes went to Macbeth, who took his place next to Zach. Macbeth was the treasurer, and responsible for the club money and making sure everyone got their fair share from any jobs we did. "Speaking of mother – did she make you feel all better?"

"Fuck off, Dante," he all but hissed at me.

"You never went crying to Mama again, kiddo?" Vienna said, needing no encouragement to wind him up. Vienna, myself and Macbeth all grew up together, alongside Zach's sons Trent and Chris. We were brothers, and with that came the typical needling.

"Enough," Crash snapped as the door opened. "Glad you could join us, Doc. How bad was it?" Doc just twisted his lips and pushed the door further open, showing a miserable-looking Monster with a bandaged hand. "He lost the tip of his little finger."

I couldn't help but burst out in laughter. "How the fuck did it get your little finger?"

"Bite me, Dante."

"Looks like something already did," I grinned at him.

"At least my old lady didn't stab me in the leg," he grinned at me.

"Just a scratch. She'll lick it better later. Can you say the same about yours?"

"Checkmate," he grinned.

"Let me have a look at the boo-boo," Vienna teased, pouting his lower lip. "Is the boo-boo sore? Does he need the hospital?"

"You're all assholes," Monster grinned. He pulled out a chair at the bottom of the table and scowled at his bandage. "I'll still be able to ride, at least."

"Could be worse son, he could have bit off the tip of your dick," Zach told him, earning another laugh from the table.

"I think that's what it was going for. It's a nasty fucker, that new dog."

"That's why it's my favourite. Right, church is in session," Crash said, banging down on the gavel.

Church was where we went to discuss our rides, our plans, and our women. It was a place of sanctuary and respect. Meetings were mandatory, and any member who missed more than two in a row, for whatever reason, had the potential to be patched out of the club.

"First item, and I think we all know what it is…" he said, his eyes flicking at me. "What do we all think of the new old lady?"

"I like her," Macbeth said straight away. "She's got our little Dante here wrapped around her finger." I flipped him the bird and flicked the ash from my cigarette into the ashtray, blowing a puff of smoke out.

"She's not who I thought Dante would bring home," Shark said. Shark was the roadrunner, responsible for organising the club rides. "But Jenna seemed to like her." Jenna was his old lady, and she worked at the bar most nights. She was a nice enough woman, always with a smile on her face and a friendly ear. It wasn't surprising she liked the look of Rachel, since Rachel looked like a *nice* woman.

A screenshot flashed in my mind of Rachel with her tongue hanging out, showing me her empty mouth, and my cock jerked in response.

Rachel wasn't as nice as she looked.

"Jury's still out on that one," Vienna grinned at me. "It's the quiet ones you need to watch out for." Vienna was the peacemaker of the group. Even when it came to Macbeth. He knew how to diffuse a situation with wit and humour unlike anyone I had ever met. He was the chalk to my cheese. Whereas I led with anger, he led with his mind. He was cool and collected – most of the time. I had seen him rip a man's ear off with his teeth. If push came to shove, he'd kill for the club, but it took a lot to get him truly angry.

"She's not bloody quiet either," I mumbled, earning a laugh from the table.

"They never are, lad," Crash said, slapping me on the shoulders.

"And she's not sweet either. Tell Jenna her judge of character sucks. I bet Jenna never stabbed you in the leg." Shark had the decency to look sheepish.

"I got to know Jenna before I brought her into my room."

"Is that the secret? Make sure women are not psychos *first?* Man, you need to learn to live a little!"

I took a heavy drag from my cigarette and sat back, listening as they all discussed my new old lady.

Hacksaw thought she seemed sweet.

Vienna was adamant she was a secret street fighter.

Shark was happy, so long as I was happy.

Rooster and Chicken – two brothers named for the fact their dad was a farmer – said she was attractive. They added "for an old lady" when I scowled at them.

And Tools – co-owner of the garage with Crash – just shrugged his shoulders, making the rest of the club members follow suit as they murmured their approval. Not that we needed approval for any of our old ladies. So long as they stayed in line, we could have whatever woman we wanted.

"That's it then. Dante will help settle her in, and I'm sure she'll be a welcome addition to the old lady team. Right," he said, slamming the gavel. "Prospects."

We had four prospects at the minute, all sitting at the end of the table. These were new members of the club who were not fully patched in. We had Monster, Noob, Shawn, and James. Monster sat up straighter, his attention on Crash.

Prospects had a year to prove themselves to the club. When the year was done, we held church to see if they would be patched in or not. We had already voted on him last week, but just for shits and giggles, we were holding him in suspense.

"As you know, Monster here has been with us for a year now," he began, and I stifled a chuckle as I saw Monster sit up even further, hiding his bandaged hand behind his back as though we wouldn't remember it. "He's been a valuable asset in helping train the guard dogs. He's organised two runs with Shark and has never missed a run himself. And he took part in dealing with the Rough Riders last week, dealing with some lower members of their club selling on our patch." He paused, and we all turned to look at him. "However, he has been late to church at least once a month, and in turn has caused Doc to be late. He had a fight with Macbeth over the dogs. He caused Trent to chip a tooth when one of the dogs got loose, and he currently has his hand in a bandage, meaning he may or may not be able to ride." Monster lowered his chin to his chest, waiting for the inevitable moment when he would be told to turn in his patch.

"With all that being said… You're in, kid." Monster's head came up sharply, as he looked between me, Crash and Zach. "You're in," Crash repeated, and then chaos descended. Every member of the club, prospects included, got up to either hug him or slap him on the back. Vienna reached under his chair and brought out his new jacket, with the complete club patch to replace his prospect patch.

"Welcome, brother," I said to him, raising my hand in the air. He grasped it tightly, and I pulled him in for a hug, slapping his shoulders.

"Thanks, Dante."

"Here. You earned this," Vienna told him, holding the leather jacket to him. We all cheered as he put it on and took his place next to Macbeth at the table, away from the other prospects.

"I think that does it for church today, lads. Behave yourself. Stay out of Mama's way, and make Rachel feel welcome. See you all next week." He banged the gavel, and one by one, we left the room. "Dante, Vienna, stay behind with Zach." He told us, his voice drowned out as everyone continued to congratulate Monster.

"Noob?" I called out.

"Yeah, VP?"

"Take Rachel some food up. Whatever you find, you mind your business. Just untie her, give her the food, and leave. Lock the door behind you. Understood?"

"Yes, sir," he nodded.

"You going to explain that or…?" Crash asked, his voice sounding amused.

"Trust me, you don't want to know," I replied, shaking my head.

Crash waited until the door was closed before he sat back down. I took my place next to him and sparked up another cigarette. "We've heard back from the Rough Riders. They're adamant they weren't the ones responsible for Mickey."

"Do we believe them?" I asked, already knowing the answer.

Mickey had been a prospect of ours for around six months before he was run off his bike last week and murdered. He was a decent bloke, never once minding that we called him Mickey because of his massive ears. He took it all in his stride and laughed along with us. He deserved better than the ending he got.

Crash sighed before he answered. "They're not going to admit it, but I think we all know they were the one's responsible. What we need to figure out is how we respond to it."

"We can't leave it unanswered," Zach hissed. "They murdered one of our own."

"He was a prospect," Vienna reminded him. "If we retaliate, we're declaring all-out war on the Rough Riders. Do we want war for a prospect?"

"He's right," I said, leaning forward with my elbows on the table and my cigarette between my lips. "War will be bloody, and we'll lose much more than a prospect by the end of it."

"So we let them get away with it? And then what? They'll think we're pussies. What's stopping them from coming after another prospect? Heck, if they know we're gonna do fuck all, what's stopping them going for a patched in member?"

I knew what he meant. The Rough Riders would never take out a titled member of the club, but his sons weren't titled members. They were just fully patched, and therefore vulnerable, as far as Zach was concerned.

"They're not going to take on a patched member, title or not," Crash reassured him.

"You know that for a fact, do you?"

"Do you know what's more important to me?" Vienna began. "Is finding out who told them where Mickey was going to be. No-one outside of this club knew his mother was sick. No-one even really knew he was a prospect. He wasn't as involved as Monster. No-one should have been following him to his mother's facility."

"You think we have a rat?" I asked him.

"I think it's a possibility. Look at last month – most of the guys were at the Greasy Spoon. And then Shark was attacked whilst picking up spare parts. Something isn't right, and my nose smells a rat."

"You have any idea who it is?" Crash said, leaning back in his chair, his eyes half closed as he contemplated what Vienna had said.

"No. All I know for certain is it's not one of us."

"One of the prospects, maybe?" Crash thought out loud.

"Maybe. Whoever it is, they'll be pretty fucking stupid. They know what happens to men who betray the club."

"I'll look into it," Zach promised. "In the meantime, let's deal with what we know for a fact. How are we going to handle the Rough Riders and Mickey's death?"

"I say we play them at their own game," I said, taking another draw of my cigarette. "They were clever. They attacked him whilst he was riding on his own, far away from the club. No witnesses, no nothing. I say we watch their prospects for a few days, find out their movements. Then, just when enough time has passed for the Rough Riders to think they got away with Mickey's murder, we'll take one of theirs, like they took ours."

"If this comes back on the club—" Crash began.

"So what? We mimic their movements. They can't outright accuse us without admitting what they did. We'll deny it, and we'll tell them there must be another club out there murdering prospects, since we don't know who killed Mickey either. They can't deny it, because if they know for a fact there's not another rival club, they'll have to prove *how* they know it."

"And if they call our bluff?" Zach asked.

"We call theirs in return."

"It's the best we've got," Vienna agreed. "If they want to declare war over a prospect, then so be it. But right now, I think retaliating on the quiet is the best way to deal with it. They'll know it's us, just like we know it's them. But it keeps things from escalating. Especially since we don't want to spook Rachel when she's only just arrived with a full-on war."

"Now that," I nodded, "is why I like you. She'll freak the fuck out if we start shooting anyone within a five-mile radius."

"I'll watch the prospects," Vienna volunteered. "And whatever I find out, I'll bring to the table before church next week. After that, we make our move."

"We all good with that?" Crash asked.

"Aye," Zach and I said together.

"So it's agreed," he banged the gavel once more. "Let's just hope this is the right decision."

Chapter 7

Rachel

Shadows crept across the room as I watched the shift from afternoon, into evening, into night.

I made a game of it, taking small bets with myself to see when the shadows would completely engulf me.

I won.

It took three guesses, but I won.

Hey, I was tied to a chair, having been kidnapped by a literal mad man. I was taking any victory I could get.

Dante didn't return, just like he swore he wouldn't, but I hadn't been clinging to that hope, anyway. I had resigned myself to being tied to this chair all night. Dante was a man of his word, especially if his word was the promise of cruelty. He was punishing me for not playing along with the narrative he made up in his own head. He had taken one look at me, and pretty much decided the script I would use for the rest of my entire life, and now that he wasn't getting it… well, the words "bitch fit" came to mind.

And yes, I realised I was judging him as much as he had judged me, but I had at least allowed myself a handful of interactions with him before I made my assessment. He assumed I was a quiet little trad-wife because I wore a nice dress. If I wasn't in such a predicament, I'd laugh about that. I'm sure even the likes of Rose West wore a nice fucking dress occasionally.

I twisted my wrists as much as the rope would allow, trying to alleviate some of the numbness that had taken over hours ago. At least the numbness distracted me from the pain in my ass from this hard seat. And the pain in my ass distracted me from the pangs of hunger.

I had been a fucking fool not to eat at the Greasy Spoon. This was my problem. I never trusted my instincts.

Instinct had warned me that I wouldn't be returning to America, and instead of fortifying my body for the battle ahead, I've gone in with no armour, no weapons, and an empty fucking stomach.

Rachel for the win!

Well… that wasn't strictly true. I had weapons, but I had played my hand too soon and used the first sharp object I had found on that stupid so-called self-defence keychain. What was a knife like that going to do to a man built like Dante? I'm surprised it even went in his stupid fucking thigh.

And of course, my twisted self was actually turned on my that. The fact that his thighs were so large and powerful, I was sat debating what size knife would be needed to penetrate skin.

I was no better than a man sometimes; I swear.

I looked out of the window and tried to determine what time it was. The moon was shining brightly on the carpet, so surely that meant it was fairly high in the sky. So that made it… around midnight, I suppose.

Yeah, good going. Since when did you become a fucking astronomer? You know as much about the moon as you do about Dante. In fact, you know Dante is an asshole, so you actually know more *about him.*

I flopped back in the chair with a thud and threw my head back, squeezing my eyes tightly as my body silently worked out the scream of frustration that had been building inside me. I strained against the ropes, my body arching as my hair spilled down my back and I let out a silent scream. When I opened my eyes again, I focused on the bed to the wall opposite me.

That fucking bed. It looked so warm and inviting, so unbelievably cosy. What I wouldn't give to be asleep on that bed right now.

My stomach rumbled loudly, but I refused to acknowledge it. Mind over matter. I was stronger than a few stomach pains, and a bit of hunger would not kill me. I'd proven that many times in the past. However, the thirst just might.

And whilst I knew I was being dramatic, and I wasn't at any risk of dying from thirst, my throat was dryer than the Sahara, and the fight with Dante earlier hadn't helped matters.

I'd let him spit in my mouth all night right now, and it would be the most pleasurable thing in the world.

Twisted. But true.

An image came to me of my room with the Gellers, with its soft bed, as though I was sleeping on a cloud, and a bath as big as some cars I had seen. Fuck me, I loved that bath. I'd probably miss that the most.

I wondered for a moment what the Gellers were doing right now. I wondered if their flight had been delayed or if they were getting ready for landing. However, I quickly shut that thought out. The Gellers were dead to me from this moment on.

I had been the perfect employee for them, never once complaining or showing how tired I was. I earned every dollar they paid me.

Speaking of which, I had quite a bit saved up in my account. If I could figure out the exchange rates, I'd be able to work out exactly what I had, and how it would benefit me.

I also needed to have a conversation with Macbeth. He was the one Dante assigned to giving Elizabeth an address for my belongings. The sooner I had those, the sooner I could make a plan. I couldn't give a fuck about the clothes or the shoes. I just wanted my documents. Or maybe I could sneak away one day and go to the bank.

Although, why should I have to sneak away? If Dante truly meant for me to be his old lady, I should be able to live a normal life, coming and going as I please. Having access to my own money and visiting a bank was hardly anything extreme or out of the ordinary.

But that was another day. Today, I was stuck here. Today, I had no chance of Dante allowing me to leave the room, never mind go to the bank or spend any money. I had pissed him off, and now I was paying the price.

Bit sensitive, really. What's one little stab in the thigh between a man and his wannabe (on his behalf) old lady?

Just as I was beginning to feel a sense of hope, thick, loud patters of rain lashed against my window, making me groan out loud.

Fan-fucking-tastic.

Hungry, thirsty, tired, and now I need to pee as well. This day was really proving to be up there with the best!

I must have drifted off, because I was vaguely aware that it was darker than it was before, but I was also pleasantly aware of the fact that I didn't feel any lack of comfort – one of the benefits of sleep, it really does make you forget your woes.

I was also aware of the thing that had woken me from a lazy slumber, and that was the sound of the door clicking open. Knowing that I wouldn't be able to see anything anyway, I kept my eyes shut and focused on my other senses rather than straining my site for, at best, a blurred shadow. I could hear footprints padding across the floor, the sound of glass clinking against a plate. I could smell the gravy, the potatoes, the juicy beef, and my mouth watered instantly.

Well, well, well, lucky me, and it's not even my birthday.

Even in the darkness, even with my eyes shut, I felt a shadow creep over me; the air shifting as someone invaded my personal space.

"Oi!" snapped a voice I didn't recognise, followed by them clicking their fingers in front of my face. I opened my eyes slowly and tried to focus on the man – it wasn't Dante, that much was immediately clear. As much as I hated to admit it, Dante had a raw, animal magnetism that screamed to the woman in me.

This dude left me cold, whoever the fuck he was.

I blinked at him, staring hard at his face, trying to see if I recognised him from the crowd of bikers that had kidnapped me earlier.

"Like what you see?" He said with a laugh, his voice deep and gruff. Dante's voice was sinful, almost like a verbal aphrodisiac. He was gruff on a primal level. This little prick was gruff, like a thirty a day chain smoker.

"Why? Do you want me to like what I see?"

He looked me up and down. "I've seen worse. You wouldn't be a bad little thing to entertain for a while."

"Helpless victim one of your kinks, is it? Get your kicks from seeing women at your mercy? What's the matter, not man enough to get your own woman, so you hit on the ones your boss kidnaps? Score!"

"If I wanted you, trust me, it wouldn't take much. I've yet to find a woman to say no."

"Go on then," I challenged.

He looked at me, not moving. He clearly hadn't expected me to call his bluff. "What you waiting for?" I opened my legs and shuffled down in the chair until my ass was hanging off the edge. "Show me what you've got, big boy. I can't wait to see your moves."

"I—" he still didn't move.

"I knew it," I said with a smirk, closing my legs. "You're all mouth, too scared of the boss man to even attempt it. I can see why your little club has such a scary reputation." The way I said scary sounded more like "scawy", and I knew from the sharp intake of breath that I had hit a nerve.

"Listen—"

"No, *you* listen," I interrupted. "It's dark, it's cold, and I literally cannot be fucked with your dick waving competition. I don't care. You win, you're such a big manly man, all the girls definitely want such a strong man like you. Now, can you just untie me, leave the dinner, and kindly fuck off out of here and leave me in peace?"

"Oh, this dinner? This one right here?" He mocked, waving the plate under my nose.

"Really?" I said dryly, rolling my eyes at him. "I'm not about to beg."

"If you want it, come and get it."

Bastard.

"Keep it," I attempted to shrug. "I can go a few more hours."

"Is that right? Are you sure Dante will bring you anything else? Especially when I tell him how ungrateful you were," he tutted, shaking his head at me. "He went out of his way to prepare this for you, and you're not even going to be a good girl and play nice so I can feed you?"

"Really?" I breathed, looking up at him through my lashes.

"If that's what you want."

"Is that what *you* want? You want to feed me?" I asked with a girlish smile. "No-one has ever fed me before."

"I think we might have just found *your* kink," he grinned. "Told you. It's as easy as pie. I know what girls like."

"I stand mistaken. Come here." I looked at him coyly and opened my mouth, waiting for him to feed me a bite. He came towards me, mashing foods together on the fork to give me a bite of everything. My mouth watered, sending a jolt of shock to my stomach, bringing it roaring to life.

I was going to regret this. It smelled so fucking good.

"Open up," he said, bending down slightly and extending the fork towards me. "What does a good girl say?"

I giggled, squirming in the chair slightly. He lowered the fork to my lips, and that's when my right leg shot out and kicked the plate out of his hands, sending the contents spilling onto the carpet. The plate shattered with the force of my kick, sounding like a bomb in the quiet room. "I don't know what good girls say, but *this* girl says fuck your dinner, fuck your weird obsession with age-play, and fuck *you!* How's that for ungrateful?" I spat at the food on the floor, taking great satisfaction in seeing some of the gravy had splashed onto his leg.

"Wait until Dante finds out about this!" He growled at me, twisting on his heel, and heading for the door.

"Oh, okay, Malfoy," I called out after him, raising my voice as he opened the door. "You off to make fun of the Weasley boys next or…?" My voice trailed off with a laugh as he slammed the door behind him.

"Too easy," I chuckled to myself, before my eyes landed back on the plate shining in the moonlight. I strained my leg, stretching it as far as possible until my shoe was on top of one of the shards. I gently scraped it under my foot, bringing it closer to me slowly but surely, until it was close enough for my foot to comfortably rest on top of it so I could kick it under my chair and slide it between both of my feet, covered by my shoes.

I'll save that one for later.

Dante

"Listen," I turned around as Noob entered the room. He was my least favourite prospect. He reminded me a lot of Macbeth

68

when we were younger. Why he was even hanging around a motorcycle club was beyond me. He had been here for two years before he declared himself a prospect. I had done everything I could to avoid him for those two years. Something about him gave me the creeps. Luckily, he couldn't be patched in unless the vote was unanimous. He had a lot of work to do if he wanted to be a full member in a few months.

He was on thin ice as far as I was concerned, which is why I had given him the simple task of taking Rachel her meal. Even that idiot couldn't fuck that up.

"I know you're sweet on her, but she's got one hell of a smart mouth."

I shrugged, turning back to the TV. I kind of enjoyed the thought of Rachel giving him a hard time. She seemed to have moved past the blank, irritating expression, and was now allowing her inner brat to shine through. I had seen a brief glimpse to know that Noob was out of his depth with her.

"You weren't supposed to talk to her. All you had to do was take her the meal, wait for her to eat, and leave. It seemed fairly simple to me."

"She was asleep."

"Okay… and?" I flicked through the channels, my tone one of boredom. I didn't even know why he was bothering me with this. Rachel either ate or she didn't. It was as simple as that. If she hurt his feelings along the way, what did that have to do with me?

"So I had to wake her up."

"You need words to nudge someone awake?"

"Have you ever spoken to her for more than a minute?"

I sighed and turned the TV off. "Where is this going?" I asked, turning towards him again.

What does a guy have to do to get a moment's peace around here? Is everyone forgetting the fact that I was stabbed in the leg only hours ago?

"Simply put, she's a fucking cunt."

"I'm sorry," I said quietly, my voice like ice. "Repeat that. I don't think I heard correctly. She's a what?"

"N-no, I didn't mean—"

"Oh," I said, getting to my feet. "You *didn't* mean she was a cunt? What did you mean, then?"

He took a step backwards as I rose from the seat. "I just meant... you see..."

"Ye-es?"

"Dante!" my mother snapped, coming into the room. "Are you playing nice?"

"I haven't decided yet. I'm waiting for Noob here to let me know."

"Bee is waiting for you," she said, a warning note in her voice.

"You hear that?" I directed my question to Noob. "My kids waiting. That's both the main girls in my life you've upset now. I suggest you hurry up and clear up this little confusion."

My mother remained in the doorway, knowing better than to get involved in any of my business, but she did shoot a pitiful look towards Noob.

"I guess I'll go read Bee her bedtime story," she sighed. "It's a good job she's fucking homeschooled, staying up until this hour!" We heard her mumble as she walked away.

"Oh, would you look at that?" I slowly made my way towards Noob. "Now my mother's mad at me. That's three for three. Things aren't looking too good for you now, are they?"

Noob swallowed heavily, backing up from my retreat. "I'm sorry, Dante. I spoke out of turn. I shouldn't have called her a cunt."

"No. No, you shouldn't."

"She kicked the plate out of my hand."

"Did she?" I said flatly, still creeping towards him.

"She didn't want it, Dante, I swear." He put his hands up, warding me off. "She told me to go fuck myself."

I was right in front of him now, towering over him as he cowered away from me. Just when I thought he was going to piss himself there and then, my face broke out into a grin, and I gave him a slap on his back.

"I'm just fucking with you, man. I'll deal with her. Seems she might be harder to break than I had first thought."

Noob laughed, both out of relief and fear. But that was his mistake. Fear made him loosen his tongue, and he started talking a mile to the dozen. "You're telling me! She's a good-looking lass. You want to make sure she doesn't go spreading her legs to any of the other guys. They won't all be as gentlemanly as me." He gave me a returned slap to the arm, his hand lingering on me.

I froze, and the smile instantly fell from his face.

"She did what?" I said quietly, blinking once, my head cocked to the side.

His face paled, his hand falling from my arm as immediate tremors ran through him. "She... Dante, I swear to God, I didn't encourage it. She took one look at me and started with her mouth. She was daring me to take her, saying I wouldn't dare because of you and—"

My fist came out and connected with his jaw, knocking him to the floor. I was on him in an instant, grabbing his shirt to lift his face close to mine as I crouched over him. "You've got five seconds to tell me fucking everything. When I'm done with you, I'll go ask Rachel. Need to make sure your story matches hers; you know? And I swear to God, if I find out you laid a single finger on her, I will personally peel the skin from your back, and then drag you round hogtied to the bikes."

Rachel

Alright. I admit it. I was rash. I should have swallowed my stupid pride and accepted the food.

The longer it was on the floor, the more I regretted kicking it there in the first place.

It mocked me.

Nothing had the right to smell that good. Even as the gravy took on a musty smell, it still appealed to me. I'd eat the skin off the gravy and not utter a single complaint, and everyone knows the weird skin it gets is the worst bit.

Hell, I'd have smothered that idiot's fucking dick in gravy and inhaled it. I was that hungry.

If it wasn't for the fact that I had so much stupid pride, I'd have rocked on my seat until it tipped over, hoping that I'd land face first in the mashed potatoes until I suffocated. At least I'd die full up.

But I wouldn't give Dante the satisfaction of knowing I'd even attempted to eat food off the floor like a begging dog.

I just had to push through it and not think about it.

Although… the thought of being on my knees and begging for things from Dante had a certain appeal to it. That's when I knew I was truly hungry. I was losing my goddamn mind. Dante was a snack, but Jesus…

The only problem was, if I didn't think about food, I was thinking about how sore my wrists were beginning to get, and the dull ache in my arms from remaining in the same position for so long. If I didn't think about that, then I was thinking about the fact that it currently felt as though there were a team of tiny dancing leprechauns doing an Irish jig on my bladder. It was uncomfortably full, and I was honestly struggling to remember the last time I had used the toilet.

My stomach let out a growl, as though it was playing the music for the stupid fucking leprechauns and once again, I was back to the food.

Round, round, baby, round, round.

Just when I was about to say a big "fuck you" to pride, and the horse it rode in on, my door crashed open with such force, it bounced off the wall behind it, the handle leaving a dint. The sound was like a bolt of thunder, and I'm not ashamed to admit that I did let out a yelp of fear.

My eyes flew to the doorway, and I saw the shadow of a giant, a giant I knew only too well.

And he looked absolutely fucking livid.

"Rachel," his voice growled through the room, sending a shiver down my spine at how low and deep it was, the clear warning tone igniting my inner brat.

Probably not the right reaction.

"Yes, Dante?" I called out pleasantly. He stepped into the room and shut the door behind him, sealing out the light from the hallway. He was just a black shadow now. A shadow that was creeping towards me.

Funny how all my earlier troubles were forgotten. I didn't feel hungry, or sore, or needing to pee. Dante had the ability to invade my entire body without doing a thing. He surrounded me, invaded my senses, and all I wanted to do was mess with him, to see the tick in his throat as I angered him.

I'd devour that tick right now.

Okay, maybe I was still a bit hungry,

My head followed him, twisting to the side as he wandered to the back of the chair and undid the restraints, finally freeing my hands. They flopped forward, and I instinctively stretched them out in front of me and up over my head.

"I hope you're not expecting thanks for that because—" My words were cut off with a gargle as he wrapped a large hand around my throat and squeezed tightly, pulling me to my feet with a choke. I tried to pull away, a cough rising in my throat that I couldn't get out, such was the grip he had on me. He walked me backwards until my back slammed against the wall. I tried to speak. I don't even know what I was going to say. Probably something stupid. But he clamped his other hand down on my mouth so hard, I could feel my teeth digging into my lips.

I looked at the broken piece of glass on the floor under my chair, and wished I had the foresight to grab it the minute he released my hands, instead of thinking about my comfort. I had just been so relieved to be free; I hadn't thought it through. That was probably the biggest mistake I had made today.

"Think very, *very* carefully about your next words. When I take my hand off your mouth, the only thing I want to hear is why the *fuck* you think being my old lady means spreading your legs to *any* of my club members, never mind one as low as him."

Ahh shit.

Malfoy tattle taled.

Chapter 8

Rachel

Dante was absolutely livid with me, that much was obvious. His hand stayed clamped around my mouth, not giving me the opportunity to answer his question – which was a good thing, because what would I have said?

What he said was technically true. I did spread my legs to that little snitch Malfoy, or whatever his name was. But I didn't *spread* my legs in the sense that I wanted to fuck him. Which is probably what Dante was envisioning. And I wouldn't have put it past Malfoy to make me seem worse than I was because his pride was injured. I wonder if he told Dante about the comments he made towards me?

Probably not.

Should I tell him?

Also, probably not.

"Are you ready?" Dante asked after taking a deep breath. His voice seemed calmer, but if there was one thing I had learnt, it was the seemingly calm people that were the most dangerous. Angry people were predictable. They weren't completely in control, so you knew they were going to lash out verbally or physically. You had to prepare for either. And if it was the latter, you had to be prepared for all forms of violence, including weapons. If you were prepared for any and all eventualities, you could protect yourself.

Calm people were in control. Which meant they were not predictable. Calm people could still feel anger, but they were able to make conscious decisions and not lash out in the heat of the moment. So a truly angry, calm person had the ability to snap your neck and clean the mess up afterwards. They weren't in a frenzy. Every move they made was calculated. Thought through. Planned.

Calmed people scared the fuck out of me.

Not a great thought when your neck was currently being squeezed by an angry, calm giant.

I nodded as much as his hand would allow me to, and he removed his other hand from my mouth and loosened his grip on my throat. Not by much, not enough to let me get away, but enough to allow me to breathe with ease.

He stayed close to me, his eyes locked onto mine. I could feel his warm breath against my skin, fanning my hair away from my face. I could see the tick in his neck as he fought for control, to remain calm whilst I explained myself.

Even in the darkness, he was close enough that I could see his body tensed up, as though he was one wrong word away from exploding.

Which made my mind up for me. I wasn't about to open my mouth and say everything wrong and end up in an even worse position. I was tired, hungry, sore, and honestly, this could escalate far more than needed if I played the wrong hand.

"Well?"

"Well, what?"

"Don't play innocent," Dante sighed. "I'll be getting answers out of you one way or another. The easiest thing to do would be to lay it all out on the table, and then I can decide how I want to deal with it."

"Hmm," I frowned. "I'm confused."

"What can I possibly have said that's confused you right now?"

"I'm confused about what needs handling. There was a situation, and I dealt with it. There isn't any need for you to decide anything. Stay out of it."

"Excuse me?" He all but spluttered.

"Take your hands off me and I'll excuse you."

He laughed slightly – not because he found anything funny; I think he was bewildered more than anything. "You spread your legs for a fucking prospect, straight after hearing you were my old lady, and this has nothing to do with me?"

"Well, first of all, that's not how it happened, and second of all, yeah. That's exactly what I'm saying."

"Tell me how it happened," he challenged.

"I'll do no such thing – you've got a real issue with ordering people around; did you know that? If I felt like you needed to know, I'd say something. But here we are."

"I've every right to order around those that belong to me."

"When you find someone that belongs to you, knock yourself out."

"You belong to me. You're—"

"An old lady. I heard it the first million times. Get a new phrase, for fuck's sake."

"Rachel…" He paused a moment. "You're beginning to annoy me."

"Malfoy annoyed *me*. Be grateful you've got the use of your hands to do something about it."

"Who the fuck is Malfoy?" He blinked at me, his anger disappearing more and more by the second, and sheer bewilderment taking its place.

"Him – Dinner boy. He wasn't polite enough to bother with necessities such as names, so I came up with my own."

He let go of my throat completely then and rubbed his hands over his eyes. He stayed close to me, placing his hands on the wall behind me, trapping me between him.

"Let's start again," he said pleasantly.

"Great. I love fresh starts. Big believer in those! If you could drop me off where you found me, that would be great."

"I meant tonight."

"Yeah, well, I meant the entire day."

"Rachel… No. for the last time, you're staying here," he sighed.

"Shame."

"So?"

"So?"

"Fuck me, you're annoying." He pushed off the wall and walked away from me, pacing the carpet up and down.

"Maybe you should do your research on people before you go kidnapping them. Could have saved yourself the headache."

"Yeah, I've heard that already today."

"Maybe you should listen to advice, then."

"Maybe you could just do as you're asked and tell me what happened."

"Maybe I could remind you of the fact that it was *you* who sent that idiot up here. Once again, had you done your research, you wouldn't have exposed me to a sex pest." He glared at me, and I shrugged. "Just a thought."

"What do you mean, 'sex pest?' Did he touch you?" He demanded, coming towards me again, and grabbing hold of me.

"Oh, for fuck's sake," I hissed, taking him off guard by shoving him backwards and moving out of his reach. "No, he did not. But you are. Constantly. You're a fucking brute. Can you have one conversation without leaving a bruise on me? Have I actually done anything to warrant this?"

"Well... you did stab me."

"*After* you manhandled me repeatedly. *After* you kidnapped me. *After* you tried to scare the ever-loving shit out of me – unsuccessfully, might I add. Other than that, I happen to think I've been a model citizen." He opened his mouth, but I was quick to say what was on my mind. "Have I kicked off in any way? Have I shouted, screamed, demanded any sort of explanation? Or did I get on your bike willingly? Did I enter your home uncoerced? Did I follow you up here, silent as a mouse? I've done everything asked of me, and all I got in return was your shit attitude, the scornful stares of the dickheads you call your friends, and exposed to whatever the fuck Malfoy was. So excuse me if I don't really feel like talking, when *not* talking has already got me tied up and starved. My mother always told me my smart mouth would be the death of me. Believe it or not, I'm playing it safe!" There was a painful silence after I finished my rant, both of us glaring at each other. I got an immense sense of satisfaction when he was the first one to turn away.

"Why didn't you?" He finally asked.

"Why didn't I do what?"

"Why didn't you fight back more?"

"What would it have achieved? You wouldn't have let me go, and it would have just made things worse for me. I'm already covered in bruises, and that's from me being *smart*. I don't want to think about what I'd look like right now had I said no. I might look simple, but I can assure you, I'm far from fucking stupid. I played it the way I thought best. But I can promise you, I'm over that. Lay your hands on me again, and you'll live to regret it."

"Are you threatening me?" He asked incredulously.

"Promising," I corrected.

"You're like five feet tall. What damage could you possibly do?" He laughed.

"You think violence is the only way I can punish you? Oh Dante, you're a big man, but you clearly don't have the brains to match. There's so much I can do; you don't have a fucking clue." It was my turn to laugh as I stepped closer to *him* this time. "What was it you called me? Submissive... Sweet? You keep thinking that." I got up on my tiptoes to whisper in his ear, feeling his breathing speed up as my chest pressed against his. "You won't even see it coming. I'll destroy this place from the inside out, and you won't realise until it's too late. Emotion owns you, and it'll be your downfall. Look how angry you were at the thought of me spreading my legs for Malfoy. How will you feel when I invite your brother into my bed? How will you react when you realise loyalty will always lose to sex? How many of your club members do you think I can fuck before—"

He grabbed my hips, pulling me even closer to him. "Think very carefully before drawing this battle line with me."

"You drew the battle line. I'm rising to the challenge. Do your worst, Dante, and I'll do mine. I might come out with a few cuts and bruises, but you'll come out of this with no friends, no family, no club, nothing. I had a home; the Gellers were my new family. You took all of that. I'll do the same to you, and I'll do it all with a smile on my face, and there's fuck all you can do to stop me."

"You sure about that?"

I brought my lips close to his, so that every word I spoke caused them to rub against his.

"You already tried. You had me tied to a chair, and I still could have had your friend eating my pussy without giving you a second thought. And that was without me even trying. What do you think I could achieve if I gave it some effort?"

Fuck, his lips were softer than I thought they would be. My breathing increased as I became aware of how close we were, how our bodies had moulded against each other. I could feel the bulge between his legs press against my stomach. I saw the way his eyes dilated as I looked up at him. I felt the familiar tingle as my nipples hardened in awareness, in *response,* and that's when I knew I was truly fucked.

I hadn't left this world behind at all. I had just buried it for a while.

The thrill of danger had always been my kink. Some women responded to flowers, I responded to wildness. People always said fight or flight, but in my case, it was fight, flight, or fuck. And I always went with fuck.

There was something titillating to have a man capable of murder, capable of killing you in a second, to have him so angry that he appeared to hate you, only to then channel that hate into fucking you senseless.

If you've never been fucked as though you were hated… I'm so sorry. But I loved every minute of it.

I would be a brat every step of the way, but once a certain point was reached, I'd submit under them and take all the nasty, degrading, humiliating sex they had to offer.

They might have thought they were dominating me, but what they didn't realise was I had won. I owned them. So long as they desired me, they could never truly leave me alone. I had them dancing to the beat of my drum. I might get off on them calling me a filthy slut or slapping me so hard my teeth rattled. I might enjoy them choking me to the point of blacking out, but it was *my* pussy they thought about before they went to sleep. *My* pussy that was their first waking thought. It was *my* pussy they were begging to tense up on their cock, desperate to cum inside.

If that wasn't erotic, I didn't know what the fuck was.

"Try it," Dante said, swallowing hard. "You've some ego if you think—"

"What? Think I'm attractive? Seductive?" I laughed again. "You came in here guns blazing because of something you had heard. You didn't even know if it was true, but jealousy had you reacting. I saw the way your jaw clenched when I wiggled my ass downstairs earlier, letting everyone in that bar get a look at the goods. And this," I reached between his legs and grabbed hold of the bulge straining against his jeans. I cupped it, massaging it with my palm. "This tells me that I don't need to think. I know. And so long as this is the reaction you have, I've more power than you think."

His lips clamped down on mine then, taking my breath away with the force of his kiss. I recovered quickly, stepping up as far as I could on my tiptoes to kiss him back with as much force as he was offering me. His fingers dug into my hips tighter as I moved my hand away so he could pull me in closer, our bodies so close, I'm surprised we didn't blend into one.

My hands crept up to his shoulders, and he lifted me up with one smooth sweep, wrapping my legs around his waist as his hands fell to cup my ass. I grabbed fistfuls of his hair as tight as I could, slipping my tongue in his mouth as his lips opened in a gasp of pain.

He met my silent challenge and grabbed hold of my ass tighter. I bit down on his lip, and he spun us, slamming me against the wall so hard my breath left my body at once. I locked my legs at the ankles and pushed on the small of his back, feeling his cock through his trousers hit between my legs. He felt it too, and his cock jerked in response. He ran his tongue along mine and then sucked my bottom lip into his mouth.

Using the wall as a support, my hands still grabbing his hair, I began to grind on him, my body leaning forward, so my tits were in his face, my lower back and ass against the wall, my hips rotating, swirling, rocking against his.

My pussy clenched in excitement as he growled low in his throat, but before I could tease him anymore, he spun once more, walking with me in his arms.

He threw me backwards on the bed with such force my teeth rattled, and I bit down on my tongue.

"So long as you react like that," he panted, looking down at me with such disgust I almost recoiled from it. "Then I have more power than you think. Get some sleep, Rachel, before I do something to you that you'll end up regretting for the rest of your life."

He spun on his heel and walked out the door, slamming it shut behind him. I jumped off the bed and ran after him, opening the door to shout after his retreating form. "If you could just point the way to Malfoy's house, I'll go let him finish what you started, since you're too pussy to do it!"

He didn't give me a reaction, so I slammed the door shut again and assessed the situation.

I could escape right now. I could genuinely leave and give it my best shot to get the fuck out of here.

How long would it take him to notice? No doubt he had people on guard, anticipating this, and would I really want to be that predictable? It would end in my punishment, that I knew for certain.

And then there was the question of where would I go? My mother wouldn't have me back. I needed visitation rights for my dad, and I had no friends left. At least, not friends I should be getting involved with.

How pathetic was my life that staying here was the safer option? At least here I had shelter. Out there, I was a sitting duck, exposed to the elements as I tried to hide, waiting for Dante to come find me. Which he would. I had no idea where the fuck we were, and he knew this place like the back of his hand.

Instead, I grabbed the chair Dante had tied me to earlier, bent down to grab the broken plate shard, and carried them both to the other side of the room with me, opening the one other door in the room, smiling with satisfaction when I saw it led to an ensuite bathroom.

I slipped inside, shoving the chair up against the handle of the closed door and gave it a quick test to prove it wouldn't open, and breathed a sigh of relief. It wouldn't stop Dante if he really wanted to get in here, but at least it would give me some warning. I placed the broken plate on the cushion of the chair and turned around, flicking the lights on to take in my surroundings.

I blinked rapidly as my eyes stung, adjusting to the light, and it dawned on me how long I had been sitting in the darkness for. The bastard probably would have left me there until the morning if it wasn't for the dinner incident.

That might actually have been a better outcome than the one I was currently living with. I had pissed Dante off, and he was either going to be the type to go away and calm down or go away and think of how he could meet my challenge and win the game.

Forcing those thoughts to the back of my mind, I scanned the room, pleasantly surprised with all that I found. There was a large bath on the back wall, with a little table next to it full of a variety of different products. There were numerous cupboards and cabinets, and a quick inspection showed me they contained medicine, towels, and hair styling tools. I grabbed one of the fluffy towels, the dressing gown hanging on the inside of one of the cupboards and threw them on the chair near the bath.

I gave the door one last test and satisfied that I would be at peace for at least a little while; I turned the bath taps on, and sat on the toilet, waiting for the steam to fill the room as I processed everything that had happened in just a few hours.

Stolen

As I slipped into the bath, breathing a sigh of relief at the way the water soothed my aching body, my thoughts soon went to Dante and the kiss we had shared.

I let out a small groan as my pussy throbbed in response. It had been so long since I was touched by a man, and Dante was just beast enough to be the perfect one to end my unwanted celibacy.

My hand slid down my stomach and between my legs as I imagined him joining me on the bed he had thrown me on, staring down at me with an animalistic hunger, wanting to devour me.

Fuck me, I really am in trouble, was my last coherent thought before I gave myself over to the fantasy, sinking further down the bath as my fingers slid inside my waiting pussy.

Dante

That woman! She was fucking infuriating!

All she had to do was tell me what had happened between her and Noob. Instead, she had been a smart mouthed little bitch, and the next thing I knew, we were grinding against each other like sex starved teenagers.

I can honestly say I didn't know whether I wanted to fuck her or kill her, and I can't be completely sure that she would have cared either way. She almost seemed to want me to hurt her, and it had driven me half mad for her. I have always been the more dominant person when having sex, but never have I wanted to squeeze someone's throat until their eyes were bloodshot whilst forcing them to take my dick in every hole they owned. And never before have I been with a woman who gave the impression that she would consider that basic foreplay.

I hadn't been expecting this. I had been expecting a nice, meek, polite woman, who would suck my dick on my birthdays and possibly anal at Christmas. I had expected her to smile, to be cordial and friendly, to be a people pleaser.

Rachel was not a people pleaser.

I didn't know a fucking thing about her, and yet I liked her. I didn't want to fucking like her. I wanted Bee to like her, and I expected to find her pleasant enough that I could stand to be in her company whilst Bee grew up.

So far, I couldn't stand to be in Rachel's company, and yet I was fast becoming obsessed with her.

I ran shaking hands through my hair as I sat on the edge of my bed. My elbows rested on my knees as I sat forward, my head in my hands, playing the scene back in my head.

It was my own undoing. I heard her groan as though she was right next to me, and I almost came in my trousers.

Get a fucking grip, Dante, I raged to myself, pushing off my knees to stand up.

I snatched the phone out of my pocket and dialled a number before I could second guess it.

"Hey, honey," Beth purred down the phone.

"You ready to make payment now?"

"I thought you'd never ask! Should I come over?"

"I'll come to you. And Beth?"

"Yeah?" she breathed.

"Be naked when I get there."

Chapter 9

Dante

After checking that my mother was okay to keep an eye on Bee, I jumped on my bike, taking the long route to Greasy, which meant driving through the town we called home.

The town was only about twenty minutes from the services on the motorway... ten on a good day if traffic felt like playing nice. The Greasy served as a meeting ground for the bikers, especially as it was one of the services off the motorway – although it was renown up and down England for being a place of violence and crime. We never bothered to correct the reputation, and we never bothered whether we lived up to it. We lived by our own rules, and we were happy with that. We weren't interested in pleasing the general population.

The commune we lived in was all but abandoned before we turned up. We had turned this into a village of everything we could ever need. My family and I ran the local bar, which served as a home for us, and a place for the bikers to unwind. We also ran the local garage, unashamedly ripping off any idiotic outsiders that were fool enough to pass through.

Many of the wives brainstormed about other shops to implement and there was now a convenience store, a tattoo shop, a cafe, doctor's office, and hairdressers/beauty – I had never been in there, so I've no idea what they offered. The women looked decent enough after coming out, though.

When we first arrived, there hadn't been many of us. However, over the years, we now had thirty families living in this village, and more members spread out through the city. Those were members who didn't play an active role in the day to day running of the club but were still loyal enough that they would come running if we rang.

My grandad had been the one to scout out the place when me and Macbeth were toddlers. Our old club lands were too small and didn't demand as much territory as this one. Over the years, we had slowly gained authority over most of Leeds, and were expanding further and further every year.

Beth had been to the village a few times, scoping out the place. Vienna (named because he had once made the foolish mistake of singing the song by Billy Joel when we were teenagers. In his defence, he hadn't known we were waiting outside the school showers, but we had never let him live it down) had said that it seemed as though she was scoping out the place to see where she would fit in – the sad truth was, she would always be Greasy girl to us. I had no interest in her outside of the café, and the odd fuck here and there.

Her sister hung around the club a lot, too. But Spunky was a well-known club whore, and none of the men were ever going to take her seriously enough to make her an old lady. We made our own destinies in life, and those two had cemented themselves so firmly in their roles, it was impossible to see them as anything else.

Greasy girl and her whore sister.

As I pulled round to the back entrance that led to Beth's home, it wasn't her that was on my mind. What did that say about me as a man, that there was a woman was mere meters away from me, naked as the day she was born, and all I could think about was the woman miles away hating my guts?

I'm sure a psychologist would have a field day with that.

I pushed open the door and headed upstairs, my boots making a loud noise on the stairs, alerting Beth to my presence. I knew straight away that she would be rearranging herself on the bed in the most seductive pose she could muster.

Beth had never said no to anything I had wanted to try with her. She jumped into any suggestion with an almost puppy like excitement, but I had never really bothered pushing her boundaries. Yet, I had already spat in Rachel's mouth, which just happened to be the most erotic thing to happen to me this year, and she fought me every step of the way.

Again, I was a psychiatrist's wet dream.

With a sigh, I pushed open the door and was proven correct. Beth was sitting on the edge of the bed, completely naked, just as I had asked. Her legs were spread, but her hands were between them, playing with her wet pussy. I could see it glistening from where I was standing. Her arms covered her tits, and despite myself, I raised an eyebrow of approval. Naked, but nothing on display that I could see. She had cleverly covered all her best bits.

But then she went and ruined it by leaning back, smiling at me as she brought her feet onto the bed and gave me a full show of how wet and ready she was.

"You're not mad I started without you, are you?" She breathed.

"Couldn't give a fuck," I replied, pulling my shirt over my head and unbuttoning my jeans, quickly pushing them down my thighs and kicking them off.

I climbed on her without another word, and she dived at me, planting kisses over my face, my neck, my shoulders. Anywhere her lips could reach, she was giving her undivided attention. I rested my hands on either side of her head and remained propped up as she did her best to bring me to her level of arousal. She wrapped her legs around my waist and clung to me, raising her body to press against mine.

I felt my dick harden against my boxers, which was hardly surprising. I wasn't in control of my dick at the best of times. But my mind refused to play along. I felt suffocated by her clinging to me, and it just reminded me of a monkey clinging to its playmates. A flash of Rachel flooded my mind. Rachel in my arms, her legs wrapped around my waist. I hadn't been thinking of anything other than her then.

Her hatred for me had made for a wild arousal, and I had felt the heat from between her legs through both of our clothing. My cock jerked in response, and Beth let out a groan of satisfaction, kissing my skin even quicker.

I wanted it to be Rachel, moaning beneath me. I wanted to have her begging and pleading. I wanted her out of control, needy, and consumed with nothing other than the thought of my cock driving into her.

All I could see was her face. All I could smell was her scent. My dick jerked wildly, sending Beth crazed beneath me. It pissed me off how much Rachel was constantly on my mind. I'd legit fucking *die* to hear my name moaning from her lips, and that angered me even further.

I grabbed hold of Beth and rolled her over until she was on top of me, and she immediately adjusted, already grinding her pussy against my dick.

"Dante," she breathed, her hands coming up to her hair to brush it out of her face. The movement made her tits perkier, her nipples two hard buds begging for my attention.

Rachel came to mind once more, and I saw fire and passion in her eyes. Beth always looked so dull. She obviously had a good time, but it was like she was going through the motions she had seen in some porno or another. Rachel was led by instinct, whereas you could practically see the cogs in Beth's brain turning as she thought about what to do next. Rachel wouldn't care what her tits looked like. I could see her clear as day, with nothing on her mind other than riding the shit out of me for her own pleasure. I imagined her greedy little pussy sinking on my dick, taking everything for herself, moving solely to get herself off.

I fucking loved when a woman knew how to pleasure herself. And if she used my body to do it, even better.

With a growl, I grabbed hold of Beth once more and sat up, bringing her to a sitting position in my lap. I looked at her face, so eager to please, and felt completely empty. I kissed her then, grabbing the back of her neck and holding her in place as I punished her with my mouth — punishing her for something she hadn't even done wrong. Punishing her because she wasn't Rachel. Beth let out a small yelp of pain as I bit down, and I felt my blood boil that she couldn't just take it like *she* would have taken it.

I pushed her off me and onto her knees, ignoring her gasp from shock, and stood up, pulling my boxers down and let my cock spring free.

"Suck," I demanded, grabbing her hair and pushing her down on me. She grabbed hold of me with both hands and stroked her tongue along the length of my cock before she took the tip into her mouth.

Instinct told me Rachel would have inhaled my dick until she was choking. She wouldn't have been bothered about looking pretty, she would have been raw and wild, sucking me like her life depended on it.

The more I thought of Rachel, the more aroused I was becoming. I tightened my grip on Beth's hair and tried to push her down on me further, and with a girlish giggle, she obliged, bobbing down on me.

I threw my head back with frustration, wanting... I don't know what I wanted. I wanted more. I wanted fire. I wanted gritty and dirty. I wanted uncontrollable.

I had to be honest with myself. I wanted to fuck Rachel, and Beth was a poor substitute.

"Get up," I hissed, pulling my cock out of Beth's mouth with a pop. She had been putting such minimal effort in that I pulled out safely, without so much as a scratch from her teeth.

She got straight to her feet and stood before me, waiting for her next command.

"I'll come collect the cash in the morning," I told her, pulling my boxers back up and picking my jeans off the floor.

"Excuse me?" She said, her eyes wide.

"Are you as shit at listening as you are at sucking dick or something?"

She didn't respond. She went over to the door and grabbed her dressing gown off the hook and wrapped it around her body, pulling it tightly closed. "This is about her, isn't it?"

"Who?" I responded as I pulled my shirt over my head.

"Her. Her from this afternoon."

"If you're talking about Rachel, then no."

"Spunky told me she was your old lady now."

"Okay. And?"

"And I hadn't been expecting you tonight."

"Are you making a point here, Beth?"

"Don't take it out on me because you haven't been able to have your way with her. I've done nothing wrong." She said in a small voice.

"I'm taking it out on you because you've done nothing right." I responded with a hiss, "Have you ever said no once in your life? Did it ever occur to you that since I have an old lady at home, you shouldn't even be entertaining me?"

"I'm not responsible for what you do and who you cheat on, Dante."

"Of course you're not. Because I tell you to jump, you say how high. And with minimal fucking effort, making sure you don't break a sweat."

"I'd like you to leave now, please. *You* came to *me*. I didn't ring you. I didn't drag you away. You came over here on your own accord. I've done nothing to deserve to be insulted like this."

"Answer me. Have you ever said no once in your life? If I asked you to get on your knees right now and pick up where we left off, you'd do it. If I told you to be my secret shag for the rest of our lives, you'd do it. If I told you to fuck every guy in the club, you'd do it. Have you never just for one second stopped and had a thought all of your own?"

"Is this making you feel better?" She asked with a hint of anger, but I just sneered at her and walked out the door, slamming it behind me.

I knew what I needed to do.

Most men would consider themselves in love with the level of obsession I had for Rachel. But I recognised it for what it was: lust. Pure, unadulterated lust. I needed to get it out of my system, and there was only one way to do that.

Rachel

I stretched in bed, waking up after the most restless sleep I had ever experienced. Even worse than after what had happened with Alex. Even after what my dad did for me. I was selfish enough to sleep easily, despite the fact one was dead, and one was in prison. The first few weeks afterwards had been the most difficult, but I soon moved on and slept with ease.

Last night had been different.

Even after a relaxing bath, I had still seen every hour on the clock. I lost count of the number of times I had woke up from a dream of Dante and was left with no choice but to fuck myself. It only took the edge off the burning heat that surged through my body whenever I thought of him.

But outside of Dante and my need for him, I was painfully aware of how much I had neglected my body and how much yesterday had worn on me. My arms hurt, my stomach was rumbling, my lip was stinging, and I was still raging beyond belief at what had happened.

Stolen

I could hear movement throughout the house, letting me know everyone else was up and alive, busy starting their day. I sat up and pulled my purse over to me, swearing under my breath when I remembered Dante had tipped all my belongings out, and I had swept them to the floor before I climbed into my bed. I got to my knees and leant over the side of the bed, scrambling for my phone when I heard the click of the door.

"Now that's a welcome I could get used to," Dante's amused voice came from behind me, and I cringed, knowing he was getting a full view of my naked behind. I hadn't wanted to put my dress back on, and the towel had unravelled whilst I slept.

"Considering you're not welcome," I said, grabbing my phone and pushing myself back up until I was sitting cross-legged on the bed, not bothering to cover myself. "I wouldn't get used to anything."

I shot Dante a nasty look, but he wasn't paying any attention to my face. His focus was on my tits, my stomach, between my legs.

"Getting a good look, are you?"

"Could be better," he responded with a smirk. "Bee's eating breakfast, so I'm up for a make-up quickie if you are."

"I'm not going to dignify that with an answer." I rolled my eyes at him and climbed off the bed, standing completely naked before him. "Clothes." I demanded.

"What's up with that?" He nodded at the dress I had been wearing yesterday.

"Oh, let me think," I said sarcastically, beginning to count on my fingers. "I wore that dress all day, including eating in that disgusting diner, and on the back of your bike. I was tied up in that dress for hours on end, had dinner more or less spilled on it, blood on it – not all mine, granted, but it's there, nonetheless. I was spat at in that dress, knocked about in that dress... I'm running out of fingers, so need I continue?"

"You missed out 'my pussy was wetter than ever before whilst wearing that dress', but you more or less covered the basics." He grinned back.

"Don't flatter yourself. Is this your attempt at shitty humour? Because it's not working. I'm not interested in being your friend or building any sort of relationship with you. The less I have to deal with you, the better. Just tell me where to get some clothes, or I will walk straight to breakfast exactly how I am."

"Be my guest," he stepped aside and gestured to the hallway.

Oh, fun! A game of chicken!

Never one to back down from a challenge, I did exactly that, walking straight past him, knocking him with my shoulder as I did so. I turned around once I was in the corridor and raised an eyebrow in a silent question. He answered by pointing to the left, so I spun back around and marched down the hallway.

My skin tingled with awareness, knowing he was watching my every move. My hips swayed of their own violation, and I knew my ass was jiggling.

I ran with it, slowing my movements down, my back straightening as I gave him the best show possible. I could hear him following me, and I got the sudden sensation of being hunted down, predator and prey, and a jolt of electricity shot straight to my pussy, making me clench in excitement.

I had just made it to the top of the stairs, committed to walking through the entire bar completely naked, when his hands wrapped around me, picking me up in one smooth movement. He pulled us into a dark corner at the same time as he spun me around, and my legs immediately wrapped around his waist. His lips fell on mine the minute I was facing him, and we completely attacked each other, each of us fighting for dominance over the kiss. I bit down on his lip, his fingers dug into my ass. I stroked my tongue along his, and he slammed me into the wall, trapping my head so he could angle the kiss how he wanted, his tongue dancing with my own. My chest pressed against his, and I hissed as my hard nipples rubbed against the material of his shirt, earning me a grunt of satisfaction from him.

He pulled away from my lips and buried his head in my neck, planting kisses along my collarbone, sucking the skin hard enough to leave an immediate bruise.

I reached between us and grabbed the bottom of his shirt, pushing it up his body. He kept me pinned to the wall with just the strength of his lower half as he removed his hands from me long enough to pull the shirt over his head before kissing me again. His hard cock was pressed against me, straining to be free, and I wiggled my hips, grinding against him, my hands clinging to his bare shoulders to steady myself.

His hands crept to my tits, grabbing my nipples and squeezing hard, testing my pain tolerance. It stung, but I just hardened our kiss, quickening my grinding. He squeezed my nipples harder and then he pulled on them, sending another sharp sting through me. My hands flew up to his hair, grabbing fistfuls between my fingers and pulled as hard as I could.

I let out a groan of pleasure, and I heard the victory growl vibrate in his throat as he somehow pressed even closer to me, letting go of one of my tits as his hand travelled to the button on his jeans. I clenched again as I heard him pull the zipper down and, with a quick tug, freed his cock.

Both of his hands grabbed my inner thighs and brought them up, bending me in half against the wall, my knees against his chin as he rotated his hips, sliding his cock against my pussy, covering it in my wetness. I tried to thrust against him, to encourage him to slide inside me and fuck me until I was screaming, but he held steady, giving me a sharp, warning bite on my lower lip. A bite that meant stop taking control.

Fuck that.

I waited until I felt his cock slide against me in just the right spot and I thrust forward again, feeling the tip of him spread my pussy open.

"Rachel," Dante growled, moving his lips to my ear. His tongue swirled around as he spoke to me, the wetness sending shivers down my spine as it contrasted with his warm breath. "From this moment on, you belong to me. From now on, whatever I say, you do. You're fucking mine, and I will kill to keep what belongs to me. Including you," he threatened.

"For once in your life," I whispered back, not at all bothered by his threat. If anything, it turned me on more. "Just shut up and fuck me."

He did exactly that, his cock slamming into me with such force the breath left my lungs as my back crashed into the wall.

My pussy stung as his huge cock spread me open, but I didn't care. I bit down on my knee and dug my fingernails into his shoulders, leaving small crescent moons behind.

"Fuck," he all but growled down my ear, and that one simple word was my undoing. My pussy clenched around him, hungrily drawing him in deeper. I pulled his head back by his hair and lowered my mouth to his, sinking my teeth into his lips.

"Fuck me, Dante," I whispered against his lips, grinding against him. He hadn't moved after the initial thrust inside me, and it was driving me mad. Nothing felt like it was enough. I needed everything he had and more.

"Dante!" A sharp voice came from behind us, making us both jump as we both came back to reality and remembered where we were. "Get some fucking control! Your daughter is downstairs waiting for you both. Put your skank down and get some fucking clothes on."

Dante growled, looking for a moment as though he was going to ignore the interruption, but another bark of his name had him whispering "to be continued" against my lips as he thrust into me once more. I moaned low in my throat, not caring who was watching. Using the wall for support, I thrust my body into him, tempting him to stay inside me, offering him all that I had. He looked almost feral, his eyes dark. He placed one hand on the wall behind us and took a deep breath. The woman I recognised as his mother threw some clothes at us and stormed down the stairs as Dante pulled his cock out of me and lowered me to the floor.

Before I had time to react, to show my disappointment, he sank to his knees and quickly buried his face between my legs, seeking out my clit and sucked it into his mouth. I brought one leg up over his shoulder, leaning back against the wall as his tongue flicked against my clit wildly. He pulled away long enough to spit on his fingers before he looked up at me, locking eyes with my own, and winked at me. Then, he pushed two of his fingers inside me and his tongue went back to its assault.

I bit down on the back of my hand as his fingers slammed in and out of me, curling inside me to rub against my g-spot. I bucked wildly, grinding against his face, quickly coming to the point of no return.

Just when I was on the brink and about to scream the entire house down in pleasure, Dante pulled away and clamped his teeth down on my inner thigh, making me scream for a completely different reason.

"What the fuck!" I pulled away from him and he stood up with a grin. He sucked his fingers into his mouth, cleaning them of my pussy juices.

"Just in case you had any ideas about fulfilling those threats you made last night. Now everyone can see you're marked. Get dressed. I'll see you downstairs."

He walked away from me, wiping his mouth with his hand. As he was halfway down the stairs, he looked up at me and winked again, laughing to himself as he continued his descent.

I could have screamed.

My pussy was aching, my thigh was stinging, and my head was spinning.

As the cold light of reality clawed its way back in, I had a sickening thought.

Had Dante really threatened to kill me?

And, more importantly, why had I liked it?

Why had I bucked against him, practically begging him to fuck me?

I was one fucked up woman, because rather than being scared, I couldn't wait for round two.

Chapter 10

Rachel

I hurried to get dressed – not because I wanted to please Dante. The guy could use a cactus as a suppository as far as I was concerned. But rather because I was quite looking forward to meeting the offspring of such a man.

I realised from a young age that I wasn't the most pleasant woman on this planet, but I had always done well with children. If she was someone for me to pass time with whilst I planned my great escape, then I wasn't going to complain. However, I had already promised myself that I wouldn't bond with her. I wouldn't grow attached. I had grown attached to Joseph in the three years I had cared for him. Of course I fucking had. You'd have to be made of stone not to. I spent more time with him than his parents did.

I knew everything about him. I knew what blanket he needed to have at bedtime. I knew what his favourite foods were, and which foods you needed to sneak into his meals without him knowing. I knew his favourite book, colour, animal. I knew that little spot below his ribs where he was the most ticklish.

I loved that little guy, and in the blink of an eye, I was taken away from him without being able to say a proper goodbye.

I refuse to give Dante that power over me.

If he saw me falling in love with Bee, of having that instinct to care for and nurture her as though she were my own, he'd use it as a weapon. I would never allow myself to form an attachment with anyone in his life, because it was all too easy for him to change the playing field and take me away from anything familiar.

Plus, besides wanting to meet Bee, I needed to put that fucking mother of his in her place. No woman was going to call me a skank and get away with it without a small tongue lashing.

I could hear my mother in my head; "don't let words hurt you, Rachel." She had always said that, because I was always determined to silence the insults. She thought I should let it run off me like water off a duck's back.

It's not that I was hurt by what they were saying. The point wasn't whether I was hurt or not. They said these things to be cruel, to *try* to hurt me. Their intention was to wound. And whether I let that happen or not, they deserved to be punished for their intentions alone.

So I threw on the hideous jeans and chequered shirt she threw at my feet and jogged down the stairs, making sure to fan my hair out as I did so, massaging my fingers into the roots to give it some volume.

The stairs led directly to the archway leading to the bar, and around the corner seemed to be the living area, which no one had bothered to give me the guided tour of so far. I was contemplating exploring myself when Dante caught sight of me and barked my name.

With a sigh, I followed his voice into the bar and saw them all sat around one of the larger tables.

By all, I meant Macbeth, what I assumed was his dad, Crash, and his beast of a mother, Big Mama. There was also a lovely looking young girl that had enough of Dante's features for me to know she was his daughter.

"You barked, my lord," I mumbled as I reluctantly made my way over. Amy – Bee – had the biggest smile on her face. Macbeth was grinning at Dante's fierce scowl, and Mama was curling her upper lip at me. Crash hadn't even looked up from his toast.

"Sit down, Rachel, and stop acting like you're in a fucking circus every time you move. You're the most desperate for attention woman I've ever known!"

"It's almost as if you've known me longer than a day to make such an assessment!"

"Sit," he barked again, kicking out the chair next to him.

"Ask me nicely," I responded, kicking the chair back under the table.

"Just do as you're told. I want to eat."

"I'll do as I'm *asked,* when I'm asked *nicely.*"

We locked eyes, both of us glaring at the other.

"Daddy, just ask her to sit down. It's polite," Bee said, nudging Dante with her elbow.

"Listen to your daughter," I said, my eyes still locked on his. "Ask me nicely, *Daddy.*"

A small growl came from Dante's throat.

"Ask her nicely, Daddy!" Macbeth grinned from the other side of the table, looking back and forth between the two of us as though he was having the time of his life.

"Don't waste your time, girl. He won't ask," Dante's father said. "Sit yourself down and get some breakfast in you."

"My stubbornness surpasses my hunger." I said back, still not stopping the eye contact war I was locked in to.

"So starve then." Dante shrugged.

"Well, there's no need to go to that extreme," I responded, reaching over the table to grab a slice of toast. "Mmm!" I murmured, taking the biggest bite possible. "Tastes as sweet as victory."

"You know what else tastes sweet?" He said, bringing his fingers to his mouth again. I felt my cheeks flame, the toast I had been about to bite forgotten as my mouth fell open. He sucked the tips of his fingers, his tongue coming out ever so slightly. I sucked in a sharp breath, my thighs clenching together. To anyone else, it looked like he was removing crumbs, but we both knew.

"What's tastes sweet, Dante?" I said, clearing my throat, hoping it didn't scream my desire. "It's certainly not victory. You've yet to have one."

"You're acting like an immature brat; did you know that? Act your age." But he smiled up at me. A smile I didn't return.

"Huh, almost as if you know my age as well. You're on a roll this morning."

"What sort of example are you setting for Bee?"

"Well," I said, chewing my bite of food and shaking the image of him licking his fingers from my mind. "For one, I'm teaching her not to allow men to bully her. Two, I'm teaching her that there's always an alternative to your demands. And three… Well, three is really more the example *you* should be setting, but I guess I'm a part of it. Don't rely on strangers to teach her how to behave. Did I cover everything?"

I pulled the chair back out myself and threw myself down on it. "Oh, four, understand when your opponent knows he's met his match, and can only win by threatening looks and being stubborn. Sometimes," I said, lowering my voice as I turned to Bee with a grin. "Being the bigger person makes these giants look so petty and small that even giving in to their demands makes you the victor. Whew!" I exhaled, looking at everyone around the table. "That was quite the educational lesson. What's for breakfast? The hospitality here sucks, and I'm starved." I leant forward and grabbed a sausage off Macbeth's plate and took a huge bite. "Cheers."

Dante

I knew Rachel was looking for a reaction, which is why I was ignoring her attempts to draw me into an argument. Bee saw a lot for a five-year-old, but she wasn't going to see me lose my shit because some woman was throwing a bitch fit that she didn't get to cum this morning.

Although, watching her with Bee, it was clear I had made one correct judgement in my assessment of her. She was as brilliant with her as she was the boy from the Greasy Spoon. She had a natural affinity with children, and I could see Bee warming to her more and more. She was telling her about her time in America, and how the boy she had looked after – Joseph – had been trying to learn English slang. Rachel did an American accent trying to do a British accent, and it had Bee cackling into her cereal.

"Can I be done, Daddy?" Bee asked me, showing me her empty bowl. I just nodded at her and watched as she scooted off the chair and rushed to the kitchen. She knew the bar would soon be filled with the bikers, so she was excited to get dressed and spend the day with them. She fitted in perfectly, a proper little biker.

I was just about to feel some hope arise out of the shitty decisions I had made, when my mother chose that moment to strike.

"You know," she said, her voice sweet enough, unless you knew her. And I knew her. I could hear the poison in it as she leaned towards Rachel. "You should be setting boundaries with that girl."

"Really?" Rachel replied, eyeing my mother up and down. "And how would you suggest I do that?"

"Well, you're not here to be her friend, are you?"

"Am I not, no? You tell me then, Big Mama," Rachel replied, sarcasm dripping from her voice. "What am I supposed to be to her?"

"As an old lady—"

"That's not what I asked. I couldn't give two flying fucks about being an old lady. I asked what I was supposed to be to her, to Bee."

"You could try being a mother."

"I'm not her mother. Next."

Macbeth and my dad must have realised this was getting serious as their tones got harder and firmer. Both of them lifted their heads from their food and paid close attention, cringing as hard as I knew I must be doing. My mother didn't take kindly to people calling her out.

"You *will* be her mother."

"Says who?"

"As Dante's old lady—"

"Well, let me just stop you there. I'm not his old lady. I have no intention of being his old lady."

"It's a good job, because you're clearly not up for the job."

"What!" Rachel gasped, clutching her hands close to her chest. "I'm not up to the job of being the old lady? Ruling over this shit hole? Oh, no… anyway…"

"How is it you think I've spent twenty years running this place? Because I can assure you, it wasn't with sarcasm."

"Pointless question, because I don't think you've spent any time running this place," Rachel replied with a shrug, stealing another piece of toast from my dad and giving him a small, flirty wink. He grinned back at her, and I could tell he already liked her.

"Excuse me?"

"You're excused. Are you off to be a grandma, since establishing the roles in Bee's life is so important to you?"

Pride made my mother's spine straighten as she ignored Rachel and went back to her point. "I've been the leader of this club for so long because I'm firm. Was I my children's best friend? No. But did I have their respect? You bet your ass I did. People might not be my friend, but I've got the respect of everyone—"

"Yeah," Rachel interrupted, stretching the word out as she sucked the breath between her teeth. "I'm just not sure I buy that."

My god, did the woman never shut her fucking mouth?

"What don't you believe?"

"Well, you're a mouthy little gobshite. I'll give you that, and you're certainly full of opinions no one asked for. And I'm sure that worked in your favour – at least in the beginning. But let's not sit here and pretend that's kept you at the top."

"Now who's full of opinions?"

Rachel laughed. "Is this your 'gotcha' moment? I'll go on record that this opinion is fact." She leant forward, resting her elbows on the table, and linked her fingers under her chin. "You're the old lady because you went on your knees and worshipped at the holy stick of every biker here, like the good little club whore you were. Crash here," she nodded her head towards my dad. "Liked your skills enough to pick you up and keep you as his little trophy. But that's not enough, is it? Because how could Crash possibly keep such a prestige position when he wedded and bedded the club whore? That's when you bred your little biker heir and a spare. That kept you in the favour of the followers for a while. Now, you get to be the loudmouth bitch, because you rely on the muscles of your sons to keep the order. Did I nail it, or have I missed some vital piece of information?"

My mum stood up, her chair falling to the ground as she leant over the table, slamming her hands down in front of Rachel.

To give her credit, she didn't even flinch. She remained exactly where she was.

"Did I touch a nerve?" She asked pleasantly.

"I am the leader of this club because—"

"Are you the leader, though? I know enough about the club to know you're nothing. Your old man is the leader. You're just the whore at his side," Rachel interrupted, sitting back in her chair and putting her feet up on the chair next to her. "If I'm to be Dante's old lady, and Dante is due to take over this club, what will that make you? Which is the reason why you're so angry right now. You're intimidated by me. You fear me, because you know that if I play the cards a certain way, I can take everything from you, all because your son is desperate to fuck me."

"That's enough," I said, standing up and grabbing Rachel by her upper arm and hauled her to her feet. "You won't speak to my mother that way."

"Her attitude receives my attitude," she spat back, ripping her arm out of my grasp. "She drew the battle line; I just had the balls to meet her head on. It's not *my* fault none of you have ever put her in her place before!"

She stormed out of the room without a backwards glance. I shot an apologetic glance at my mother, who looked absolutely livid, and went to chase after her.

"Don't walk away from me, Rachel." I called once I was out of the bar. She was already halfway up the stairs, and instead of stopping, she just lifted her hand and raised her middle finger over her shoulder. I raced up after her, taking the stairs two at a time, and grabbed hold of her once more when we were both at the top.

"I'm getting real fucking sick and tired of your hands on me, Dante. I'm not a fucking rag doll."

"What the fuck is wrong with you?" I hissed in her face, noting the way her green eyes were sparkling in her anger, the way her blonde hair framed her face. It was still mussed up from our interrupted session earlier, and it absolutely reeked of sex appeal.

"I might have problems, Dante, but they're nothing compared to the fucking God complex—"

I kissed her. I was sick and tired of her fucking attitude, and this was the only way I knew to shut her up. I didn't realise it was possible to both love and hate a mouth so fucking much.

She leant into me almost immediately, her body surrendering to mine, but just as I pressed us closer together, she clamped her teeth down on me and tugged her head sharply to the side, taking a chunk of skin with her. I felt the blood drip down my chin the second her lips left mine.

She threw her head back defiantly and placed her hands on her hips. "Don't fucking touch me. I don't need you chasing after me playing the saviour. I don't need your mother's approval. I don't fucking need *any* of you."

"What the fuc—"

"You might think you're a fucking god, Dante, but you're just like your mother. And like her, you need knocking down a peg or two. Don't delude yourself into thinking a simple kiss can silence anyone, least of all me. And don't think so little of me to believe I'm that sex starved and desperate for attention that I'd fall for your tricks!"

She turned, and all but ran to her room, slamming the door behind her.

I almost followed.

Almost.

But if I followed her into that room, I would kill her.

Chapter 11

Dante

"You look how I feel," Vienna said as I entered the bar, still wiping blood from my lips. I had spent at least half an hour trying to stem the flow, but every time I moved my mouth, the blood poured freely. "That was quite the argument between Mama and your old lady."

"How would you know?" I said, eyeing him suspiciously. "Did you even leave the bar last night? No wonder you feel shit."

"I did," he nodded proudly.

"Did you fuck!" Jenna hissed. "I kicked you awake on the floor this morning!"

"I wasn't at the bar, though, was I?" Vienna grinned, tapping his temple with his index finger. "It's all in the wording."

"Yeah? You're cleaning the puke up this time. Before noon. How was my wording there?"

"Ambiguous at best."

"Do it," she snapped with a smile, slamming the cleaning trolley into Vienna's hip. "Before Big Mama sees."

"I have Big M wrapped around my little finger tighter than a stripper on the pole," he said, narrowing his eyes as he wiggled his pinkie in the air.

"Who's wrapped around what pole?" my mum asked as she came through the door behind me. Vienna hurried to lower his hand and sat up straighter on his stool.

"Vienna here was just saying how close you two are," I grinned, looking back and forth between the two of them.

"Why?" my mum said, a confused frown on her face.

"Dunno," I shrugged, looking innocent. "He just started bragging about how he has you wrapped around his finger."

"No," Vienna gave a nervous chuckle as my mum scowled at him. "That's not quite – heh, what I meant was…"

"Oh, come on," Jenna said. "What happened to 'it's all in the wording'"?

"Do you know? I'm sure I have a shift at the garage today," he mumbled, getting up from the stool. "I'm gonna go and give Tools a hand—"

"Stay where you are," Mama laughed at him. "I'm going to deal with Bee. You," she said, narrowing her eyes at Vienna, "are a naughty boy."

"Ooh, Mama, don't toy with me like that. Not in front of the big man," he breathed, nodding his head in my direction. "I don't want him finding out about us like this."

"I'd eat you for breakfast."

"I'd cover my dick in your favourite food and tell you to eat until the cows came home. I like to keep my ladies satisfied."

"Please," I muttered, rolling my eyes. "No wonder you don't have an old lady, if that's how you talk to women."

"Didn't need to kidnap one though, did I?" He said, still eyeing my mum up, licking his lips at her.

"I'm off to find Crash. Dante… get new friends."

"I plan to." I laughed as she walked away and Vienna threw his upper body over the bar, holding his arms out towards my mum.

"Come back, Mama. Come baaaaaack."

"You're a weird, weird man."

"Hey, what can I say? Your mam fires up all those unresolved mummy issues I've got. You think Crash would be up for a little menage?" He wiggled his eyebrows at me.

"I'm not having this conversation with you."

"What's one little threesome amongst friends? I'm a very gentle lover." He reached out and stroked the back of his hand down my face.

"Get the fuck out of here," I laughed, slapping his hand away from me. "You need to lay off the drinking."

"Lay off the drinking and lay on your mama? Sold. Point me in her direction."

"Dante," a familiar voice came from the entrance, making me freeze on the spot.

"Maybe not," Vienna said under his breath, sitting back down. The amusing, friendly atmosphere left and was replaced by a chilling coolness. His slurring stopped, immediately sobering up. This was club business, and Vienna never fucked around when it came to the club.

"Officer Bradley. Bit early for a drink, isn't it?" I said as Vienna twisted in his stool to face him.

"Not a social call, I'm afraid," he gave a fake apologetic twist of his lips. "Maybe next time."

"So, what can we do you for?" I asked.

"I'll just cut to the chase. We've had a report from a concerned citizen that a woman is being held against her will here. Thought I'd do my civic duty and come check it out."

"A report from who?" I asked, cocking my head to the side. "You always check out every report you get on us? I'm flattered."

"Only the important ones. But I'm not at liberty to say where the report came from, only that we received it. What I *can* say, however, is that I have it on good authority, that one," he paused as he pulled the notepad out of his pocket. "Miss Rachel, no last name given, was last seen being forcibly removed from her employees by a gang of bikers."

"Those Rough Riders can be bastards at times. Have you spoken to them?" Vienna asked, his face the picture of innocence.

"We'll be asking all those we feel need to be asked," Bradley replied cooly.

"Well, there's no-one being held here against their will, officer. Anything else we can help with?"

"See, the man in question was very concerned about this lady on a professional level. He says her career is at risk because of a gang of 'thugs'," he smirked as he made the air quotes. "Apparently kidnapped her. He was also able to confidently recollect the patch he saw on the leather cuts. And would you believe the name he was able to recall?"

"Enlighten us," I muttered sarcastically. That bastard. Seems Rachel's old boss wanted her back.

"Would you believe, coincidence of all coincidences, it said Devil's Disciples. And, even bigger coincidence, a day after we receive this report, I get word that you have a new old lady. Fancy that."

"Fancy that," I repeated. "As much as I'd like to play into your little conspiracy theory, it is just that. A coincidence."

"A new old lady who moved in with you less than a day of knowing you?"

"I'm irresistible. What can I say?"

"I'm sure you are. But in this case, I'm afraid I'm going to have to question your irresistibility and err on the side of caution. So you mind if I take a look around and see for myself what the situation is?"

"Not at all. You got yourself a warrant there, officer?"

He gave me a small smile. "Not at the minute. Do I need one?"

"To wander around the house my daughter calls home? You bet your ass you do."

"There's no need for the hostilities, Dante. I just came to have a friendly chat and offer my best wishes."

"Much appreciated. If that will be all.. busy day, I'm sure you understand." As soon as the words left my mouth, Vienna was up and out of his seat, ready to escort officer Bradley out of the pub.

"Just one more thing, if you don't mind," he paused for a moment. "Who is the lucky lady? I'm assuming she has a name?"

"My name's Rachel," came a soft voice from behind us. Vienna and I both froze as Rachel came out of the bar and around to my side. "As I'm sure you're well aware."

The officer's face flashed with shock, but he recovered quickly, giving her a beaming smile. "Morning, Miss." He held his hand out to her, but she looked at it with distaste and then back at his face, never once extending her own hand in return.

"We're going to need you to come down to the station," Bradley said, his tone firm and cold in the light of her rejection.

"For what?"

"We need to get your report on—"

"No." Rachel said simply.

"I'm afraid it's not optional. There's been a very serious allegation made in regards to your safety and—"

"And what?" She snapped. "As you can see, I am perfectly fine. Do I look like I've been harmed? Do I look like I'm fearing for my life?" She linked arms with me and looked up at me, beaming a smile that made my stomach flip. "I'm not going to deny it and say Dante was… less than kind with the way he asked me to become his old lady. But I am fine. I am safe. I am *happy*."

"With all due respect, ma'am, I've seen this before. In cases like this—"

"What case might that be?" I snapped. "You heard her. She's here because she wants to be here. That's all you need to know."

"I'd like to ask her once more. Whilst she's away from you. Coercion is a powerful tool."

"I'm not being coerced into anything, and I don't need anyone interfering in my business, either. And I'm guessing it was Mr Geller that rang you?"

"I'm not at liberty—"

"Forget about it. Well, just so you know, Mr Geller is a sex pest. He has been pestering to get me in bed for just shy of three years. I have always said no. He sees me as his property."

"And what does that have to do with Dante?"

"Isn't it obvious? He's lashing out because he's feeling rejected. I never once looked at him the way I look at Dante. I have never once felt for him what I feel for Dante. He's jealous. You want to talk about coercion? Maybe you should have a chat with him about how he used to try to coerce me into bed." She paused, allowing officer Bradley to absorb what she had just said. "And whilst we're talking about Mr Geller, can I just add that leaving his employment was the best thing that happened to me. Second to meeting Dante here, of course."

"I see..." officer Bradley said softly. "Whilst I sympathise with you – I'm sure it wasn't pleasant to live with all those years – no actual crime has been committed. We can't arrest someone purely because they fancied a woman."

"And no crime has been committed here, either. You can't arrest someone for being forthright and bold."

"We have to investigate all reports, miss."

"But not a report of sexual misconduct. Understood."

"If you were to make a formal—"

"I'm not going to, but you were quick to dismiss it, though, weren't you? This almost feels like a personal vendetta against Dante at this point. Do you get extra donuts at the station if you bring in a biker, or is this just a special thrill for you?"

He gave her a tight-lipped smile. "I'm sorry to have bothered you."

"I don't accept your apology. Maybe get all sides of the story before you come here next time."

"With all due respect miss, the Devil's—"

"Have a reputation. I know. So, if that will be all..." her voice trailed off, and Vienna held the door open for the officer to leave.

"Okay. Well, you know where we are if you need us. Have a nice day, ma'am."

"Have the day you deserve." She responded, giving him a kind wave.

The minute the doors shut behind him, she dropped my arm with a hiss, as though it was a hot poker searing her skin.

"Drop my arm faster next time, Rachel. Wouldn't want anyone thinking you actually had feelings for me."

"I've more feeling for the dead squirrel I saw on the side of the road."

"I'm wounded," I said, clutching my chest. "Why are you even down here? Decided you had enough sulking for the day?"

"I was saving your ass. You're welcome, by the way." She snapped back, looking at me as though she wanted the floor to open and swallow me whole, dragging me straight down to hell.

"Ahh yes, quite the actress, aren't you?" I muttered, scowling at her. "I almost believed you for a second there. How many guys have you practiced that look for?"

I'm man enough to admit I was being irrational. But the way she had smiled up at me... How could that not be real? It fucking irritated me how much I wanted to see that look again. And have it be genuine this time. The way she went from hot and cold was baffling. I was beginning to miss that blank expression. At least it was easy. I didn't like how easy it was for her to toy with me with just a simple look. And it was at that moment, I realised she was under my skin. She was gaining power over me.

"One or two. What's it got to do with you?"

"No wonder you had such a rich family to work for. You know your way into getting doors to open for you, huh?"

She just laughed at me. "Jealous, Dante?"

"Curious."

She scoffed at me and shook her head. "Whatever. I'm not being drawn into another argument with you. I'm going back to my room."

My hand snatched out and grabbed her by the elbow, stopping her from walking past me. "Thank you." I said, swallowing my pride. "I appreciate you getting the officer out of here."

She ripped her arm away from me. "I didn't do it for you. I have *never* been able to trust the police. They say one thing and do another. They bring nothing but trouble. I did it for *me*. When I get away from here, and trust me, I *will* be getting out of here. It will be through my own choices. Not because an officer came and rescued me."

"You're still holding on to the belief that I would ever let you go?"

"Yup. Just like you're still holding on to the belief that you would even have a choice in the matter."

"Who are you kidding?" I laughed at her, spinning her around by her shoulders so we were face to face. "You're not going anywhere. Admit it. You *like* being here. Oh, I'm sure you'll scream and shout about how you hate it, how I'm so cruel and awful, how you've been kidnapped and held against your will. The doors open, Rachel. It's been open all morning. You could have left last night, early this morning, now… But you've chosen not to. I can see it in your eyes. You're here because you're waiting for the moment I decide to take pity on you and finally fuck you like you've been gagging for."

My head snapped to the side as her hand lashed out and slapped me over the face. I grabbed her wrist as she brought her other hand up, ready to repeat it, and hauled her against my chest. She struggled, trying to remove her wrist from my grip, but I tightened, turning her hand yellow with the force of my grip.

"Out," I barked at the bar that had fallen into a deathly silence at the sound of Rachel's slap. I didn't look at them. I kept my eyes on Rachel, her own eyes burning with a hatred. "Now!" I roared, barely even hearing the noise as they scrambled to the exit.

"I knew you were a bit thick, Rachel. I didn't think you were fucking moronic."

Rachel

Dante's words sent a chill down my spine. They were said so softly, but the coldness in his voice chilled me to the bone.

"I like to keep surprising people." I muttered back, trying once again to remove my wrist from his grip. He smiled cruelly at me, squeezing my wrist to the point of pain. He lifted it higher, stretching my arm up high, and brought my body closer to his own. "Oh, look, we're back to the part where you use your giant size against me. I've never read *that* chapter before."

"Do not," he hissed. "Do not keep testing my patience, Rachel. This is not going to end well."

I rose to my tiptoes and brought my face close to his. "So, it's okay for you to basically call me a whore, and say I slept my way through the ranks of employment – which is a bit rich coming from someone who takes the riding life a bit too literally, if you catch my drift. But it's not okay for me to clap back? Fuck off, Dante."

"Why are you like this?"

"Like what?" I let out a rough laugh. "Not submissive? Not quiet? Not bending to your every whim and need? Because I have a fucking brain. Because I'm my own person, and not an extension of your wants. Because I'm a goddamn human being, and my thoughts and feelings are just as important as your own!"

"Oh Rachel," he said, placing two fingers under the bottom of my chin, tilting my head back as he brought his head down to whisper against my lips. "If only you were as important as you think you are."

That did it.

I reacted on instinct. My knee came up, kneeing him straight in the balls, and the heel of my hand came up to connect with his nose. A loud crack resounded out as Dante let go of my chin and stumbled backwards. I stumbled back myself, rubbing my arm as he finally let go of the iron grip he had on it, and braced myself for retaliation. I straightened my spine and threw my head back in defiance. It would be a cold day in hell before I cowered.

"Are you fucking psychotic?" Dante growled. He crossed the small distance between us and grabbed my jaw. "You want to talk about being treated equally?" His warm breath hit my face as he spoke, and I forced myself not to flinch under his anger. "How about I hit you back? My safety is just as important as yours. How would you respond if I slammed my fist into your nose?"

"Do it," I said, pushing my face up to his so my nose was pressed against his. "I fucking dare you. You wouldn't be the first man, and I guarantee you won't get the fucking reaction you're looking for."

He wiped the blood from his nose with the back of his hand and smeared it down my face. "How much do you want to bet?"

I curled my lip in disgust, but I didn't recoil from it. "Try it. See what happens."

We both stared at each other, our breathing hard as we faced each other off, silently daring the other to be the first one to break the hold.

"You are infuriating," Dante said finally.

"You—" I said, but I never got to finish. Dante crashed his lips onto mine, stealing the scathing words I had been about to spit at him.

"You are infuriating," he murmured against my lips. "But fuck me, you are the sexiest woman I have ever known."

His lips came to mine again, and this time, he ignited a fire inside me. I grabbed hold of the back of his head and kissed him harder. He tightened the grip he had on my jaw and walked me backwards until my back crashed against the edge of the bar.

He picked me up easily and sat me on the wooden top, knocking away the pint glasses without once breaking the hold of our kiss. I spread my legs immediately, and he stepped between them, grinding himself against me. I pawed at his shirt, my hands slipping underneath it to feel the solid muscle of his chest, and he pulled away from me for a second to pull it over his head, giving me complete access to his upper body. He grabbed hold of the hideous chequered shirt I was wearing and tore it open, buttons flying across the room. He pushed it down over my shoulders, leaving me in just my bra and kissed me again, his hand coming around my throat and gently squeezing.

It was the middle of the day. Anyone could walk in here at any time, and the thought just thrilled me more. There was a primal urge inside me to claim Dante as my own. I didn't even like him. He was cruel, vicious… a complete brute. But at this moment, I wanted the world to know that he belonged to me.

I pushed myself to the edge of the bar top, my ass hanging off the edge of it so he could grind against me properly. The material of my trousers rubbed against my pussy, and I could feel the bulge in his trousers, creating the most delicious friction that had me craving so much more.

I reached between our bodies and undid the button to his trousers and used my feet to push them down his hips, my hands greedily grabbing his cock the second it sprung free from its prison.

He let out an animalistic grunt as soon as my hands touched him; the sound vibrating through my throat as his tongue danced with my own. "Stroke me," he murmured against my lips. "Show me what else those hands can do besides deliver a mean right hook." He smiled against my mouth, eliciting a small laugh from me as he spoke.

I fisted his shaft and pumped up and down, doing small flicks with my wrist to rotate my movements. "You're such a good girl," he whispered, and I was lost. So fucking lost. Wanting to be praised by him. I wanted him to be pleased with what I was doing. Any other time, I fucking hated to be praised, but turn me on, and I can't get enough of it.

My pussy was throbbing, and all I wanted was for him to take away this ache. To shatter me and tear me apart as he pounded inside me.

"Fuck me, Dante," I whispered, and he needed no further encouragement. He picked me up once more, and I wrapped my legs around his waist as he lowered me onto one of the tables. I placed my feet on the edge and opened my legs wide for him, showing him how wet I was, how much I wanted him.

"Fuck," he breathed, his eyes never once leaving my body. I reached between my legs and opened my pussy lips for him. He grabbed his cock at the base and stroked his length as he positioned himself at my entrance.

I waited, my breath held as he rubbed his cock along my pussy, covering the tip of it in my wetness. The tip of his cock circled my clit once, twice, and then, without warning, he slammed inside me. My head fell off the edge of the table as I opened my mouth on a silent scream. He didn't give me a chance to adjust. He grabbed hold of my hips and hauled my body further to the edge, and fucked me relentlessly. I pushed my body up, resting the palms of my hands on the table so I could look between our bodies and see his cock pounding in and out of me, getting slicker and wetter every time.

"Dante," I breathed, and his hand came back around my throat, holding me in place.

"You're such a good girl," he growled, fucking me even harder. "Take my fucking cock, Rachel. I want to feel your pussy clenching around me. I want to feel you drawing me in, taking all I've got."

My eyes rolled into the back of my head as wave after wave of pleasure screamed its way through my body. He let go of my hip and his thumb came to circle my clit, sending my pleasure even higher.

"Fuck, Dante, harder, harder..." I breathed, thrusting my hips up to meet his every move. My pussy was beginning to hurt with the force of his fucking, but I welcomed the pain – enjoyed it even. His hand on my throat squeezed, cutting off my breathing.

"Do you want to cum, Rachel?" He said, bringing his head to mine again and ran his tongue along my bottom lip.

I nodded, unable to talk with him squeezing my throat.

"How bad?" he asked, squeezing even tighter, cutting off my breathing completely. My vision began to sway, the lights dulling. My orgasm came crashing forward the more I felt like I was going to pass out. I swear, I would happily have died, so long as he kept choking me and fucking me like I was worthless. The table creaked across the floor with the force of our movements, and yet he still managed to fuck me even harder. My pussy tightened around him, and he let out a growl so ferocious I moaned as well. It was such an erotic sound, and I would have sold my soul to hear it again.

I hated when men were silent in bed. Give me moans, pants, groans, growls... give me it all. There was nothing hotter than when a man let go and gave in to what he was feeling. The noisier the better as far as I was concerned.

I deliberately tensed my muscles again, earning another growl from him. His hand left my throat and grabbed a fistful of my hair, tilting my head back.

"Dante, I'm so fucking close," I breathed, and he grinned at me.

"You want me to make you cum?" I nodded. "Tell me who you belong to." He said simply, slowing down his movements.

I almost cried. I tried to rock against him, but it he pulled away from me, his cock almost leaving my body.

"Dante, please," I begged, doing my best to shuffle back towards him.

"Who do you belong to?" He repeated. "Tell me whose old lady you are. Tell me who's cock you're craving. Tell me where you belong, and I'll make you cum, Rachel."

I locked eyes with him, meeting the challenge in his gaze. I shook my head, refusing to say the words.

"Tell me," he said, breaking the eye contact to whisper in my ear. He gave one small thrust, enough to make my body crave more. His tongue came out to swirl around my ear, leaving a small wet trail in its wake. The next time he spoke, it sent chills down me as his cool breath hit against the wetness. "Tell me who you belong to, and I swear I'll make you feel so fucking good. I'll make this pussy purr for my cock like you've never done before. But you need to be a good girl, Rachel, or else I'll think you don't want it."

I shook my head, and he picked up his movements, fucking me harder once more. I grabbed his shoulders so he couldn't pull away from me this time and pulled him closer to me.

"Nice try," he whispered, burying his face in my neck, and biting down where he could see my pulse beating frantically. "Say it. Say you belong to me. Say you're mine."

I gasped as he bit down hard enough to leave a bruise. "Last chance, Rachel." His other hand squeezed my clit tightly at the same time he pulled his cock out of me. The minute he left my body, I said it.

"I'm yours, Dante. I belong to you. I want you to fuck me." I rushed out, my voice full of longing, almost pleading and begging, and we both knew it.

He grinned at me, both hands grabbing my hips and flipped me over. I barely had a chance to steady myself before he slammed back inside me, fucking me from behind.

I gripped the edge of the table, my knuckles turning white. "Yes, Dante, yes," I screamed with relief. My orgasm built higher and higher, and before I knew it, I exploded into a white-hot flash of pleasure that had me screaming as I saw stars. He continued fucking me, drawing out every last millisecond of my orgasm, until I thought I couldn't take any more.

And then, just as soon as it happened, it was over, and he was pulling out of me, hurrying to pull his trousers up. I climbed off the table and looked at him.

"Did you…?"

"Nope," he said simply, doing up the button.

"Why?"

He let out a cruel laugh. "You're really going to ask why? Why the fuck would I want to cum inside you, Rachel? You're fucking nothing. And seeing how easy it was to get you to submit to me after the pathetic act of bravado you've been putting on this past day, I'm not even sure it's worth even trying again. You're not old lady material, you're not much of anything at all." He spat at me before walking away, leaving me feeling like complete shit.

I knew I shouldn't let his words get to me, that he was just lashing out, deliberately trying to hurt me, but I couldn't help it.

I hadn't had sex in years. And even when I had been having sex, most of it hadn't been consensual. There was a lot about me Dante didn't know. That I didn't want him to know. But, other than a handful of occasions as a teenager, I had never willingly given my body to anyone.

Apart from him.

"I wouldn't want to be your old fucking lady," I shouted after him, feeling the anger rise through my body, replacing the hurt. "You made me cum, big fucking deal. You're still a fucking cunt, Dante. A cunt that no one wants. No-one could ever want. I know it, you know it, and it won't be long before Bee knows it and she gets the fuck out of here too. The sooner you leave this world, the fucking better it will be."

I grabbed my shirt off the floor and hurried up the stairs, never once bothering to look back down and see if he had even heard what I shouted.

Fuck him.

Chapter 12

Rachel

Fuck Dante.
Fuck him!
Fuck his mother, his father, his stupid brother, his bar. Fuck everything about him. Fuck his biker club, fuck his "my old lady" bullshit.

Fuck his controlling attitude, fuck his brutish nature.

Fuck him.

Fuck him.

Fuck. Him!

The issue being: I *had* just fucked him, and it was the most amazing sex I'd ever had in my life. I was madder with myself for giving into my lust for him. I had never felt such an animalistic need to fuck the brains out of a man before. My skin was always on fire around him, my body burning to be touched.

By the time I got back to my room, I was so angry at myself I was directing it at everyone else. The day had barely started, and already I wanted to kill everyone.

I was still livid with myself for letting that fuckwit of a mother of his get a rise out of me. I was livid with myself for having sex with Dante not once but twice today – if the first time actually counted. I was livid that I didn't say more to Dante, that I didn't swallow my mistrust and leave with the police, and I was livid that I was still fucking here, the last place I wanted to be.

And that's when a plan came to mind.

I wasn't sitting here any longer, waiting around for the next time Dante wanted to either fuck or fight. He told me the door was open, and I was walking through it come hell or highwater.

I didn't have many people left in the UK, but I did have one I could go to. I couldn't promise the reception would be a welcome one, but it had to be better than staying here.

I didn't exactly know where "here" was, but I would figure it out. I knew roughly how to get to the motorway, and once I was there, the road signs would direct me to familiar territory. Failing all that, I'd just ride until I came to somewhere far away, enough for me to stop and ask for help.

If I stayed here any longer, I'd end up hating myself. Twice I had given into Dante and allowed sex to win. I wasn't going to allow him that sort of power over me. He knew I wanted him, and it was fucking humiliating how easily he got me to surrender. Already I was craving his body again, imagining his hands on me, his teeth biting into me. I couldn't do it anymore.

I crept to the door and poked my head out, silently listening for any sounds of life. I could hear Big Mama talking to Bee at the other end of the corridor, getting their literacy lesson done for the day so Bee could go and enjoy her free time. I could hear noise from downstairs telling me the guys had been invited back in – most likely by Dante. That would keep him nice and occupied since they would be busy greeting each other or ordering drinks. No-one was going to be looking in my direction.

If ever there was going to be a time for me to slip away unnoticed, this was it. I couldn't fuck it up, or Dante would never leave me unguarded again. I'm surprised he left me alone after what happened with Malfoy. The man had a deep level of distrust within him, and he half expected me to go fucking all the men here.

I slipped into the hallway and closed the door behind me, hoping Dante would see it as a sign I was still in there, and walked towards the stairs as normally as I could manage – I didn't want anyone coming up here at the same time and think I was up to no good by sneaking.

I reached the bottom step and paused, bending down to see into the bar. Dante was there, laughing with an absolute unit of a man with a beard down to his chest and radiant green eyes that I could see from this distance. They were already drinking together, looking as though they didn't have a care in the world.

The bearded man looked around, and I ducked before he saw me. I peered through the gaps in the banister, and finally realised who he was. He was one of the men who had been shouting abuse at the Gellers when I was kidnapped. Which must mean he was one of the more important members of the club. He scanned the bar, seemingly absentmindedly, but something told me not to underestimate this man. There was a sharpness in his eyes.

I took great satisfaction in seeing Dante's lip swollen and scratches on his arm. The lip was in anger; the scratches were another emotion completely. But no one else knew that, so at least they weren't sitting there celebrating Dante's victory in getting his leg over.

Or at least I hoped they weren't.

One of the other men, someone I couldn't see, shouted over to Dante, and asked about the "pig" that had been creeping around. Knowing that they would be well immersed in their hatred of the police, I took that as my cue, slipping past the archway and to the coatrack nearby. I grabbed a leather jacket, slipping it over my arms, and grabbed one of the helmets off the long cabinet next to it. Once done, I took a quick glance behind me, saw that I was still alone, and grabbed a pair of boots and some keys off the wall and slipped out the back door, keeping a hold of it until it was almost closed. I couldn't risk it squeaking or banging shut.

Once outside, I pushed my feet into the boots, zipped the jacket up, and frantically pressed the key fob, pointing it at the many bikes until I saw one blink in response. I ran over to it, throwing my leg over and took a deep breath, absolutely shitting myself at the sheer beast underneath me.

It's fine. It'll be fine, I told myself, resolving to dump the thing and hitchhike the rest of the way if needs be. So long as I put some distance between me and Dante, that was all that mattered.

You know you're never supposed to ride another man's bike; I thought to myself. The club would more than likely be madder about that than me leaving. Weird logic around these parts.

Without another thought, I slipped the key in and twisted, feeling it roar to life.

For the first time in a long time, I was grateful for my teenage rebellion. Dante wasn't the first biker I had been around. Granted, the others weren't part of a club, but they had still owned monster bikes, and I had ridden more than my fair share. As intimidating as this bike was, I just had to have confidence and believe in myself. With a deep breath, I pushed off, feeling the weight on my shoulders lessen the further away I got.

I took one last look at the pub in my mirrors, and then I was gone.

Dante

"How's the little spitfire treating you?" Vienna grinned at me.

"Don't ask," I sighed back. "She's fucking insane. She slapped me earlier. Like a proper Eastenders, Peggy Mitchell, bitch slap." The bar had filled back up quickly, and it wouldn't have surprised me if they were all waiting outside for me and Rachel to be finished. It wasn't even five minutes after before I heard Vienna yelling out for his usual.

I felt another flash of guilt as I remembered the words I had spat at Rachel. I knew I had taken it too far. I was just too stubborn to go ahead and apologise. Especially as I knew she didn't even mean the shit she had said to me. Fuck, I had almost asked a woman to marry me when I lost my virginity. Sex makes you do weird things. You say things you wouldn't usually say. So I lashed out, and it fucking annoyed me that she could get that sort of response from me.

Vienna laughed into his pint, shaking his head. "At least she didn't stab you again, brother. I'll drink to that."

"Mate, don't. I could fuck her and kill her, and not necessarily in that order, either."

"I warned you. Those quiet ones are never as innocent as they seem."

"Yeah, but come on. I thought you meant she'd be decent in the sack once she was confident enough. I didn't think you meant she'd stab me before she'd even said hello."

Vienna just laughed again. "That's the risk you take when you just pluck a random woman from Greasy."

"Never again, my friend. I can promise you that."

"Here, here," he replied, raising his pint to me. I clinked my glass against his own and thought of Rachel sulking upstairs.

It wasn't common for *every* biker to be here this early. They had jobs and lives to be getting on with. They were here because they'd heard about Officer Bradley's unannounced visit, and they were here to meet the new old lady of the club. Except she was too busy sulking over the fact that she'd been giving a good dicking and she *loved* it. After all her bravado about never surrendering, she had folded and thrown herself on me like a woman starved.

"I'll say one thing for her though, brother," Vienna began. "She knows not to talk to the law. She really saved your ass back there."

"I had it handled."

"Handled by letting Bradley wander around your home? You sure did. Give credit where credit is due. She saved your bacon. Poor Bradley didn't know how to handle her," he said with a chuckle, shaking his head in approval. "She just kept interrupting him every time and tore him a new one. I like her." He said firmly.

"Because she told a police officer to politely fuck off? You're easily pleased."

"Well… that, and the slap she gave you, are two big positives as far as I'm concerned."

"I'm gonna go get her," I decided suddenly, getting to my feet.

"Sit down, Dante," Vienna replied. "Give her time to cool down. There's no point causing an argument with all the lads as witnesses. If she's not going anywhere, we'll meet her another time. Don't go running to a woman's command. She wants the attention. You mark my words. When she realises you're not playing her game, she'll make her way down here herself and get all the attention she craves."

"I highly doubt that."

"Maybe. This is why I don't fuck around with the old lady business. I haven't got a fucking clue what I'm doing."

"Here, fucking, here," I sighed, clinking glasses with him once more.

"She'll come around, though. I'm sure of that. I'm not saying she'll ever actually *like* you… but she'll come around to the idea of living the club life. You'll see."

"Maybe you're right. That's if we both make it out of today alive," I replied, thinking how many times we had already shouted at each other today. "Oh, by the way, any news on "

"Dante," Jenna called from the other end of the bar. "Isn't that your bike?" I looked at her with a scowl and saw she was pointing out the window.

My ears pricked up, and I heard the sounds of an engine roaring over the noise of the bar, and I shoved Vienna out of the way to get a closer look out of the window.

"That little bitch!" I said through ground teeth.

"What did I say? Attention, attention, attention." Vienna threw his pint back and slammed the glass on the table. "What's the score, boss? We going chasin'?" Four other men immediately stood up, ready to follow any order I issued.

"Don't worry about it," I replied, throwing my own pint back and signalling for two more to be brought over. "She's took one of my bikes. They're all marked. There's nowhere she can go that I can't track. Let her think she's safe. We'll get her when I'm fucking ready, not when she demands. Drink up lads," I said, looking at my brothers. "We go hunting tonight."

Rachel was about to find out exactly what I was capable of. Maybe then she'd be grateful for how easy I had been on her so far.

But those days were gone.

When I found her – and make no mistake, I *would* find her – she'd live to regret ever daring trying to leave.

Chapter 13

Rachel

It had taken over four hours, but I finally made it. It could have been sooner, but I spent the first two hours absolutely shitting myself that Dante would be following me instead of concentrating on where I was going. The second two hours were making up for the mistakes of the first.

It was further away than I thought, roughly three and a half hours away, but I made it.

I was outside the little slice of suburban heaven. A modest detached house, with its cute white picket fence, sat atop a flimsy brick wall surrounding the entire property. The grass was neatly cut by the gardener, who came twice a week. The windows sparkled under the sun, clean as a whistle. The car was parked on the road ahead of me, where it always was. God forbid it went on the driveway and left tyre marks on the stones!

This place had been my own personal prison in hell. This house was an exact copy and paste replica of all the surrounding houses. You could be an individual on the inside, but the outside must be neat, and it must be uniform.

Except no-one was individual on the inside. You were either grey, or you were beige. There was a mild crushed velvet stage, but that disappeared as soon as it arrived.

I took in a deep breath to steady my nerves, and it dawned on me where I was. I knew where I had been headed, but since I had not been back here since it happened, it took a second for it to really register with me.

I was here. Back at the scene of the crime.

Back where everything changed forever. Back where I had left something much worse than tyre marks on the driveway.

I was at my mothers, the sad beige queen.

Her clothes were beige, her furniture was beige, she rocked the same sad, beige hairstyle for decades, and always had her nails painted the same beige. Unless it was a special occasion, then she went a shade darker to "spice things up a bit".

She had even wrapped my books up as a teenager in some weird beige paper, so that the bookshelves looked more aesthetically pleasing. The colourful designs were an eyesore, she said. Didn't match the décor.

There was nothing wrong with this life. My mother was a very, very happy woman. And it genuinely pleased her to have such neatness and order in her home. Or at least I used to. Nowadays, I think it was the comfort of familiarity that kept her going. My mother was happy, so long as everyone else thought she was happy. She thrived in this world.

But it wasn't me.

I wasn't even allowed the sanctuary of my bedroom to reflect my personality, because, and I quote: "What if the window cleaner looks in and sees? What if he *tells*? Don't be selfish, Rachel."

I sat on my stolen bike and exhaled heavily. "Don't be selfish, Rachel," was a phrase that had been uttered since I had learned to walk and talk.

Doing badly in school? You're embarrassing us. Don't be selfish, Rachel.

Struggling to make friends? You need to learn to play nicely. Don't be selfish, Rachel.

Wanting to eat something that wasn't on the set weekly menu? Food costs a lot of money, and she spent a lot of time and effort planning and cooking for me and my father. Don't be selfish, Rachel.

I was always "selfish Rachel", and things hadn't changed. My mother had kicked me out and ordered me never to return over a decade ago, and yet here I was, ready to bring my problems into her world and destroy her perfect life.

Selfish Rachel.

No point putting it off any longer, I thought to myself and, with a sigh, climbed off the bike and pushed open the gate to the gardens, practicing my grin as I made my way down the path.

Smile at her. Be friendly. Don't alert her. You're not here to cause issues. You want to put the past to rest. You want to make amends. Do not let her think anything is wrong. Smile. Smile like you mean it. Smile like you used to before it all went wrong. Smile like she needs.

My cheeks were beginning to hurt I was smiling so much, and I caught a glance in the window and realised I looked more psychotic than friendly. I dropped the smile and knocked on the door. I knew I wouldn't be waiting long. My mother wasn't selfish Rebecca. She didn't keep visitors lingering at her door. She answered in a timely manner, and either invited them in or sent them away with a friendly dismissal.

I saw a shadow through the glass in the door, and my breath caught in my throat as it moved closer, bringing forth more colour as it did so, until the shadow was no longer a shadow, and instead the blurred form of my mother.

I heard her unlock the door from the inside, and I almost threw up as she opened it wide – no fear here, not in suburban heaven – a big smile on her face.

"Can I help you—Rachel!" She gasped, stumbling backwards, her eyes as wide as saucers.

There was no turning back now.

"Hi, mum. Can I come in?"

Chapter 14

Rachel

"Thank you," I murmured politely as I accepted the cup of tea my mother offered me. I hadn't been surprised that she had let me in. Appearances were everything, and she'd welcome Satan himself into her home if it meant her neighbours didn't suspect anything was amiss. And I'm almost certain she thought I was the spawn of Satan.

What had surprised me was how calm she was being. She had recovered quickly from her little stumble. She had simply straightened her smile and responded to my question with, "I think that's probably for the best. I'll put the kettle on." And that was it. We hadn't spoken a word since.

A cup of tea solved everything as far as my mum was concerned. You discover the paint is too dark after decorating? Cup of tea. Burned dinner? Tea. Your husband is spending life in prison? Endless tea. Your daughter has just returned home, having washed the blood from her hands? Tea. All the tea. Nothing but tea.

I had closed the front door behind me, taking a quick glance over my shoulder, and kicked my boots off at the door, straightening them into a neat line just in the nick of time. My mother had thrown many a fit over the years over something so simple as me not making sure my shoes were neat and uniform against the edge of the wall. It just didn't *do* to leave them wherever they were kicked off. Civilised people just didn't *act* that way.

I slipped off my leather jacket, hanging it on the hooks on the wall, and looked in the mirror hanging over the radiator cover, quickly straightening my hair. I had left the helmet over the handles of the bike.

I didn't look the most presentable, but I looked less threatening out of the leathers and massive boots.

I walked into the front room, which was the same as it had always been, except my pictures had been removed from their frames on the fireplace, and the one award I had received as a child removed from the cabinet in the corner. I had been erased from this room completely.

But that was typical of my mother. She removed the dark stains in her life and never thought about them again. Plus, the fewer reminders there were of me, the fewer people would ask questions. Time was a healer, but my mother was in a rush. There were no awkward questions to be had if she stopped acknowledging my existence at all. She didn't want to be healed. She just wanted to forget it had ever happened at all. You can't be healed from something that never happened.

I sat on the small beige sofa, right on the edge so I didn't mess up the cushions at the back, and that's when my mother had come back in with the cup of teas, almost as though she didn't trust me enough to leave me on my own for too long.

She sat on the opposite sofa, the coffee table between us, and crossed her legs, one over the other, straightening her dress over her knees.

An uneasy silence fell over us. My mother had her nose in the air, refusing to look in my direction. She had taken a quick glance when I first knocked at the door, but had quickly looked away again.

"How have you been?" I asked finally.

"Fine," she replied, swinging her foot gently. "And yourself?" She asked out of politeness, out of habit, more than genuine interest, but I didn't want to begin on the wrong foot. So I answered, determined to keep any tone out of my voice that she could take offense to.

"I'm okay. I've been in America."

"I know."

"Oh," I said simply, not really knowing what else to say. My mother and I had never really had much in common and hadn't had much to say to each other at the best of times. And that was before we had the massive elephant in the room coming between us.

"I did write you a few times…"

"I know. I read them." She nodded back.

"Oh," I repeated with a nod of my own. "I, err… I like what you've done with the place."

"No, you don't," she said with a small smile. "You always hated my taste in decor."

"I didn't hate it; it just wasn't me. We're just different."

"Yes."

"Mhmm," I replied awkwardly, and looked around the room again.

"You look… Well, you look healthy. Good." My mother said, and I almost fell off the sofa in shock.

"Thank you."

"That hair colour suits you."

"Natural is best, as you always told me."

"Mhmm," she repeated my earlier mumble, and we fell into an awkward silence again.

Fuck me, this was painful.

"Do you… do you visit much?" I asked, nodding my head to the picture on the fireplace.

"Every week."

"And he's… he's okay?"

"Well, he's not the one who's dead," she responded coldly, meeting my eyes for the first time since I had arrived.

"Mum—" I began, leaning forward to place my cup on the coffee table. She cut off anything else I had been about to say by standing up, snatching my cup off the table, and tutted at me. "Coaster. Are you staying for dinner?"

"I err… what?"

"I need to start dinner. Are you staying?"

"I… yes."

"Fine. You can go upstairs and freshen up. You still have some clothes up there, and it looks as though they'll still fit you. Don't come back in that hideous thing. You can have one night, Rachel. One. And then I want you gone. I don't know what's brought you back here, and I don't want to know. I don't care. You are my daughter, but that doesn't mean I want you here bringing all your troubles and drama. You're running out of parents to take the blame for your actions. I will let you stay here for the night because it's the right thing to do. But in the morning. I want you gone."

"Mum…" I began, but she cut me off.

"No, Rachel. I won't hear it. You have never had something to tell me that didn't come with problems. I can't deal with any more of your problems. You are my daughter," she repeated, tears in her eyes. "And I will always love you, but you are not welcome here. Not until he," she nodded at the same picture I had nodded at, "is back home where he belongs. Then we'll talk. For now, you get one night. Dinner will be at seven. I'll see you then."

Her eyes had teared up as she spoke, but she didn't give in to her emotion. She sniffed, turned, and walked towards the kitchen.

I looked at the clock, noting that it was only two in the afternoon. Dinner was at seven, same as it had always been. She wouldn't speak to me before then. My mother was more stubborn than Dante. More stubborn than myself, even. Once she set her mind to something, she saw it through to the end. She'd give me the bare minimum, and nothing more. And after what I had done, I couldn't really ask for anything else.

With hours stretching ahead of me, and being left to my own devices, I started doing some mental calculations.

I had set off around nine. It took me over four hours to get here, but that was accounting for half an hour's worth of mistakes.

If Dante had been right behind me, he would be here by now. I had sat outside the house a good fifteen minutes, and inside another fifteen.

He would have definitely noticed my absence by now. Which meant he would be looking for me.

I had stupidly left my purse behind, but I hadn't kept my ID in there, anyway. The Gellers had my ID, along with my passport and boarding pass. He had no way of finding out my surname unless he rang them. I had only been away from them a day, and they'd be recovering from jetlag and getting used to being back on US time zone.

They were eight hours behind, so it would be six there. They were not answering the phone at six in the morning when they had just returned from a summer long trip around Europe, so even *if* Dante somehow managed to find their number and ring them, they wouldn't answer. And I had to hope they weren't stupid enough to give him any information.

So Dante would have to find another way to find out my surname. The police hadn't given it to them, thank God.

I'm sure a man like him was more than capable of finding out who I was, but it would take a hot minute. And then he had to join the dots to find out my parents and where they lived.

I should be okay here. I should be fine to stay until the morning, and then I could get out of here and put more distance between myself and Dante until I could either get my passport back or apply for a new one. My mother would have the documents I needed. She always filed away documents.

I could make this work. I just had to get through tonight.

Dante couldn't possibly know where I was. He didn't know my name, my mother, or anything about my life prior to the moment he saw me, other than the fact I had worked in America.

He couldn't even tell you my age.

I was okay.

With those reassuring thoughts in mind, I decided to head upstairs to my old bedroom and try to take a quick nap. There was no point dwelling on it. I had nowhere else to go right now. Dante either found me, or he didn't. It was out of my hands. I just had to have hope and trust I had made the right call.

Chapter 15

Rachel

I woke refreshed from the best nap I'd had in years. I knew there was a chance I was in danger, but I never felt more secure than I did when I was in my childhood home.

I was never comfortable growing up here, but there was an instinct that home meant safety. As a young child, this place was my sanctuary. I had outgrown my parents, but this had once been my safe haven, the place where I was safe from harm. Whenever I was hurt, I came home to be tended. If I was sad, I came to my parents – my dad – for comfort. Teenage Rachel may have hated it, but toddler Rachel, child Rachel, the Rachel who didn't know any different, had always been taken care of here. Scraped knees were mended here. The monsters under the bed had been chased away here. This was the only home I had ever known. Home was where things were made better, and I was home.

Even if I knew deep down I no longer belonged here, and this was no longer my home.

I reached for my phone out of instinct, and cursed when I remembered I had left it at Dante's place – which I suppose was a good thing, as it meant he couldn't track me through that.

I had also gone out and inspected the bike thoroughly and hadn't found any sort of tracking device on there. Which is a thought that had occurred to me just as I had been drifting off for a nap, shaking me awake completely as blinding panic set in. But it seemed I was in the clear there too.

Which meant I was free to enjoy this moment of luxury. Free to wake without a child immediately demanding my attention until the moment they fell asleep. Free to stretch my arms over my head and not be restricted by restraints. Free to enjoy the moment of peace before I went downstairs to join the one-man firing squad that was my mother. There was no way she had sat and made dinner without giving me a second thought. She was either going to give me the silent treatment, or she was going to give me hell.

I was never sure which one I dreaded worse. But right now… right now, I was just free.

I wasn't selfish Rachel, or nanny Rachel, or old lady Rachel, or new step mum Rachel. I was just Rachel. And I liked the ring that had to it.

Just Rachel.

It was at that moment that my stomach let out the loudest rumble, and I realised just Rachel still hadn't had any more than a few bites to eat since the service station, and I was beginning to feel sick with starvation.

With a sigh, I threw the covers back and slid out of bed, feeling more and more like the rebellious teenager with every step I made towards the kitchen.

I deliberately hadn't changed out of the clothes I had arrived in. It was immature, but I didn't care. I enjoyed annoying my mother, and it was hard to shake the habit of a lifetime. There were worse crimes than bad fashion sense. We knew that better than most.

It had always been the same growing up. I always annoyed my parents one way or another. And I hadn't found it in me to care if I'm being completely honest. They were embarrassed by the most stupid things that it bordered on ridiculous and created nothing but resentment within me. I wasn't even a bad child. I pushed boundaries, and certainly didn't abide by all their rules, but for the most part I knew how to behave. But with all their criticism came the need inside me to live up to the reputation. If they thought they had a bad daughter, I'd give them a bad daughter.

I heard my mother putting plates on the dining table, and hurried my step, an offer of help on my lips.

"Sit yourself down. Dinner is ready. I have an awful headache, so you'll understand if I eat and retire for the night." Her lips tightened as she looked at my clothes, but she didn't say a word about them.

"If that's what you want to do," I said simply, not bothering to argue. I wasn't all that bothered about spending the evening with her, either. It was nice to see her, nice to see that she was managing to live with the events that happened without completely breaking down, but other than the basic welfare check, I had no more desire to know her than I did when I lived here.

I did as she asked, and took the same seat I had always had, which was to her right. She sat at one end of the table, facing the window, and my dad would be at the other end, facing into the room. Because of the way this room was positioned, there was a window opposite me, which gave a view of the vast back garden my parents owned. Unfortunately for me, it was dark, and I could barely see a thing.

My mum placed the plate of casserole on my placemat and took her seat, folding her napkin over her lap, and held her hand out for me.

"Mum—"

"Don't be selfish, Rachel. Hand."

I gave her my hand, but I didn't close my eyes.

Of course *she* did.

"Dear Lord, thank you for the food we are about to eat today. Thank you for your ever-present grace and love. Help us to stay grounded in your teachings and practice them in all that we do. Give us the strength to show understanding and kindness to those around us, even in the most trying times. Help us to be patient with ourselves and our peers, remembering that you are always with us. Amen."

Well, if that wasn't the most pointed fucking grace I've ever heard in my li —

"Rachel!"

"Amen. And thank you for bringing me back to such a welcome and loving flock."

"Just eat, Rachel."

"Please don't interrupt me and the Lord. I'm thanking him for my blessings."

"Eat!"

I smothered a grin and waited until my mother had taken her first bite, and then I tucked in myself. The first spoon to my lips was all I needed for the beast to unleash. I thought I had been hungry walking into the dining room, but I had no idea just how ravenous I was until faced with a full bowl of food.

I grabbed a hot bread roll, lathered butter on it and used it as a spoon to shove casserole into my mouth. When the bread was done, I grabbed another, and another. I used the last crust of bread to scoop portions of casserole onto my spoon and threw it into my mouth. I even picked the bowl up at one point and tipped it, making it easier to fill the spoon to capacity.

I had been so engrossed in getting as much to eat as quick as I could; I hadn't noticed my mother put down her cutlery and eye me cautiously.

Just as I was scraping the last bits of gravy out of the bowl and into my mouth, the hunger gave way to reality, and I smiled out of embarrassment as my surroundings came back to me.

"Sorry about that. It's been a while since I had a home cooked meal."

"Are you clean?" My mother asked, her lips a thin, tight line.

I blinked at her for a second, shock ricochetting through my body. "I beg your fucking pardon?"

"I don't want to argue with you. Are you clean? Show me your arms." She reached out for my wrist, and I pulled away sharply.

"I shall do no such thing."

"Show me your arms, Rachel, or leave."

"You're being ridiculous. I never injected. I took cocaine. You sniff cocaine, mum. Besides, that's in the past."

"You're white as a ghost. You've not stopped shaking since you got here, and you've eaten that casserole like a stray dog. Show. Me. Your. Arms."

"It's been a rough few days, that's all. And fuck you for assuming the worst."

"I assume the worst because all you've ever given me is the worst!" My mother screamed, standing up so hard her chair tipped backwards.

The veil had slipped.

"In case you hadn't realised, I've been doing pretty fucking good for myself since then. Not that you'd know, because you never bothered to check. You never bothered to ask! I had to pass a drug test to get my job, mother. I had to have regular drug tests to *keep* my job. Hell, I had to have a drugs test to leave the country and come back to England. I am fucking *clean!* I'm not part of that crowd anymore!"

"You should never have been part of that crowd in the first place!"

"Well, I fucking was!" I finally snapped, standing up myself. "And I'm sorry for that, but it happened and I'm not going to spend the rest of my life feeling bad about it! I could get on my knees right now and apologise to every cunt I harmed, but it's not going to change the past!"

"Your dad is spending the rest of his life in prison because—"

"Because of a decision *he* made. Get that through your thick fucking head, mother," I jabbed at my temples with my index finger. "I didn't ask him to take the blame—"

"What else was he supposed to do? His only child, addicted to drugs at seventeen, had a string of petty crimes against her, a criminal record waiting to catch up with her! You threw your life away at fifteen, Rachel, and when it got too much for you, you took your dad's place in freedom and let him take your place in jail!"

"Oh, fuck off! You had no idea what Alex put me through, what he did to me—"

"You killed him, Rachel! Whatever he did to you, it did not warrant you stabbing him to death!"

"You weren't fucking there! You don't know what he did to me, the things he said, the things he *used*! Your tiny brain could not comprehend the evil in some people. So yes, I stabbed him, and the only regret I have is that his autopsy says *almost severed* and not fucking headless!"

"What are you?" my mother whispered, shaking her head. "You flew off to America the day after your dad was sentenced, and every time you've been back, you've been in trouble."

"How the fuck would you know? I have never been back here, never so much as—"

"People *talk*, Rachel! You think I haven't heard about you terrorising his family?"

"Terrorising?" I laughed, sounding almost hysterical. "They hunted me down, mother! They almost fucking killed me." I pulled the sleeve up my arm to reveal the scars I had there. "They sliced me open and left me on the fucking pavement to die. And you have the nerve to say I terrorised them? You're fucking mad."

"So what is it this time, Rachel?" my mother said, ignoring my scars, as she always did, and changed the topic. "What drug lord do you owe money to? Whose precious child have you murdered?"

"I've been back to England plenty of times. And how many times did I get in trouble? I'll answer for you, once. *Once!* And I didn't go looking for trouble, it found me. I could have answered the police's questions when I was on my deathbed, and they wanted to know who my parents were. I could have made the hospital ring you. But I didn't. I left you in fucking peace and quiet, despite desperately needing someone, anyone, to be by my side. Obviously Alex's family were after revenge, which is exactly why I never came back here with my drama!"

"Until now, obviously."

"Yes! Until now! Do you know how fucking embarrassing it was to have my employees question why no one visited me in the hospital? Do you think it was fucking easy to lie? To say that it was a random attack? That I was in the wrong place at the wrong time, and I was jumped by thugs? They knew my parents weren't dead. Don't you think they questioned why you never bothered showing up at the hospital?"

"You could have told them the truth," she said with a sniff.

"And what would that have achieved? I didn't want to stick around lest Alex's family came and finished what they started! I said the easiest thing that would allow me to return to America as soon as possible."

"Well, Alex's family is no longer around here themselves. They got into more trouble than they could handle. Last I heard, they had moved to London and were hiding with relatives. So you can leave whenever you're ready. There will be no drama for you to cause."

"How can you be so cold?" I demanded. "I am your daughter. How can you just turn your back on me so completely?"

"It's easy when your daughter is the reason you sleep alone every night. When your daughter is the reason you were friendless for years, at a time when you needed friends the most. When your daughter is the reason—"

"I won't take the blame for those stuck-up bitches turning their back on you."

"That's not surprising. You don't take the blame for anything."

"Why should I? I have my dad ready to jump to my defence and take all the blame for himself. I'm feeling pretty damn good over here."

Too far.

My mother's hand whipped through the air and slapped me across the face with such force I felt blood fly from my mouth and land on the table at the side of us.

"That," I said through ground teeth, spitting the rest of the blood onto her expensive carpet. "Is the only time you get to lay your hands on me without consequence. Do it again, and—"

"Do you smell that?" My mother interrupted.

"Aren't you too old for 'it smells like bullshit' jokes?"

"I'm being serious, Rachel. Don't you smell that? It smells like... oh, God!" My mother's eyes went wide. "Is that smoke?"

I followed her gaze and saw that the front room was completely engulfed in thick, black smoke that was headed towards us. How had we been so caught up in our argument that we hadn't smelled it until now?

My head snapped around, looking out the windows, and saw the fire surrounding the house as the wooden fence flickered in the flames.

And that's when my stomach dropped.

Because when I listened, I heard the laughs and the whoops as the flames got higher. I heard the roaring of the bikes as they teared up and down the garden. I smelled the petrol they poured on the ground.

The windows shattered as they threw rocks at them, followed by petrol covered pieces of material.

The loudest crash came from the front room, and I ran forward, clutching at the walls as I struggled to breathe in the thick smoke.

I saw the small bead of light raise and squinted, a strangled scream getting stuck in my throat as I saw him.

Dante was stood in the frame of the shattered window, casually smoking. I was captured under his gaze as raised the cigarette to his lips and grinned at me, breathing in deeply. My body froze. He looked fucking terrifying, and he wasn't even doing anything. He didn't move, other than to bring the cigarette to his lips. He kept his gaze on me, and I'm woman enough to admit it scared the shit out of me.

With a small flick of his wrist and a tight, evil grin, the cigarette left his grip and landed on my mother's carpet with the loudest roar as the flame met the petrol, and the room was engulfed in seconds.

"Get down!" I yelled, running back to my mother and tackled her around the waist. The dumb bitch had been using her *corded* phone to ring for help. Jesus fucking Christ.

"Are you fucking thick woman?! You get *down* in a fire! Smoke fucking rises. You don't stand waiting to meet it!"

"Rachel," my mother sobbed, and for a moment, just a moment, my heart broke for her. "What have you done this time? What evil have you brought into my home?"

Chapter 16

Rachel

"Fucking move!" I yelled at my mother over the roar of the flames, shoving her even further to the floor. "Crawl on your belly and get to the front door!" She fell to her stomach with such dramatics, I was half tempted to kick her to get some sense into her. "You realise these are actual fucking flames, mother?"

"What's happening?"

"Your house is on fire! Are you thick? Get out of the goddamn house before you get us both killed!"

"I can't go out with those animals out there?" She croaked back, tears streaming down her face.

"It's the animals or the flames. Take your pick. I'm going!" Breathing was getting difficult, and I was either going to have to drag her out of here kicking and screaming, or she was going to die. It was as simple as that.

"What do they want?"

"They won't hurt you! Just fucking move!"

"Friends of yours, are they?"

"Do you want to sit here and discuss all of my failures and die together, or do you want to at least try? So help me, I will leave you in here if you don't *move,*" I spun on my ass and kicked her thigh, nudging her along the floor.

At that moment, there was a huge crash as the fire licked through the kitchen, shattering the glass oven, and melted the wood of the cabinets. My mother finally took that as her cue to move, and began crawling through the house, coughing the entire time.

I got down low to my belly and crawled along the floor, squinting through the black smoke to make sure I was following my mother.

She slowed down, her breath coming out in heaving gasps, and it took all my strength to keep pushing her, to encourage her to move. "Come on, mum. We have to get out of here, we have to. No-one deserves to die like this."

"I can't," she spluttered, her arms shaking under the weight of her body. Tears were streaming down her face, smudging with the black of the smoke clinging to her skin.

"You can, mum, you can. The door is right there, and then we'll be okay."

"Rachel," she coughed, but I saw her nod and she mustered the strength to keep pushing.

"I'm here, mum. I'm right behind you. Don't worry about me. You're doing amazing. You can do this. Just a few more seconds and you'll be out. Keep going. Think of Dad. He needs you to stay strong."

She nodded once more and picked up her pace, heading for the safety of the outside.

But encouraging her had zapped all my strength. She started gaining distance and my vision blurred as my eyes teared up, the thick smoke clogging up my breaths, feeling as though the flames were in my throat. I took my shirt off and wrapped it around my mouth, but it was too little, too late.

I started choking, feeling the roaring heat of the fire as it closed around me. If I didn't get out of here within the next minute, the entrance would be completely blocked off.

I screamed inwardly, forcing myself to remember who the fuck I was. I would not come this far just to die like this. I pushed myself to my elbows and dragged myself out of there, my hands black with the smoke. I screamed as my hand reached out and touched the metal of the door arch, feeling as though I had reached into hell itself.

I gritted my teeth and heaved myself forward, doing my best to ignore the searing pain in my palms.

Just when I thought I wasn't going to make it, I felt the coolness of the doorstep and, with a sob of relief; I got to my knees and tumbled out of the fire, landing flat on my stomach on the gravel path.

I coughed with relief, trying to rid my lungs of the smoke that was still choking me.

And that's when I saw two huge boots stomp in front of my face as two hands clamped around my neck and hauled me to my feet.

Spit flew from my mouth as the hands squeezed around my throat, choking me even further as they lifted me off the ground. I tried to speak, but nothing came out other than wet sounding gargles. I tried kicking, tried clawing at the hands around me, but it was useless.

Dante growled low in his throat, slamming me against the brick wall so hard the rough stone ripped open my bare back. The force of hitting the wall had my head flinging forward, cutting off the tiny bit of air I had left. My eyes widened, my teeth bit my tongue, and my legs flopped underneath me as my spine went into shock through pure, painful trauma.

I was completely helpless to do anything as my body spasmed, rejecting what had happened to it. I willed my legs to work, to kick against the wall and propel myself out of Dante's vice, but nothing worked.

"Dante," I breathed, vaguely registering the screams of my mother in the background. "Don't do this."

"Do what?" He barked at me.

"Don't hurt my moth—"

"I couldn't give a fuck about your mother."

"Dante," I choked, every word agonising. "She's screaming. Leave her alone."

"No-one is fucking touching her. She's screaming because she's upset. I'm not going to hurt those who are not out to cause me hurt. And you," he hissed, slamming me against the wall again. "Are out to cause hurt."

"Dante…" I wheezed, closing my eyes against the pain.

"Shut the fuck up," he roared at me, making me flinch as his spit hit my face. "You want to be counting yourself lucky I'm not throwing you back in there. But mark my words, you *ever* try to leave again, I will kill you with my bare hands."

"Fuck you," I said weakly, using the last of my strength to spit at his face. "I'll gladly throw myself back in the flames if it means I get to escape you." My voice sounded weak and pitiful. The smoke had made it hoarse, and I barely recognised the sound leaving my mouth.

"You're being dramatic. You haven't even given it a chance. You haven't given *me* a chance."

"You're being dramatic!" I tried to yell back, but it came out as a sad little croak. "You don't even know me, yet you've just burnt my mother's house to the ground."

"I know enough to know that you belong to me." He brought his face close to mine and murmured against my cheek. "I've gone easy on you so far, and you were too fucking stubborn to see it. And now you'll never know what you were missing out on, because from this moment on, you will follow my every command, or face the consequences."

"Bring it on," I breathed, trying to swallow against his painful grip. "I will make every day of your life a living hell. You can break my body, but you'll never break my spirit. I promise you, Dante. You, your parents, your brother, your club, your daughter—" my words were cut off with a gargle as he pressed his nose against mine and growled at me.

"Choose your next words very carefully, Rachel."

"Burn in hell." I hissed back.

"I swear—" he didn't finish what he had to say. I gathered whatever moisture was left in my mouth and spat in his face.

"Fuck you, Dante."

The next thing I knew, Dante threw me away from him, sending me skidding across the grass. I howled as I placed my hands in front to steady myself and ripped open the burns from the door. I landed on my face, my cheek ripping open as I flew across the floor. "Asshole," I panted, getting to my knees and coughing, barely able to breathe through the pain.

"Vienna!" He barked. "Get her back to the club and out of my sight before I do something I regret."

"You don't regret any of this so far?" I spluttered, my body dry heaving.

"Consider this mercy compared to what I want to do. I shouldn't be showing you remorse at all."

"You don't have a remorseful bone in your body," I spat on the ground next to his boots. Dante gave me a filthy look, looking as though he wanted to stomp my head into the ground. He clenched his fist and stormed off, taking long, angry strides towards his bike, and went roaring off into the night. I closed my eyes and took some deep breaths, grateful that he was gone, that I was safe from him.

Vienna stormed over and hauled me to my feet, oblivious to the searing pain in my back that had me screaming. "Get your fucking hands off me," I roared, my body coming to life as I fought to get away from him. He didn't break his stride. He simply hauled me into his arms, my agonising back pressed against his chest, his arms tight around my stomach. I strained with all my might, clawing at his arms.

"Get off me! I swear to fucking God, I will—"

"Nice to meet you, Rachel. I'm Vienna," he said pleasantly, laughing at my feeble attempt to get away. I twisted my head and sank my teeth into his bicep, but he simply removed one of his arms from around my waist and slapped me around the face – not hard. It was as though he was waving away a pesky fly.

"I hate the lot of you," I said on a sob.

"That's not fair. Shark is a lovely man. He doesn't deserve your hate."

"Fuck Shark."

"Okey dokey," he laughed, and then started hauling me towards his bike. I dug my heels into the ground, my bare feet dragging, slicing them open too. His arms tightened around my waist, oblivious to the damage he was doing to me.

"So they are friends of yours," my mother said coldly as we passed her.

"Look at me, mother. Just fucking look. Does this look like I have any fucking choice?"

"Play nice," Vienna murmured in my ear. "We'll all be one big, happy family soon enough once Rachel and the big man tie the knot, won't we, Rachel?" He crushed me further to his body and spun me around so he could pin me to his side. My mother just shook her head sadly.

"Mother," I attempted weakly, but she held her hands up to stop me.

"Even after your dad's sacrifice, you couldn't get your life together."

"You're not seeing me. You never saw me. You're supposed to help me. I don't want to be with these people."

"Rachel..." she paused, looking at me with pity. "There's obviously a history here. People don't just burn houses down for no reason."

"You're still going to blame me?"

"Who else should I blame? You brought your shit to my door. You caused this. Even after everything that's happened, you're still dancing with the devil."

"Maybe I am the devil," I said back, my tone flat and emotionless. When would I ever learn? My mother was never going to help me. She didn't care. She thought the worst, because she only ever saw the worst. I didn't fit in with her life.

"Maybe. You know what you're getting yourself into here, don't you?" She raised her voice, directing her question towards Vienna. "She killed her last boyfriend in cold blood. No-one is safe around, Rachel. Her dad even took the blame for her, landing himself life in prison, and she still behaves this way."

"Mother, shut up," I warned. "The club can find out for themselves exactly what they've done and how they've destroyed their own lives. Get me the fuck out of here," I croaked at Vienna and walked away. I was surprised he let me go willingly. But I didn't question it. I guessed he figured I was too damaged to get too far away from him.

"You're a match made in hell, the pair of you! Especially if this is how your new man behaves!"

"I won't bother inviting you to the wedding then," I called over my shoulder, a pit of dread forming in my stomach.

I had really done it this time.

I was truly, truly alone.

I never should have come back here.

My mother was never a safe space. She was never an ally. She was never a parent. I was an inconvenience to her, and I was no more alone now than I ever was. She had proven to me once again that as far as she was concerned, her daughter had died the night she murdered another man.

Chapter 17

Rachel

"You could do a lot worse; you know?" Vienna said as we made our way over to where I had parked the stolen bike.

"Worse than a kidnapper and an arsonist? True, I suppose there's always rapists and paedophiles – or does Dante want the crown for those too?"

"Watch it," he said, his face darkening. "That man has saved my life on more than one occasion. I won't have you—"

"Cut the shit, Vienna. Good men can do bad things, and bad men can do good things. I'm sure there's people who said Hitler was an outstanding citizen, who only wanted the best for his people. Doesn't mean he was a good man, though, does it?"

"What's your issue with him?"

"Hitler? Well, the holocaust for one…"

"Ha, ha," he muttered dryly as we came to a stop. "Dante."

"Where should I begin?"

"I know the story. I was there. He kidnapped you, blah, blah, blah. But was that really the crime of the century? He took a liking to you, and he did what he needed to do. You should be complimented."

"Complimented?" I laughed incredulously. "You're as mad as he is. How can you possibly think that's an acceptable thing to do? There's a million and one other ways he could have approached this. Talking to me would have been a good start."

"Would you even have listened? I've heard from Beth—"

"Who the fuck is Beth?"

"The woman who works in the Greasy Spoon. She told me what the family was like. She said you were all snobby assholes. Would you even have given Dante the time of day? No, you wouldn't. And he didn't have time to wait. You were off to the airport. He did what he needed," he repeated with a firm nod of his head.

"And you're deluded. The bar is literally in hell. How do you men not trip over every time you walk with the standards way down low? Did you know he kept me locked up the entire night? Did you know he grabbed me, threw me about—"

"You stabbed him before he did any of that."

"Because he fucking kidnapped me! I've heard him speak, so I know he's not fucking mute. He could have tried speaking to me and building a relationship with me! How is it even normal for someone to have to repeat that so often, and yet people still aren't hearing it or understanding it?" I flung my arms out, exasperated with the logic of these people.

"We are listening. But you're not listening to what we're saying either. Talking to you wasn't an option. Wooing you—"

"Wooing?" I howled.

"Courting."

"Okay, we're heading in the wrong direction. How about 'dating'? That also works."

"Dating. Fine. How long would that have taken? Bee needs a mother now, not in five years' time."

"Bee deserves someone who *wants* to be her mother. I can assure you, that's not me."

"You were practically a mother to that boy, weren't you?" Vienna shot right back.

"No, I wasn't. I was contracted. If Dante is looking for an au pair, we can talk about money and hours. But I'm not wanting to be anyone's mother. I don't want any child of mine coming back in nearly thirty years' time and burning my house down." I said dryly, attempting a joke.

"Homes can be rebuilt." Vienna shrugged his shoulders. I looked at him then, leaning back on the bike as I assessed him.

"The point is, I want to be wanted for me. Not because I'm going to be a good mother to someone else's kid!"

"Dante does want you. There's a million women who would be a good mother to Bee. He chose you."

"Vienna," I said, pinching the bridge of my nose. "You don't treat someone like this if you want a relationship with them. In fact, I'd argue you should be doing the exact opposite of all of this."

"I don't think either of you has given this a fair shot. But, look on the bright side. You stabbed him, he burnt a house down. You've already shown each other the worst you have to offer. It can only go up from here."

"That's not true. It could get a hell of a lot worse, and you know it."

"I choose to believe in happy endings," he shrugged.

"Then why haven't you got one?"

"Not my time yet."

"I don't think it's Dante's time either. He's forcing a new timeline that wasn't in the plan."

"Dante makes his own plans."

"You really would defend him no matter what he did, wouldn't you?" I said, frowning at him. In a way, I had to admire it. No-one had ever had my back like this. The best I had was people pretending to be my friends, but they would stab me in the back the second they had the chance. I could never let my guard down with anyone. And yet here Vienna was, ready to defend Dante to the death.

"We're brothers. You don't break that sort of loyalty."

"And yet he doesn't extend the same sort of loyalty towards his actual brother – I've heard the way he speaks to Macbeth, and there's not a smidge of the respect he shows you. What's the deal there?"

"They're *brothers*. It's sort of the way it works. Hang around here often enough. You'll see we're always winding each other up."

"Nah, I feel like there's more to it. What aren't you telling me?"

"Not my story to tell. You'd have to ask him. But since we're asking questions, I've one of my own."

"Fire away, I suppose."

"Who did you kill? And does Dante know?"

"Wow," I whistled softly. "You're going straight for the big guns, aren't you?"

"I don't beat around the bush."

"Hmm. You and Dante have that in common."

"It's a club trademark," he grinned at me. "So, I'll ask again. Who did you kill, and does Dante know?"

"That was two questions."

"One was more an extension of the other, but humour me. You owe me for avoiding the question the first time I asked."

"No," I sighed, and folded my arms. "Dante doesn't know, and it's not really any of your business, either. As I said to Dante, had he taken the time to get to know me, he could have found out these things before he brought a murderer around his child." I threw my leg over the bike and kick started it. "I take it we're going back to the club?" I waited for Vienna to nod and then put my helmet on. "Come on. Those sirens are getting closer. I'm sure you want to deal with the police about as much as I do. Oh, before I go… How did you know I was here?"

Vienna gave me a lopsided smile. "Trackers, lovey. Everything is chipped."

"Trackers? But… I checked—"

"We're mechanics, darlin'. I assure you. You didn't check where we placed them."

"Of fucking course I didn't," I sighed. "Race you back. Last one there has to be Dante's old lady."

Arriving back at the club fucking sucked.

Dante wasn't there – surprise, surprise, the pussy didn't want to face me. But everyone else was. And they all looked at me with disgust as I entered the door with Vienna.

"Oh, won't somebody call the church elders!" I said dramatically, throwing my hands over my eyes and pretending to faint into Vienna's arms. "The skank decided to run out on our amazing, lovely, loving Dante. Oh, the humanity. Get fucked, the lot of you," I hissed, pushing back to my feet. "I'll be in my prison. Don't bother disturbing me." I walked through the bar with my head held high, refusing to let the bastards get to me, despite all the whispering I heard behind my back.

When I got back to my room, I saw my mobile on the bed with a note underneath it.

Went ahead and charged this for you. I'll be at poker tonight. If you need me, call me. It's the only one in the phone book – I deleted all your other numbers. I think we both need a night away from each other to cool off. D.

Yeah, you're a fucking D alright.

Who the fuck did this guy think he was, deleting all my numbers? Who was I going to call? The Gellers? I think they made it perfectly clear where I stood in their life. I had no other friends, and he'd just completely alienated the only other family member I could call.

Or should I make a call to daddy dearest in prison?

Moron.

But then, a wicked smile played on my lips as an idea came to mind.

There wasn't much I could do to get revenge on Dante. I was hardly going to burn his house down, was I? Though the idea had crossed my mind. But what I could do was play on his insecurities.

Dante saw himself as the Alpha male – touch her and you die sort of man.

And oh boy, was I about to test that resolve.

I pulled out my phone and loaded up Amazon, praying they did Prime same day delivery in this area, and actually whooped out loud when I saw they did.

My bank details were already saved, so I set about loading up Google maps, found the address, and quickly pressed order. The delivery time was in a few hours.

Grinning even harder, I threw the phone to the bed and sashayed into the bathroom, ready to wash all this soot off me. I had to look good for what I had planned.

Dante might have started a literal fire, but there was no one on this earth who knew how to play and dance in the fire quite like I did.

Chapter 18

Dante

"Tell me you're joking," my mother all but shrieked. I closed my eyes and mentally counted to ten. I had come to the kitchen for a beer. That was my first mistake. I had sat down at the small dining table. That was my second mistake. I should have disappeared to my room. But seeing the bikes outside, and knowing Rachel was hidden away in her room, I really couldn't be fucking arsed with going up there. I knew if I went past her door, I'd be compelled to go in. And God knows where that would have led.

We started off this morning almost fucking at the top of the stairs. How did it end like this?

And now here I was, being almost tackled to the floor by an angry mother who came flying through the kitchen like a woman possessed.

"Don't fucking ignore me, Dante!" I rubbed my hands over my tired eyes and looked at her.

"I'm not ignoring you. I'm taking a second to wait for the ringing in my ears to go away."

"Did you burn the house down?" She barked at me, placing her hands on her hips.

"What house?"

"Dante, don't piss me off. Have you burnt that many houses down that you can't remember which one?"

"Obviously not." I said, trying my hardest not to roll my eyes at her. "Yes, mother. I burnt the house down. What of it?"

"You decided to do this *after* we had the police at our door? The police came here looking for Rachel, you're on their radar—"

"I'm always on their radar."

"Brilliant. Now you can add kidnapping and arsonist to your rap sheet. Crash!" She snapped as my father walked into the kitchen. "Are you hearing this?"

"Canada is hearing this, Mama. Calm down." He said cooly, pouring water from the kettle and giving it a stir.

"Calm down? Calm fucking down! And what if this comes back on the club?"

"We'll deal with it," he said, bringing the drink to his lips.

"I want her gone."

"Katherine..." my dad warned, using her real name.

"No, don't 'Katherine' me! This will end in tears, mark my words! He's already neglecting Bee in favour of *her*."

I had to laugh at that.

"Mother... it's been a day. I'm not neglecting anyone, least of all my daughter. I'm sure she's been perfectly fine. I saw her this morning, and I'm going to go up and see her before I go to poker tonight."

"Win big," my dad said, heading towards the door to leave.

"Is that all you have to say?"

My dad looked back at my mother's words. "What else is there to say, Kitty? I trust that Dante is doing what he thinks is best. Remember your place."

"What's that supposed to mean?"

"It means that you're an old lady," I said coldly. "*Just* an old lady. You're not a member of this club."

"I am your mother."

"And I am a grown man. I will do as I please. You don't have to like what I do, but it's not your business. Whether my actions come back on the club or not is none of your concern. If the club is affected, we'll take it to church."

"He's right. And he's the future leader. The club will go in his direction once I've stepped down, Mama. You know this. It'll be his vision we're following. You don't get a say in this. You certainly don't get to tell him to get rid of his old lady."

"Fine," she snapped and pushed past my dad, out of the kitchen.

"Well... that could have gone worse," I said with a twist of my lips.

My dad sighed heavily and took the seat opposite me. "It's not the end of it, lad. You know it, and I know it."

"Not my problem. I'm at poker tonight."

150

"Cheers. Start the war, but leave it to me to finish. Typical." He grinned at me. "Speaking of new leaders, though. Have you thought any further about when you'll be ready to take my place?"

"We've been through this. There's no rush for you to step down. The club loves having you at the head of that table. It's where you belong."

"No-one can rule forever, Dante. You know that as well as I do."

"Macbeth won't be happy."

"When is he ever happy? He's not leader material. If I hand him the reins to this club, I'm handing him the nuclear red button. He'll destroy everything we've built. Everything my father built. I'm not going to let that happen."

"And I'm not sure I can rule a club knowing there's a brother hating me and begrudging every breath I take."

"Then you bring it up in church. The club sees more than you think, Dante. They know Macbeth is a spiteful little bastard. He's my son, and I love him, but I know the jealousy he has. I know he's coddled by your mother, and he always looks like he's up to no good and scheming. I'm blinded by love, and even I can see that. I promise you; your brothers see it too. If he's jeopardising the club, you bring it up at church. It's the right way."

I thought about that for a moment.

The club always came first. It was our biggest, most strongly enforced rule. It's the main reason a lot of the men chose not to have old ladies or start families of their own. Our loyalty was with the club. It was in our blood. If the other guys thought Macbeth a danger to the safety and longevity of the club, they would have no problem voting him out. It wouldn't get rid of him. He'd still be a pain in the ass, but we wouldn't have to abide by club bylines when dealing with him, and he wouldn't be privy to any club details or secrets.

"When are you thinking of stepping down?"

My dad grinned at me. "Today. But… I'm going to put it off. I'll let you get settled in with Rachel and put her mind at ease about living this sort of life. And I'll see this through with the prospects and the Rough Riders. Did Vienna find out any information?"

"Not yet. It's been a long day."

"The fire. I know. Okay, well let me know as soon as you hear anything. We'll deal with that, and then I'm done, Dante. I'm looking forward to seeing my son take the leading role. It's what you've been preparing for your entire life."

With that, he got up and gave me a friendly slap on the shoulder. "Just think about it. We've got some time now that Rachel is here, but just… think about it. That's all I ask."

Chapter 19

Dante

"I'm telling you, mate," Vienna said with a small laugh. "I stood right there when the old broad said it. Killed a man, she said."

"I still don't believe it. Rachel?" I laughed back incredulously, taking my seat at the poker table. "Blonde haired, green eyed, five foot tall, Rachel? The one who looks like painting her nails is hard work? *That* Rachel?"

"That's what she said. And," he said, pausing to drink out of his bottle. "Rachel didn't deny it either." He finished, pointing the bottle in my direction. "In fact, she said she regretted that the autopsy didn't say beheaded. Seemed quite upset about that."

"Fuck off," I laughed again. "You've either misunderstood or they were joking."

"I heard it clear as day, so I definitely didn't misunderstand, and they didn't look as though they were joking. The mum said Rachel got her dad locked up for it."

"She's got a temper on her. I'll give her that. But a murderer? Pull the other one."

"I'm just saying what I heard, that's all," he shrugged at me.

"I mean, I can hardly condemn her for it, considering the shit I've done. But I don't believe it."

"Believe it or not, condemn her or not, it makes no difference to me. The only thing on my mind is there's a woman in that house who we know nothing about, left alone with your daughter… a woman who may very well have killed in cold blood. Just food for thought."

"She wouldn't hurt Bee." I waved away his concerns.

"You also thought she was sweet and innocent. And then she opened her mouth. I'm going to repeat this again, and I want all you fuckers to pay attention: those quiet ones are *dangerous*."

"You must be a newborn kitten then, Ven! Least dangerous man ever because I've never heard you fucking quiet!" Hacksaw shouted over, earning him the middle finger from Vienna.

"She's far from fucking quiet," I laughed again. "She's a set of pipes on her to rival Big Mama, and that's saying something!"

Still, though, I did pull out my phone and fired off a quick text to my mum to keep Bee in her sights for tonight. She was angry with me, but she'd do anything to keep her grandchild safe. I had stopped in to see Bee before I came here, just like I promised I would, and she was excited about the thought of spending more time with Rachel. She was a bright child and completely understood that I was busier than usual today, helping her settle in.

Since I was on my phone anyway, and since Rachel was on my mind, I did happen to have a little check for any new messages. I wasn't obsessively checking or anything. I needed to use the phone, anyway.

Oh, who the fuck are you kidding?

I'd been waiting all evening for Rachel to send me a message. Even spewing venom - which seemed to be her speciality - would have been preferable to the complete silent treatment. I fucking hated her silence.

Yet every time I thought of her sat there in stubborn quietness, that blank look on her face – the blank look I had once thought I hated – it made me harder than fucking steel. Sometimes I didn't know which I preferred. The blankness trying to challenge me to get a reaction, or the fiery storm that set us both ablaze.

Every instinct in my body screamed at me to go and confront her, to demand a reaction from her. And it annoyed me that deep down, the real reason was because I wanted her attention.

She was fast becoming the object of my every waking thought. Not five minutes would pass where I didn't think about her, about what she was doing, what she was thinking, what she was *wearing*.

She was like a poison, working its way through my body. Even thinking about her had my body humming, electric stinging in my veins, a silent wind at my back pushing me towards her.

Being in her company was torture. Every animal instinct I possessed told me to grab hold of her and take her, to sink my cock into her over and over. I wanted to drag her off by her hair, to hide her in a cave and keep her as my own forever.

I had never had to worry about attention from women before. They were all over me from the moment my balls dropped and my voice broke. They quickly became more of a nuisance than anything else once the novelty wore off. They were a means to an end. An extremely satisfactory means, but they weren't something I craved in my life.

Because you've never had to crave it, I thought to myself.

That much was definitely true.

My mother used to lose her shit with me with all the women I had in and out of my bedroom in my teenage years. She had once walked in on me and Vienna with this one girl- Vienna balls deep in her pussy; me balls deep down her throat and had all but beat us black and blue.

But Rachel wasn't like that. Rachel was something I craved, because she was making me earn every interaction with her. If I wanted her angry, I had to work for it. If I wanted her horny, I had to push the right buttons. Otherwise, it was that damning blank stare she had perfected. Every emotion in her body was like a reward for me, especially now I knew how easy it was for her to hide what she was thinking. I thought back to when she first arrived and hadn't so much as flinched or shown a flicker of fear. That took some serious self-control. So, for her to lose it with me – whether it be in anger, laughter, or anything else, was a serious turn on for me. As fucked up as that sounded.

I was becoming obsessed, and for every tiny growth in my obsession for her, she seemed to add another block to her hatred tower for me.

It made me want to both fuck her and kill her.

The bored, almost dismissive look on her beautiful face was burned in my memory. I fucking hated that expression. But I had still had it on my mind as I jerked my cock last night, cumming harder than I ever had as I imagined finishing all over that fucking annoying face.

She was toxic for me, and I knew I was already in far too deep to walk away.

She was my Achilles heel, and I hated myself for discovering that I had one, when I had always thought myself immune.

She would be either my greatest victory, or the death of me. There was no in-between. I wouldn't settle for less. I would have all of her, or I would have nothing. But if I couldn't have her, I'd be damned if anyone else could either.

Every time I thought about pulling away from her, sending her on a plane back to where she came from, my mind screamed in protest. My entire body rejected the possibility of this woman not being a part of my life, despite the fact I had no knowledge of her existence a mere few days ago.

"You in or out, Dante?" Shark asked. He'd been with us a few years now and had never caused any issues. We started inviting him to poker night around a year ago, and he quickly became the host of all our nights. The man rode a bike like a nasty bastard, but fuck me if he didn't make a nice charcuterie board – hence the nickname Shark, a short version of charcuterie.

"Throw me another slice of cheese and I'm in. I'm ready to win a couple hundred quid." I grinned at them, putting my phone back in my pocket. I had three bikers outside each entrance of the clubhouse, so Rachel wasn't getting out anytime soon. I could settle for knowing she was in her room. If she wanted to do that in a sulking silence, then more fool her.

Three hours later, and a couple thousand pounds thrown across the table, we were all feeling more than a little drunk, and getting bolder with our bets. Macbeth had thrown Crash's prized watch into the mix – which he promptly lost.

To me.

It was now taking pride of place on my wrist, and I took great pleasure in twirling it under the light every time I moved my deck of cards.

He was silently fuming, but that was Macbeth all over. He knew there would be hell to pay with not only Crash, but Big

Mama when they realised he had all but pawned the watch they had given him for his fortieth birthday last year. Mother had given Crash the watch on their wedding day, and it was going to be a tradition that it went to the first-born son of the first-born son.

And now I had it, I thought with a sly grin.

"Hey, Macbeth," I said, shuffling the cards for my deal. "You got your head on this time, or you ready to part with something else?"

"Go fuck yourself," he snapped back.

"I've a woman at home for that – have you?"

Vienna visibly winced, but quickly recovered himself. Macbeth's relationships had always been a sore topic for the club. He found his women by bragging about the club and how he was the firstborn. They latched on to the power he promised. And then they realised that I held all the power. It was inevitable they turned to me. I've never touched any of them, but it didn't stop the last one moaning my name when she was underneath him.

"A woman that can't stand you. Something worth bragging about, that is," he scoffed, rolling his eyes.

"Eh, she's playing hard to get. I'll tell you what is worth bragging about." I grinned again, unable to resist the urge to poke to bear. "This might fine watch I've earned myself. Tell me, do you like losing all your valuables to me, or is it just some perverse kink at this point? There's the club, the women, the bikes, the watch… you're getting quite the rap sheet."

"Say that again," he hissed, standing up so quickly his chair fell over behind him. My eyes followed the chair before I eyed him up and down.

"Sit down, boy. You're embarrassing yourself. We're all friends here."

"You're not a fucking friend," he spat back. Vienna placed a warning hand on his shoulder as he came to sit at the table, having left to grab another round of beers from Shark's fridge.

"Get your fucking hand off me," he shrugged angrily. "You and me, outside. Right now. Leave your buddies behind and fight me like we did when we were kids. I'll kick your ass now, just like I did then."

"A ten-year-old repeatedly punching a five-year-old in the face is hardly winning a fight, Macbeth. Besides, you've not been able to connect a punch since I was six. Don't take this to a level you're not ready for," I finally made eye contact then, looking up at him with a small warning. "Sit down, Macbeth. Or go home and help Mama with the knitting. Either way, make your decision because the men are ready to play."

"Fuck you and your men."

"Any takers?" I laughed as I addressed the room. "Macbeth wants to fuck the men." He stormed out then, muttering something about us getting our comeuppance, but it was drowned out by the noise of the boys taking the piss out of him, calling him feminine and emotional.

At that moment, I felt my phone vibrate against my thigh, and I forced myself to count to ten before I snatched it out of my pocket.

Why was I even lying to myself? I was keen, okay? I'll admit it. I wanted it to be Rachel texting me.

I opened the message and my eyes almost fell out of their sockets. I felt a warmth creep over my cheekbones, and my cock instantly strained against my trousers.

It was a picture of Rachel on her knees on the bed. Her arms were raised, one hand clenched in her hair, the other squeezing her tit. She was completely naked, and between her legs was a black rabbit vibrator. Her back was arched, her eyes closed in absolute ecstasy. I could see the black of the dildo, her plump pussy lips wrapped around it. I pinched my fingers against the screen and almost groaned out loud as I zoomed in and saw the streaks of wetness along the length of the dildo from where she had slid it in and out of herself.

"What's brought that grin to your face?" Shark asked, grabbing his cards.

"Let's just say my luck has come in. I hope you've brought your wallet, lads; the odds have turned in my favour," I said, closing down the picture of Rachel – even though my mind screamed at me to do anything but that – and fired off a message back to her.

Naughty girl. I take it this means I'm forgiven?

My phone buzzed again within twenty seconds.

Who says I'm thinking of you?

Nice try, Rachel. But you know better than to think of anyone else. I don't actually remember giving you permission to fuck yourself.

Fuck your permission.

Despite myself, I grinned at her response. It seemed like my Rachel had the touch of brat within her. I decided to challenge her, to see how far she was willing to take this.

Hey, I'm not one to look a gift horse in the mouth. Even if she was mad at me, even if she had the cruellest intentions behind texting me… I was still getting nudes. It was a win as far as I was concerned.

If I can't be there to watch, I want to at least listen.

I popped my phone on my knee and looked at the poker game for a second, catching up on what was happening. It took me a moment, as all the blood seemed to be rushing to my cock. It was so hard it was painful, straining against the zip of my jeans to be free. "Fuck it. I'm out this round," I said, tapping the table as my phone buzzed again.

"You pussy bitch," I heard Vienna say, but it barely registered. I only had one thing on my mind, and that was whatever Rachel had said to me.

I opened the text to see a voice note, and I got up from the table with the pretence of getting more snacks and headed for my jacket to grab my air pods. I slipped them into my ear and pressed play, almost cumming on the spot as Rachel's moans filled my ear.

Her voice had a seductive tone to it at the best of times, but hearing it now made me genuinely believe she could read the menu of the Chinese takeaway and still get 100,000s of subscribers on Only Fans. It was as rich as silk and seemed to speak straight to a man's dick. The breathy hitch, the louder moans, the one gasp of "oh God," was absolute fucking ecstasy.

I was hoping more for the live show, I sent back, immediately saving that voice note to my phone. To my surprise, Rachel didn't hesitate. She rang me straight away, and as soon as I pressed answer, I heard her.

She sounded fucking heavenly. I could hear the subtle vibrations of her dildo, the catch in her breath as she rode it. Her moans were mainly breathy, but every few seconds there would be an earthly groan low in her throat as she hit the right spot.

"Dante!" Hacksaw yelled. "Vienna is betting your bike if you don't get back here in thirty seconds!"

"Fuck you, prick! I told you that in *confidence*!"

"I've stolen everything else from you tonight. May as well take your confidence too!"

"You're not losing your bike, Dante! My winning streak is coming, I'm telling you. I'll just pop the keys in the centre here. He won't mind."

They could take the fucking skin from my back; I was not pressing hang up on this phone call. The devil himself could have his hounds snapping at my ass ready to drag me to hell, and I'd arrive still clutching this phone.

I heard Rachel laugh down the phone, sending a jolt of arousal straight through my dick, my balls tightening. "Go to the table, Dante. I dare you. Play with your friends whilst I play with you. Let's see some of that VP composure, Mr Future Leader," she challenged me.

This was a new one on me. Never had a woman issued me a command, but I was willing to play along. I had a feeling these moods would be few and far between when it came to Rachel, and I wasn't about to close the door on the first one to come my way.

So I went to the table and did my best to concentrate on the game, but it was difficult when Rachel was whispering sweet nothings down my ear.

"My pussy is so, so wet. Listen to me riding my dildo," and I knew, just knew, she moved the phone closer as the vibrating got louder. But I could also hear her wet pussy clearer now, and my mouth watered for a taste.

"This feels so good. Oh, God... yes," she breathed.

Her moaning increased, her breathing coming faster, and I knew she was getting close.

Stop, I quickly fired off to her in a text. **Don't you dare cum yet.**

The vibration stopped, and I sent her a text calling her a good girl. My phone pinged with a message, and it was Rachel with the dildo in her mouth, looking up at the camera the same way she would look up at me if it was my dick in her mouth.

I made a mess, but I don't mind cleaning it.

My fist clenched and banged against my knee under the table. I threw a random card into the mix, ignoring the mocking as I lost another round and the hundreds I had won earlier began to dwindle away. They could take the entire lot from my bank for all I cared round about right now.

"Losing, Dante?" the minx breathed down my ear. "I'm on my back now, my legs spread so wide. Shall I fuck myself again, Dante? Shall I take this dildo and slide it inside my wet pussy?"

Yes.

"As you wish," she giggled, followed by a sharp intake of breath. I could picture her laid on the bed, her blonde hair fanned out on the pillow, her perfect pussy growing pink and plump with arousal, glistening under the light, waiting for my tongue finish what she started.

Tell me what you're thinking about. I text her, desperate to know what her fantasy was right now, my ego needing to hear the words.

"I'm thinking of being all alone in this strange house. How anyone could have their wicked way with me, especially since I have guards on my doors preventing me from leaving. But I'm not alone. I can sense him here with me. I can always sense him before I see him. There's a knock at my window, and a man climbs through, dressed in black, a mask covering his face. I recognise his build, I know him, and I'm not scared. He comes over to me and places his hand over my mouth and tells me I belong to him, that he wants me as his old lady."

Cute spin she put on our story, but at least she had proven me right. She was submissive. Even her fantasies proved that. She wanted to be dominated, to be taken. Possibly even a little of consensual non consent, and I was more than man for the job.

"The masked man forces me to stand up and to strip for him, his eyes never leaving my body. I do as he says, too scared to do anything else. Not for fear that he'd hurt me, but because I don't want to disobey him and him leave me – again." She said pointedly, and I silently took the hint.

"He reaches out, running the back of his hand down the length of my body, making me quiver with excitement. Oh god," she moaned, and I could picture her with her head thrown back, her back arching even further.

"He approaches me then, like a predator stalking its prey. He circles around the back of me and pulls me against him. His body feels strange, but familiar. I feel like I know him, but there's doubt there. He peels his mask off and dangles it in front of my face before dropping it to the carpet. I could turn around and see him if I wanted to, but I don't want to break the fantasy. I hear him unzip his trousers, and his cock springs free, hard against my spine. His hand slips between my legs and finds my clit, squeezing it between his fingers before he slides his fingers inside me. One, then two," she breathed harder.

"He tries for a third, but my pussy tenses around him and he uses his other hand to grab my thigh and lift my leg off the ground, widening me for him as he slips the third finger inside. Fucking hell," she groaned, and I hear shuffling as she picks up the speed.

"His arms are the only thing supporting me as his fingers relentlessly slide in and out of me, curling to find that one spot that will make me weak and helpless. I can feel my orgasm building, but I don't want to cum without seeing him. I twist around, and immediately cum all over his fingers. I knew it was him. I knew he wanted me just as much as I wanted him. All those stares, the sneaking into my room… Fuck, I'm gonna cum," she nearly screamed. "It was him; his fingers were inside me, making me cum harder than before. Oh god, Malfoy. Fuck, yes."

The blood rushed out of my face, out of my dick, and pooled into cement at my feet at the mention of Noobs' name – or at least what she called Noob. She was still in my ear, still screaming that bastard's name, still screaming yes, yes, yes, *yes, fuck God, yes.*

The anger that rose through me was a burning heat, scorching me from the inside out. Angry puffs of air flared my nostrils, my fists clenched so hard I lost all feeling in my fingers.

And still she wouldn't give up. She was still screaming from her orgasm, and I could feel my phone pinging as she sent me picture after picture. She was doing small, breathy laughs of disbelief, telling me she had never felt anything this good before.

I could hear the lads asking what was wrong, but I couldn't speak. I had never felt such burning anger. If I opened my mouth and let it free, I'd be bursting the dam, and I'd kill every cunt here, whether they deserved it or not.

Rachel was screaming that she was going to cum again, followed by more of *his* name.

I was going to kill her. I was going to fucking kill her.

I hung up the phone and stormed out, slamming the door behind me.

I was going to fucking kill her.

Rachel

I actually cackled out loud when I heard the disconnect sound. Dante hadn't said much as I screamed Malfoy's name, but even in the silence, I could hear his anger. I could practically feel the heat of it radiating from the phone.

I hadn't been lying when I came a second time, but it wasn't for Malfoy. Hell, even the first time wasn't for him. I had been thinking of Dante, but it was just too fun to tease him. I got a sick, almost perverse pleasure in knowing my revenge plan had been successful, and knowing Dante was so riddled with anger and jealousy that it had sent a second orgasm rolling through me before I had been able to stop it.

Still laughing, I climbed off the bed and stripped the sheets, noticing the huge wet patch that had been beneath me. Another wicked idea came to mind.

I slipped on my dressing gown, grabbed the sheet off the bed, scooped up the dildo, and left my room, marching down the hallway to where Dante slept. I crept in and placed the dildo on his pillow, and left the bedsheet crumpled up next to it. He'd know what it was.

I laughed all the way back down the hallway, holding on to the wall as my legs were still a bit shaky.

He'd be absolutely fucking livid, which is why I made sure to put the chair under the doorhandle again.

I was stupid, but I wasn't *that* fucking stupid. He wasn't storming in here without an effort. And, more importantly, he wasn't storming in here without me knowing exactly when he was coming. He'd have to break the door down to get to me, and I'd be ready and waiting.

Chapter 20

Rachel

I had no idea how much time had passed, but I awoke to the sound of a loud bang, and my eyes flew to the door. A sigh of relief escaped me when I noticed the chair was still there, followed by a cut off scream when a hand clamped around my mouth.

I tried to bite down, but it was no use. The hand pressed down more firmly, making my teeth bite into lips that had not yet healed, and then a masked face came into my view.

Just like my fantasy, I recognised the hand trapping me and the body it was attached to. As much as I hated myself for it, I had memorised every inch of Dante's frame – from his broad shoulders, his huge arms, his muscled chest, and trimmed waist. He was built like a mountain, and there was no mistaking him.

My eyes went wide, and I couldn't help the dart of arousal that shot through me, making my thighs clench together.

He pushed me back, climbing on the bed as he straddled me, my back pressed against the headboard.

"Do you like to play games, Rachel?" He whispered down my ear, followed by an evil laugh that was like a shot of cold water down my spine. He was livid. And he was calm. I hated calm, angry people. This meant he had a plan, and I knew I wouldn't fucking like it.

He pushed off me, knocking my head to the side as he pressed all his body weight on his hands, shoving himself off the bed. I went to snap at him, to tell him he was a fucking prick, when my eyes adjusted to the darkness, and my breath caught in my throat.

Malfoy was tied to a chair, the same chair I had been tied to only a few nights earlier. He was straining against the ropes, his face bloody and swollen. I leaned to the side and flicked on a lamp, cringing when I saw the pool of wetness in his lap.

It was bad enough to get kidnapped, then the poor lad had to go and piss himself. At least I had performed better than that.

What sort of sickened me was the fact I thought less of Malfoy's welfare, and I was more concerned with how the fuck Dante got them both inside my bedroom without me hearing.

A good solo session makes a girl sleep well. I did my best to suppress my grin. Instinct told me Dante would not find my attempt at humour funny right at this moment.

"Alright lads?" I said, breaking the silence that was growing more awkward than anything. "It's a bit late for a cosy chitchat, but I'm nothing if not accommodating. What can I do for—"

It was the wrong thing to say. Dante growled and rushed forward, grabbing hold of my hair and hauled me off the bed, roughly throwing me down at Malfoy's feet.

"How many times have you two fucked?" He roared, his eyes wild behind the mask.

"Dante, I swear to you—" Malfoy began at the same time as I said, "that's none of your business."

"I will rip your eyeballs out and force you to eat them in five second flat," he warned Malfoy, and a terrified, strangled sound was the only response he got.

"You're being a bit dramatic," I said from my place on the floor, resisting the urge to trip Dante up as he paced back and forth.

"Dramatic? *Dramatic?!*" He roared, hauling me to my feet, his words leaving drops of spit on my face. "This is entirely your fault!" He hissed, gesturing to Malfoy.

I simply shrugged. "It's not really the face I was interested in, to be honest. You heard the fantasy. He kept his mask on most of the time…"

Dante was completely out of control. I barely recognised him as the mask of anger completely took over. He dropped me again and grabbed hold of Malfoy, his fists pounding down on him.

I cringed against the sound of flesh on wet flesh as Malfoy's face became a blur of blood and tears.

I don't know what I had been expecting when I toyed with Dante, but I was an idiot if I hadn't thought this was a possibility.

Is this what I wanted?

Deep down, was this a test? Had I been craving Dante showing he would actually care?

What did that say about me?

Malfoy pleaded for Dante to stop, but it just seemed to make him madder. Against all logic and reason, I threw myself at Dante, jumping on his back to try to pull him away from the poor boy.

I could have left. I could have just gone. Dante was far too distracted to stop me. But I couldn't let this boy die through something that had been a joke.

"Are you fucking insane?" I screamed down into Dante's ear, yanking on his hair to get his attention.

"How many times?" He roared at Malfoy. "How many times have you two looked at each other? How many times have you been behind my back?" Malfoy was incapable of talking. Both of his eyes were swollen, his lips were split open, he was missing at least one tooth, and his nose was a bloodied mess spread over the centre of his face.

"You're being ridiculous!" I snapped, biting down on his ear, because I didn't know what else to do. Dante roared like a beast and shook me off, sending me flying into the corner in a painful heap. I hissed as my back made contact with the wall, reopening some of the scabs from my earlier run in with Dante. I pushed myself back to my feet and crouched, ready to pounce when the time was right.

"Have you been watching her? What exactly happened when you were in her bedroom?" He demanded, pulling a knife from his pocket and holding it against Malfoy's eye.

Malfoy vomited, the fear causing his body to shake uncontrollably. But his fear was also his undoing.

I closed my eyes as he began to speak, an icy clamp forming around my heart. "I swear, D-Dante, I swear. I was just t-teasing her. I wanted to impress you. I-I d-didn't think she... she," he began sobbing, drawing in great hiccupping breaths. "S-she flirted with me, s-she was c-cute and g-girly and I went along with it. Sh-she trapped me, and I-I-I—"

"Spit it fucking out," Dante growled low in his throat, pressing the knife against the thin skin of his eyelid.

"I-I thought she was... I w-wanted to impress you. I don't... I don't know what I was th-thinking. She a-asked me to feed her and then she k-kicked the plate—"

He didn't say another word. Dante cut him off, his fist connecting with his nose with a crunch. Malfoy's head flopped forward, out for the count.

That's when Dante spun on his feet and set his eyes on me. I scrambled to my feet, refusing to let this man kick me whilst I'm down. I'd meet him square on, face to face.

As much as I showed bravado, my feet moved of their own accord, until I was backed up against the wall. Dante grabbed hold of my jaw and smeared Malfoy's blood on my face. The smell of copper and sweat made me turn my face away, but it lingered, invading my nostrils.

"That," he breathed, his face dangerously close to mine. "Was entirely your fault."

"Like fuck," I breathed back, ashamed that fear gave my voice a slight tremble. "I will not take responsibility for the fact that you cannot get your jealousy under control."

"And I," he said in a voice so dangerously cold it felt like icy claws wrapping around my brain. "Will not take responsibility for you not thinking your actions through and provoking me. His blood is on your hands."

"That's typical, isn't it? What sort of man are you? You beat a man senseless, but blame it on a woman because she upset you and hurt your feelings? If jealousy controls you this badly—"

"It's got fuck all to do with jealousy," he roared at me. "I can't fucking stand you. You are everything I despise in this world. But you are mine, and no one, *no one*, touches what belongs to me. Is that fucking clear?"

"You talk a big game, Dante," I hissed at him. "But this," I grabbed between his legs, feeling his erect cock. "This tells a different story. It has everything to do with jealousy. You want me so fucking badly and can't stand the thought that I don't want you back. Hide it all you want, but jealousy caused you to beat Malfoy and jealousy had you racing over here. And *that* is why you're so annoyed. You're becoming obsessed with me and it's eating you alive."

My words caught him off guard, so when I shoved him, he took a step back. "I'm going for a shower. Make sure you're gone by the time I'm done, and take *him* with you," I hissed, nodding my head in Malfoy's direction, and slammed the bathroom door shut behind me.

Once in there, I sank against the door, finally letting loose the breath I had been holding. My heart was beating so hard I could almost hear it. My entire body was shaking, and all I could do was sit on the floor and pray he didn't follow me in here.

Dante

I wanted to follow her.

I wanted to break down the bathroom door and take her there and then. I wanted to fuck her into taking back the words she had just said.

But I was so fucking angry with her, I was genuinely scared I might hurt her.

Hearing those words on her lips had cut me deeper than I thought.

You can't stand that I don't want you back.

They were designed to hurt, and despite my best intentions, she had won.

And that pissed me off.

I knew it wasn't true. I had her respond to my touch numerous times now. I could smell her arousal every time I was within two feet of her. She was gagging for it, even if she didn't want to be. But she had shot low, and it worked.

She was vicious with her tongue. It was her greatest weapon, and she knew how to wield it for maximum damage.

I hated that she had that power over me, and I fucking hated her.

At that moment, I hated her so much. I wanted to smash her head off the tiled bathroom floor and dig around in her brain until I found the fucking issue with her. I wanted to rearrange everything inside her until it worked and responded exactly how I wanted it to.

I wanted her to want me, so I could shoot her down and hurt her as she had hurt me.

But I knew I couldn't do that.

Because I wanted her so badly, it was becoming a physical ache inside me.

I couldn't stand to be near her. She made me irrationally angry, and yet I couldn't bear to stay away.

I roared away from my thoughts, punching at the door, putting my fist straight through the wood. I kicked at it, unleashing all my anger.

But it wasn't enough.

I didn't dare look at Noob.

I stormed down the hallway, ripping off the mask as I did so, and pounded on my father's bedroom door. "Deal with it," I barked as soon as he answered, pointing in the direction of Rachel's room. "Take Noob so far away from my fucking line of vision before I slice him open and mail his insides to his mother."

"What about the patch?" He asked me. "We can't take his patch without taking it to the table. You know that, Dante."

"I couldn't give a flying fuck about the table—"

"You watch your tongue, boy. You know the rules of the club."

I sighed heavily. "Leave him with his cut. We'll talk about it at church next time. If the vote is unanimous, I'll send Vienna to go retrieve it."

My dad simply nodded and pulled out his phone, knowing he'd need assistance with this one.

My mother came out of the room and her lips thinned at the scene before her, but she knew better. Especially after the earlier telling off my dad had given her. One look from me had her mouth clamping shut.

I went to my room, slamming the door behind me and sat on the edge of my bed, my head in my hands as I digested what the fuck had just happened.

I waited long, long minutes for the anger to leave my body, not trusting myself to do anything other than breathe until then.

What was it about Rachel that invoked such a visceral reaction from me?

What was it about her that was so different to all the other women that all logic and reason went out of the window, leaving no room for anything than all-consuming jealousy?

I wanted to lock her away so no one could ever look at her body again, clothed or otherwise. And yet I wanted her on my arm, so everyone knew she was mine.

I hated her so much. I wanted nothing more than her head on a stick, and yet I couldn't stop thinking about her, about how our life could be. Or could have been. I'd fucked it now.

I had kidnapped her, tied her up, hit her, teased her, toyed with her, fucked her, burnt her mother's house down, and beaten a man close to death in front of her.

It was no wonder a flicker of fear had been in her eyes this time.

I didn't even know her fucking last name. I knew nothing about her.

It didn't make any sense. I shouldn't be this obsessed. But her soul called to my own. They were locked together in this lifetime and the next. I knew it. I could feel it with every breath I took.

"Fuck," I roared, swiping at the lamp and knocked it to the floor. I took another deep breath, letting go of the anger and laid back on the bed, only to shoot up again as my head hit something uncomfortable. I reached behind me, and the anger was back.

Had the psychotic bitch actually left her dildo on my pillow? The dildo she had used to pleasure herself with whilst thinking about another man. I reached over the bed and flicked on the other lamp and saw the bedsheet, the wet patch strategically placed so it was on full display.

My animal instincts kicked in, roaring at me to go and claim what was mine once and for all. And this time, there was no stopping it.

Chapter 21

Rachel

I laid in the bath, listening to the noises from the other room as the clean-up process started.

Poor Malfoy. He hadn't deserved that. He was an arrogant piece of shit, but he hadn't done anything wrong. Other than being annoying. But that was hardly a crime worthy of the punishment he had received.

The more time I spent with Dante, the more I was beginning to realise he had a temper to rival my own, but also a possessive streak that had never really been a part of me. But then again, I had never had anything in my life I valued, so I had no reason to be possessive about it.

Dante seemed to think he was owed the world and was possessive of things he had no right claiming ownership of.

The really sad thing was, I would have been fine with a relationship with him. All he needed to do was approach me, get to know me like a regular person, and I would have been putty in his hands.

He was exactly my type – the cliché of tall, dark, and handsome. He was covered in tattoos; he had scars; he had piercing, icy blue eyes that sent shivers down my spine. He screamed trouble and a good time, and I wouldn't have been able to resist.

And whilst I did understand that he felt as though he was against the clock, everything after that kidnapping had been shit because we were the definition of starting at rock bottom.

We were both hot-headed and stubborn, but with the right amount of work and mutual respect, we could have made it work. But there was no respect for me, so I had no respect for him. Right now, we were locked in a battle to hurt each other, but it could have been so different. So much better.

But instead, he chose this route, and I was too stubborn now to give him the power over me. And whilst my body might scream out to be owned by him, my mind never would.

And yet, I was stuck here with him. I had nowhere else to go, and I wasn't stupid enough to try to leave again. I would have to find the one corner of this world where he couldn't find me. It would take a lot of time and effort to even find the right continent, never mind pinpoint the exact location.

With a sigh, I pushed myself out of the bath, slipped the most hideous nightdress over my head and brushed my teeth, wanting nothing more than to go back to bed and put an end to a hideous day.

However, upon opening the bathroom door, I was met with Dante barrelling through my bedroom door, with a face like absolute thunder. My heart dropped when I noticed the object in his hand.

For fuck's sake, Rachel!

Why? Why did I have to keep pushing his buttons? Why did I have to keep giving him excuses to come and find me?

What round were we on now? Round five? I was growing tired of the constant back and forth.

We had argued more than the number of days I had known him. Double the number of arguments, in fact. I was tired. Life wasn't supposed to be this difficult.

Dante drew up short as he saw me, and quietly closed the door behind him – a stark difference to the way he entered. And it put my nerves on edge.

Refusing to be the first to break the silence, I made my way over to the bed and began fluffing the pillows and pulling back the sheets. I felt his eyes on me the entire time, and I grew conscious of the fact that the dress only reached my mid thighs, and whenever I bent over, I risked giving him a full view of my naked body beneath.

"Take your time," Dante said pleasantly enough.

"Mhmm," I responded, not allowing myself to be drawn into whatever argument he had planned.

He leant against the wall, his arms crossed, his eyes following me, and I felt the room shrink around me, suffocating me with the growing tension.

"Dante," I sighed, finally having had enough. Sometimes it just wasn't worth the effort of being stubborn. "I'm tired. What do you want?"

"I need permission to enter a room in my own home?"

"You need permission to enter the room that's been assigned as my prison, yes."

"I own the house, which would make me the prison guard. I don't need permission to do shit."

"Fair enough, warden. I'm going to bed." I clicked off the lights, surrendering the room to the darkness, and climbed back into bed. I pulled the covers up over my chin, hearing Dante move in the darkness. I deliberately ignored him, and he answered me by reaching below the covers, grabbing my ankle, and hauling me to the edge of the bed.

I sat up, ready to hiss venom at him. However, the minute my back left the bed, he slapped me around the face with the dildo I had left on his pillow and waved it in the air. The slap wasn't hard enough to hurt me, but it did make a gasp leave my throat.

"I am getting fucking sick and tired—"

"Did you leave something behind?"

"It was a gift," I slapped it away.

"Is that so? The issue is this…"

"Gift." I finished for him when he paused.

"Gift," he said through gritted teeth. "Isn't for me, is it? I heard loud and clear who you named it after."

"Maybe I was hoping it would whisper to you in the night and give you some tips."

He chuckled at me, placing his fingers under my chin, and lifted my head until our eyes were locked. "What tips would they be?"

I opened my mouth, but he cut me off. "Because as I remember it, the last thing I needed was tips on getting you off. In fact, I remember clearly that I had your pussy weeping for my touch. I had your entire body burning, your heart racing, and I had barely even begun. So try again, Rachel. Why did you leave me it?"

"You did not," I hissed, ignoring his last question.

"Didn't I?" I gritted my teeth as I saw him smirk in the darkness. He bent down low and licked my neck, leaving a wet trail from my collarbone up to my ear. A shiver ran down my spine before I could stop it, followed by another as he whispered in my ear. "Are you going to tell me that you weren't panting and begging for more as my cock slid inside you? That your greedy pussy wasn't tensing up around me to draw me in deeper? That you weren't loving being pinned against that wall, your legs spread wide, your wetness dripping down your thighs? That you didn't love being fucked from behind, bent over that table? Are you going to deny that, Rachel? Is that really what you are trying to say?"

I tried to nod, which was difficult with his fingers gripping my chin, holding me in place. "That's exactly what I'm saying," I whispered back to him.

"We both know that's a lie, Rachel," he stepped closer to me, spreading my legs as he settled between them. "If I reached between us right now, I guarantee I'd find your pussy soaked, your clit throbbing for my touch."

My clit did exactly that, throbbing with every word he said. His voice was deep in my ear, sending vibrations straight through my body. My thighs tensed as my pussy clenched, my body betraying me as my mind raged at how easily he had me worked up.

"I'm right, aren't I?"

"Fuck you," I spat at him, pulling my head away from his grip.

"It's tempting, kitten. Believe me, it's tempting. I'd love nothing more than to fuck you on this bed right now, to show you exactly who you belong to. How many times do you think I could get you to scream my name? How many times do you think I could bring you right to the edge of orgasm, giving that tight little pussy of yours exactly what it's craving before I pull away and keep you waiting? Would you whimper, kitten? Would you sob in frustration when I denied you your orgasm?"

"Don't call me that," I hissed, closing my eyes and swallowed hard, knowing that everything he said was true.

"Kitten? But that's what you've been since the minute you opened your mouth. A bad-tempered, spitting kitten."

"And you've been nothing but a condescending dickhead."

"Look at you," he whispered against my lips. "Even when you're trying to look like you couldn't care less, your body is calling for me. It won't hurt you to admit it. I've seen this look in your eyes before. Do you think I haven't learnt your signs by now? I saw it against the wall, I saw it over the table, and would you believe? I saw it when I was beating on Noob. Admit it, me fighting for you turned you on more than anything since you've been here."

"You're fucking sick," I spat.

He laughed again, standing up straight. My back arched instantly, wanting the warmth that his body brought me.

"There's that mouth again, always ready with some smart remark. I know one way to shut you up, though, and it'll be a lesson you won't forget."

Even in the darkness, I saw the warning glint in his eye, and my body stiffened, ready to flee. He noticed the change and, quick as lightning, his hand shot out, grabbing my hair in a painful grip. "Planning on going somewhere, kitten?"

"Get your fucking hands off me!"

"When you've learnt your lesson, I will." His other hand went to the zipper on his trousers, pulling it down, letting his cock spring free, inches away from my face. He fisted it at the base, slowly pumping up and down, the tip almost touching my lips.

I tried to pull my head away, but he tightened his grip on my hair. "Ah, ah. I don't think so. You're going to suck my cock and swallow my cum like a good girl." He let go of his cock and grabbed my cheeks, squeezing them tight. I tried to clamp my lips together, but he squeezed tighter until my lips parted and he thrust his hips, pushing his cock forward and pulled my head down by my hair.

I tensed, ready to strike, but he just laughed at me. "If you bite me, Rachel, I promise you, you will leave this room black and blue."

A growing anger started low in my belly, threatening to spread upwards and spew out of my mouth. I wanted to tell him he was a cruel bastard, that I'd rather choke before I sucked his dick.

But we both knew it was a lie, and the mocking gleam in his eye proved that.

The minute I heard him undo his zip, I knew what was coming and my body had responded. My nipples hardened, my skin flamed, and my mouth watered.

I hadn't really put any effort into escaping his grip, and that was the truly embarrassing thing. Despite everything he had done, despite what had just happened in this very room, despite all the blood, pain, and devastation that had happened, I still wanted this. I still wanted *him*.

I was completely fucked, inside and out.

He rotated his hips, sliding his cock along my lips, and before I could think twice, my lips parted further, my tongue darting out to taste him.

Fuck, but he tasted good. I couldn't stop my body from shuffling forwards, getting closer to him. My head leant back, opening my throat, my lips parting further.

He hissed as my tongue stroked along the length of him, and that hiss was my undoing. I grabbed the base of his cock and slid my lips down him, taking him deep into my mouth. He thrust his hips again, encouraging me to take more of him, and I obliged, swirling my tongue around him as I did so.

"Fuck, Rachel," he breathed. His grip on my hair tightened, threatening to tear it out. But I didn't care. The sound of his voice as I brought him pleasure was like heroin to me, and I wanted to hear it again.

I *needed* to hear it again.

I started moving quicker, bobbing my head up and down, taking him as deep as I could. He grabbed my hair with both hands and thrust his hips wildly, making me choke as his cock hit the back of my throat. My hands fisted, refusing to give in to the gag that threatened to spoil my fun and slipped off the bed, kneeling on the floor in front of him so I could tip my head back further, taking more and more of him.

His growl of approval had my pussy weeping, the juices spilling down my inner thighs.

My head fell back against the bed, and Dante was over me in a second, fucking my mouth, taking all control away from me. All I could do was open wide and grasp his hips as spit dripped down my chin.

"Fucking hell," he groaned with a thrust of his hips. My lips reached the base of his cock, and he held still, holding himself deep down my throat. I choked, my eyes flying wide as I struggled to breathe, but he kept me pinned there, his cock throbbing in my mouth. I clawed at his thighs, and he responded by pinching my nose, completely cutting off all breathing. My chest heaved and my throat made a gargling noise, spit dripping down my chin. Just as my vision began to blacken, he finally pulled out with a pop. I pulled in heaving gasps, my eyes watering. "The noises your throat makes gagging on my cock are fucking unreal," he whispered, his throbbing cock rubbing my lips again.

I flew forward, sinking my lips down on him and sucked him like my life depended on it. His knees buckled as my tongue swirled around the tip, my hands coming up to play with his balls, feeling them jerk against my palm. He tried to push me back again, but I held firm, pushing at the same time as he pushed, and once again his cock slipped down my throat, but I kept going, refusing to let the power slip to his side.

He wasn't going to dominate me, and throat fuck me on his terms. I took control, humming low in my throat, sending vibrations through his body. He growled in response, and I did it again, this time deliberately allowing myself to gag on him, loving the way his cock jerked in response to the noise. There was a power vortex at play, both of us fighting to be in control. I was violently sucking his dick, and he met me move for move with a violence of his own.

I picked up the pace, bobbing up and down faster than ever, my hands gently squeezing his balls. He growled low in his throat, and I hummed in response. I grabbed hold of his hips and opened wide, and he took the hint, thrusting so hard I felt his ass tense beneath my hands with the force of his movements.

I wasn't going to let him win. Despite how much I was enjoying myself, I wasn't going to allow him to think his so-called punishment had worked. I wasn't going to wait until after it was over to hear his mocking tone as he called me a good girl for making him cum. I wouldn't give him the satisfaction.

And an idea came to mind.

I put on a good show, gargling on his cock, letting the spit fly from my mouth.

When I felt his thighs tense, I tightened my grip on his hips, and with one final jerk of his cock, I pushed him with every ounce of strength I possessed and dipped low, slipping between his legs and scrambled to my feet.

I looked back long enough to see his cum land on the bed. His back arched as he fisted his cock, pumping up and down, too far gone to stop his orgasm, even if he did have to finish himself.

"When I said go fuck yourself, I meant it. Looks like I won." I hissed at him when he turned wild, animalistic eyes on me.

And then I ran.

I ran like my life depended on it.

I heard him roar and begin to give chase, his footsteps barely making a noise behind me. I didn't need to hear him. I *felt* him. I could feel the anger, the desire, the need to punish.

I gritted my teeth and willed my legs to go faster, flying down the stairs at superhuman speed, cursing the small spiral towards the bottom as I tripped. I heard the banister creek beneath my hands, and then a flash of movement in the corner of my eye, followed by a loud thud.

A scream caught in my throat as Dante jumped the banister and landed in an angry crouch at the bottom of the stairs.

I skidded to a stop, both of my hands clinging to the banister rail. He stayed crouched, but his head lifted, his eyes locking onto mine.

"That," he said with a ferocious snarl. "Was a very foolish mistake."

My breath hitched in my throat as he slowly began to rise, stalking towards me with slow, deliberate steps.

I tried to think of a smart response, but I came up with nothing. I knew I was going to get caught, and I knew I was going to get punished for it, and the thought fucking thrilled me. I had wanted him to chase me. I wanted to feel hunted by this beast of a man.

My pussy was soaked, my clit beating in response to his steps.

"Dante," I breathed, taking a step back. My voice sounded breathy and excited, and I knew he heard it, too. He grinned at me, a sadistic, cruel grin that still somehow managed to make my pussy tense with excitement.

"Try again," he challenged. "Run, kitten. Because when I get hold of you, I can promise you, you won't be able to sit for a week."

I turned, and I ran.

Chapter 22

Dante

I chuckled as Rachel fled, tripping over the steps, taking them like an animal on all fours to keep herself steady. I closed my eyes and took a deep breath, waiting until she was at the top before I followed.

I had been pissed at her little stunt, but the minute I saw her chest heaving, the excitement shining brightly in her eyes; I understood. She wanted to go down with a fight. She hated that she loved sucking my dick and didn't want to surrender willingly. She wanted to feel as though I was forcing her, chasing her down like the bad bastard I was. But as she had scrambled up the stairs, I caught a glimpse of her pussy, swollen and soaked.

She was gagging for it, and the minute I caught up with her, her pussy was going to swallow up my cock like it was the last meal it would ever have. But if this gave my kitten the feeling of being in control, of having some power, of being able to justify what was about to happen, I'd let her have it. The night would end the same, regardless.

I was going to have my cock so deep in her that she would be screaming my name and clawing at my back for more.

I climbed the stairs slowly, listening for her movements. She was pounding along the corridor, and I chuckled as I heard a door slam near the study.

As quiet as a mouse, I made my way to the door I knew she was behind. "Kitten," I called, trying the handle, and finding it locked. I knocked on the door and I swear I heard her moan from the other side. "You have five seconds to open this door. Don't make me force it. One… Two…Three…" I heard her gasp, and I didn't bother counting any further. With one forceful shove with my shoulder, the flimsy lock cracked, and the door swung open. "Five," I grinned at her.

"You missed a number," she breathed, her chest heaving up and down. She could barely stand still, her body was so worked up.

We both stood still for long seconds, doing nothing but staring at each other. Then, just as I saw her tense up, I pounced, flying across the room. She went to run, but I grabbed her around her waist and easily swung her off her feet and brought her back tight against my chest.

She tried to scratch at my arms, to kick my shins, but I just laughed at her. "Shh, kitten," I whispered down her ear, biting down sharply on her sensitive lobe. I spun her around and pushed up her dress as her legs wrapped around my waist.

I ground my cock against her, noting the way her eyes rolled into the back of her head at the friction I was creating. She tried to mimic me, gyrating against me, her hands on my shoulders, to pull herself closer.

But I wasn't about to let her have it all on her terms.

I grabbed her hips at the same time I pushed her against the wall, pulling her body up until her legs were wrapped around my neck. She let out a squeal as I grabbed her knees and pushed them upwards, bending her body in half, pushing her pussy forwards into my face, her ass resting on my chest.

She grabbed her knees, keeping them pinned by her ears, and planted her feet on my shoulders, offering herself up to me.

"What do you want, kitten?" I teased, blowing on her soaking pussy. She didn't answer. She just stared at me intently, willing me with her eyes to give her what she so desperately wanted.

"Is this what you want?" My tongue came out, and with one big lick, I lapped at her pussy, from her opening to her clit. She bit down on her lower lip, nodding frantically, her feet digging into my shoulders as she silently asked for more.

"Or do you want this?" I teased, dipping my tongue slightly inside her slick opening.

Fuck me, she tasted divine. The tiniest bit of her creaminess on my tongue had the beast in me demanding that we take it all, that we have her shuddering against our mouth. But I wanted to take my time with her, to have her out of her mind with frustration before I took mercy on her.

"Or maybe it's this," I took her pussy lips between my teeth and bit down, working my way up to her clit and scraped my teeth down it – just once, but once was enough. Her stomach caved as she drew in a deep breath, her head banging against the wall.

"Which is it, kitten? This," I lapped at her pussy again. "This," bite, "or this," I said finally, slipping my tongue inside her once more.

"All of it," she ground out through her teeth.

"A greedy kitten," I laughed at her, ignoring her growl of warning as my tongue pulled out of her. "You're so wet for me. Can you feel your pussy juices running down onto my chest? Your body is saying all the words your mouth is refusing to say. Your pussy is weeping for me," I whispered, licking along the length of her once more, my tongue flat, greedily lapping up all that she was offering. "If you tell me what you want, I'll have it singing, Rachel."

"Dante," she breathed, wiggling her hips.

"Words, kitten. Use your words. What do you want?"

"This," she groaned, trying to push her forward.

"Just this? Just as we are now? What if I did this?" I brought my hands between her bodies and grabbed her ass, spreading her ass cheeks as I teased around her tight hole with my index finger. She gasped as I toyed with it, teasing my entry. "Would you like that, too?"

She had initially tensed, but she relaxed against me, nodding once more.

"We just went over this. Nodding isn't enough. If you can't say what you want, I can't give it to you."

"You know what I want."

"Do I? Because you just ran. I don't want to confuse things here. Tell me. Tell me in explicit, filthy detail what you want, and I'll be happy to oblige." I twisted my head and planted a kiss on her inner thigh, biting down when she remained silent and wrung a scream from her as I clamped my teeth into her sensitive skin and sucked it into my mouth, leaving a ferocious bruise.

"I want…" she swallowed deeply, her eyes burning with a fierce hunger.

"Hmm?" I asked, licking the bruise I had just created to take away some of the sting.

"Don't make me say it, Dante. You know what I want."

I pretended not to hear her, twisting my head to the other side to bite down on her other thigh.

"Fuck," she screamed, tensing her pussy, causing more of her nectar to spill onto my chest. The pain was only heightening her arousal.

"Put us both out of our misery, kitten. Tell me to eat your pussy. Tell me to have you sobbing against this wall as you cum all over my tongue."

My words pushed her over the edge and released all the things I had been needing to hear.

"You win, Dante. You win," she gasped, almost sobbing. "I want you to eat my pussy. I want you to stick your tongue so deep in me. I want you to bite me, suck me, lick me. I want it all. I want it all. I want it all." She breathed, frantically writhing against me.

That's all I had needed.

With a smirk up at her, I pushed my face into her soaking folds and ate her like a man starved.

My tongue lathered her up, licking along the length of her slit, circling around the sensitive bud at the top. Every so often, I'd take it gently into my mouth, squeezing my lips together before releasing it with a pop and repeating my movements.

She was panting above me, biting down on her knees to stop herself from screaming. I slipped my tongue inside her and pushed her ass forward, deepening my tongue as my nose rubbed against her clit.

I shook my head gently, rubbing my nose on her, inhaling the scent of her, as my tongue darted in and out of her. My cock throbbed, desperate to copy my actions, especially when she tensed around my tongue, greedily trying to draw me in further.

I pulled away long enough to spit on my finger, and then I sucked her clit into my mouth at the same time I slipped my index up her ass.

She banged her head against the wall over and over as my teeth scraped against her, my finger sliding in and out of her ass. My tongue flicked wildly against her clit, side to side, up and down, drawing my name on it, marking my territory.

I was relentless with her as her stomach tensed against my forehead, letting me know she was getting close.

I pulled away and slipped my tongue down to her opening, lapping up all the juice that had spilled out of her, and gathered it in my mouth, spitting it onto her clit and went back to flicking it with my tongue.

She moaned louder; the sound being drawn from low in her throat. Her ass tensed around my finger, her feet dug into my shoulders, and I grabbed her clit between my teeth, holding her right on the edge as I stilled my movements. I pulled away slowly, her clit stretching between my teeth, and she screamed a frustrated, anguished scream, her legs shaking against my head.

"Dante, please," she all but roared at me. She tried to push her knees together, to create her own friction, desperate and wild to finish what I had started.

I pulled my finger out of her ass and grabbed her thighs, pulling her legs wide apart. She gasped as she slipped down the wall slightly and dug her feet into my shoulders even tighter. I could see her pussy opening clench and unclench as she throbbed on the edge of her orgasm, and it was my undoing.

I sank my face into the heaven she was offering and brought her over the edge with a few flicks of my tongue.

Her body flew forward as her orgasm shook her entire body. I forced her legs to remain open, drawing out every last bit of pleasure as her body doubled over, her head resting against mine, her mouth clamping down on my ear as she screamed out an almost anguished moan.

Finally, her legs stopped shaking slightly, and she flopped back, her back smacking against the wall as her chest heaved. I kept flicking at her clit and every so often she would spasm, jerking against the wall as small aftershocks wracked through her.

My hand went to my jeans, pulling my cock out as I withdrew from her just enough to slide her back down my body until her legs were wrapped around my waist once more.

I wasted no time positioning my cock at her pussy, and with one quick thrust, I was buried inside her. She wrapped her arms around my neck, her fingers sinking into my hair, her legs locking at the ankles as she sighed in relief.

"Fuck me, kitten," I breathed against her lips. "You're so fucking tight. I can barely fit my cock inside your sweet pussy."

She tensed up, and I grabbed her ass, pulling her away until just the tip of my cock was inside her, then roughly pushed her back down, burying myself to the hilt. Her greedy pussy lips dragged along the length of me, not wanting to let me go, and as

I pushed inside, she clenched so hard I had to grind my teeth to stop myself from cumming on the spot.

"That's it, baby," I whispered as she began to bounce on my hands holding her ass, creating a steady rhythm. "Fuck, I can barely pull out of you. Your pussy is clenching my cock so tight."

Every word I spoke to her had animalistic noises coming from low in her throat as a response. I picked up the pace, lifting her ass up and down at the same time as I thrust my hips. I could feel her tits bouncing between our bodies as I fucked her with such force, the sounds of our bodies slapping together almost sounding violent.

"Cum for me, kitten. I want to cum inside this tight pussy of yours, but only after I feel you tense around me as you cum first. I want your pussy to milk me inside you."

She moved her hands to my shoulders and bounced with all the might she could muster, and I met her rhythm equally, slapping her down on my cock.

I felt the tingling in my spine as my cock jerked, my own release seemingly closer than hers. I growled, refusing to finish without having her orgasm running down the length of me. I pushed us away from the wall and towards the chair next to the bed. I spun her around with my cock still inside her and bent her over the arm. Her toes barely scraped the floor, her ass high in the air.

I slammed my cock in and out of her, wringing screams from her throat. I lifted my leg and planted my foot on the cushion of the chair, slamming into her harder and faster, her entire body jerking at the force of my thrusts. Her hands reached out to grab the opposite arm to hold on for dear life as I continued assaulting her pussy with my cock.

"Cum for me, Rachel," I demanded, slapping her ass.

"Dante," she screamed, biting down on the arm of the chair. "Jesus fucking Christ. Please, please, please…" she begged over and over, shaking her head as her orgasm built higher and higher. I could tell by the way her body moved that she was close.

"That's it, baby," I muttered as I felt her tense again and with one final slam into her, I pushed her over the edge. The scream that left her was wild and frantic, her fingers clinging to the chair as her entire body bucked wildly.

She was tensed around my cock so hard it almost hurt, and with a small laugh I thrust into her as fast as I could until I felt myself spilling deep inside her, bringing out another moan from her.

My legs were shaking as much as her body was, and as I slapped her ass for a final time, her entire body sagged, completely spent and satisfied.

Chapter 23

Rachel

I hadn't been able to look at Dante when he pulled out of me. As soon as we were finished, the humiliating way I had begged him to fuck me came flooding back to me, and pride wouldn't let me meet his eyes.

For all the back talk I had given him, he had forced a surrender from me with an ease that was humiliating. And not only that, but he also had me begging and pleading for more.

I'd shuffled out of the room with a mumbled goodnight and hurried to my bedroom, still throbbing with pleasure. I heard his cruel laughter behind me, and I had wanted to hit him.

Now it was morning, and I was still too embarrassed to leave my room. So much for slicing him open if he so much as touched me again.

The orgasm he had wrung from my body was like nothing I had ever experienced before. As it was building, all I could do was shake my head in denial of the pleasure I had felt coming over me.

I buried my head in my hands and groaned as I remembered getting him to chase me. How he had seen right through my act and knew exactly what I had wanted.

And that mouth.

Fuck me.

I had always, *always* fallen victim to a filthy mouth, and he had known just what to say to get me worked up.

And his tongue… my god, his tongue. My thighs clenched together as my pussy responded immediately to just the memory of it deep inside me.

At least I had the justification that he might be able to wring a response from my body, but he had no chance of ever getting any response from my mind. A shag was a shag, and bodies were designed to respond to being touched a certain way. He was a talented fuck, knowing which buttons to press, but that was it. I didn't want him as a person. I wanted his body. I still hated him as much as ever.

Which brought me the reminder that I still had to get some sort of revenge for the stunt he had pulled at my mother's house. She could rebuild, and it would probably do her the world of good to realise that nothing in that house had any meaning, but that didn't mean Dante could go unpunished for it. The whole dildo scene wasn't enough. Especially as he had enacted his own revenge later that night. I had to make him pay more.

And so long as I was here, I may as well play judge, jury, and executioner.

A knock at the door pulled me out of my thoughts, and I jumped out of bed, pulling on the hideous nightdress once more – I hadn't been able to sleep in it. Every dream I had was of Dante, and I woke hot and bothered too many times to count to keep it on. I cringed as I pulled it over my head, smelling my arousal on it, smelling *Dante* on it.

Fucking hell, why must I always be punished like this?

"Come in," I called, dreading seeing his large frame on the other side as the door opened.

"Hi," a small voice giggled, her head popping around the gap, giving me a big, toothy grin. "I brought you breakfast." She pushed the door open further with her shoulder and came towards me with the biggest smile, pride shining in her eyes.

I couldn't help but grin back at her, my eyes scanning the wooden tray she carried.

"Here, I'll get that," I hurried forward and took the tray from her arms, closing the door with my foot as I nodded towards the bed and sat down next to her.

"Thank you, Bee," I grinned, noting the pancakes with the toppings turned into a smile. "This is amazing. Did you do it yourself?"

"I had a little help," she admitted, her thumb and index finger coming together with the tiniest gap in between, showing me how much help she had.

"That little?" I faked a gasp. "Well, in that case, I am extra thankful. But I don't think I can eat all of this on my own. Are you going to stay and share with me? I'd hate for you not to benefit from your hard work."

She happily accepted my invitation, and I smiled down at her as her chubby hands grabbed at the bacon that had once been the pancakes smile and shoved it into her mouth.

"Bacon is life, am I right?" I laughed. "Try this," I gently grabbed the last piece of bacon she had clenched in her fist and dipped it into the eggs for eyes and held it out to her.

"I love bacon," she said with her mouth full. "But Papa always eats it all. Daddy says he's a greedy fat bastard, but he always smiles when he says it, so I don't think he's really that mad."

"Is that right?" I laughed again, ripping the pancake in half, and offering her the biggest slice before I folded it in half and shoved it into my mouth. I didn't bother correcting her swearing. She wasn't my child, and if she had learnt that word, she had learnt it from her own family. Let them tell her off.

"Best pancake ever," I smacked my lips together, drawing a giggle from her as she did the same.

She was a charming little thing, with huge, bright blue eyes, and hair as dark as a raven's wing spilling down her back and ending at her hips. There was a small dusting of freckles on her nose, and a small cut on her chin – other than that, her skin was absolute porcelain, and it didn't take much to realise she was going to grow up to be a phenomenal beauty.

A small part of me wondered if she looked like her mother, but I squashed that thought. I refused to compare myself to anyone else, and I knew that's where my mind would have gone. I especially refused to compete with a dead woman. I would never, ever see another woman as an enemy. I would never see another woman as an obstacle to gaining a man's attention.

"My mummy had blonde hair like you," she said, stuffing more pancake into my mouth.

Well, that answered that question.

"Did she?" I asked hesitantly, not wanting to say anything to upset her. I would take whatever information she offered, but I wouldn't pry.

"Yep. I've seen it in pictures."

Is that why Dante was interested in me? Did I remind him of her?

A feeling stirred in my stomach. It wasn't jealousy; I knew that much. But I didn't like the feeling all the same. I just couldn't quite put my finger on what it was.

Perhaps it was because I knew Bee's mother was dead, and I had no intention of being a replacement and allowing history to repeat itself and ending up with the same fate.

Jump to conclusions much?

"What are your plans for the day?" I asked her, changing the topic.

"I'm supposed to be doing schoolwork with my nanny."

That must be what she called her grandmother. I knew enough to know she didn't have a babysitter nanny. Mary Poppins would not be welcome here.

"Ooft," I breathed, my eyes going wide. "On a day like this, stuck in with Big Mama?"

She giggled, her little body squirming on the bed. "You don't have to call her Big Mama."

"No? What's her name then?"

"She's Nanny," she said, still giggling.

"She's not my nanny," I grinned back, unable to resist the urge to reach out and tickle her sides. "I'll tell you what. How about me and you go and speak to your nanny and see if she will let us spend the day together? I've been cooped up in this room for so long. Maybe you could show me around?"

Her eyes grew wide with excitement. "I could show you where Daddy works!"

"Hey, that's an idea."

I had no fucking intention of going anywhere near Dante today, tomorrow, or anytime soon. I didn't have it in me to burst her bubble, though. I'd just steer her away from whatever direction she tried taking me in.

"Why don't you take this to the kitchen," I nodded down at the now empty tray. "And give me ten minutes to freshen up, and I'll meet you there. Then we'll go find nanny and start our adventure. Deal?"

"Deal!" she squealed, jumping off the bed.

"No running!" I yelled after her, hurrying to the door to watch her sprint down the hallway. "Bee! Steady!" I warned, wary that she had a plate on the tray. Dante would peal the skin from my back if she hurt herself. "I'm not going anywhere. There's no rush!"

"Promise?" She grinned at me, and that one word hit me like a sucker punch to the gut.

"I promise," I cleared my throat as I croaked, but Bee didn't hear it, or if she did, she didn't pay it any attention.

And why would she? She was a child. She had no idea what was going on in my mind. She heard the word, and that was good enough for her.

But could I actually keep that promise?

The more I bonded with her, the more it would hurt to leave.

I might be a nasty bitch to the rest of the world, but I wouldn't want to hurt her feelings. No child deserved to feel unloved – it was feeling hated by the world that had caused me to act out as a child myself. I'd protect anyone from feeling the same.

I shrugged, knowing it was pointless to dwell on these things. I was here for the foreseeable future – not because I wanted to be, but because I had nowhere else to go. So I may as well have some fun whilst I could.

I snatched my phone off the side and brought up Dante's text exchange.

Where the fuck are my clothes? I fired off, whilst making my way down to his room.

Do me a favour, princess, pull up Google Maps. Does it look like America is around the corner? Be fucking patient. He text back within the minute.

I don't need a geography lesson.

Shut the fuck up and maybe take a lesson on patience.

You wanna play around with learning new things?
It was almost too easy.

I pushed open his bedroom door, and with a hum on my lips, I went around, opening all the draws and cupboards I could find, and gathered all the clothes on his bed. Taking a quick picture of them, I sent it to Dante.

In today's lesson, we're learning the concept of consequence. All crimes must be punished. Especially one as serious as arson. With that in mind, what do you think is going to happen to these?

> **I'm warning you, Rachel.**

I didn't reply, and another message came through.

> **I can't be fucked with any more of your shit. I'm warning you, and I fucking mean it.**

I warned you first. You didn't heed my warning. Here are the consequences. Isn't this a fun lesson? Hey, maybe I am cut out for this motherhood malarky. I've already taught *you* so much, and you're the most stubborn cunt I've ever met!

I found a lighter in Dante's bedside drawer, so I made my way to the bathroom, dumped the clothes in the bath, and set them alight without a second thought.

Don't the clothes look pretty when the flames are licking them? I text him, followed by another picture.

He rang me then, but I cut him off and switched aeroplane mode on. Not my problem.

I skipped out of the bathroom and headed to the stairs, another tune on my lips.

Today was going to be a good day.

Chapter 24

Dante

"Dante, phone," Crash said to me as the other members clambered into the room.

I growled low in my throat, knowing there was fuck all I could do about what I had just seen.

The fucking psychotic bitch! I raged to myself, drumming my fingers on the table. She had gone too far. Burning my fucking clothes, for what reason? We ended last night on a good note. Yet today she had woken up and, for some reason had chosen violence.

I just wanted one day with her where it was peaceful! Was that really too much to fucking ask?

And here I was. Stuck in church. The club would always, always come first for me, but by God, she was testing my loyalty.

"Rachel, I take it?" Vienna asked.

"Just… just don't." I sighed.

"Oh, but I'm going to," he grinned. I clicked on the picture and showed him, knowing there would be no peace until I did. "Ooooh," he hissed between his teeth. "She is pissed."

"Let me see," Shark nudged Vienna, looking over his shoulder. Vienna tipped the phone in his direction and Shark, helpful as ever, did nothing but shake his head. At least he suppressed the laughter. Before I knew what was happening, Shark passed the phone to Rooster, who let his brother Chicken look at it. Doc snatched it out of their hands and smirked whilst handing it to Trent. The entire club, minus that useless brother of mine, was loving this.

"Was that the leather jacket that…?"

"Yep."

"Shit. I'm sorry, son."

"It's fine." I rubbed a hand over my eyes. "I'll deal with it. Are we getting started or what?"

"Macbeth isn't here yet," Monster said.

"Makes a fucking change from you being the one holding up church," I snapped. It wasn't his fault, but I was too pissed to apologise.

"Has anyone seen him today?" Crash asked.

We all either murmured a negative or shook our heads.

"For fuck's sake. We'll give him ten minutes. If he's not here by then, Dante, you go looking for him. I don't care what it takes, just bring him back in one piece."

"I can do that," I grinned. "There are still ways to fuck a man up and keep him in one piece."

Rachel

"Are you ready for our adventure?" I asked Bee, who was sitting at the dining table eating her breakfast – well, her second breakfast, considering she had already polished off mine.

"My nanny says I'm not allowed," she muttered, her eyes low and her lips pulling down at the corners.

I approached her and crouched down at the side of her, brushing her hair out of her face and behind her ears. "Your nanny isn't the only one in charge here. If I say we're going out, then we're going out."

"She'll be mad."

I paused. "Does your nanny get mad at you a lot?"

"Sometimes," she mumbled, her little foot kicking off the table leg. "She says I'm not easy. She gets frustrated."

An icy fist clenched its way around my heart. It was one thing to lose your temper or get frustrated. It was another thing completely to get so frustrated that you lashed out at the child and had them believing they weren't easy to deal with.

"Sometimes adults say silly things, and we should ignore those silly things, even if they hurt sometimes. Don't worry about your nanny. You finish off your breakfast, and I'll go speak to her. Where is she?"

"Bar," she mumbled, and then grinned at me. "Thank you, Rachel."

I gave her a small wink and pushed myself to my feet and went to find Big Mama.

She wasn't in the bar, but I heard thunderous feet upstairs, followed by shouts of anger with a hint of fear.

I climbed the stairs and leant on the banister at the top, watching her frantically pouring water onto the burning clothes.

"Need a hand?" I called to her.

"Did you do this?" She hissed, whipping around, when she heard my voice.

"Me? What possible reason could I have for wanting to burn…? What do you have there?" I said, straining to look in the bath and faked a shocked gasp. "Oh dear, are they Dante's clothes? Hmm, he's not going to be a happy camper, is he?"

"He'll whip the skin from your back when he finds out."

I lifted one of my shoulders in a shrug. "Ahh, well, he wouldn't be the first."

"I don't think you understand the gravity of what you've done. This," she whipped up a charred leather jacket and marched at me, branding it in my face. "This was given to him by Bee's mother when they were married."

"Doesn't look as though it has the club patch on it. Can't be that important."

"Bee's mother gave him it!" She repeated.

I gave her a blank look and shrugged again – even I was getting sick of the amount of shrugging I had done this morning. "But it's not his patch – lucky him. He can always buy another shitty leather jacket."

"But it won't have the sentimental value behind it!"

"So?"

"What do you mean 'so'? Are you that uncaring?"

"Memories should be in the mind, not the possessions. He'll get over it."

"And what if your little stunt had burnt the house down? Then what?"

"I don't really like to play what ifs, but I'll humour you this once. *If* the house had burnt down, then one – it would have been funny and two – he'll have understood how my mother feels."

"I heard about that." she pulled back slightly, her lips twisting. "I can't say I agree with what he did, but Dante… He doesn't always think things through. He lets his emotions get the better of him sometimes."

"Funny how you can excuse an entire house burning down – a house that was filled with a lifetime of memories and sentimental belongings. But you can't excuse a harmless bonfire in the bath. It's not like, ha-ha funny, but more... funny weird... you need to reevaluate that moral compass of yours."

"Do you know what? I'm not dealing with this. Clean up your own fucking mess, and God help you when Dante gets home."

"Yeah..." I said, drawing out the word as I sucked in my breath. "I'm not cleaning that up. I've got my own bath; it makes no difference to me if that one stays like that forever. I'm taking Bee out anyway, so looks like Dante won't have a sparring partner when he gets home."

"Excuse me?"

"Did I mumble?"

"You're not taking Bee anywhere."

"I am, though. That's the thing."

"Over my dead body."

"Bit dramatic, but feel free to jump in the bath with those clothes. I'd only planned on the one fire today, but I can make an exception since it's you."

"Dante said—"

"You've really got to stop mentioning him. I don't give a fuck what Dante says, does, thinks or feels. The sooner everyone realises that, the happier we're all going to be. I've made a promise to her, and I intend to stick to it. Unless you're going to personally pin me to the wall like our Lord and saviour, there's not really much you can do about it."

"Macbeth!" she called, her face like thunder. I burst out laughing, shaking my head at her.

"I called it the minute I saw you. Hiding behind the muscles of your son."

"Macbeth!" she screeched louder. He poked his head out of his bedroom door, looking back and forth between his mother and me.

"I don't like the look of this," he muttered.

"Would you kindly inform our guest that she won't be taking Bee out of this house now, or any other time, for that matter?"

"And would you kindly inform your mother that she doesn't get to tell me what I can and can't do?"

He sighed, closing his bedroom door and came towards us. "Why are you dragging me into this?"

"I'm not dragging you into anything, but I don't mind sitting back and enjoying the view," I said, eyeing him up and down.

He was an extremely good-looking man – he was slightly smaller than Dante, but his muscles were just as big and defined. There was just something about him that was lacking – a quality about him that wasn't there. When Dante entered a room, he owned the entire space. Macbeth wasn't easy to miss, but he didn't have the presence that made you feel as though the entire air had been sucked out of the room. Dante had an air of imminent danger, as though he could kill you ten different ways without breaking a sweat. And whilst Macbeth was certainly intimidating with his height, his scary tattoos, and scars, he just didn't have the aura around him that said his soul belonged to the devil.

"Behave yourself," he grinned at me.

"Yes sir," I said, standing tall and saluting him. He laughed and looked back at his raging mother.

"Look... Wasn't she one of those... fancy nanny things?"

"An au pair. Yes, I was."

"There we are then. She knows what she's doing. Let her take the kid. What's the worst that could happen?"

"Dante said they *both* had to stay here," she said, almost stomping her foot in frustration.

"Then let Dante deal with it when he gets back. If he wanted to keep her under lock and key, he should do it himself. I'm certainly not going to keep her prisoner. Leave her be. It will do Dante the world of good if we all stopped pretending his word is law."

"Macbeth, you are my favourite. Finally, someone who speaks a bit of sense!"

"She's not taking her—"

"Oh, for fuck's sake, mother!" Macbeth hissed at her. "What was the fucking point in Dante spending an absolute fortune installing cameras all over the bloody village? If they're that useless, we can't even let Bee go for a walk with her, then what's the point? Dante can't come storming in here saying that Rachel is his new old lady and then not even let her spend time with the kid. If he's got a problem, he can speak to me. I'm gonna walk them out. I'm late for church, anyway. Come on," he directed to me, and I grabbed him, linking my arm with his.

"S'later big mama. Don't scrub the bath too hard now, you hear?" and allowed Macbeth to lead me away with a triumphant glare over my shoulder.

"You really shouldn't poke her like that," he smiled as we walked down the stairs together. "She tells Dante everything."

"I can list a dozen things I care more about than Dante's opinion. I could probably do two dozen if I really thought about it."

"You really don't like him, do you?" He said with an amused shake of his head.

"I don't care either way. I nothing the man."

"You... 'nothing' him?"

"Yep. Nothing. He's not important enough for me to feel anything. He's not on my radar. I don't love him. I don't care enough to hate him. I nothing him. No love, no hate, no dislike, nothing. He's not that important to me. Is that clear enough for you?"

"Crystal. Ouch, by the way. Can I be there when you tell him that?"

"Ooh, you cruel man," I grinned back at him. "You don't seem to like him much either. What's the story there?"

He paused a moment. "Let me ask you something first, please. What do you know about him?"

"Nothing, and I've no intention of learning anything either. So don't start with any tales of how he's big and dangerous and how I should be listening to his every command, because it'll fall on deaf ears."

"Hey," he said, holding his hands up in surrender. "Don't shoot the messenger. If you want to play games with him, I'll cheer you on from the sidelines. But I'd look into his past, Rachel, and really think it through before you provoke him any further."

"What's the worst that could happen?"

"Uhm, death? I'm serious, Rachel," he said when I laughed at him.

"Dante isn't going to kill me. Honestly, everyone in this place is so dramatic. You know there's a middle ground, right? It doesn't always have to be death this, and murder that."

"Not in Dante's world. This isn't a normal, law-abiding community. You should know that by now. We do things our own way and Dante... Well, Dante is the future leader for a reason. He doesn't take kindly to what he would see as betrayal or weakness. And you constantly disrespecting him would be seen as weakness."

"Then he needs to sit down and have a conversation with his ego. I think it will do him good to be knocked down a peg or two."

"Just know I'm writing 'I told you so' on your gravestone. And I'm not visiting you, nor bringing you flowers. You can have an ugly grave."

"Noted. I'm not a fan of flowers, anyway."

"You're not listening to a word I say, are you?" He asked with a small grin.

"Sure I am! And for the sake of peace and harmony around here, I'll do my best to be nicer to Dante. How's that sound?" He nodded, even though we both knew it was a complete lie and I had no intention of being nice to Dante any time soon.

"So... Before I dive into the history between you and Dante, can I ask you about my clothes?"

"Err... They're fine? Is this a trap? I feel like it's a trap. No, you don't look fat."

"Not the clothes I'm wearing, dummy! But thank you... I'm on about the ones from America. You were going to sort it with Mrs Geller?"

"I gave her an address."

"This address?" I said, eyeing him with suspicion.

"Why wouldn't I?" He replied, looking at me as though I had grown two heads.

"Well, what's taking so long?"

"You realise America is on the other side of the world, right? Including the time it takes them to return home, pack up your shit, and get it posted. It's gonna be a while. Go spend Dante's money if you want more clothes. Lord knows he's got more than enough."

"I don't want to spend Dante's money!"

"Spend your own, in that case. Surely you got paid from your fancy nanny job?"

"I did."

"So, what's the problem?"

The problem was, I didn't want to waste my savings on clothes when I would need them to start afresh. "Bit hard to go shopping when I'm not allowed to leave."

"It's 2024, order online. Sounds like you just want to be a martyr. There are options."

"Brilliant. Thank you."

"Listen, you can be miserable and spend some money, getting yourself some nice clothes or whatever you want. Or you can be really miserable and do nothing. You're stuck here, but it's up to you to make the best of your situation."

"Hmm, maybe. So, are you going to tell me what the deal is between you two?" I asked, changing the topic.

"Can't. Club meeting." he winked at me and then began walking away.

"Bastard! Hey," I called out. "Before you go. What's your mum's real name?"

"Katherine. My dad calls her Kitty. She hates that."

"I *love* that."

"I knew you would."

"Macbeth, I see a friendship forming that could land us both in trouble."

"I won't tell if you won't," he winked at me again, and the evil streak in me had an idea forming.

"I'm good at secrets. But for now, I'll settle on owing you a debt and taking Bee out of here before she goes thinking I'm letting her down too."

"Have fun." he stepped out of the way to let me pass. As I brushed past him, he grabbed my arm and whispered down my ear. "And make no mistake, I will be calling in on you to repay that debt sooner or later. Enjoy your day," he said, his voice returning to normal as he released my arm.

I stiffened.

I fucking hated being grabbed. Dante had done it once too often, and it was something Alex used to do all the time. People assumed because I was short, they could manhandle me and there wasn't a thing I could do about it.

That's not how things would be here.

"Consider the debt repaid as of now for not retaliating. Grab my arm like that again, I'll rip yours from the socket and beat you to death with it," I said in a cold voice, looking up at him from under my lashes.

200

I didn't wait for a response. I pushed the rest of the way past him, nudging him with my shoulder as I did so, making sure a big smile was on my face by the time I got to Bee.

"I thought you had changed your mind!" Her entire face lit up when she saw me.

"Now, why would I do that? Are you ready?" I held out my hand to her. "Let's go on that adventure."

Dante

"Glad you could join us," Crash said sarcastically as Macbeth waltzed into church as though he hadn't kept the club waiting for him.

"Excuse me, I was cleaning up the mess Dante left behind." he shot a nasty look my way as he took his seat at the table. "Interesting old lady you have there."

"What happened?" I snapped.

"It's a surprise," he grinned at me. "So, what's church in session for to—"

"I already know about the clothes. What else?"

"If you already know about the clothes, then you know everything."

"Ha. You wouldn't piss on *me* if *I* was on fire, never mind clean up my clothes. What else?"

"Macbeth…" our dad sighed in frustration. "Could you stop behaving like a child that got the last sweet and just tell him so we can get on with this fucking meeting?"

"Jeez, everyone is so tense around here." I growled at him, and he held his hands up in surrender. "Okay, okay. It seems Rachel wanted to take Bee for a walk around the village. Bee was offering to show her all the sites. Mother wasn't happy about it, especially as she was already trying to put the fire out – which she did, by the way, but she's refused to clean it. Good luck getting the smell out of everything else. Your bed is black with smoke."

"Yeah, I figured it would be. Leather tends to do that. I still don't get what the problem is. Why shouldn't Rachel and Bee go out?"

He shrugged. "Beats me. Mama was kicking off something rotten. Tried to get me to lay down the law. I didn't, before you start growling again. I told her she could go, and if you weren't happy with it, you would deal with it when you got back."

"Thank you," I said begrudgingly. "And that's it? Nothing else happened?"

"Not that I can think of," he said innocently. I eyed him suspiciously, but kept my thoughts to myself. Things were never that simple when it came to Macbeth. I'd have to wait to get Rachel's side of the story.

"If we've finished gabbing like a bunch of women, can we get this meeting on the go?" Tools said. "I've four cars booked in today, and from the sounds of it, Crash ain't gonna be there to help. Time is money."

"He's right," Crash nodded. "Since everyone is here, I'll begin," he banged the gavel off the table. "I'm sure you've all noticed the absence of one of the prospects." A couple of eyes drifted to the end of the table, noting Noob's absence. "Dante... do you want to explain?"

I took a cigarette from the packet and sparked it up, taking a long, deep draw before I began. "You all heard at the end of church last time that I asked Noob to give Rachel some food. It was her first night here, and she was a bit... bad tempered. I wanted to give her some space. He took her the food up. And I'm not a hundred percent on the details, but it seems as though there was some flirting going on. He says one thing, she says another. I left it there and moved on from it. However, something else happened, and, without going into too much detail, I lost it with him." I paused a moment and let them all digest what I had said. They probably knew where this was going.

"I beat him in the middle of Rachel's room and made her watch. In my mind, it was justified. Looking back, I realise I probably went too far. But I'm sure you'd all do the same if it was your own old lady."

"So where is he now?" Sunshine asked. Sunshine worked part time at the garage. He should have retired years ago. He was a grumpy old cunt, but he was as permanent as the furniture at this point.

"Away," Crash answered for me. "And I'd prefer it if Dante didn't know where 'away' was at the moment. What I need from you all is an answer to what we do with him."

"Do you want him patched out?" Hacksaw asked.

"No," I said slowly. "If he wants to come back, then I'll be happy to accept him. He can stay the fuck away from Rachel, and we won't have a problem. Let him see out the rest of his prospect year, and we can decide what to do with him from there. What I want to know is, what do you guys want to do with me?"

"Dante…" my dad began.

"No. We vote. That's the way we've always done things. I might be VP, but I'm not above the club laws."

"Dante…" Zach said with a small pause. "There's nothing to vote on as far as I'm concerned. I've been a member of this club long enough to remember having to break up more fights than you've had hot dinners. Fuck, you and Trent here used to be little fuckers for fighting and bloodying each other up."

"Be that as it may," I said, taking another draw of my cigarette. "I'd like to hear it from everyone else. I'm going to be the leader of this club soon enough. I should know better than to lose it like that."

"We're all guilty of it. Like you said, we don't think straight when it comes to the women," Sunshine said. Every man around the table murmured their agreement.

"I respect you telling us," Shark said. "But what happened between you and Noob is between you and Noob. Neither of you are dead, and I'm sure the two of you can talk it out if he decides to return."

"If that's decided…" Crash said, pausing with the gavel hovered in the air, waiting for any objection. "We can move on," he slammed the gavel down and then sighed heavily.

"It's time to discuss the Rough Riders. Ven, do you want to take this one?"

We listened as Vienna told us what he had found out. He had a contact close to the Rough Riders, and he had said that he'd heard that a man from out of town had been paid – very handsomely – to kill Mickey. He was supposed to use the money to disappear, and it seems as though he had succeeded. Last the contact had heard, he had boarded a ferry to France, and had no intention of returning. Meaning we had no way of interrogating him.

The Rough Riders had covered their back's, and as far as the law was concerned, the man had left enough evidence to make sure the crime couldn't be pinned on the club. Not that we would be using the police to deal with this, but it made our life more difficult. The police tended to stay out of club rivalries, and often brushed crimes under the table, so long as there wasn't a public uproar.

However, officer Bradley was up our asses lately. If we went and killed a member of the Rough Riders, it would seem completely unprovoked.

"So what do we do?" Zach asked.

"I say we stick to the original plan. An eye for an eye," I said firmly. "We can't let them walk all over us. They're already taking fucking liberties selling on our patch. We need to nip this in the bud before they grow any bolder. We need to take a stand."

"Agreed," Crash said. "Ever since their VP took to the head of the table, they've been unpredictable. We need to show them that we are not pushovers. That we are willing to go to war if need be. And yes, I know it was only a prospect they killed, but I've been thinking over this the past few days, and prospect or not, we should be going to war to defend our brothers."

"We do it today," I said, looking at Crash. "We can't risk them hearing about this somehow. We need the element of surprise."

He nodded, understanding what I meant. We still were not sure if there was a rat amongst us. The sooner we did this, the better.

"If everyone is in agreement…?" He got the affirmation of everyone else as they went around the table one by one, giving their approval.

"Ven, Crash, Zach, and I will go and deal with this. Shark, I need a favour from you."

"Anything, brother."

"I want you to stay here and keep an eye on Rachel and Bee for me. Make sure my mother is staying out of their way, and that they're not getting up to no good."

"On it. If she sees me, I'll tell her I went to see Jenna."

"Keep her nearby when you find her. Don't have them wandering everywhere. Not until Rachel has been formally introduced. People are bound to have questions for her, and I don't want her dealing with them unprepared. Fuck knows where that will lead." I rubbed a tired hand over my eyes. "Plus, as beautiful as she is, she looks a little… worse for wear compared to when she arrived. Hey, here's a thought. Do you think Jenna will have something she could wear?"

"She has no clothes?"

"They're in America."

"Take her clothes shopping, then," Zach snapped.

"We all know she wouldn't accept my money, Z."

"I'll sort it," Shark promised. "I'm sure Jenna will be happy to help."

"Perfect. Oh, and Shark? Don't be drawn into an argument with her. She's got a vicious fucking tongue on her."

"Oh, believe me, I'll be avoiding talking to her at all costs. I like my patch," he grinned.

"Okay. Let's get to work, brothers." Crash said, banging the gavel. "We've got a prospect to find."

Chapter 25

Dante

"Is that him?" Crash asked as we brought the bikes to a stop.

"That's him," Vienna confirmed, leaning forward to rest his arms over the handles of the bike. "They have him doing the same run every day."

"What's he doing?"

"Collect money as far as I can tell."

"Here?" Zach asked incredulously. I understood.

We were on the outskirts of Leeds, which meant this was our patch. The Rough Riders had no business dealing here, but they had slowly but surely crept closer and closer with their drugs. It's not a business I liked fucking around with. But I understood drugs made the club a lot of money, so we kept it going, dealing here and there. We had been slack, probably not being as frequent as we should have been. Maybe this can be something Monster can take over now that he is a fully fledged member of the club. But that didn't change the fact that right now, our customers had gone elsewhere, and the Rough Riders had been more than happy to pick up the slack.

"How many do they have?" I asked.

"A couple dozen," Vienna replied with a twist of his lips.

"Shit," I spat. "And they trust a prospect with that level of responsibility?"

"I guess they were hoping if the prospect got caught, we would assume they were acting without the president's permission."

Fucking hell. Our prospects didn't so much as grab an extra pint from the bar without checking that they weren't needed by Crash first. If the Rough Riders expected us to believe that one of their prospects was dealing hard core drugs without the president knowing, we may as well just declare all-out war now, because clearly they have no control over the club, if that was the case.

"How do you want to deal with this?" Zach asked.

"You two keep watch," I said, nodding to Crash and Zach. "Ven, you flag him down. Ask him about scoring a deal. I'll come out when he's not expecting it and deal with it."

Crash nodded his approval. I knew he wanted me to slowly start making the bigger decisions, so I hadn't run this past him beforehand. Ven and I were more than capable of handling this alone, and it was clear to everyone that Ven would be the VP when I took to the head of the table. We needed to do this without the other two.

"Sounds good to me, VP," Zach said, and kick-started his bike, roaring off to keep a watch on the corner for any cops. Crash nodded his head at the both of us and sped off in the opposite direction. We'd meet up with them when this was over.

"Ready, Ven?"

"See you soon, brother," he grinned, shrugging off his patch and handing it to me. He left his bike next to mine as he set off on foot to speak to the prospect.

I watched from the shadows as Ven approached the prospect and spoke to him. They were both looking around, making sure no one was listening in, until finally, the prospect nodded, and they both headed in my direction.

"Who are you dealing for?" I heard Ven say, doing a brilliant job of twitching and fidgeting, as though he was strung out on a comedown.

"My boss prefers to stay anonymous."

"I dunno, man. I've had some bad shit before. There are certain people I won't deal with."

The prospect laughed, looking Ven up and down. "I don't really think you're in a place to be picky. Beggars can't be choosers."

"Doesn't Marius usually deal here?" He said, referring to one of the members of the Rough Riders.

"You know Marius?" The prospect asked in surprise.

"Look at me." Vienna stopped and gestured up and down his body. "Does it look like this is my first hit?"

"I suppose not," he grinned back. "Marius got a promotion. He's in production now, that's all I can say. I'm taking over for a while."

"Production?"

"Trade secret," the prospect said, tapping his nose.

"Is that so?"

I crept towards them as they continued talking, moving on to discuss how much Vienna wanted, and how often he was looking to buy. I stuck to the shadows, keeping my head low. If the prospect was to look up, he'd just see another man walking the streets. As they rounded the corner to an alley, I picked up my pace, hearing the engines from Crash and Zach as they approached us, having kept an eye on us too.

They cut the engines short, and, still on the bikes, scooted them over to the exits of the alley.

The prospect didn't so much as look up. He was so confident that the Rough Riders would keep him protected, it didn't even occur to him to be concerned about the roar of motorbikes that could be heard. He probably thought it was his own brothers.

I walked over to them, nodding at Ven as I came to stand at the prospect's back.

"Rider," I said, making him almost jump a mile in the air. I grabbed him, wrapping my arm around his mouth as my hand clamped around his neck. In one quick move, the knife came out of my pocket, and I sliced his throat, holding him tight and steady as he thrashed against me. As he stilled, I lowered his body to the ground and cleaned my knife on his patch.

"Ven, dump him in the bins."

"Got it, boss," he said without hesitation. It was broad daylight, and whilst most people had the common sense not to go entering any alleyways in sketchy neighbourhoods, there was always some idiot with a big mouth just around the corner. We knew we didn't have long to get the fuck out of here.

"I'm going to race to Greasy and get a change of clothes. I'll meet you there."

"I've got this," he nodded. "Go."

I spun on my heel and headed towards Crash. "It's done," I murmured as I passed him without slowing my movement. I handed him the knife in one smooth gesture and continued walking. If I was caught with blood on me, at least they wouldn't have the murder weapon. If Crash was caught, at least he wouldn't be covered in blood. We both went in the opposite direction, knowing without saying a word that we'd catch up later.

It didn't take me long to reach the Greasy. We had a change of clothes in a shed at the back, so I quickly shrugged out of my clothes, bagged them up, and sent a text to James and Shawn to come and collect them. They were the last two remaining prospects until Noob decided what to do, and they knew the protocol well. They'd get this sorted – probably more efficiently than usual, since they knew all eyes were on them with Monster being promoted and Noob having fucked up.

As I pushed my way into the cafe, I cursed under my breath, noting that Spunky and Beth were already here, and they looked pissed.

"What can we do you for, VP?" Spunky said, stressing the 'VP'.

"You finally decided to shift your bony ass and prop up the bar somewhere else?" I said to her, eyeing her in disgust.

"There's a more welcoming atmosphere here."

"Oh good, you're getting the message then. I was beginning to think you'd never click on. Two beers, Beth."

Spunky had been hanging around the club for years now. It was her hope that if she slept with enough of us, one of us would eventually make her an old lady. None of us were that fucking stupid. We slept with the club whores because it was easy access at any time of the day, but none of us were even considering them as anything more than a quick fuck.

Spunky had become more and more a pain in the ass with every passing year. We kept her around because when push came to shove; she did as she was told. Especially because she knew I was sleeping with her sister, and she wouldn't do anything to jeopardise her sister's potential old lady status.

"We're out of beers," Beth said apologetically, just as Vienna walked into Greasy.

"Beth," he said firmly. "Don't fuck around when it comes to booze. Two beers."

"You need your guard dog to speak for you?" She said, finally looking at me, a flash of hurt in her eyes that she quickly disguised.

"It's been a long morning, Beth," I sighed.

"Why don't you have a beer at home with your old lady?" Spunky all but spat at me.

"Because I want one here. So I'm going to give you two choices. You give them to me, and Ven and I will sit in that booth over there and not bother you. Or, you don't give them to me, and we come back here with the actual guard dogs and set them free on you two bitches. Your choice."

"Typical," Spunky coughed. "You're not shit without your weapons and protection, are you, Da—" She didn't get to finish. I shot out and backhanded her across the face hard enough to send her flying off her seat.

"Beers, Beth. Last time I ask."

Spunky held her cheek and looked up at me, spitting at my feet. "Fuck him, Beth. You're well rid of scum like that."

"That's enough," Vienna snapped. He jumped over the bar, grabbed two beers, and handed one to me.

"What the fuck do you think you're doing?" Beth hissed, stepping out of his way.

"This," he grinned. He grabbed hold of one of the snooker cues off the wall – Beth always had them on the wall to make sure people paid for their games – and began smashing bottles one by one. The girls screamed, ducking from the flying glass as he took long swings at all the bottles. Some of them he hit one by one, others he got behind and swooped them all off the shelves in one smooth sweep. He knocked the expensive liquor to the floor, smashed the taps off the bar, and didn't give up until every last bit of alcohol was in a broken slop on the floor.

"Is there anything else you'd like to get off your chest, or are we free to enjoy our beers now?"

"You're fucking insane!" Spunky spat.

Vienna hopped over the bar and crouched down low in front of her, resting his arms on his knees. "Maybe so, princess. But do you know what else we've always been? Loyal. Not once have we ever fucking turned you away, or been rude to you. No matter how you acted, we protected you and stayed loyal to you. And now you've fucked it," Vienna said coldly.

"I'm sorry," Beth said softly, looking down at the floor, refusing to meet our eyes.

"You should be," I said coldly. "You still owe us payment from last month," I reminded her. I had been on my way to collect payment when I had set sights on Rachel. "And it doesn't look as though you're going to be able to make payment this month, either."

"Dante—" she began, worry flaring in her eyes. She knew we didn't give a shit about the money. But for her, without us, it meant no protection. The Rough Riders were known to hang about near here, too. The only thing stopping them from coming into Greasy was that they knew we were never far away. "Look—"

"I've nothing more to say. I'll ring you in a few days for the cash. Your sister has made it more than clear we're not welcome here anymore." I downed my beer and headed for the door. "And Beth," I said, pausing and throwing her a glance over my shoulder. "You better have the money. Any agreement we had before is finished."

Rachel

"Where would you like to go first?" I asked Bee as we went outside. It had taken us over ninety minutes to get ready. First Bee wanted to change her shoes, dragging me upstairs to her bedroom. Then she had shown me all the teddies she had and introduced me to them one by one. Then she wanted to have a quick tea party with one of her dolls. When I finally got her back downstairs, she got distracted by something on the TV, and then had wanted another snack. I was exhausted already, but she was practically jumping on the spot with her excitement to get going. We had packed a picnic to eat somewhere. It had taken us so long; we were almost at lunchtime by the time we set off.

"The park!" She all but shouted, grabbing my hand and dragging me along before I even had a chance to respond.

"You don't need to drag me, Bee!" I laughed. "You're in charge today. If you want to go to the park, then the park it shall be. Although I thought you wanted to show me around."

"I'll point things out," she said, still tugging on my hand.

"Lead the way."

"At least you don't have to worry about getting dirty playing in the park. Nanny is always mad when I come home dirty," she said, looking me up and down.

She wasn't wrong.

Since my clothes still hadn't arrived from America, I was left with no choice but to wear the same hideous clothing I had worn to my mother's house. They stank of smoke, but there wasn't a chance I was about to ask Kitty if I could wear something of hers. I'd rather empty a room with my stench than ask her to spit on me if I was on fire.

I was self-conscious as we walked along, though, aware of the image I presented. I had spent so long meticulously planning every last detail of my appearance, dressing my body in expensive clothes and manicured nails. It was a shock to the system to be dressed so grungy.

Bee didn't have a care in the world, and definitely didn't share any of my worries as she happily skipped along beside me, pointing out this person, or this place, and everyone gave a friendly wave back, and then frowned when they saw me with her.

I knew there was a lot of interest in me. Everyone knew who I was, but since I hadn't been formally introduced, all they could do was guess what mine and Dante's relationship was like, and how long I would be here for.

The majority of them had been in the pub the night I arrived, but even I knew that the brief glimpse of me didn't give much away. They knew I was Dante's old lady – or meant to be; I corrected myself. But outside of that, all they could do was speculate.

Keep them guessing as far as I was concerned. I had no intentions of satisfying their curiosity.

Just like Dante, they'd soon learn I wasn't going to play along with whatever made up rules they had.

I waved back with a big smile on my face, taking a petty delight in the frowns and uncomfortable expressions I got in return. No doubt they had heard stories about me – places like this always had an impeccable gossip mill, and I knew for a fact I would be the number one hot topic.

"Hey look!" Bee exclaimed. "There's Shark! Shark!" she shouted at a young-looking man. He stopped and waved back, changing direction to walk towards us.

"Who is he?"

"He's my daddy's friend. He has the best cheeses!"

"Cheeses?" I questioned, but she didn't answer. Instead, she went charging forward to throw herself into Shark's outstretched arms.

"There's my favourite mini biker!" He said, bringing her in for a huge hug. "What are you doing out without your nanny?"

"I'm with Rachel!" she said happily, pointing an almost accusatory finger at me. Shark did a double take, seeming to notice me for the first time.

It's the fucking clothes, Rachel. You're a far cry from the pretty girl in the beautiful grey dress from a few days ago!

That much was true. It wasn't even the clothes. I had changed. My lips were still cut, there were bruises on my face, my hands were cut to shreds. There were bite marks on my neck from Dante, and my back was still torn to pieces. Not that he could see that, but it did make me walk more stiff and awkward. There were shadows under my eyes. My hair was a mess, and I could still hear the hoarseness in my voice when I spoke from the smoke.

"Nice to officially meet you, Rachel."

"I'll reserve judgement," I murmured back.

"Charming," he grinned back good-naturedly.

"You know Dante, right?" I smiled softly back. "If he's the precedent of what to expect from you people, I'm approaching everyone with caution."

"Dante isn't so bad once you get to know him."

"So people keep telling me," I said bitterly. "I believe in first impressions."

"Fair enough. I believe you might have seen my old lady, Jenna?" he asked, changing the topic. "She works at the bar."

"I might have. It's been a busy few days," I replied with a twist of my lips.

"You could say that again. I'll take you to meet her now, if you want? It would be nice for her to have some female friends for a change." His eyes flicked to my hair and the outfit I was wearing, and I knew what he was offering. Jenna might be able to help out with some clothes. At the very least, she might have a brush for me.

"We're going to the park!" Bee said, almost stamping her foot in frustration.

"We're going to the park," I repeated.

"I'll come with you," he said quickly. "Maybe Jenna can meet us there." Then again, maybe I was wrong about the hairbrush. I eyed him suspiciously, alarm bells ringing.

"No, it's okay—"

"Yes!" Bee grinned. "Will you teach me to do the monkey bars again? I can do it this time, I promise!"

"Sure thing, little Bee."

I frowned at him as Bee rushed forward and he began walking with us, always a step behind me.

"Either you're checking out my ass, or you're about to murder me. I've seen the documentaries."

He gave me a tight grin.

"You know I have permission to be with her, right?" I almost kicked myself. Why did I feel as though I had to explain to this man? But I couldn't stop the blaring alarms ringing in my head. Something wasn't right here.

"I'm sure you do. She's got quite the family around her. I know they wouldn't have let her out of their sight if they didn't know exactly where she was going."

"Right... so why are you playing bodyguard?"

"Because if I know Dante, he'll be looking for you when he's finished with club business. Once he finds out you're not at base, he'll start searching. I don't want Bee upset when her park trip ends early. I'll stay with her whilst you sort things out with the boss."

"Look," I said, stopping dead in my tracks. "I'm not sure what you've heard—"

"I've not heard a thing." He mumbled, refusing to make eye contact or even look my way.

"Sure you haven't That's why you're acting as though if you step too close to me you'll catch Ebola. I know you had... what the fuck do you guys call it? Church?"

He nodded.

"Right. I caught Macbeth on his way there, so I know you've seen Dante. Which means I'm guessing he told you about Mal...Noob. You're a shitty liar, Shark. Has he told you to follow me?"

"Bee is waiting," he said, trying to continue walking, but my hand reached out and snatched his arm before he could go anywhere.

"You're not moving until you tell me what the problem is and why Dante has sent his spies after me."

"I don't have a problem and he hasn't."

"Are you always this evasive, then? Because you're giving off the vibe of a man who has something to hide."

"Rachel... For the sake of honesty, I'll admit I know you burnt his clothes, but that's it. Nothing more, nothing less. He has club business to attend to, and I don't. I figured I'd go and see Jenna, and then get some work done. I happened to bump into you, and here we are. That's it. You don't always have to think so suspiciously of him. You could try being nicer to him, you know?"

"And make things easier on Dante? Not a chance. What's the worst that could happen? He'll burn my house down? Oh... wait... Hey, were you there?" I asked.

"I'm a member of this club. Do you really have to ask?"

"Well then. You see why I don't want to be nice to him. What can happen that's worse than my mother losing her entire home?"

Shark looked as though he had a very good idea of what Dante was capable at his worst, but if he had any specifics, he didn't elaborate.

"I'd really rather take you back to the pub, Rachel. I don't think the park is a good idea."

"I'm not going back to the pub. I promised Bee and I keep my promises. You either follow, or you don't. Either way, we're going."

"I'm leaving the second Dante arrives. I have enough arguments at home," He mumbled again, looking back down at the floor, and heading towards where Bee was waiting to cross the road.

"So me and Dante will be arguing then? So he is in a bad mood?" I shouted after him with a laugh, but he didn't answer me.

I hurried to catch up with him, and once I had held Bee's hand over the crossing, I tried again to draw him into conversation.

"What's the deal here? Why are you so scared of Dante? Aren't you both members of the same club?"

"Dante isn't a member. He's the VP."

"Yeah, that's what I meant."

"So you can see why he'd have an issue with me discussing him behind his back with his new old lady? I don't want to look like I'm playing happy families with you. I know what happened to the last bloke."

"Happy families? By taking his daughter to the park? You people need to get out more, you take things way too seriously. Am I just supposed to never speak to anyone again without a chaperone?"

"If you know what's good for you, you won't. Not until you've been formally introduced to everyone."

"You guys realise you're not the royal family, don't you? In fact, I don't think even they have this many protocols in place."

"I also don't think the royal family bounces their enemy's heads off the pavements like it was a basketball, but I've seen Dante do that."

"What a delightful, delightful man. I'll tell you what, I'll do you a deal," I said as he held open the gate to the park for me. "You can text Dante right now and tell him you've found me, and that you'll keep an eye on me until he turns up."

"Why would I text—"

"The act is over, Shark. I know he's told you to keep an eye on me. Tell him you're keeping an eye. In return, you answer a few questions I have. And you have to answer honestly."

"What kind of questions?" He asked, eyeing me suspiciously.

"Deal or no deal?"

He sighed heavily. "Fine."

"Text away." I waved at his phone and waited until he had nodded.

"He said he'll be here soon."

"You best talk fast, then."

We both sat down on a bench at the edge of the railings, and I shouted to Bee to be careful. She went squealing off to the slides, and I whipped around to face Shark.

"What happened to Bee's mother?"

"We're jumping straight in, are we?"

"Time is of the essence."

"She died."

"How?"

"An accident." He said, leaning forward to rest his elbows on his knees and kept his eyes on Bee the entire time he spoke.

"What type of accident?"

"A fatal one."

"Shark, I will jump up from this seat and run as fast as my legs can carry me. How pissed do you think Dante will be, then? Answer the questions properly."

"A motorcycle accident."

"Huh," I said, my eyes widening with surprise. "She wasn't an experienced rider?"

"She was. She was practically born with a bike between her legs. But she wasn't in the right frame of mind when she climbed that bike. Bee was only a few months old if I remember right, and Laura – that's Bee's mum."

"Yeah, I got that," I snapped, rolling my eyes.

"Anyway, Laura and Dante had been arguing. She came flying out of the clubhouse and said she needed to get away. She didn't have her leathers on, no helmet, nothing. Dante chased her, more out of anger to start with. We all followed. But it went from anger to genuine concern real quick. She lost control, like we all knew she would."

"What were they arguing about?"

"I don't know."

"Are you telling the truth?"

"Why wouldn't I?" He was still looking at Bee. He had yet to move a muscle other than follow her with his eyes.

"Hmm. Fair enough. Did they argue often?"

"Fairly often. I've heard whispers that maybe she was depressed, especially after having Bee. She didn't bond with her very well. She said having the baby prevented her from having a life. You'd have to ask Dante about that, though. He doesn't discuss it much."

"I've more chance of spontaneously combusting right here, right now, than getting any sort of answers from him." I paused for a moment and then asked my next question. "Has he had any other old ladies since?"

"No. Believe it or not, declaring someone your old lady is a huge commitment. It's not something you'd do for everyone you've shagged."

"So why did he say that about me when he doesn't even know me?"

He shrugged. "Again, you'd have to ask Dante."

"This is like having a conversation with an AI. Are you programmed with just a few replies and that's your default or something?"

"What do you want from me, woman? I don't live inside Dante's head." He gave me a nasty side eye, but he soon went back to looking at where Bee was.

"Are you afraid to look at me?"

"I'm not getting drawn into your games."

"I'm not playing any games."

He scoffed in response. "You have trouble written all over you. No disrespect, but you smell of drama. I can practically see little shivers of delight running through you at the thought of angering Dante. I'm not getting involved. He said to keep an eye on you, and that's all I'm doing. You seem nice enough, Rachel, but I'm not looking for any drama."

I simply smiled. "How long have you been here, Shark?"

"A while."

"How'd you get your name? You got a nasty bite? Like to eat humans? You climb in the bathtub and thrash about whilst your old lady chucks you chunks of meat?"

He gave me a bizarre look and shook his head. "I make the food for poker night."

"Excuse me?"

"The food. I do charcuterie boards."

I actually laughed out loud at that. "If I had a thousand guesses, I never would have guessed that."

"My mother did them. Not as a profession or anything, she just liked to feed everyone all the damn time. The first poker night I joined, Macbeth threw a packet of crisps on the table that he had stuffed down the front of his trousers, and Vienna brought beers. Two of them he drank on the way there. Dante said he ate earlier, and the other guys weren't much better. There was nothing more than scraps on the table. They spent the entire night getting drunk, growing hangrier and hangrier, until Dante punched Macbeth in the face because Dante wanted pizza, but Macbeth had slept with the delivery guy's daughter, and he refused to deliver to anyone even vaguely related to the family. So I went out and bought some stuff, whipped up a quick snack, and the job's been mine ever since."

"That's strangely cute." I laughed.

"Daddy!" Bee screeched, running out of the gates. I noticed Shark stiffen and slide further down the bench away from me.

I turned around and my breath caught in my throat as Dante picked Bee up and spun her around. The sun was behind him, casting a glow around his massive frame. He grinned at her, a genuine grin that lit up his entire face as he looked down at the tiny child in his arms. She gave him a cuddle, her arms barely reaching around his chest.

Fucking behemoth. I spun back around, refusing to look at him.

"Rachel!" Bee shouted. "Daddy's here!"

"Yeah, Rachel," he repeated, a note of humour in his voice. "Daddy's here." He placed Bee on the floor, and she went charging back into the park. Shark stood, nodded at Dante, and followed Bee, offering to take her to the monkey bars.

"You," Dante hissed from behind me, bending low to speak directly into my ear. "Get up and come with me."

Chapter 26

Rachel

"No," I replied simply, not turning my head to look at him. I couldn't look at him. He looked like a fucking God, with the sun shining on him like that. My mouth was already watering, and we all knew where that landed me.

"Did I phrase it as a question?" He growled down into my ear; the warning note clear.

"What are you going to do, manhandle me in front of all these children?" I shot him a quick look over my shoulder and quickly regretted it. "I hardly think so."

I silenced the yelp that left me as Dante grabbed me under my arms and hauled me over the back of the bench as though I weighed no more than a sack of flour. I fought against his hold, my legs dragging across the floor, struggling to get my balance as he dragged me over the grass and towards the trees.

"I swear to fuck, Dante, if you don't let me go right now!"

"You're making a scene in front of all these children, Rachel," he mocked me, but he did haul me up enough for me to get my footing.

I spun on him then, my fist connecting with his jaw with a crack that had a few heads turning. "That," I spat at him. "Will be the last time you ever use your height and strength against me. I am sick and fucking tired of you dragging me about! If I say no, I fucking mean no!"

He held his chin, looking at me with both astonishment and blinding anger. I planted my feet firmly on the floor and met him with a furious look of my own, refusing to be intimidated by him.

"Hit me again and—"

I swung at him once more, cutting off his words. He was prepared for me this time, his huge hand clamping around my fist, stopping it dead in its tracks. "I could break this with a single move," he said, squeezing my fist. "One twist, that's all it would take."

"Do it," I challenged. "It will heal, and once it does, I'll come back for round two."

He twisted slightly, and I willed myself not to show the pain of the bone straining. "Have you done it yet? Is it broken? Is this the part where I start crying for mercy?"

He let out a humourless laugh. "Are you done being a brat yet?"

"Are you done being a bully?"

"Are you done being an arsonist?"

"Are you?"

Every question had us taking a step closer to each other, until we were practically nose to nose, our breathing heavy. The only thing separating us was my fist, which he still had trapped between his, and was now squashed between our bodies.

"You're testing my patience, woman."

"Likewise. Do you think this has been fucking easy on me? I think I've behaved like a model citizen, compared to how I could have been. You're not exactly easy to get along with."

"Give over. No harm has come to you."

I almost barked with a dry laugh. "Are you fucking kidding me? Can we just break down what's happened to me since I've been here? In two days, I've been kidnapped, I've been tied up, I've been denied basic necessities like food and water. I was even denied going to the toilet. I had an idiotic Malfoy try hitting on me, and then I had to watch him get beaten half to death. I've had nothing but arguments with you, your mother… your brother is a weirdo. My mother's house was set on fire, I've been dragged about, I've been choked to within an inch of my life, I have no belongings, not even a pair of underwear I can call my own… need I go fucking on?" I said, holding my one free hand palm up so he could inspect the damage.

"Oh, I see. You were expecting prince charming, were you? And that your life would be nothing but comfort and roses?" He raised an eyebrow at me sardonically.

I pulled my hand out of his grip and shoved his chest. The fucking behemoth didn't budge an inch, so I shoved again, the sarcastic smirk pushing my anger higher and higher. "I wasn't expecting anything. I've learnt to hope for nothing, and yet somehow still expect the worst. The only person that seems to have any expectations here is *you*. You're expecting me to be this wonderful, traditional housewife. One who sucks dick like a pro, and expertly handles all household affairs. You expect me to be mother to a child I'm not allowed to be around, to be happy that I've had to leave my entire life behind, and you want me to do it all with a happy-go-lucky, positive, sunshine attitude! It seems to me, the only one here with deluded expectations, is you!"

"I never said you couldn't be around Bee. I just didn't want you taking her out alone right now."

"And whys that?"

"Because I don't know you."

I almost roared with frustration. I spun around and took a couple of steps away before wheeling back and marching towards him, shoving him once more with every ounce of strength I possessed. He still didn't budge, and it made me want to kick his stupid fucking shins. "You're right, you don't know me. So you shouldn't have fucking taken me!"

"I'm not going over this again, Rachel. I did what needed to be done."

"Oh, fuck off. You never do what needs to be done. You do what you want to do. Look at Bee—"

"What about Bee?" he said, his body stiffening and his voice colder than ever.

"Oh, come on. You can't tell me you do everything that needs to be done as far as she's concerned. She doesn't even go to school, for fuck's sake!"

"Not that it is any of your business, but she doesn't go to school because it's not safe for her to be there. I have a lot of enemies—"

"If that's the case, you had no business bringing a child into this world and raising them in an unsafe environment!"

"Besides," he carried on as though I hadn't interrupted him. "There is absolutely nothing wrong with homeschooling."

"No, there isn't. I actually love home schooling – *if* it's done correctly. And this isn't correctly. What is she learning, Dante?"

"My mother sees to all that."

"Stop it. If you're going to forgo conventional education, then you, as her parent, should be stepping up and making sure she's getting everything she would have been getting at school. That means actually putting the effort in to ensure she's not getting left behind! And before you start," I warned when he opened his mouth. "No-one is saying you have to sit her down for six hours a day and mimic a classroom environment, but locking her in a dusty old house, with a grandma who has no patience for her, and refusing to socialise her with anyone else, isn't the way! Do you know how often your mother loses her temper with her? How often Bee is left to her own devices because your mother is manning the bar? Lord knows there's no love lost between me and your mother, but even I know this isn't fair to either of them. Your mother has already raised her children – although the jury is out on that one. If you ask me, you were dragged up, not raised—"

"Are you finished?"

"No. The point is, why should she have to raise Bee too? She doesn't deserve that, and Bee doesn't deserve to be rotting away in a house where people can't be bothered with her! She deserves friends her own age, Dante. She deserves to have fun where she's not surrounded by drunken, angry bikers. She deserves some essence of normality! You should have seen how excited she was to come to the park! Look at her now, Dante! The smile hasn't left her face, because she's playing with other children!"

He was silent for a moment as I broke off, breathing heavily. "Is that it? Are you done now? Because that's quite the assessment you've made after only spending a morning in Bee's company."

"Sometimes an outsider's perspective is the clearest one. You're too blind to see what's right in front of you. But let's try a different angle here. What sort of message are you sending to her if you bring a woman home, publicly declare her your old lady, but then deem that woman unsafe for her to be around? Children see more than you think. What sort of message is Bee getting, if the only adult interactions she sees is her dad throwing his weight around, and bullying women? Because that's what you've done, Dante. You've tried your best to bully me. I stand up to you, but that could have very easily been different. And let's face it, that's what you wanted. You didn't want me to fight back! Would you be happy with Bee growing up thinking this is acceptable? What if her future partner puts their hands around her neck and chokes her? Or kidnaps her? Or sets your house on fire?"

"I wouldn't let that happen."

"Would she even tell you? If she grows up thinking this is normal behaviour, she's not going to even think about telling you, because she won't think it's wrong! You can't always protect her. She has to live her life. And if someone was to treat her badly, then the damage was already done. She will have to live with the aftermath, no matter if you deal with the person who caused the hurt or not! Physically, you can heal her, but can you heal her mentally?"

"You're getting all of this because my mother said you couldn't take her out?" He grinned at me, and it was as though he had set me alight with the way the anger ran through my veins.

"Fine!" I all but screamed at him. "Have it your way and keep your daughter locked up like you're some fucked up, tattooed, giant version of Mother Gothel. Don't let her have friends, or relationships, or a life outside of you, your mother, and your shit fucking bikes! I'm beginning to understand now why Laura ran off. And mark my words, Bee will end up doing the same if you keep her living like this!" I was breathing heavily by the time I was finished. And it was only when I saw the flash of pain in Dante's eyes that I realised what I had said.

I wanted to reach out and snatch the words back, to gobble them back inside my mouth and pretend they were never uttered. But it was too late. They were out there, clear for all to hear.

A darkness fell over Dante's face, and his eyes flashed with a murderous rage.

"What did you just say?"

A smarter woman might have backed down. A smarter woman may have apologised and said she didn't mean it. Unfortunately for me, all the smarts in the world could not replace my stubborn streak. The angrier Dante looked, the more my pride screamed at me not to be intimidated by a man.

All my life, people had tried shouting over me. They had used my small frame against me. After Alex, I had sworn I would never let that happen again. Dante might be double the size that Alex had been, but it made no difference to my bad-tempered self. I would not be intimidated.

"You heard me," I challenged. "You can pull all the scary faces you want, and you can also try roaring and intimidating me. It won't change anything. Facts are facts. Someone needed to say it, so why not me? You've surrounded yourself with yes men, too afraid to stand up to you and speak up for what's right. That won't ever be me."

As I spoke, Dante closed the distance between us, causing me to have to crane my neck back to look up at him. "What? Are you going to grab me now? You're going to inflict some sort of punishment on me for being right? You're mad because you've been forced to face reality. Bee deserves better than what you're currently offering her, and I have the qualification to allow me to state that as a fact."

He didn't need to know that I didn't have any formal qualification. I had got lucky in America and found myself in with a family who were desperate, and they didn't ask. They took my word for it. After them, I had a glowing reference, and no one bothered to check if I was lying or not.

"A piece of paper makes you more qualified than a parent?"

"It makes me more qualified than a negligent parent, yes."

"Rachel, no offense, but I'm hardly going to trust a word you say, considering I know for a fact you killed a man — something you wouldn't have disclosed to any employees."

"Irrelevant." I waved away his accusation, but my stomach flipped at the way he uttered it so casually.

Thanks mother and your big fucking gob. And thank you Vienna, and your fucking loudmouth. You gossiping little shite.

"You also think the sun shines out of your own ass—"

"Maybe it does."

"I can assure you it does not. Considering I had your ass in my face, up close and personal, only twelve hours ago, *I'm* qualified to make *that* assessment."

"Don't be fucking vulgar. But why am I not surprised? Typical Dante. Ignore the fucking issues and turn it into a sex thing."

"Rachel," he began with a heavy sigh. "Believe it or not, I didn't come here to argue with you."

"Yeah, right," I scoffed, rolling my eyes at him.

"I didn't. I came to call a truce."

"Sure you did. That's why you sent the cheese man after me."

"I beg your fucking pardon?"

"Him," I said, pointing at Shark. "And no, he didn't tell me. I'm not a fucking moron."

"Can't you ever just call someone by their actual fucking name, Rachel? It's impossible to know who you're on about when you just make things up!"

"Ha! That's a bit rich coming from the man who's part of a biker club with the likes of Macbeth and Vienna. You're really going to lecture me on nicknames?"

"Fair point. Well made," he paused for a second before sighing heavily when I raised an eyebrow at him. "Okay. Fine. Yes. I did send Shark to watch you. And yes, I was pissed at you burning my things, but that doesn't mean I don't understand why you did it. And I also do appreciate the fact that you have Bee's best interests at heart. I don't want every day to be a fight. I—" he sighed again. "Look, do you want to go for a ride?"

"I—Excuse me?"

"Do you want to go for a ride?" He repeated, enunciating each word. "Shark can stay with Bee. We need to clear the air and draw a line in the sand. We got off on the wrong foot and—"

"No."

"No?" he repeated, as though he had never heard the word before.

"That's what I said. You're asking me to leave Bee behind. To be like everyone else in her life and ditch her when something better comes along."

"No, I—"

"No means no, Dante. But thanks. I'll stay with Bee. And for your information, we didn't get off on the wrong foot. We got off exactly how things should be. What, did you expect me to go riding off into the sunset with you? You'll talk, I'll listen, you'll explain yourself, and suddenly everything will be okay. 'Ooh, he might have spat on me, starved me, and strangled me, but he is just sooo mysterious and handsome, and sooo misunderstood. He'll change for me. I can tame him.'"

"Are you forgetting you also stabbed me?"

"In response to everything you had already done to me! I stabbed you with a self-defence tool! But that just proves my point, doesn't it? There's no 'getting off on the wrong foot' here. We're trying to squeeze feet into shoes that just don't fit.

It's never going to happen. Nothing excuses abuse Dante, and that's all I've received since the moment I met you. I don't want half assed efforts and lame excuses."

"I'm trying to offer you an olive branch," he said through gritted teeth.

"Unfortunately for you, I don't like olives. If this was a movie, I'd be screaming at the heroine to run a mile, track down the nearest cop and report you for all your crimes. Lord knows there's enough. But luckily for you, I hate the cops. But that doesn't change the fact that I'm not going anywhere with you. Not now, not tomorrow, not ever."

I tried to walk off then, but the minute I turned my back on him, he once again grabbed me, picked me up, and hauled me over his shoulder in one smooth move.

"Put me fucking down!" I screamed at him, my legs kicking at his chest and my fists beating down on his back. He slapped my ass in response and called out to Shark. "Take Bee home in an hour!"

I saw Shark salute in response, and I cursed him under my breath.

"Oi, Shrek!" I hissed, kicking him again. He laughed and pinned my legs at the back of my knees.

"Does that make you princess Fiona?"

"It makes me princess fucking pissed. Put me down. Now."

"Let me guess, 'I'll suffer the consequences'? I've seen the movie. I know the lines."

"I fucking hate you. Did you know that?"

"Well, good job I'm taking us somewhere where we can hash out our differences, isn't it? You'll love me by the end of the day."

"I won't love you by the end of my fucking life. Get off!" I heaved, but it made no difference.

I pushed myself up the best I could, my arms straight against his back as I lifted my head up. I saw Bee waving at me, and I gave her a sad little wave back, doing my best to smile. She went running off after Shark; her smile radiating her entire face.

I wasn't smiling, though. And the minute Dante let me down, he was going to pay for ruining my morning.

Chapter 27

Dante

Rachel might have small legs, but they didn't half deliver a hefty kick to the chest. I had resorted to pinning them down behind the knees, and still she lashed out the best she could.

Her fists rained down on my back, her nails dug into my shoulder, and at one point she had even bitten my ear – although a sharp slap to her ass soon put an end to her trying that again.

We passed a few people on our way, but none of them gave Rachel the help she needed. I tried my hardest not to laugh at the frustrated scream she let out when people just waved at us, shaking their heads with a smile on their lips. They knew better than to intervene.

"Oi!" Rachel shouted to the couple at the end of the street. "How common is it to see a fucking brute manhandling a woman around here? How often have you seen women dragged about without their consent that it's just become so commonplace you don't even attempt to intervene?"

"They won't answer you, you know. They've no interest in getting involved in a lover's tiff."

"What the fuck is wrong with you?" Rachel shouted at the couple, completely ignoring me. I didn't mind. If past interactions between us had taught me anything, it was that Rachel and I had around fifteen minutes before one of us was hurling insults at the other. I didn't want to waste any of those minutes on idle chitchat.

It was time to clear the air and come to some sort of truce before this situation got way out of hand.

I carried on marching down the street until we reached my bar. I pushed the door open with one hand and went straight to a booth at the back, ignoring everyone else that was in there.

I plopped Rachel down on the seat, simply placing my fingers to her lips to shush her when she tried to speak and went to the bar, grabbing a bottle of whiskey, and then returned to her.

"I don't like whiskey," she muttered, pushing away the shot glass I had put before her.

"What do you want, then?" I said with a frustrated sigh.

"To leave."

"Tough," I snapped, taking the seat opposite her. "And today you like whiskey." I poured us both a shot.

"Here are the rules: one of us asks a question. The other takes a shot for Dutch courage, and then answers. We take it in turns. No question is off limits."

"It's not even lunchtime," she pushed the glass away again.

"I'm sure you've drunk this early before. Stop being a brat and play the game."

"This is pathetic."

"Do you have a better idea? Because believe it or not, Rachel, I would like to get to know you better. I would like to know your likes and dislikes. I would like to know what goes on in that pretty little head of yours. I would like to at least try to be friends. But if you're too coward…" I brought my drink to my lips and let my words trail off.

Predictable little hell cat that she was, she sat up straighter, snatching the glass back close to her. "I'm not a coward."

"Then you should have no issue playing along. I'll even let you go first, my drinks waiting." I tipped my full glass her way.

"Fine. Were you born a cunt, or was it your big-time aspiration?"

I gave her a lop-sided smirk, throwing my drink back, my jaw clenching at the burn. "Aspiration. I think it's safe to say I achieved it, wouldn't you?" I picked up the whiskey bottle and motioned to her shot glass. She pushed it forward reluctantly and snatched it back the minute it was half full.

"Fire away."

"Where's your dad?" I asked, her eyes growing wide as I went for the kill. There was no point beating around the bush. The drinks were designed to get us to loosen up and be more honest, but the game was flawed. The more we drank, the more drunk we were going to get. It was best to get the important questions out in the open.

"Prison," she said shortly, throwing her drink back.

"Why?"

"Isn't it your turn?" She hissed, snatching the whiskey bottle and filling my glass to the top.

"Why were you and Laura arguing the night she died?" She challenged, raising one of her eyebrows.

My stomach flipped at her question. But the rules were the rules. I'd answer honestly and hope that it showed her I was at least taking this seriously.

"She didn't like her life. She wasn't happy. She had a baby thinking it would fix our marriage, then soon found out she hated being a mother. She had no patience for Bee, and would leave her crying for hours on end. I tried to help her, but I also didn't want her to feel as though I was taking over and not allowing her to even try to be a mother. Laura also hated it here. She was born a biker. Her dad was one of my dad's right-hand men – he committed suicide not long after Laura died. But Laura wanted more freedom. She said she had wasted the best years of her life with a man who couldn't stand her."

"Is that true?" Rachel asked. I didn't point out that it was two questions, I just raised my glass, and she filled it without question.

"Partly," I said after throwing the brown liquid down my throat. "I thought I loved her. I was too young to realise what love really was. I wasn't faithful to her either, and I wasn't exactly careful about keeping the affairs secret. People talk and she easily found out. I was a cocky shit – probably still am," I grinned, my stomach fluttering when Rachel gave me a small grin back.

"I'll drink to that," she said, clinking her empty glass against mine.

"Bitch," I playfully huffed, and her smile widened. "The night Laura stormed out of here, Bee had been teething. We tried for hours to settle her, but nothing was working. My mother suggested rubbing some brandy on her gums, and Laura lost it. She was screaming that it was outdated advice, and no one did that anymore. She was screaming all sorts. Most of it didn't even make sense. It was months – no, years - of pent-up frustration, finally releasing in the most incoherent way. And then, out of nowhere, the screaming stopped, and she said she needed to get out of here. She snatched up the keys to her bike and was out the door before I had a chance to hand Bee to my mother and follow her."

I paused for a moment, letting Rachel digest what I had just said. "When I saw she was without her gear, I called the lads, and we followed her. I will say, I don't think Laura had any intention of suicide, and what happened was a tragic accident. But it happened, and here we are."

Rachel stayed silent. I thought she might have had follow-up questions, and I was prepared for them. But instead, she raised her glass for me to pour her turn.

I raised my eyebrows in surprise, and she shrugged. "It's your turn. Fair is fair."

"Okay," I said, pouring her a generous shot. "Who did you kill?"

The drink paused at her lips, and for a second I thought she was going to back down. The blank look that had irritated me so badly a few nights ago descended back over her face as she completely froze. But then, a familiar spark came to her eyes, and she threw the drink back, tossing her hair over her shoulders as she did so, and slammed the drink on the table.

"My ex," she said, her eyes meeting mine.

"Can I ask why?"

"He was an asshole, and he deserved it."

"Why?" I pushed, not wanting to accept such a generic response. I had no doubt he'd done something to deserve it. From what I knew about her, she wasn't stabbing people for the fun of it. There was a reason there, and I wanted to know exactly what that reason was.

She grabbed the bottle and took a swig directly from the top, no longer bothering with the glass. She shook her head, closing her eyes as the liquid burned down her throat, and then she took another, keeping her hand on the bottle as she put it back down on the table.

"Alex was an asshole. But more than that, he was a dangerous asshole. My home life wasn't terrible, but it wasn't ideal. My parents loved me, but they didn't really have much time for me. They wanted me silent and had no idea how to handle a child that was struggling in that oppressive world they called their own. I started acting out. Nothing major. Pretty typical teenage rebellion stuff – getting into trouble at school or skipping it altogether. Answering back. Drinking. Smoking weed. When I was sixteen, I met a guy who immediately showed an overly keen interest in me. He invited me to a party that night, and because I wasn't used to the attention, my stupid ass felt flattered and went along." She paused and took another drink. "When we got there, he immediately changed. Gone was the charming man who had lured me in, and instead was this... I can only describe him as an octopus. His hands were everywhere, and he was spitting all sorts of vile words at me. I tried to push him away, but he had laughed at me, saying I was a silly little girl trying to play the big bad grown up, when in reality I was immature and pathetic. He said he would make me a woman. The next thing I knew, the man was on the floor, and Alex was there. He introduced himself and said he was sorry that had happened. A couple of his female friends rushed around me and said they saw the whole thing, and how horrible it was, and they would look after me for the rest of the night." Another drink.

"They looked fucking terrifying – all of them had crazy hair colours, spikes in their ears, dark clothing with chains hanging off them. But they proved looks can be deceiving, because they were nothing but nice to me." she twisted her lips in a mocking smile. "Surprise, surprise, they were not nice. Not underneath the fake surface."

"What happened?"

"I found out later that the guy who brought me to the club was a recruiter – they called him a 'buffer', which is a fucking ridiculous name. Basically, he would get young girls from the street, bring them to the club, and Alex would play the hero, rescuing them from the dangerous situation they were in. He and his gang made it seem as though they were the safe haven, and by the time people realised the truth, it was too late to leave. Alex was in his thirties, and I wasn't the first girl he had done this to. He went for messed up teenagers, with parents who either didn't care, or who gave up when they were too much trouble. When they went missing, the police gave it a half assed attempt to look into it, but those girls were trouble. They were always listed as runaways, and the case would grow cold. Alex either had them murdered when he had enough of them, or just discarded of them and left them to the streets." Another drink. I was almost tempted to take the bottle away from her, knowing her small frame couldn't handle this amount of alcohol in this amount of time, but I was too scared that she would button up, and I'd never find out what had happened to her back then.

"But that wasn't the Alex I knew," she continued. "I know now he groomed me, but obviously it didn't feel that way at the time. I relished getting so much attention from this older man. He piled me with cigarettes, alcohol, and drugs. I would brag about my older boyfriend, who took me to parties and who treated me as though I was his equal, not a child. I willingly slept with him, and he was so happy that he got to take my virginity. He took the sheets and pinned them to the wall of the club," her cheeks coloured with embarrassment at the memory. "It didn't even occur to me to be mad about that. He said it showed everyone I belonged to him, and it was proof that I wanted to be there. I gave him the ultimate gift. Sick, I know."

My stomach flipped at the thought of the humiliation she must have gone through. And flipped once again as I remembered Rachel's earlier words about how I would react if anyone dared treat Bee the same way.

"My parents knew there was a change. My style changed. I dyed my hair black and pierced my ears a bunch of times. When I came back unable to speak due to my tongue piercing, they called me a mess and said I needed to sort my act out. Alex laughed and gave me my first hit of cocaine that night and said if my parents wanted to complain, let's give them something to complain about. I went back home a complete mess. My parents rang the police, but they couldn't do much as I refused to give up the names of the people who had supplied me with the drugs. They took pity on me and issued me a caution, but said I was well on my way to a young offenders' institute." She took another drink, her eyes watering at the burn in her throat. The harsh liquor only intensified the hoarseness in her throat, and once more my stomach flipped. I had caused that, and now I was causing her such misery as she relived her horrific adolescence.

"Alex loved that. He was so proud of me, and kept his arm around me the entire night, showing me off to everyone. I wanted to keep that happy light in his eyes. He was the only one who was ever proud of me – even before I rebelled, my parents were always disappointed. Nothing I did was ever good enough. Alex wasn't like that. He lavished praise on me. He would always whisper how much he loved me. He said he would kill anyone who tried to take me away from him. As a sixteen-year-old who read one too many romances, this was music to my ears. I didn't realise he was love bombing me, and essentially emotionally abusing me. I would have done anything for him. Which is why, the first time he hit me, I didn't do a thing about it. He told me I deserved it, and I accepted it. He had wanted me to steal money from my parents and I had refused. Once he hit me, I went and stole a couple hundred, and he went on his knees apologising. But the line had been crossed, and so the next time he hit me, he didn't feel as bad." She went to take a drink, but then seemed to think for a moment, pushing the bottle away from her.

"Over the next year or so, Alex hit me for various reasons. I stopped going home during the worst of it. I didn't want my parents to see me like that. They worried enough as it was. I couldn't imagine what it would do to them to see me with black eyes, or burn marks, or whip marks. At one point, I even had a shoe print on my back from where one of Alex's friends had stomped on me. All the friends I had before Alex were long gone. They had been rebellious, but in a 'testing the boundaries' sort of way that all teenagers do. They didn't want to get involved in anything hardcore. I had no one other than Alex, and he made sure I knew it. He stopped apologising for hurting me, and instead spat all the reasons why I deserved it. He had officially moved on from stage one – love bombing to earn my trust and had now turned to stage two. He wanted to make me feel worthless, as though I should be grateful for the tiniest bit of attention he threw my way. And I was. I'm embarrassed by some of the things I did to earn his affection."

I stayed silent, waiting for her to continue. She looked at me, a defiant light in her eyes, as though challenging me to be disgusted by her next admission. "He said I needed training and stood by and watched as I fucked his friends. They were not gentle, yet if I cried, I was punished for it. I learnt to act as a sex doll, letting them do whatever they wanted to me. The girls would help clean me up afterwards, but they weren't exactly kind either."

"Jesus," I muttered. That's where the blank look came from. It was training, but not the type I had expected. Rachel gave me a wry grin.

"Be grateful you're only getting the cliff notes version."

"What happened next?"

"One of the guys made an offhand suggestion one day that I would suck dick much better if I had no teeth. He said it jokingly, but Alex latched onto the idea. For weeks, he tried to persuade me to have my teeth removed and said he would pay for the best dentures out there. I laughed to start with, but when I realised he was serious, I stood my ground for the first time ever. He was mad and said no one would even know. It would be our secret. He went back to phase one Alex, being nice to me, stroking my hair to get me to sleep, washing it for me, cooking for me. He was so lovely; I was almost convinced to do it. I stopped fighting as much, and he took that as agreement. He told me he had me booked in with a dentist friend of his, and that they were going to make a pretty penny from me, as there was always a market for teeth. I told him I wanted to go home for the night and see my parents, since I was obviously not going to be able to see them for a while whilst they made my dentures and whatnot. He agreed and dropped me off at home, arguing with my parents. He was no longer bothered about them seeing him. He knew I was well under his control. He actually enjoyed mocking them. He gave me the biggest kiss in front of them, groping my ass and tits as he did so. When he left, I went straight to my room. My parents followed, and we had a huge argument. For the first time in years, I looked at them and saw the damage I was really doing. My dad looked older than ever. He almost appeared ill. My mother wasn't much better, although she had the luxury of makeup to hide the bags under her eyes, and she dyed away all the grey hair." She paused, and this time I pushed the bottle at her. She fucking needed it. She took a long swig and gave me a grateful, sad smile.

"Guilt ate at me and made me lash out. I ran away, telling them I would never be back. I went back to the club that was now my home. I didn't let Alex know I was coming – how could I when he didn't even allow me to own a phone? But when I arrived, I heard them all. They were laughing about me; about how desperate I was and how easy I was to manipulate. Alex said I was perfect, and that there wasn't a thing I wouldn't agree to. A model student. One of them even laughed that they could break my arms and legs so I couldn't fight back. I'd be the perfect little submissive then. They were talking about advertising me, selling my entire body for whatever man was interested. My heart shattered. Despite all the abuse, I genuinely believed he loved me. It was a reality check. I carried on listening and heard their plans for their new victim. They wanted me to get a new girl for them, to help train. They said it wouldn't be so difficult if it was me doing the recruiting. I was still only seventeen, and it should be easy for me to get the trust of a younger girl. I would seem exciting. Thanks to the internet, girls were getting more wary of being approached by men, and they were finding it difficult with their current recruiters, but they had never tried a female before. Instead of showing a sexual interest, they wanted me to become their best friend."

"Rachel... I'm so sorry."

She waved my apology away, and I noted that her hand was shaking, and her words were beginning to slur. "I was horrified. I had heard whispers that there had been girls before me, but I had never been shown any proof, so I hadn't believed it. Stupid little me. I thought I was special. Alex wasn't a paedophile or a groomer. I was just special. Different. This proved I wasn't.

"I went up to my room and stripped off – more out of habit than anything else. Alex didn't like me to wear clothes in the bedroom. For some reason, I looked in the mirror for the first time in God knows how long, and I really saw myself. I was on the dangerous side of skinny, covered in burn marks and bruises. My skin looked grey, my cheeks were sunken, and I had this haunted look in my eyes that scared me. Did I really want another girl to go through this? I looked in the mirror, and it wasn't even myself I saw. It was my old friends, my nieces, random kids I had seen on the street. This was their fate if I let this continue. It was the wake-up call and reality check I needed. When Alex came to bed, he was surprised to see me and got angry that I came home by myself. He wanted to know who I had been with. We ended up arguing, and I confronted him about what I had heard. He laughed in my face. The illusion shattered. He asked me if I really thought I was that special I could keep his attention forever? I had an expiration date, and it was fast approaching. I asked him why he wanted my teeth removed then, if he no longer wanted me, and he grabbed my face and said he was planning on selling me to the highest bidder every night. He hadn't wasted so much time training me not to reap the rewards."

She swallowed thickly, her voice breaking.

"He said something along the lines of reaping the rewards right there and then and pushed me to the bed. I tried to fight, but it was pointless. His friends heard the banging, and they came rushing into the room. Two of them pinned my arms and legs to the bed, and they all took it in turns to rape me. It went on for hours. They were laughing the entire time. One of them even said this proved how fun I'd be when I had no working limbs. When it was finally over, I ran. I went back to my parents and when they asked what had happened, I refused to tell them. I had always kept my body covered around them, and they just assumed I was involved with a bad man who did drugs. They had no idea the extent of it, and that's what I told them. I was too ashamed to admit what I had put up with all those years."

She paused, and wiped away a tear before it had the chance to fall. She sniffed and sat up straighter, all emotion gone.

"About two months later, Alex reappeared. My dad had given me his old phone, and he got my number from the local weed dealer. He would send me messages saying he wasn't done with me, and I was foolish if I ever thought he was letting me go. One day, my mother was cooking for a dinner party she was hosting and had sent my dad out to get something she had forgotten. Alex had been watching the house and saw that as his opportunity to strike. He text me to tell me he was coming to get me. I panicked. I had only just started to heal. I was finally beginning to leave the house again after weeks of being shut away in my bedroom. I never went far, just for a walk around the garden, but it was progress. I was recovering. And with one text from him, I was back to square one. When I heard his car, I didn't even think it through. I waited at the door for him, and when I saw him coming down the garden path, I rushed at him and stabbed him in the stomach. He was so shocked; all he could do was look at me. I ripped the knife out and stabbed him again. I went manic, stabbing him over and over, until someone dragged me off him." She took a deep breath, and I reached out to hold her hand.

"My dad was screaming in my face, asking me what the fuck I had just done. They assumed I did it through crazed withdrawal symptoms – at least my mother did. I think my dad recognised that something more was going on. The police arrived, and my dad took the blame."

"Why did your mother say you killed him in cold blood?" I asked, my own blood seething with an uncontrollable rage.

"Because that's what it looked like. He hadn't done a thing to me that day, and I attacked him. Like I said, my parents had no idea the extent of what I went through. I don't ever want them to know. They don't *deserve* to know."

"What? Why? They should know how much they failed you, Rachel. They should leave with that guilt and shame for the rest of their lives. You were a child, and you were let down. Why wouldn't you want them to know?"

She snatched her hand away from me. "Because they assumed the worst of me. I don't want them to forgive what I had done because they feel sorry for me. They automatically assumed I was high, or on a comedown, or whatever else. Let them spend the rest of their days hating me. I don't care. If they didn't love me enough to see that I was going through some pretty messed up shit, then they were shitty parents. I want them – mainly my mother – to spend the rest of their lives wondering where they went so wrong that their daughter turned into a murderer. I'm not having them justifying it because I was groomed, or whatever else. Let them think I'm truly psychotic."

"You do realise that doesn't make any sense, right?"

"Yep," she said, popping the p. She swigged from the bottle once more, taking giant gulps. "I don't care," she said, her jaw clenched. I took the bottle from her hands and put it back on the table. "They failed me, Dante. I swore to myself I would never explain myself to them. My mother still believes Alex didn't deserve to die. She's a Christian woman and truly believes he could have repented for his sins. Jesus would have forgiven him. I took away his chance to turn his life around, and now she has to live with the shame of having a husband in prison. She can't see past her own selfish existence."

I closed my eyes and took a deep breath, my anger close to erupting.

I don't know what I had been expecting Rachel to say, but I definitely hadn't expected anything I had heard.

"I want the names," I told her in a voice I didn't recognise. My eyes snapped open and locked with her own.

She dismissed me with a wave of her hand. "Its history."

"It's not fucking history."

"Listen," she said, standing up on wobbly legs. It sounded more like "lishen", and I realised how much the alcohol had gone to her head. "I don't need you coming in here and p-playing shaviour."

"Saviour," I correctly dryly.

"Whatever." she swiped her hand again, knocking over the whiskey bottle. "You concentrate on your life; I'll concentrate on mine. You're no better than them, anyway."

"I beg your fucking pardon?"

"You and Alex are peash in a pod."

"You're drunk. Go to bed, Rachel. Sleep it off," I warned through gritted teeth.

"What's the saying? Drunk words, shober thoughts."

"I'm going to give you a pass, because clearly it's hurt from bringing up old memories, but I suggest you remove yourself from my company before you say something you regret, and I do something I regret."

"No," she said stubbornly, her hands planted on top of the table to stop herself from swaying. "Look around. You have club whores, throwing themselves at any of you. Is that any different from the trained girls Alex had? You kidnapped me. You kept me for yourself, just like Alex. You throw your weight around—"

Before I knew what I was doing, I was up on my feet and grabbing her jaw, squeezing her cheeks together to stop her from talking. "Watch it," I hissed in her face.

The noise of the bar quietened as everyone turned to see what was happening.

"Point proven," she spat at me. Literally spat at me. Her spit landed on my cheek, and I saw red.

I slammed her body against the wall, her head ricocheting off the wall. "Don't take it out on me because you've got a shitty past. You think for someone that was raised on alcohol, you'd know how to handle it better. I guess Alex didn't train you as well as you thought."

You fucking asshole, Dante.

I hated myself. I knew it was too far. But it was too late to take the words back.

"And you'd think since one woman already killed herself to escape you, you'd consider treating them better. Old habits die hard, I guess." She shot back, all traces of slurring gone.

I wanted to slam her into the wall so hard there would be a Rachel shaped hole in her place. She had taken a healed wound, and with one cruel sentence, she had ripped the scab off and exposed it all over again.

Which is exactly what I had done to her, too.

"Isn't this the part where you call Vienna to come deal with the aftermath whilst you run away from the thing you caused?" She mocked me, not even bothering to try to get out of my punishing grip.

"Fuck off, Rachel."

"Gladly. Show me the door and you won't see me for dust. I never wanted to be here, and I certainly don't want to be with you."

The game was a mistake. Introducing alcohol to two people who couldn't spend five minutes in each other's company was a mistake. Hindsight was a brilliant fucking thing.

But I wasn't going to let her speak to me like that unpunished. I never pretended to be anything other than a cruel man who liked to get his own way. And I needed to take that smug smirk off her face.

And so I did it in the lowest way I could.

I brought my face close to hers and hissed down her ear. "Ordinarily, I'd hit someone for a remark like that, but you've already been used as a punching bag. No doubt you'd revert straight back into the role you were born to play. It's time you face facts, Rachel. Hate me as much as you want, but I'm all you've got. You leave here, and it wouldn't take much for me to find Alex's remaining family and friends and tell them where you are. You're as trapped now as you were then."

"Good," she whispered back. I pulled my head back and looked at her, expecting to see tears, or anger, or something. But once again, that blank expression was back. It made me want to rip her skin off and rearrange her features. She pushed her head away from the wall and brought hers close to mine.

"I thrive in this environment," she grinned at me. A cold, evil grin. Her tongue came out, and she licked my face, from my chin, all the way up to under my eye. "I'm not a scared seventeen-year-old. And as you've just learnt, I rectified my mistake and dealt with the problem. Just as I'll deal with you if you ever push me too far. And this time, I promise the autopsy won't say 'nearly beheaded'. Now go fuck yourself."

She pushed me away, and I was shocked enough to let her go. "Oh, and whilst we're handing out threats. One phone call from me to social services, and Bee will be ripped out of here without a second thought. No wife, no old lady, no daughter. Think about that next time you threaten me. We all have our fucking vices."

She shoulder checked me as she walked past and grabbed another bottle off the bar.

"Hope you enjoyed the show, ladies and gents," she shouted to the crowd. "Long reign, the new old lady." She looked back at me. "Cheers," she said in a voice like ice, bringing the bottle to her lips and took a long drink before letting it drop from her hand and smash to the floor.

She didn't even flinch as it shattered and splashed up her legs. She just turned around and headed back upstairs without a word, leaving the entire bar in stunned silence.

Chapter 28

Rachel

I laid in bed in that awkward stage of not being quite sober, but not quite drunk either. I had come upstairs and immediately threw myself down on the bed. I woke up hours later, face down, dry mouth, and wide awake. Enough time had passed between now and my last drink to clear my thoughts, and I didn't like any of the memories that came back to me.

After brushing my teeth, and changing my clothes, I filled a glass with water, already knowing that this calm was deceptive, and I'd wake up tomorrow with a raging hangover, and climbed back into bed. Not that it did any good. I stared at the ceiling, picturing Dante's face as I hurled insults at him.

I cringed as I remembered us both yelling at each other in front of his club. His intentions had been good ones. It wouldn't hurt to get to know each other better, but we both went for the jugular, wanting to pick at the scars that weren't fully healed, rather than focusing on the smaller stuff first. And, of course, when we were hurt, we lashed out, each in a competition to hurt the other more than we were hurting ourselves.

How many more times were we going to go at each other? How many more rounds did we have in us?

I stared at the ceiling, replaying the entire evening in my mind, when I heard the door creek open, letting in a stream of light, before it was blocked out by a formidable shadow.

I smelled him before I could see him properly – that unique smell that was half leather, half man, whole Dante. My body reacted immediately, jumping in excitement, my heart rate accelerating, my mouth drying up, my skin tingling.

God, I hope it wasn't as obvious to him as it was to me how easily my body responded to him on such a primal, physical level.

But what does he want?

I wasn't up for round two so soon. It would take me a while to recover from the effects of the alcohol, and no doubt I'd let my temper get the best of me and say something I'd really regret.

I heard Dante moving around, but I didn't dare turn my head to look at him and let him know I was awake.

It was only when the bed dipped on the other side that I realised he was climbing into bed with me and I came to life.

"What the fuck do you think you're doing?" I hissed, pushing on his back. Only to snatch my hands away as they came into contact with his bare skin.

"I'm getting into bed and going to sleep, Rachel. Isn't it fucking obvious?"

"Well, you're not sleeping here," I huffed, bracing myself to prepare for the feel of his muscles under my hands as I pushed at him again. "You have your own bed."

"My own bed that stinks of smoke. I'm not sleeping there. If you don't want to share a bed with me, you can go and sleep in it. You're the one who caused this issue."

"Go and sleep on the sofa!"

"Be for real right now," he chuckled softly, and pulled the covers up over his lower half, completely oblivious to my shoves.

"This is ridiculous," I said, flopping down on my side and shoving him so more. I pulled away sharply, almost falling off the bed as I made contact with his bare hip.

He laughed, "I'm naked, Rachel. By all means, keep pawing at me. I won't say no."

"Why do you have no clothes on?"

"I'm a 34-year-old man. Did you expect me to have baby shark pyjamas?"

"There are more options between nude and baby fucking shark!"

"I'm too old to learn them. Good night, Rachel." He said and rolled over, presenting me with his back.

I sighed heavily, knowing I wasn't winning this argument. My back was too sore for me to sleep on the hard sofa, and I didn't want to wake up with a hangover in the morning only to see Big Mama glaring at me. I had no choice but to put up and shut up.

I laid down, careful to lower my body down on the bed, inch by painful inch, so I didn't so much as brush against his leg hair, never mind make contact with any of his skin. I rolled over onto my side, so we were back-to-back, and tucked my arm under my pillow, willing myself to fall asleep as fast as possible.

I could feel the heat radiating off his body, burning straight through my nightdress. I could hear his steady breathing, in complete contrast to my own wild breathing that wouldn't seem to calm down. There was no way he couldn't hear the gulping breaths I was drawing in.

For fuck's sake! I hissed to myself as my legs began twitching – I always got restless legs when I was stressed. *It's all in your fucking head! You're fine. Your legs are fine!*

But they weren't fine. It felt like I had a million centipedes crawling through the veins of my legs. I wanted to move them, but I didn't want to keep drawing attention to myself.

The more I tried to stay still, the more my legs jerked. My entire body stiffened, and still my legs burned with the need to move.

I tried rubbing one foot over my other leg, but all that did was raise my ass up, bringing it closer to Dante. I soon put an end to that and put my leg back down.

I rolled my eyes and stifled a groan, feeling as though my legs were being stabbed by a thousand needles.

This was fucking torture!

"I've had women twitch less during their tenth orgasm than this. Stay fucking still!" Dante hissed at me.

"Go to your own bed if you don't like it!" I snapped at him in a whisper. He rolled over, tucking himself close to my back, and stroked his hand down my leg. I stiffened and tried to pull away, but he wrapped his arm around me and pulled me back into his chest, holding me steady.

"Shh. Stay still. I can help." He whispered against my cheek and went back to stroking my leg. Only this time, he dug his fingers into my skin, rotating his fingertips as he did so.

"I can do it myself."

"And I'd like to get some sleep sometime tonight. Just accept the massage, and we'll both be much happier."

I said nothing and let him get to work. He expertly massaged my legs, his fingers dancing over my skin until I forgot all about my restless legs, and thought of nothing but Dante's hands on me, of his fingers delicately stroking me. I had to bite down on my lip to stop myself from groaning out loud when I thought of how if his hands just slid further up, he'd be able to stroke me where I was craving him, where I had grown wetter and hotter for him just from a mere touch of his hand. I thought of how he could massage the inside of my legs, opening them wide for his entry. How this time, I wouldn't run. I'd take what he had to offer and –

"Better?" Dante asked suddenly, making me jump out of my skin as though he could read my thoughts.

"Y-yes," I stuttered. "Thank you."

"Good," he whispered back and pulled away from me. He didn't roll over, but no part of his body was touching me anymore, and I hated the way that made me feel. In spite of our height difference, he fit against me perfectly, my body moulding into his like a matching jigsaw piece. "Goodnight, Rachel."

"G-goodnight, Dante."

I swear I heard the bastard chuckle. He knew what he was fucking doing!

Every breath he took fanned against the back of my neck. Every beat of his heart seemed to resonate with my own. I was so aware of him; I knew what his body was doing more than my own. My skin tingled, craving his touch. I burned for him. But pride wouldn't let me do anything more. I bit down on my lip once more and almost banged my fist in frustration. How was he so unbothered by all of this? Why wasn't he this affected by me as I was him?

He coughed gently, and I was so tightly wound up, I jumped, suppressing a yelp of fright just in time. I shuffled further away from him, clinging to the edge of the mattress to stop myself from falling off, and forced my eyes shut.

Count fucking sheep, Rachel. Count sheep.

I tried to remember some breathing techniques my old high school councillor had taught me, breathing in deep, holding it for five seconds before releasing it slowly.

A few rounds of this had me calmed down enough to not be so tightly tensed up it was bordering on painful, but then Dante shifted in his sleep, and I was a tight coil once more.

When will this night fucking end?

I forced myself to stretch my legs, instead of being curled into a ball, and once again, made contact with Dante's skin. The fucking behemoth was everywhere, taking up the entire space!

Dante sighed, and I felt him sitting up. "You," he said, grabbing hold of me, wrapping his arm around my stomach, and rolled me over onto my back. "Are one stubborn little bitch." I saw his grin in the darkness as he shuffled our bodies until I was underneath him. "I've been hard as a fucking rock for the past half hour. Ever since I saw the mere silhouette of your body in the darkness, I've been fucking hard. I can't spend the night like this, Rachel. I need to fuck you. I *want* to fuck you. I need to feel you underneath me. I need to hear you moaning my name. I need all of you so fucking badly, its driving me half mad." He was propped up on one arm, looking down at me as his other arm stroked over my stomach.

I looked at him, my breath catching in my throat. "If you want me to go, Rachel, I'll go." He lowered himself down, burying his face in my neck, delivering small kisses all the way up to my ear and back down again. "But if you want me to stay, please, for the love of God, touch me. I'm burning for you. I need you. I can't stop fucking thinking of you. Every time I'm awake, you're on my mind. Every time I sleep, you're haunting my dreams. I spend all my time thinking about you, and what you're doing, wishing you were with me instead. I'm obsessed with you, addicted to you, and I never want to be cured."

"Dante," I breathed, reaching up and grabbing his face, lowering it down to mine. I hesitated at the last second, my lips hovering beneath his, but he closed the gap, capturing my lips with his own.

Just as I relaxed underneath him, the door flew open, and Dante's dad stood there.

"Church," he snapped, slamming the door behind him.

"Fuck," Dante hissed, climbing off me without hesitation.

"Where are you going?"

"I have to go to church," he said, pulling his trousers back on.

"Right now?"

"That's the way it works," he said shortly, searching for his shirt.

"You've got to be fucking kidding me."

"I'm a brother first and foremost, Rachel. I don't get a choice in this."

"So your dad says jump, and you say how high?"

"It's not like that," he sighed. "It's just the way it is. The club always comes first. We pledged our loyalty. It's not something you can pick and choose to participate in."

"Fine!" I snapped. "I fail to see what could possibly be so important at this time of night! But if you'd rather be there than here, then go!"

"I'm not going to argue with you. I don't want to argue with you. It's not as simple as you're making it out to be. Don't you think if I had a choice, I'd be back in bed with you, finishing what we started? I have to do this."

"If you leave, don't bother coming back!" I heard myself saying. I was both hurt and humiliated, and I couldn't believe after what he had just said to me, he could drop me so easily at just one little word from his dad.

"If that's how you want it to be. I'll spend the night at the main house. Night, Rachel."

He opened the door and shut it softly behind him, refusing to be drawn in to any disagreement with me.

I grabbed my pillow and screamed my frustration into it.

Chapter 29

Rachel

It was dark when I woke up, and I immediately hated myself.

I brought my hands to my eyes, rubbing them awake, and then squinted as my head exploded into a million stars.

My mouth felt like sandpaper, my throat felt like I'd been chewing glass, and my stomach was threatening to bring up every piece of food I had ever eaten in my life.

But none of that even began to compare to the band of Irish dancers currently performing a jig in my head. It erupted with pain, and I hissed, drawing the covers up over my chin.

What the fuck happened?

I tried to sift through my memories, but everything was a blank.

One step at a time, Rachel.

What had I done?

I took Bee to the park.

I met Shark.

Dante came.

But then what?

We were drinking. I didn't need to remember that. The hangover from hell was evidence enough.

Had we argued?

I had a vague memory of Dante grabbing me again, but every time I tried to focus on it, it slipped out of reach.

What had we been arguing about this time?

I tried to swallow and scowled as my mouth protested. It was so dry, and my teeth felt fluffy. I know teeth can't be fluffy, but that's what they felt like.

A vision of Dante hovering over me flashed behind my eyes, and it all came flooding back – the empty words he had used to get me beneath him, the way he had forgotten me so easily for his pathetic club, the way I had almost begged him not to go. I had really shown my hand this time. So much for the perfect blank expression.

I threw the covers off the bed and pushed my legs off, letting them dangle off the edge for a moment before I pulled my body up.

The room immediately swayed, and I leant forward, leaning against the table as I waited for the moment to pass.

It didn't pass.

The movement caused all the alcohol in my stomach to swish about. I clamped a hand to my mouth and ran, knowing I didn't have long before I emptied the contents of my stomach.

I made it to the bathroom, forgetting I had left the light on this morning.

My hand flew up to my eyes as the light blinded me, knocking me off balance.

I crashed against the wall; my movements unsteady.

"You think for someone that was raised on alcohol; you'd know how to handle it better."

It all came flooding back in a dizzy wave. Not just being in bed with him, but the whole evening.

Why had I said those things to him? I knew I had pushed him, and whilst I can't take the full blame and be responsible for the words and actions of anyone else, I was aware enough to know I had provoked him to the point of no return.

I cringed as it all played out in my mind.. Drinking. Spilling my past. Lashing out because I was hurt. Trying to make Dante hurt. Him grabbing me. The bar watching.

The room spun faster as every event of the past few days played in my mind, taking over every sense I had. Words, the smell of smoke, the blood, being tied up… it made me feel sicker than I already was.

And that's when my body gave up.

My legs buckled underneath me, my head spun, and my stomach pressed eject.

I landed on my back, smacking my already pounding head off the tiled bathroom floor, at the same time vomit rushed from my throat.

The back of my head felt wet, and I saw the crimson from the corner of my eye, staining the white flooring.

I tried to push myself up as the vomit crept back down my throat at the same time as more came up.

I knew at that moment, I was fucked.

My body was done. My head was too sore to move it to the side. My eyes were already growing heavy, my lungs burning as my throat blocked.

I closed my eyes and the last thing I saw was my chest as it heaved, convulsing on the floor, choking on my own vomit.

What a fucking way to go out, Rachel.

Chapter 30

Rachel

I was underwater.

The waves dragged me further under, enveloping me in their welcome embrace as they took me far, far away.

Far away from the hurt.

From the anxiety.

From my own fucked up mind.

The silence followed, offering me peace and comfort.

Nothing was scary there.

But the waves couldn't take me. Not completely. Not whilst I was stuck here.

Someone was calling my name, breaking through the waves, stopping me from leaving. I wanted to leave. I wanted the peace they offered. The blackness of nothing. I wanted nothing. I wanted quiet.

There was screaming.

A little girls scream.

Whose scream was that? Was that mine?

Definitely not mine. My throat was constricted. Something was there, lodged deep. I couldn't breathe past it. The waves were slipping further away from me as panic set in. Why couldn't I breathe?

My eyes were heavy. I tried with all my might, but they wouldn't open.

My panic grew to almost a frenzy. My body was no longer my own. It didn't respond to any of my commands.

Everything around me was muffled and muted. I was surrounded by people, and yet I felt alone. I couldn't talk to any of them.

"Is she breathing?"

"Oh, God. Rachel! Hold on."

There was nothing to hold on to but the darkness. And the darkness was calling my name.

I liked the darkness. There was no pain there.

I sank into it, willing it to take me.

I was done.

I was done fighting. I was done struggling every day of my life.

I was happy to befriend the darkness and live in the empty nothing it offered.

I surrendered, the roaring scream of a heartbroken man following me.

The waves kept bringing me in, then forcing me back out.

They couldn't claim me. Someone was fighting for me, even when I was too weak to fight for myself.

But no one had ever fought for me.

If someone wanted me to stay, it wasn't for my benefit. The waves were uncaring, retreating away from me and taking sanctuary with it.

I slowly became aware of no longer being in the darkness. Of no longer having nothing.

The lights.

There were so many lights.

I didn't open my eyes, and still I saw them.

Blue flashing lights.

White, bright lights.

They pierced through the darkness, dragging me from its welcome embrace.

"She's lost... blood."

"Rachel, can you hear me?"

"Her heart rate is dropping!"

The darkness changed its mind, and it was stronger than the lights. Blackness crept back in, creeping from the corners until it enveloped my vision.

"Rachel, hold on!"

There was no holding on.

There was nothing left to hold on to.

In truth, there was never anything for me in the first place.

The wave pulled me away, taking me back to the darkness.

Back where I belonged.

I didn't fight.

There was no longer any point.

The blackness had its icy fingers wrapped around me, and it dragged me along, taking me to its lair.

There was no pain here. No noise.

It was just silence.

I liked the silence.

"... she's stable for now... touch and go... recovery... we're doing everything we can... up to her..."

Why were there noises?

They were piercing the darkness, punching holes in the peace it gave me.

My eyes fluttered open and immediately clamped shut again.

So much white. So much harsh lighting.

I called to the darkness, but it was ebbing away, further and further, this time without me.

It had let me go.

It didn't want to compete with the outside forces that willed me away from it. Darkness didn't need complication. I either came, or I didn't. And someone else was making the choice for me, regardless of what I wanted.

I wanted its warmth. It's emptiness. The ability to take away all my pain, to make me stop thinking.

To make it all just stop.

I wanted the nothingness.

As the blackness faded, the world welcomed me back. And it was not a warm welcome.

The world fucking hated me.

My head screamed out as the noises exploded. The beeping of machines, the voices, the patter of footsteps.

My eyelids fluttered as shadows fell over them, and a man I didn't know looked down at me, writing something on his clipboard.

Where the fuck was I?

I closed my eyes again and tried to remember where I was.

My body ached, and for a heart stopping moment, I forgot the past few years and was reminded of Alex. I hadn't hurt this bad since I was with him.

My eyes fluttered again as my heart started racing. I saw the man with the clipboard shoot a worried frown as the beeping intensified.

I couldn't breathe.

I couldn't move.

I was stuck here, and Alex would be coming.

He would never let me go.

The beeping was incessant, the noise coming faster, entering a competition with my heart as it thudded to a dangerous rhythm.

A searing heat on my arm had my eyes pinging open.

I looked around frantically, noticing the needle in my arm, the drip attached to it. I reached up and winced as I touched the bandages on my head.

What had he done to me this time?

He would make me pay for drawing attention to myself!

I scanned the room, looking for a friendly face. Looking for anyone that could tell me I was going to be okay.

The heat on my arm intensified and my gaze rushed to it, seeing a hand rubbing my skin. My eyes followed up the arm to the face.

And there he was.

This fucking giant of a man that used his huge hands for comfort and not hurt. He wasn't Alex. He was offering me kindness, offering me peace. I scanned his tattoos and noticed how dark they were.

He was my darkness. It hadn't left me after-all. He had joined me in the real world, letting me know I wasn't alone.

He was looking at me with such tenderness; the worry creasing his forehead, his eyes shining with concern.

"Rachel... don't worry... you're okay. I'm here."

He brushed the hair off my face, and my eyes closed.

My darkness was the first man to hold me in a long time without hurting me.

Even my own dad had grabbed me and shook me, screaming at me that I was driving him into an early grave.

"Don't…" I tried to whisper, immediately missing the warmth of his hand as he snatched it away.

I opened my eyes again.

I didn't know who he was. I was lost in time, stuck with the man who groomed me. But this stranger was offering kindness. There was a hurt in his eyes.

Had I caused that?

"Maybe you should leave," the man in the white coat said.

The man next to me shot him a fierce look. "I'll stay by my girlfriend's side until she tells me to leave."

Girlfriend?

My heart started racing once more. Why was he calling me that?

What was I missing?

Why couldn't I piece any of this together?

"Sir, as we have already explained to you, this is an ongoing investigation. You shouldn't even be here. Your presence is clearly causing her distress."

"I already explained to you, I did not fucking do this. She's distressed because you're confusing her!"

"And if that's true, the investigation will prove that. We have to put the interest of the patient first, even if it means upsetting you. So in the meantime—"

The man stood up. "In the meantime, what?" He growled, making me recoil in pain as his voice vibrated around my already throbbing head.

"As I already said, Rachel is under distress. Your presence here—"

The man took a step towards him, and I willed myself to stop it.

My hand shot out and grabbed his arm.

He looked down at me in shock.

"No," I whispered. "Please don't leave me. Don't let him come for me."

"For whom to come for you, Rachel?" The man in the white coat asked kindly, shooting a cruel look at the man at my side.

He sat back down and grabbed my hand, hugging it between his own, and planted a kiss on my knuckles.

"Don't let Alex come. Don't let him take me. Stay with me, my darkness."

And then the blackness came back for me. But this time, it was not welcoming. It was not my darkness. My darkness was out there. This one was an imposter, and it wanted to imprison me.

It snatched me up and stole me away, dragging me under. I didn't have time to say any more. Like an angry predator, its mouth swallowed me whole and ate me up, making me fall, fall, fall...

And this time, I wasn't so sure it would let me go.

Dante

"How is she?" Macbeth asked, looking up at me for a brief moment before he returned to bouncing the tennis ball off the wall.

"I don't know," I sighed, flopping down next to him. The tennis ball bounced back towards us, and I grabbed it, slamming it on the bench. "This," I muttered through clenched teeth. "Is getting on my last fucking nerve."

Macbeth huffed, budging up slightly, and muttered something about me sitting on his knee. I didn't have it in me to start an argument with him.

"Do they still think you're to blame?" My mother asked, handing me a disgusting cup of slop. "It's coffee," she said, pushing the polystyrene cup towards my mouth.

I took it anyway, despite the vile way it smelled. I needed it more for the warmth it gave my hands than anything else.

I'd been frozen to the bone since I saw her.

I couldn't even think about it.

She was on the floor, looking as pale as death. Her blonde hair was matted as the blood seeped through it and coloured the floor around her. Her lips had been turning blue. Her skin was taking on an ashen tone, and the most horrendous gargling noise was leaving her lips, a sound that would haunt me until my dying days.

I shook my head, wanting to rid myself of that picture forever, but I knew it was burned into my soul. I would never forget. It had shaken me to my core.

"Fucking wankers," my dad hissed. "Took one look at us and assumed we beat the poor girl."

"Sir, we've already asked you to keep the noise down. Next time, we'll have to ask you to leave," a nurse warned from the reception desk at the end of the waiting area.

"And I've already told you cunts, I'll leave when my daughter-in-law is ready to come home and not a minute earlier." He growled at her.

"Sir, we will not tolerate such foul language. Please don't make me call security."

My dad went to march towards her. "Leave it!" I snapped.

He growled low in his throat, but he listened. He knew as well as I did that sometimes we had to pick our battles. Let them think the worst of us. Most people did anyway. And usually, we had no problem proving them right. But now was not the time, and it certainly was not the place.

We needed to be here when Rachel woke up.

Properly woke up. Not stuck in whatever reality she was currently in.

This was all my fault. I made her relive her time with her ex, and now she was trapped in the past.

My heart clenched as I saw her face as she pleaded with me not to let Alex come near her. She had looked on the verge of fainting through panic, her eyes wide and wild.

She had called me "her darkness" and though I didn't have a fucking clue what it meant, she said it with such longing and possessiveness, I had to hope some part of her recognised me, that some part of her wanted me.

My dad shot the receptionist a filthy look and resumed his position of leaning against the wall, his arms folded, and his legs locked at the ankle. He looked at me with concern as I held my head in my hands, wracked with guilt as the same scene played over and over in my mind.

"They don't know what to think," I said to my mum after a long silence. "Until Rachel wakes up—"

"I thought she was awake?" Macbeth frowned.

"She was. Kind of. They don't know if she was half awake and confused, or if she was fully awake and had memory loss.

She doesn't know where she is. She doesn't know what year it is. She doesn't know who *I* am. She's trapped in her mind somewhere. Until she wakes up properly, we won't know for sure."

"What happened to her, Dante? What happened in her past that's trapping her?" My mother asked, worry creasing her brow.

"What makes you say anything happened?" I snapped. I knew it was uncalled for, but I couldn't seem to get my emotions under control, and I was taking it out on all the wrong people.

I knew who I should be taking it out on, and I vowed to get revenge for her. Rachel belonged to me. Her hurt was my hurt. Her pain was my pain. I would heal what time had not. I would destroy all those who dared so much as look at her in a way she didn't like. I would track her rapists down and make them bathe in acid. They would all pay. She would get her vengeance.

"People don't start screaming about not letting them take her if they weren't terrified of the people doing the taking," my mother said, her lips twisting.

I sighed heavily. "It's not my story to tell, and truthfully, I don't fully know. But I'm going to fucking fix it." I got to my feet and shot my dad a look.

"Dante, are you sure this is a good idea?" My mother frowned.

"I've never been more sure of anything. Rachel is terrified of these people. There's one surefire way to make her believe that she's safe."

"What if she wakes up?"

"Comfort her then, for fuck's sake. I have to do this."

"We're right behind you." My dad reassured me, pushing himself off the wall. "Aren't we, Macbeth?"

"Not really," he shrugged. "What?" He muttered when our dad shot him an angry look. "I don't even know the lass. She's not my old lady. Let Dante go bash some heads together. He's more than capable."

"Mac," my dad warned.

"Leave him," I said in disgust. "He's fucking useless, anyway. Round up the rest of the lads. We've got some people to take care of." I stormed away, but not before I hissed down

Macbeth's ear. "Just so you know, when I'm president, you're fucking gone. Even if I have to kill you myself."

Chapter 31

Dante

"What did you find?" I all but shouted into my helmet as I raced home, ready to meet up with everyone else.

"Not much." I could hear Vienna's disappointment through the phone. "Hacksaw is doing his best, but there's not much to go off. Did she tell you anything else?"

"That's all I know, man," I sighed, revving the bike as I picked up more speed.

"Do you know her mam and dad's names?"

"I don't know a fucking thing," I all but roared, taking the corner at dangerous speed. "I wouldn't even know where to find her fucking mother these days, either."

"Well, that's sort of what happens when you burn someone's house down. They move elsewhere. And even if you were to find her, I doubt she'd talk to you."

"Yes, thank you for that, Vienna."

"Happy to help," he said pleasantly as I overtook a car and raced through a red light. I was being fucking reckless, which I never was. But we had reached nothing but a dead end so far in our investigation, and it was driving me mad.

I wanted to find these fuckers and make them pay.

Mainly for what they had done to Rachel, but also for every other woman they had hurt over the years.

I wasn't perfect by any means, but there are some lines you just don't cross, and grooming little girls was one of those lines. Especially when you abused those girls to the extent those bastards did.

"Look, dude, I'm nearly at the club. I'll see you in a moment." I told Vienna, shutting off the Bluetooth call before he had a chance to reply.

I'd find the cunts even if it took me the rest of my goddamn life to do it. Rachel deserved closure on that chapter of her life. She might have thought she was over it, but all she had done was suppress those memories, and was living as a shadow of her former self. I had seen glimpses of the real Rachel before the veil fell back over and she continued her act of being a robot, and I'd just about do anything to keep the Rachel I was obsessed with around permanently.

I pulled up to the clubhouse, and all but jumped off the bike, slamming open the door. I did let out a little laugh as I saw the massive hulk of a man that was Hacksaw with his teeny, tiny, reading glasses on the end of his nose.

"What the fuck are those?" I said, snatching them off his face. "You steal these from one of Bee's barbies?"

"Fuck off, Dante," he huffed, ripping them out of my grasp.

Vienna slapped him on his back and held out his hand. "Fifty bucks," he said, rubbing his hand under Hacksaw's nose. "Come on. Cough it up, spectacles."

"For what?" I asked, looking back and forth between the two of them.

"He bet me fifty you would comment on the glasses within a minute. I stupidly thought better of you, seen as though I'm doing you a favour and all. But I guess assholes will be assholes." He dug into his pocket and slapped the notes into Vienna's waiting hand.

"Ahh, smell that? It smells like victory." Vienna beamed, stroking the notes down Hacksaw's cheeks. "No, don't let him take us," he said in a singsong, high-pitched voice. "We loved living in your back pocket, never getting spent. Hush, hush," he said, his voice returning to normal. "You will live a good life with me."

"You're a weird man," Hacksaw frowned.

"A weird man that's fifty bucks richer. Now scoot on over, let's have a look," Vienna said, kicking the seat Hacksaw was sitting on, sending the wheels flying across the floor.

I snapped to attention, looking at the laptop Hacksaw had set up. "We've searched for an Alex on the database, but nothing is coming up." Hacksaw said as he scooted the chair back over to us.

The database was the police database. We had no business being in there, but we had a few contacts at the station, and they allowed us access so we could keep our members safe. If a crime was committed, they would face our punishment based on our club rules. They were not facing a jury that would judge them harshly, just because of the way they looked. We had our own bylaws and expected members to stick to them. The issue was, what was acceptable to us wasn't always acceptable by British law.

"What about her parents?" I asked, frowning as I scanned the list, going back the last two decades.

They were right, there wasn't an Alex to be found.

"Without her last name, it's proving difficult to even find out what her parents are called. Are you sure she never told you?"

"I never asked," I admitted with a huffed breath. "Her dad is in prison. We'll have to look up court cases from the past decade and go from there. We can cross reference names to the local news pages, can't we?" I asked, directing my question at Hacksaw. He was a whizz at computers, hence the 'Hack' in his name. The saw came from the fact that he was a fucking brute with the weapon. I had once seen him saw a man's fingers off for brushing up too close to him at the urinals.

"We can, but it'll be time consuming."

"He went to prison for murder. Stabbed a bloke to death. By all accounts, it was brutal. He was nearly beheaded and stabbed a fair few times. Does that help?"

Vienna shot me a look, but I gave him one of my own, warning him to stay quiet, and he gave me a small nod of his head.

Rachel's mum had told him that Rachel had murdered a man in cold blood, and it didn't take a genius to put two and two together and realise what had happened. His eyebrows raised slightly as he chuckled and gave a nod of approval. He was a weird bastard, and Rachel had just climbed up in his estimation.

"Roughly how long ago?" Hacksaw asked, his fingers flying over the keyboard.

"About ten years ago. Rachel is twenty-seven, and she said it happened just before her eighteenth. I don't know when the court date would have been, though."

"Doesn't matter. Something like that would have made the papers somewhere. If not, it should be on record the day he was admitted to prison. Was he kept on remand until the court date?"

"I haven't a fucking clue. I would have assumed so."

"Give me a minute," Hacksaw murmured, more to himself than to us.

"How is she doing?" Vienna asked, drowning out the clacking of the keyboard.

"Fucked if I know. She didn't even know who I was."

"She's had a bang to the head, mate. A nasty one at that. Are you surprised?"

"I don't know what I am. She called me darkness, so whoever I am to her right now in her confused state, it can't be fucking good with a name like that, can it?"

"Maybe she likes the dark."

"Shut up, Ven," I said, rolling my eyes at him. "There's a lot of things Rachel likes – albeit I don't know any of them, but I do know I'm not one of them."

"None of us like you either, pal, but we're still here. Give her time."

I didn't bother dignifying that with an answer.

"It might turn out to be a good thing," Vienna said after a pause.

"How do you figure?"

"You two didn't exactly get off to the best starts. Maybe if she forgets everything, you can start fresh."

"Aye, right. Because that's a brilliant way to begin a long-lasting relationship."

"Better than the beginning of the one you currently have?" Vienna shot right back; his eyebrow raised.

"It is what it is. There's no point wishing things were different now. And I don't wish anything was different. I did what I wanted, and I have no regrets about it." My tone was harsher than I meant it to be, but Vienna didn't react.

"Got it!" Hacksaw said, a triumphant note in his voice. "Rebecca and Chris Brooks. Daughter Rachel Brooks. Chris was jailed for life for the murder of local club owner Alex Saint."

"Ironic name," I muttered.

"And here's our girl. Looking mighty different, but I'd recognise those eyes a mile away." He clicked on the picture to enlarge it, and my heart jumped at a picture of Rachel as a teenager.

Her hair was jet black, with awkward bangs framing her face. Her eye makeup was heavy, her lips overdrawn and dark.

Her skin looked pale as paper in comparison to all the dark makeup, and you could see all the bones and veins in her neck and shoulders she was that thin. She stood awkwardly next to her mother and father, one of her hands clasping the other at the elbow. She looked vulnerable and afraid, and once again, my temper roared to life at the fact that these idiotic parents of hers couldn't see the signs that she was in trouble.

One look at her here and you could see she was haunted.

"It's her, right?" Hacksaw said proudly.

"Oh yeah," Vienna said, squinting at the picture. "Her mother hasn't changed a bit."

"Damn," Hacksaw whistled. "She's a fine looking broad for her age. She looking for a toy-boy whilst the old man is banged up?"

"I think Dante burning her house to the ground might have fucked that idea up for you, Hacksaw."

"For tits like hers, I'd be willing to throw him to the wolves," he grinned, nudging me with his elbow playfully.

"Right, people, let's stop thinking with our dicks and get a plan together," I said, slamming the laptop shut, ending their fun. "We have a name. Alex Saint. You ring every low life dirt ball you can think of. He owned a club a decade ago, and from what I gathered, he had a lot of the punk/gothic scene as regulars. Even the tiniest thread is a lead. By the end of the night, I want the name of his closest friends, his ex's, his parents… hell, if he has a dead hamster, I want to know the name and location of its burial. Do I make it clear?"

"Yes, boss," Hacksaw said, bringing out his phone immediately.

For as much as these guys fucked around, they had my back. They knew when it was time to be serious and right now, I was as serious as a heart attack. "Pass the message on to every club member here. I want everyone on this as a priority. If anyone can get me the address of the club in the next hour, they can have free drinks for the rest of the year."

Both men murmured their agreement and went off, their phones already at their ear. As the door closed behind them, I pulled up the laptop lid and looked at the picture of Rachel again.

I couldn't save her as a teenager, but I'd make damn sure that she spent the rest of her adult life never having to fear anyone again.

Anyone except me, that is.

Chapter 32

Rachel

The darkness calmed down.

This time, when it let me go, it was more like a gentle washing up at shore, rather than launching me from its arms.

There was no aggression. It was almost like the darkness caressed my body as it left me, letting me know that it was okay. It would be back for me when it was my time. But now was not my time, and it was okay letting me go.

I awoke silently, my eyes fluttering as I adjusted to the bright lights.

"Welcome to the land of the living," a cheery woman greeted me as she took down notes. "Don't mind me. I'm just here doing your hourly observations. You gave us all quite the scare," she smiled, her voice light and airy.

"I did?" I croaked.

"Here, honey," she brought a cup of water to my lips and pressed the button on the bed to raise me up slightly. She looked at the machine and gave a pleased nod as my blood pressure remained normal. "Can't sit you up any further than this. You had a nasty knock on the head. We'll take it slow and steady and make sure you don't go fainting on us again!"

"Again?"

"You don't remember?" She asked, her voice still as pleasant as ever. "Not to worry," she scribbled away on her notepad. "It's normal not to remember the first few times you wake after a concussion. I'm Doctor Ezra. No relation to George," the joke rolled off her tongue, her most rehearsed line. "Can you tell me your full name, sweetie?"

"Rachel Brooks," I said automatically.

"Wonderful. And how old are you, Rachel?"

"Twenty-seven."

"Do you know what year it is?"

"2024."

"Fantastic," she carried on scribbling down her notes, and then sat on the end of my bed. She brought a light out of her breast pocket and shone it in my eyes, noting down whatever reaction she saw.

"Okay, this is all brilliant so far, Rachel. Can you remember who brought you here?"

"I don't remember. But I assume it was Dante."

"Mmm," she said absentmindedly. "And what is your relationship with Dante?"

"Boyfriend," I said without thinking.

Why the fuck are you calling him your boyfriend?

I knew why.

Because those in a position of authority tended to believe the worst of people like Dante. And my instinct told me to protect him. I didn't need the likes of the police getting involved – which they would if they had any sort of hint that he was to blame.

"Okay," the doctor nodded. "And do you remember what happened to you, Rachel?"

"Ish. I had been drinking. It had been a long few days, and I probably hadn't eaten as much as I should have. I went to bed, and I awoke with the fiercest hangover."

"Uh-huh," she nodded, her pen flying over the paper.

I knew what she was doing.

Verbal fucking nods.

It was what everyone did when they were pretending to be interested.

My mother was the master of verbal nodding. I could have told her the whole sordid events of what happened with Alex, and she'd still nod away, a pleasant smile on her face.

"I went to the bathroom to be sick, I got faint, and I passed out."

"Anything else?"

"Nope."

"Who were you drinking with?"

"Does it matter?"

"No need to get defensive, Rachel," she looked up through her lashes. "I'm just trying to get the full story."

"That is the full story. It doesn't matter who I was drinking with, because they were not there when the accident happened."

"Any particular reason you were drinking?"

"I'm an adult. Do I have to have a reason to be drinking?"

"No, but getting so drunk you can barely stand... you can see our cause for concern, can't you?"

"I was in a pub. Like I said, I hadn't been eating as much as I should have, and I had one too many."

"Okay... and this pub you were in. Would this be the same one your boyfriend owns?"

"That's right. It's not a crime to drink in a pub, is it?"

"Certainly not," she said, the happy smile back in place. "Was Dante drinking?"

"He had one or two."

"And where did Dante go when you went to bed?"

"He was with me," I said, my cheeks colouring as I remembered. "He left early hours in the morning, and I have no idea after that. I was still in bed. I can't see through walls."

She looked at me and simply smiled again.

"Alright, everything looks okay here. How are you feeling?" She changed topic to my physical health, knowing she wasn't getting any more details from me.

"My head hurts."

"I bet it does. You're due some painkillers soon; the nurse will bring them around for you. Are you hungry? I can buzz for the auxiliary to bring you some toast?"

"Starving," I admitted.

"Tea, coffee?"

"A tea would be great."

"Wonderful. I'll have them bring it to you. Okay," she said, her pen finally stopping. "I think I'm done here. I'll be back to see you in the morning, Rachel. If there's anything you need, don't hesitate to buzz. Visiting hours start in an hour. I'm sure your boyfriend will be in to see you. He hasn't left the hospital since you were brought in."

"How long have I been out?"

"A little over two days. He slept at your side the first night, and then stayed by your side as long as we would allow yesterday. We asked him to leave last night, but he was right back here this morning, bright and early!"

"Was he here when I woke?"

"I believe so," she murmured, already moving on from me and mentally preparing for the next patient.

"Did I talk to him?"

"You'd have to ask him. Okay, so if there's nothing else you need, I'm going to leave you at peace."

"There's nothing."

"Great. Take it easy, Rachel, and I'll see you in the morning. All going well, we should be able to let you go in a day or two." And then she left the room, leaving me with nothing but my thoughts.

I had no recollection of waking up previous to now. I vaguely remembered being on the brink of consciousness and hearing the ambulance and the flashing lights as we raced to the hospital, but other than that, I was drawing a complete blank.

A knock at the door had me jumping as a nurse brought me in some tea and toast and left me with the menu for the evening meal. She didn't hang around, and for that I was grateful. Sleep was calling my name again. For once, I welcomed the thought of sleep. I wanted this memory fog to pass as soon as possible, and the more sleep I got, the quicker that would happen as far as I was concerned.

I quickly bit down on some toast, my throat protesting at the rough texture, and flopped back on the pillows, sifting through my memories as I tried to piece together what I had missed when I had been out.

I thought I could remember Dante tenderly kissing my hands and asking me not to leave him, but the memory seemed so out of place and so wildly out of character that I dismissed it as false. Dante wouldn't show such an open display of emotion, and he certainly wouldn't do it in front of other people.

I'd have to take the doctor's advice and ask him when he turned up.

I quickly scribbled down my choice for the evening meal whilst I remembered and then allowed my eyes to close, drifting off into a restless sleep.

A soft knock at the door had my eyes flying open, bringing a welcome end to the nightmares that had plagued me.

Stolen

Alex was on my mind, and in my dreams. He kept shifting into Dante as he delivered his punishments. One minute Alex was shouting at me, the next Dante was hitting me. It was Dante who ordered his friends to rape me. It was Dante who punched me so hard blood flew out of my mouth.

Dante had hurt me, and he wasn't above hitting a woman, but he was miles away from the monster that Alex had been. But that didn't excuse the pain he had put me through and the trauma he had already inflicted. It's no wonder my subconscious was mixing the two together. There were different ways to hurt a person, and Dante was to blame for a lot of my current pain.

"Dinner," the nurse smiled, wheeling in a trolley. My stomach grumbled, and I thanked her, realising how starving I really was.

"Your tea has gone cold, my love. Would you like another?"

"Yes, please," I accepted with a grateful nod. "Do you know when visiting hours are?" I asked her as she set up my plate, taking the knife and fork out of the napkin they were wrapped in.

"Been and gone for today."

"Already? I slept through it all?" I lifted my arm slightly as she slid the table over my lap, the smell of the food invading my nose.

"Sure did. You must have needed it."

"Did... did anyone come?"

"I believe your boyfriend's mother was here. She didn't come in when we said you were sleeping, though. She left you those flowers."

I followed her pointed finger to the roses in the corner and thanked her.

I fucking hated roses.

"Enjoy," the nurse said as she retreated out of my room.

I picked up my fork and poked at my food, my appetite leaving.

He hadn't fucking come!

I don't know why I was surprised. He had made it clear that he couldn't give a flying fuck about me.

So why did it hurt so much?

Maybe I was clinging to the memory of him tenderly kissing me. If there was any doubt that I had completely made up that little interaction, it was quickly squashed.

Dante couldn't even be bothered to take the time out of his day to come visit me. He certainly wasn't going to be sitting at my bedside, begging me not to leave him.

He was probably more concerned about what I would say when I woke up. Especially after the crack I had made about informing social services if he ever threatened me again. He probably put on a good show of being the concerned boyfriend, pretending he gave a shit, just for the doctor's benefit. Since I had woken, and the police hadn't carted him away and put Bee in a home, he knew I wasn't pinning this on him, so the pretence was done.

As if I'd ever be low enough to blame him for something he hadn't done. He had enough crimes behind him, crimes he had actually committed. He didn't need my help adding to his rap sheet.

I stabbed into the chicken curry and shoved a forkful into my mouth, turning my lips at the bland taste.

Food is food, Rachel. Be grateful. There was a time you didn't get any without earning it.

That much was true. Food was Alex's greatest weapon, and Dante certainly hadn't been the most hospitable either.

Even thinking his name had my heart leaping, but I steeled myself, refusing to give in to the feeling.

I had made up any affection he had towards me, and now I had to kill my own growing affection towards him. I wasn't going to let a fake memory manipulate me.

I had been through something traumatic. I was feeling more vulnerable and exposed than usual. That's why I was clinging to Dante. As soon as I was over this and out of the hospital, it would be back to business as usual. I just had to keep telling myself that whatever softness I was feeling towards him right now was a lie. It was manipulated by hormones that were out of whack. It wasn't fucking real.

I was alone in this world. I'd always been alone, and I was happiest that way.

Fuck everyone else.

I'd recover, and once I was out of here, I'd make my own way in life. Fuck what Dante had to say.

He had no control over me. His threats of telling Alex's friends and family had no merit. I left the country once; I could do it again.

I just had to deal with his company long enough to get my passport back.

Chapter 33

Dante

Rachel hadn't allowed any visitors to the hospital the next day. The staff informed me she had woken up the night I was researching Alex, and I had turned up the next morning ready to apologise for not being there, but she had refused my company. I had tried to convince the staff to let me in, but they said the patient's wishes must always come first, and Rachel wished to be alone to get some sleep.

The nurses said she seemed herself, and her memory seemed fine. The doctor had visited, and they were satisfied that I was not to blame for her injuries, and so the investigation was dropped before it was reported to the police – which didn't really matter, as my guy was ready waiting to intercept any report made, anyway. But it was less of a headache this way.

My men had also pulled through on the Alex front. We had the names of his closest contacts and had proof they were close when Alex was alive. We had the name of his club, the new owner, and the new location it had moved to.

It seemed after Alex died; the club fell apart for a while. But Alex's best friend, Ben, had taken over around six months later, moving the headquarters to a bigger, more popular location and, as far as we could tell, they were all still together and still up to their old tricks.

Shark and Macbeth spent the day there yesterday, working on getting an in with them, and finding out as much information as they could.

It surprised me that Macbeth had been willing to help at all. Crash held a brief church meeting last night and gave the other members a rundown of what Rachel had gone through – we didn't go into explicit details, because that was her story to tell, but they knew enough to know that Alex and all concerned had to be dealt with. Especially as Rachel was the old lady of the VP.

Macbeth had volunteered to help after he heard the story. When I questioned it, he said that Rachel was a decent lass, and she didn't deserve what had happened to her. Even more so because she was already going to be punished enough for being my old lady for the foreseeable future.

I ignored that part. I had shaken his hand, thanked him, and we set about planning how we were going to approach this.

I had been excited to share all of this with Rachel, but I was refused in the morning, and she didn't change her mind come afternoon or evening visiting hours either.

I put it down to her memory returning, and that she was still seething over our argument. Understandable, but I had to hope this would show her I was sorry, and that I was willing to fix things. If I could just explain to her why I had left for church that night, and why I was so busy right now, she would understand. I was doing this for her.

And I hope she would also realise that by doing this, I was also taking away any threats I could make in the future about informing Alex's family. It had been a disgusting thing to hold over her, and this was putting the power in her hands. I would be as guilty as she was once all this was said and done. She would have all the power.

I would make it okay for her. She would no longer have to fear any of Alex's gang. I would protect her.

I was waiting outside the hospital, as the nurse had rung me and let me know Rachel said she was ready to leave. She wanted to leave herself, but it was against hospital policy to allow her to leave alone with a concussion. She conceded to me meeting her outside in the car park. She didn't want me coming up to the ward.

I leant against the wall, my eyes trained on the doors, waiting for her arrival.

She came out half an hour later than planned, a paper bag in her hand from the pharmacy. Her long blonde hair was pinned into a messy bun atop her head, and her clothes hung off her. I tried not to smile at the picture she presented, but it was hard not to when she was in my shirt and my mother's trousers.

Rachel was a curvaceous woman, but this outfit made her look frumpy in all the wrong places.

She saw me leaning against the wall, and her eyes burnt with an emotion I couldn't quite decipher.

"How are you feeling?" I asked, as she silently shoved the paper bag at me.

"Fine," she said pleasantly enough, and my stomach dropped. The fire in her eyes went out and the blank expression was back in place.

I knew her well enough now to know the blank expression was her trained default mode. She did it when she was hiding. And that pissed me off even more.

I had always hated that fucking blank look, and now I knew the reason behind it, I positively loathed it.

She didn't need to hide from me. I wanted her to show me her worst. I wanted her to know I would love her no matter what. Just like I wanted her to love me at my most horrific, cruel, sadistic moments.

It was the main reason I didn't regret kidnapping her. She needed to know I was not the hero. I was fucked up. I had my own moral compass. But it was best to show her this. She would love every side of me, not just the good guy most men pretended to be.

"How are we getting home?" She asked, her lips curling at the word home.

"My bike is in the carpark."

"I'm not getting on that thing."

"Would you rather walk?"

"Funnily enough, Dante, yes, yes, I would. In case it escaped your notice, I have stitches in the back of my head. Six of them, to be precise. I don't fancy squeezing a fucking helmet over my head and riding on your fucking death trap."

It was on the tip of my tongue to make a cock joke there, but the stern expression on her face had me clamping my lips shut.

There was a time and a place, and judging by the thunderous look on Rachel's face, this was not the time.

Rachel

If he made the joke, so help me God, I would kill him. I could tell by the childish grin on his ridiculous fucking mouth just exactly what he was thinking: "My cock is a deathtrap," har har fucking har.

I would gut him right here, right now, and I'd play skipping rope with his intestines if he even so much as dared. I was in no mood for stupid jokes.

"The bike's all I've got, Rachel," he said with a shrug. "Unless you'd prefer to walk…"

"Fine," I snapped, walking to the car park, immediately spotting the huge monstrosity he was so in love with.

Funny, I didn't know his mother was here.

Now that *was a good fucking joke. I should share it with him since he's in such a jolly fucking mood.*

I was in a bratty mood, and I knew it. Nothing Dante could say was going to make any difference. If he said right, I was going to fight to go left. If he told me not to jump off a cliff, I was going to go right ahead and do it, just to piss him off.

And then I'd haunt him all the way through my afterlife, so he never knew a moment's peace until he joined me in death. And then I'd annoy him until the end of time.

I was still bothered about him not visiting me the other day. So much so I had banned all other visitors for the rest of my stay. A part of me felt bad about that, thinking maybe Bee had wanted to visit, but I couldn't just ban Dante alone. I couldn't let him know he was under my skin and affecting me to the point I had to lash out.

So I banned everyone, and if he asked, I would just tell him it was because I couldn't stand the fucking lot of them. It was difficult enough dealing with them when I was okay. I didn't want anything to do with the cunts when my head was throbbing and being held together by bastard string.

It wasn't a massive lie.

I stayed silent as Dante pulled two helmets out and ignored the sting as he pushed it down on my head.

"Sorry," he said, and all I could think was, "my God, he's good. He actually looked apologetic."

Probably worried I'd get blood all over his fancy fucking helmet.

He clasped the safety buckle under my chin, his fingers soft and gentle as they lingered against my skin for a moment, leaving a tingling sensation wherever they touched.

Hormones. A girl's worst enemy.

"I'll drive as steady as I can," he promised as we climbed onto his bike. I shuffled close to him, wrapping myself around his back. I heard his sharp intake of breath as my tits pressed against him, but I ignored it.

"Just get me home, Dante. The sooner the better. I want a bath, a warm meal, and my bed. In that order. And I want it alone."

I glanced at the bed and then at Dante, my brow arching in a silent question.

"Mum and Bee went out last night and got you everything they thought you would need. That woman you were staying with in America has sent your belongings, and they should be here by the weekend, but I figured it wouldn't hurt to have a few extra bits."

"You've spoken to her?"

"Macbeth has. He said it's all arranged."

I looked at the dresses and leggings, none of them in my style. I preferred dark colours and closer fitting clothes. All of these were bright, flowy, girly things, and I knew for certain it was Bee's influence. His mother would have brought home a black bag of potato sacks and told me to make the best of them.

I couldn't hate the clothes when it was Bee that chose them. I did, however, hate the fact that I had needed clothes for days on end, and the only reason Dante had bought them for me was because he felt sorry for me.

He could have done this at any time. Hell, he could have given me his credit card and I could have done this myself. If he was feeling particularly cheeky, he could have taken me shopping himself and made me do a strip show for him every time I tried an outfit on. I probably would have done it.

But he chose not to. He was perfectly happy to keep me in filthy clothes. Clothes that had blood on them. Clothes that stunk of smoke. Yet he hadn't wanted to sleep in bed because of a bit of smoke.

"Great, thanks," I said, my voice devoid of emotion.

"Do you like them?"

"They're fine."

"We can take back anything you don't like—"

"Dante, I'm currently dressed as though I'm on day release from the fucking circus. The clothes are fine. I will deal with it. Just like I deal with everything else," I muttered under my breath. If Dante heard me, he didn't show it.

"Bee wants to know if you would like to share a McDonald's with her tonight?"

"And where will you be?" I questioned, my warning radar blinking rapidly.

His lips twisted apologetically. "I have to go out."

Ahh. There it was.

"Of course you do. The radar never fails."

"Excuse me?"

"You're excused," I said, pushing the clothes off the bed and climbing beneath the sheets. "Tell Bee I would love a McDonalds. You guys get UberEats here?"

"Why wouldn't we?"

"Shark told me about the pizza incident. I thought maybe you were blacklisted."

"I... He... yes," he said finally.

"Great. Tell your mother to send her up in an hour or two and we'll order. Leave your card."

"Bee has the UberEats account details."

"Even better." I gave a fake smile and turned over, pulling the covers up to my chin and presented him with my back.

"Rachel—"

"I'm fine, Dante. Enjoy your evening out."

I willed him to leave as my chin wobbled. Ridiculous tears sprung to my eyes, and I frantically wiped them away with a clenched fist, hoping Dante didn't see.

Tears don't make you weak, Rachel. Cry tonight and come back fighting tomorrow. You're allowed to feel, it's not a crime.

I certainly felt fucking weak right now. I was crying because the sexy biker didn't want to spend time with me. How pathetic was that?

You've been through a lot. Be gentle with yourself. Be kind. You're the only one who will be.

That much was true.

I was crying angry tears. Frustrated tears. Sad tears.

Why had Dante ripped me away from my small, comfortable life? Why had he taken everything away from me when he couldn't stand to be in my company?

What was the fucking point?

"Let me explain to you. Let me tell you where I'm going—"

"You don't owe me an explanation, Dante. You don't owe me anything. In fact, I think it would be better the less we said to each other. It never ends well. Enjoy your evening," I repeated.

Dante sighed, but he didn't argue. I heard his footsteps walk to the other side of the room, and the minute I heard the click of the door, I opened the floodgates and let my emotions wash over me.

I would be back to being a robot tomorrow.

Tonight? Tonight I needed to cry.

Chapter 34

Dante

I walked away, because if I didn't, I would strangle her.

Rachel was too stubborn for her own good. All she had to do was talk to me, and allow me the chance to explain, and she wouldn't have been upset.

She had tried to hide her tears, but I heard the telltale sniff as she forced herself to hold back, and I saw her clenched fists swipe at her eyes to clear away the drops that couldn't be contained.

I'd brought enough hurt into her life the past few days, and I felt a complete asshole to be adding more, but this had to be done. She would thank me in the future. I would have loved to spend the evening with her and Bee, all three of us finding a way to connect and move forward as a new, blended family. However, when I spoke to my mam and dad about bringing Rachel home today, Macbeth had been listening, and told me I might want to put the happy reunion on hold. He told me he had an in with Ben – the new club owner who Alex had once considered his best friend. I couldn't pass on the opportunity to size the place up and figure out the best plan of attack.

"All good, brother?" Vienna asked as I entered the bar. The rest of the lads were already there, gathering whatever information they could. Vienna waited for me, as he always did. He was my right-hand man, and where I went, he went.

"Better than expected, I suppose."

"She'll come around, man," he said, giving me a reassuring slap on the shoulders. "Think of what she's been through. Can you blame the girl for wanting to be alone for a while?"

"I can't blame her for thinking the worst of me."

"Well… I didn't want to be the one to say," he joked, flashing me a grin. "Ahh, come on. We'll go take care of some of her demons. You've got the rest of your lives to make it up to her – although might I suggest not pissing her off too much, or else the rest of your life might be much shorter than planned."

Ben's club was in the heart of Leeds – bold move for someone who was part of the grooming scene. He took hiding in plain sight to a whole new level.

Hacksaw had sent a text just as we left the clubhouse telling us that they were all inside and were talking to various people.

Macbeth was last seen talking to Ben himself, and so it was him who I scanned the floor for, wanting to know what information he had found.

"There," Vienna muttered, his head nodding ever so slightly in Macbeth's direction. I knew better than to look directly at them, so I turned slightly, looking at them through my peripheral.

Macbeth was laughing at something Ben said, and the pair of them clinked their glasses together in response to Macbeth's answer. "Looking awfully friendly for two people that just met yesterday," Vienna muttered.

"He's either playing his role well—"

"Or he's living up to his name." Vienna finished for me.

Feeling a growing lump forming in the pit of my stomach, I made my way over to my brother and Ben, ready to find out for myself.

"Ahh, here he is," Macbeth boomed, his speech already beginning to slur. "The little brother, in the flesh!"

"Alright, Cole?" I said, using his real name for a change. The less these guys knew about who we were, the better.

Most people in the country had heard of the Devil's Disciples, and I had no doubt in my mind Ben was well aware of all the clubs local to him, motorcycle or otherwise.

"Cole, is it?" Ben asked with a wry, calculating grin. "When did we stop using Macbeth?"

Ahh, fucking hell.

The useless bastard hadn't kept his mouth shut.

"And I take it you're Dante?" He addressed me.

"In the flesh," I said, using Macbeth's earlier line as I shot him an angry look.

It didn't matter. It wasn't public knowledge that I was with Rachel, and even if he did know about her, she had changed so much from the pale, skinny, dark-haired girl he had helped abuse, it was doubtful he'd know she was the same person.

"Macbeth here tells me you're looking at expanding your club?" He says to me, and I shot another look at Macbeth.

"Did he?"

"Don't be mad," Ben said, a happy beam on his face. "I'm glad we respect one another enough that you came to me beforehand. I've no problem where you place your club, so long as my business remains my business, and your business remains your business. Which, I'm sure we'll be in agreement there," he laughed, looking between me and Macbeth.

"Go and get us some drinks," I said to my useless brother. "Now, Mac. And ask Vienna what he wants. He'll be parched."

He knew what I meant.

"Dante," he warned, but I brushed him off.

"Go, before our new friend here gets bored with us."

I kept my eyes on Ben as Macbeth left, and the minute he was out of eyesight, I let the happy grin fall from my lips.

"Something on your mind, Dante?" Ben asked, having also lost the pretence of there ever being a friendship between us. His eyes were as cold as I knew mine were.

"How did you come to own this club? Seems an awfully big place to run for someone so young. Don't most new businesses crumble within the year?"

"There's always an exception to the rule."

"And you just so happen to be the exception, right?"

He gestured around him, "what do you think?"

"It's not what I think, it's what I know. And I've heard other things about how this club came to be so popular, and how it came to be in your hands."

He paused for a brief moment before answering. "I inherited it from a friend."

I gave a low whistle as I looked around. "That's one generous friend."

"You know what they say. It's not what you know, it's who you know."

I saw a shadow move around the edges of the club, and my spine stiffened. However, I made sure to relax in time before Ben realised I had noticed anything.

"That's true. You've just got to know the right person."

"Here, here," Ben said, but he didn't raise his glass.

"I think we might actually have someone in common, you and I – since we're speaking of people we know."

Ben's eyes snapped back to mine, eyeing me with growing caution. "Oh, yeah?"

"Yeah," I gave a small laugh. "It's been some years now, but I'm sure you haven't forgotten her."

Ben laughed, the relief evident. His eyes cleared up, the suspicion clearing away. "Sorry about that, man. For a second there, I thought I might have fucked over one of your friends." I grinned back, trying not to recoil as he slapped me over my back.

"Easy mistake to make around here. Everyone's fucked over someone at some point."

"Ain't that the truth? So who's the female? Shit, I didn't fuck her, did I?"

"Something like that."

"Man…" he half whistled; half laughed. "These women. They don't half get about. What's her name? I'll see if I can place her?"

"Rachel."

"Rachel?" He frowned. "I haven't met a Rachel in years."

"I didn't say how long ago it was," I muttered. The shadow kept moving, and so I moved closer to Ben. He strained his neck to look up at me.

"What's her surname?" He asked, the sweat breaking out on his forehead.

"You know which Rachel I'm talking about. You see, I've been researching you, Ben. I know all about who you got this club from, and what the pair of you used to get up to with underage girls. I'm sure after all these years, you thought you had got away with it. It's just unfortunate for you that one of those girls turned out to be my future old lady."

"Look, man," he said, backing up from me. "I don't know what she told you, but whatever happened between her, and Alex was their business."

"So, you do know which Rachel I'm talking about?" I said through clenched teeth, still backing him up to the edge of the room.

Ben looked back and forth, his eyes frantically looking around the room.

"It's ancient history. She killed him. He paid for his crimes."

"He did, didn't he? Shame it wasn't earlier, but at least my girl got her vengeance in the end. He paid with his life."

"Exactly. He—"

"But did you?"

"What?" He spluttered.

"Did you pay, Ben? Did you suffer the consequences of your actions, or were you happy to let Alex take the blame entirely?"

"I—"

"I know everything, Ben. Did you think you would spend the rest of your life going unpunished?" I nodded into the corner, and Ben spun his head around at the same time as Vienna clamped a hand around his mouth and dragged him kicking and screaming into the shadows. I took a quick look around the room, meeting the eyes of Shark and Hacksaw – fuck knows where Macbeth had gone. I nodded to them, and they followed as we dragged Ben out of the back door leading to the alleyway.

Chapter 35

Rachel

Bee convinced me to watch *Moana* with her, and the pair of us laughed our hearts out at her doing her impression of Tamatoa. She went around my room gathering anything with the slightest bit of shine, or that she deemed valuable, and she hunched over at the back with all the items piled on top of her, singing how shiny she was.

At one point, I almost choked on my burger when she crawled at me, her behind stuck high in the air, her arms and legs rigid straight.

The girl was a pure character, and I felt myself fall in love more and more every time we spent time together.

She even convinced me to act out Maui, and she kept throwing things at me whenever I was supposed to shapeshift into something else, calling it the "magic blast."

When *Moana* was finished, she snuggled up to me, her raven hair draped over my chest as she cuddled into my side, using her hair as a pillow. We put on The Lion King, but she was yawning by the time Simba the lion was outcast from his pride.

Boy, I know how that little fucker felt. I felt I was an outcast no matter where I went.

A small kiss to Bee's forehead had her eyes closing, and she stopped fighting her sleep. Her tiny fist clung to my shirt, resting atop my stomach, and I soon found my eyes growing heavy. Just as I was drifting off into a blissful sleep, I felt her stir below me.

"Rachel?" she whispered.

"Yeah?" I whispered back, opening one of my eyes and pulling a sleepy, funny face.

"Please let me keep you." And her eyes closed once more, a happy, content sigh leaving her lips before her breathing evened out into the deep breaths of sleep.

My heart clenched. This little firecracker had stolen the small amount of love I had left in me to give. She made the days here bearable, and that terrified me.

I didn't want to be second guessing leaving. I wanted to be able to cut ties with this club and never look back.

It was different with Joseph. I was under contract to care for him, and I kept my guard high. But with Bee... I had already been through so much whilst being here, and my usual defence mechanisms were not in place. She had shimmied her way through the holes in my armour, and I would always worry about her wellbeing if I wasn't around.

I had seen enough to know that club life wasn't like a regular life. Whilst there was an incredible sense of loyalty and camaraderie here, it was also filled with danger and betrayal around every corner. How long could Bee be kept away from this? How long before someone used her as leverage against Dante?

It made me want to stay, just so she would always have me around to protect her. Sure, she had her nanny, but I doubt Big Mama had it in her to do much against the more evil people in this world. I had already proven I was willing to do what it takes to survive. I would protect Bee to the death.

I looked down at her and snuggled in closer, holding her tight against me. This girl was precious, and she was the one thing stopping me from hating it here completely.

Dante

Hacksaw and Shark rode ahead of us, clearing the way to the garage that Crash and Tools owned. We had to make sure no one saw us bring Ben in. Not that I had ever cared about other members seeing before, but I didn't want word getting back to Rachel until I was ready. I wanted to extract every piece of information from Ben by any means necessary, and then I would allow her to watch as I delivered the killing blow.

Crash would understand, and he would know to keep his mouth shut. Tools would complain, and Sunshine would live up to his namesake more than ever. No doubt we'd never hear the end to all the grumbling and moaning, but he would still know better than to spill club secrets. We'd bring it to church when the time was right.

Ben was hogtied to the back of my bike, and the fucker had not stopped trying to scream through his gag the entire ride back.

Every so often, I would reach behind me and deliver a slap around his head. Or I would take the corner too fast and listened to his terrified screams as his face came dangerously close to scraping across the tarmac road.

It was quite cathartic in its own way, and I was already in a much better mood than I was when the night began.

When arriving at the village, the roads were quiet and clear, so we went straight to the garage, and Shark closed the doors behind us.

"Chair," I instructed Hacksaw before I'd even shut off the engine. He had Ben removed from my bike and swung him into the chair by the time I removed my helmet.

These three men were with me every step of the way, and our operations worked like clockwork. It made me feel more positive about taking over when Crash stepped down. I knew Zach was looking to step away from his role as Sergeant at Arms, and I knew these men would be my new team. They had never let me down before and would fulfil their roles perfectly.

As I removed my jacket and rolled up my sleeves, Hacksaw had Ben tied down, and Vienna was already attaching the chains to the hooks.

"W-wait," Ben spluttered as he saw me pick up the hammer. "We can talk this through. Let me see her. I'll apologise!"

"If I were to take these pliers and remove every one of your fingernails and shove each one up your ass, would an apology suffice? If I carved my name into your stomach until you were close to bleeding out, would an apology be enough? Would you forgive me?"

Ben blanched, his mouth opening and closing like a demented fish as he struggled to find the words.

"It doesn't matter," I grinned at him. "I'm going to enjoy this too much to want an apology, anyway."

The sounds of Ben's screaming had given me a headache like no other. The three men had stood and watched as I used the hammer to smash Ben's kneecaps. Once I was done there, I threw the hammer to the side and rained blow and after blow down on his face, releasing all the pent-up aggression that had been building since Rachel walked into my life.

The screams that had started loud and piercing, had soon turned into gargled wet pleas as the blood filled his mouth. And still I hadn't stopped.

My fists ached by the time I was done, and my fists were stained with blood belonging to both of us – my knuckles had split long before I was finished. His face was unrecognisable beneath the crimson that covered it, but since he was going to be here a while, he'd soon recover.

As I cleaned my hands up, Hacksaw pierced the hooks into his chest and back, and both he and Shark had carried Ben to the wall, whilst Vienna tightened the chains, suspending him from the ceiling against the wall. I could see the skin on his chest straining from the hook beneath it, but he would hold for the night.

For good measure, Vienna had silently grabbed a pair of scissors that we used for cutting down tyres and sliced at his Achilles Heel. If by some miracle he did get down from the chains, he wasn't going anywhere with his bust knees and snipped heels.

When I arrived back home, I went straight to Rachel's room, hoping and praying she was still awake. But as I pushed the door open, I found both her and Bee fast asleep. Bee was curled up in the foetal position, with Rachel spooned up behind her. Rachel had her arms around Bee, holding her close to her chest and their fingers were linked against Bee's torso. Her head was tucked into Rachel's neck, and her chin was resting atop Bee's head. They looked so peaceful and serene; I didn't dare wake them.

Crossing the room, I grabbed a blanket from the closet since they were laid on top of theirs and laid it over them. Rachel stirred slightly, and before I knew what I was doing, I leaned forward and kissed her forehead and smoothed the hair back from her face.

I laid the back of my hand against her skin and noticed that she was feeling a bit warm, so I went to the bathroom and filled up a glass of water for her and placed it on the bedside table alongside some painkillers for the morning.

I walked to the other side of the bed and crouched down in front of Bee. I placed a kiss on her cheek and whispered that I loved her – something I had done every night since she was born and then decided I had pushed my luck enough for one night. If Rachel woke up, it would only mean an argument. I was aware enough to know it was my presence that would disturb their peace.

Going back to the door, I shot one last look at the two ladies in my life and quietly shut it behind me.

Rachel

The man moved like a fucking beast. I now understood the issue the troll had with those irritating billy goats trip trapping across his bridge.

Shit was annoying.

I kept my eyes shut, not wanting to disturb the peace that had fallen over my bedroom for the past few hours. I heard him as he picked up the rubbish from our dinner. I heard him as he opened and closed the closet. I felt the blanket being laid across me, and then the fucker had gone and lingered on my shoulder as he pulled the blanket up to my chin.

I couldn't help the way my body reacted to him. Luckily, he thought I was stirring in my sleep. Then he surprised me by laying a gentle kiss on my forehead before he checked my temperature.

I slyly opened my eye as the bathroom light clicked on and quickly slammed it shut again when I saw him come back in with a glass of water and some paracetamol from the medicine cabinet.

He placed them on my bedside table and then walked over to Bee's side of the bed.

"I love you, my mini-B," he whispered, followed by the sound of him giving her a kiss.

And then he was gone.

I didn't quite trust that my spying had remained undetected, so I only half opened my eyes and then breathed a sigh of relief, opening them fully when I noticed he had left the room.

"What the fuck was that about?" I whispered to myself.

So he was capable of being gentle when he wanted to.

I still needed answers though, so I gently shifted Bee to the side and placed the pillows I had been using behind her so she would think I was still there, and softly padded across the carpet, following Dante.

Chapter 36

Rachel

I saw the light shining under Dante's bedroom door, and walked straight towards it, pushing the door open without bothering to knock.

The sound of the running water told me he was in the shower, and so I sat on the end of his bed and waited for him, picking the skin around my nails as my nerves grew.

I didn't know why I was so nervous. Dante and I had argued so many times already, so this time should be no different. And yet I couldn't help but think that there was something more final about this.

Every game had to come to an end, and we were both growing tired of the cat and mouse, will they/won't they game we had been playing.

If we couldn't find common ground soon, there was no point even trying anymore – not that either of us had really been trying up to now.

Dante had been right the other night when he said we needed to get to know each other. We had to learn to get along; we had to find a friendly middle ground, or else we were doomed. Dante wasn't the type of person to be content with living in total peace – he wouldn't be part of the Devil's Disciples, if that was the case. And if I was being honest, I didn't want total peace either. Some part of us enjoyed the drama, and no doubt we would always goad the other into an argument. But the situation we had at the minute couldn't continue. Every argument was an escalation on the last, and it wouldn't be long before we did some serious damage – both emotional and physical.

The shower clicked off, and a moment later, Dante entered the room, fixing the towel he had tied around his waist.

My mouth immediately dried up, and yet somehow filled with my own drool at the same time. I had yet to see Dante without his clothes on, and he was fucking magnificent.

His body was covered in tattoos – a tribal tattoo up one arm, a snake slithering around the other. A small bee rested on his collarbone, with a little beehive underneath. At the right side of his stomach were two little stick figures, and "Bee and Daddy" written underneath them. It didn't take a genius to work out he had tattooed one of Bee's early pieces of art.

There were scars over his chest, his shoulders, and even a nasty one down his ribcage near his heart.

His muscles rippled with the movements he made, the veins on his forearm protruding.

My blood fired up, and I clenched my thighs together at the immediate heat that raced between my legs as small droplets of water ran down his face and onto his body.

"What are you doing here, Rachel?" Dante asked, frowning at me with suspicion.

"I came to talk," I replied, clearing my throat before I spoke, and yet it still came out husky.

"About what?"

I gritted my teeth against his hostile tone. "I just wanted to talk."

"You were asleep ten minutes ago."

"I woke up."

"Clearly." he rolled his eyes at me and walked over to his chest of drawers, pulling out a pair of boxers. He dropped the towel, completely unashamed in his nudity, and pulled them on in one smooth move.

I dragged my eyes away from the impressive bulge and forced myself to look at his face. Thank God he wasn't paying attention to me and hadn't seen me drooling over his dick like a savage beast.

"Why are you being so hostile?"

"Am I?"

"Yes."

"Maybe I'm just matching the energy."

"What's that supposed to mean?"

"It means I tried to talk to you earlier, Rachel, and you turned your back on me."

"I'm here now, aren't I?"

"So we can talk whilst it's on your terms?"

"Yes," I said simply, and had to bite my lip as he swung around, shock flashing in his eyes before it was replaced with a growing anger.

"At least you're honest."

"Exactly. I'm a difficult woman, I get that. I'm not the easiest person to have a conversation with at the best of times. It's best to try when I'm in the right mood. I know my faults, and that's one of them. But I'm here now," I repeated. "So, can we talk?" I asked after he didn't bother responding.

"I've had a long night. Can we leave it until the morning?"

"No, we can't. I don't want to start another day with bad feelings. I'd like to clear the air."

"What is there to clear?" He asked in exasperation.

"You've got to be kidding me? How about we start with why you didn't visit me at the hospital?"

"I did visit you!"

"Not when I was awake! I was left on my own all evening!"

"Not all evening!" He responded in mock horror. "And yet somehow you survived? You fucking warrior! Do the terrorists know about you? I'm sure they'd run a mile when faced with such bravery and sacrifice. A whole evening!"

"Wow," I said, elongating the word so it came out more like "woooooow." "I have never seen such a good-looking man look so unattractive. That was… that was quite something."

"Just leave, Rachel. I'm not in the mood."

"You brought this on yourself. You could have spent the evening with me and Bee, and yet you decided to go out gallivanting God knows where."

"Jealous?" He said, flashing a grin at me.

"Of what?" I made a point of looking at the digital clock on the table. "You were gone only a few hours. Hardly a raunchy marathon, was it?"

"Can't beat a quick and dirty roll in the hay once in a while."

"If you've got issues with premature ejaculation, you can just say that. You don't have to dress it up all fancy."

"I didn't hear you complaining."

"I've got low standards."

"That makes two of us," he fired right back.

"Like I said, you made the choice to go out tonight. You lowered your own standards."

"Touche," he grinned, and my back relaxed as some of the tension left the room. I didn't really believe that he had been with another woman tonight. My gut told me he wasn't that kind of bloke, and since I really didn't know him that well, my gut was the only thing I could trust.

But still... I had to push a little. I had to know for sure.

"Besides, you can't handle me on my own. I don't think you've got it in you to handle two women." I joked.

Half joked.

Me and my big mouth.

I should have known better than to mess with a man's pride.

"I can handle you just fine. I could always tie you up again and repeat my night with Beth."

"Who the fuck is Beth?" I bit out, watching the blood drain from Dante's face as he realised he'd said the completely wrong thing.

I wasn't a jealous woman, that much was true. But if someone was going to throw it in my face that they had slept with another woman, I was going to react.

"Beth owns the Greasy Spoon," he said simply.

"And what does she have to do with this?"

"Nothing. Nothing at all. You're right. What did you want to talk about?"

"Nah, mate, that's not how this works. You brought her up, have the balls to finish what you were about to say. What does Beth have to do with this?"

"I was just being a dick, Rachel. Me and Beth used to sleep together, that's all."

"But you said you would tie me up and repeat the night with Beth." I persisted.

He visibly cringed. "Can we just forget what I said? I don't—"

"You slept with Beth after bringing me here, didn't you? You're fucking unbelievable."

"What? We weren't together – we're still not together!"

"Oh, I'll go fuck Malfoy then, shall I? In fact, where's your friend Vienna? Now *that* is one fine looking man. I'll happily take a ride on his—" Dante grabbed hold of my arms and launched me on the bed, throwing his body down on top of mine. My head hung off the edge, and he grabbed my hair in a tight fist with one hand, pushing my head forward until we were practically nose to nose.

"Don't even fucking think about repeating that," he snarled, grabbing hold of my face and forcing me to look at him.

"If it's good for you, it's good for me."

"You belong to me!"

"And yet the first night I was here, you slept with someone else! Fuck you, Dante! You absolute fucking hypocrite, bastard, cunt," every word I said, I accompanied it with a punch to his chest before I gave up speaking and just rained punch after punch down on him. "What was the fucking point? You wanted me so badly you had to kidnap me, and yet once you had me here, you couldn't wait to run off elsewhere! Get off me, you fucking brute!" I all but screamed. "I swear to God, I will sleep with every fucking member of this club by the time I'm done here!"

He let go of my head and gathered my hands, pulling me down the bed as he pinned my arms to my side.

"I didn't fucking sleep with her," he snarled in my face. "And if you ever even think about sleeping with someone else ever again, so help me God, I will skin you alive."

"Is that supposed to intimidate me, Dante?" I hissed back at him. "Jokes on you. I'm fucking into that shit. Go on, give me another threat. Get me all worked up so I can go find Vienna."

"Get out of my sight before I do something I regret," he growled, pushing himself off the bed with such force my body bounced against the mattress.

"Now who's jealous?" I laughed, jumping to my feet.

"It's got fuck all to do with jealousy. But once I say something is mine, it stays that way until *I* decide I'm done with them!"

"I was never yours to take in the first place," I hissed, storming over to the door. "Come find me in the morning. I'll be the blonde in Vienna's bed, having been ravished to within an inch of my life. Something which *you* have been incapable of doing."

The door was slammed shut before I even had it open an inch. He grabbed my elbow and spun me around, trapping me between his body and the door.

"Vienna wouldn't bother," he hissed at me. "He knows damaged goods when he sees it."

"And yet he's got to accept these damaged goods as his VP's old lady. Make it make sense, Dante."

"Everyone is allowed to make mistakes. But unlike some of us, I'll see my mistakes through to the end."

"You're so full of shit. And your attempts at hurting me are pathetic. This," I reached between our bodies and cupped his stiffening cock. "Is evidence of how much you want this mistake. You don't want me to go near anyone else, because you know if you don't keep your eye on me, they'll fuck me too. Malfoy was evidence of that." I brought my face close to his and whispered against his lips. "Isn't it funny that for someone who sees me as damaged goods, you're hard every time I come near you?"

His cock grew even harder against my hand, and I felt the familiar blaze run through my body.

Was it normal to get turned on by arguing?

I was fucked if I knew.

All I knew was that the angrier I got this man, the wetter my pussy was. There was something wired up wrong with me. Insults were like foreplay to me.

Yeah, I'm one messed up woman.

"For once in your life, how about you put that smart mouth to good use and do something about it," Dante whispered back to me, grinding his cock against my hand.

The same fire that had burned inside me had spread to him, burning him alive as quick as it had burned through me.

"What's up, Rachel? Scared?"

Oh, but the man was good. He knew what he was doing. He knew I couldn't back down from being challenged.

Most normal people were whispering love and affectionate words to each other when they were having sex. And yet for some reason, every time me and Dante pushed each other's buttons by arguing and insulting each other.

"What is there to be scared of? I've had this inside me." I gently squeezed his cock. "Your dick game is shit. I've had better orgasms from something battery operated."

"You're still talking. Something tells me you are scared."

My heart was pounding as he spoke into my neck. His breath was hot against my skin, and my pussy clenched as my hands fisted at my sides.

"If you want me to suck your dick, Dante, you only have to ask. Don't try to manipulate it, so it's my idea. It's not hard. 'Rachel, please suck my dick. I need it.' Give it a go—"

"Rachel?"

"Yeah?" I almost squeaked.

"Shut the fuck up," he laughed, knocking my ankle with his foot, sending me dropping to my knees.

I immediately pulled his cock out of his boxers and gave up the pretence of not wanting this.

I ran my tongue along the tip, licking up the drop of pre-cum I found. He let out a moan, and I looked up at him with a small laugh, repeating my movement. I kept my eyes locked on his as he fisted my hair, watching me as I rang my tongue along the length of him.

"Fuck," he breathed as my hand reached up to cradle his balls. I gathered the saliva in my mouth and spat on the head of his cock and used my other hand to spread it along the length of him, squeezing him gently as I rotated my wrist whilst stroking him.

His other hand steadied himself against the door as he tightened his grip on my hair, encouraging my movements.

I fisted him at the base and brought his cock to my lips, rubbing it along them as I gave him one last smile before I shut my eyes and sucked him as deep into my mouth as I could.

His legs immediately shook as I went from zero to a hundred, bobbing down on his cock as fast as I could. I swirled my tongue along the length of him as I went down and then sucked my cheeks together to tighten around him as I went up.

I felt his knees buckle as the different sensations went through him, and he let go of my hair, placing both hands on the door above me. I hummed my approval, earning myself another throaty moan as the noise vibrated through him.

He shuffled slightly closer, and I opened my mouth wider, taking him to the back of my throat and held him there until I felt myself beginning to choke and pulled my head back, letting the noise of my gag escape.

"Jesus fucking Christ," he bit out as I repeated the move. He thrust his hips forward this time, choking me even further, and I let it happen, knowing he loved the noises I made when I struggled to breathe. As he pulled out of me, the spit dripped down my chin, and he brought his hand to my lower lip and ran his thumb over it. "That's a good girl," he whispered, his jaw clenched. "You look so fucking sexy sucking my cock. There's nothing better than that brief moment of wide-eyed panic on your face when you think I'm not going to let you breathe."

He slid his cock back between my lips, and we locked eyes as he slowly pushed it to the back of my throat. I clenched my fists and tipped my head back, opening my throat for him.

"Fuck, Rachel. Look at you, determined to take it all," he gave a hard thrust of his hips, sending his cock to the back of my mouth. My eyes went wide with shock, and I banged my fist against my knee, refusing to give into the gag that rose up.

He grabbed the back of my head with one hand as he pulled out of my mouth, but a mere moment later, he thrust back in, hitting the back of my throat. His other hand came up to pinch my nose, cutting off all breathing as his cock smothered me. I kept my eyes on his, my throat convulsing around him. My chest heaved and became heavy. Spit dripped down my chin, and all the while his cock throbbed in my mouth.

"You're fucking amazing. I could spend the rest of my life having you choking on me," he breathed, letting go of my nose and pulled out of my mouth.

I drew in a grateful breath and fisted the base of him, pulling him back towards me and wrapping my lips around him once more.

I moaned on his cock, my pussy throbbing at his words. "Is that what you want, Rachel? You want to choke on my cock?"

I didn't answer. I just sucked him to the back of my throat once more and looked up at him, the tears springing to my eyes as he thrust forward, pushing himself further down my throat. "Fuck yes, take my cock like the good little slut you are." His thumb was no longer stroking my lower lip. His fingers had clamped around my cheeks, and he pushed my head back, smacking it against the wall as he thrust his hips. My hands came round his hips and my fingers dug into his ass as he thrust in and out of my mouth, each time going further and further down my throat.

My chest grew tight, unable to breathe as he fucked my mouth and I dropped a hand and pushed it between my legs, my fingers immediately getting covered in my own wetness.

I let out a small, strangled scream as I pushed two fingers inside myself. Dante's legs shook even harder and the veins in his neck protruded as he held back, not wanting the feeling to end. My other hand squeezed at his ass, encouraging him to keep taking me as hard as he wanted.

He pulled out of my mouth, and I dragged in huge breaths of air, the spit dripping onto my chest as I panted in relief. He gave me less than ten seconds to recover before he noticed where my hands were, and with an animalistic moan, he thrust his cock right back into my mouth.

"I can hear how wet your pussy is, Rachel. Is that how much you love having your mouth abused?" I gave a small nod, taking back control as I dragged my mouth up the length of him, squeezing him tight. I pushed on his ass as my head moved up and down his cock, and then I pulled out and blew cool air over the tip of him. His entire body jerked at the sensation, and I felt my pussy clamp around my fingers in response to the power I had over him.

I pulled my fingers out of my pussy and brought my hand up to his cock, spreading my juices over him as I massaged him at the same time as I took him in my mouth.

Dante's hand covered my own, encouraging me to wank him faster, and I knew he was getting close.

I felt him stiffen up, his cock jerking in my mouth, and my head moved even faster, wanting to taste his cum down my throat. His hand squeezed mine to the point of pain, my knuckles grinding against each other as I death gripped him, but his wild groans spurred me on, encouraging me to be as rough with him as he was with me.

Just as I braced myself to choke on his cum, he pulled out of my mouth and pushed my hand away, stroking his own cock and finished on my face.

"Fuck," he breathed, his legs shaking. My tongue came out and licked at the cum that dripped down to my lips and, with a small laugh, he hauled me to my feet and whispered in my ear. "Look at you, so greedy for my cum. Maybe one day, kitten, you'll be worthy enough for me to want to cum in your mouth. But right now, all you're worth is this."

He planted a painful kiss on my lips and then he left me alone in his room, wondering what the fuck had just happened.

Chapter 37

Dante

I was a fucking bastard, and I knew it.

I shouldn't have done that. I shouldn't have degraded her and then left her. But I panicked.

I'm man enough to admit it.

There was something about that woman that brought out the worst in me.

Whenever me and Laura argued, she would turn on the waterworks, using her tears as a weapon to get her own way. Rachel hadn't done that, no matter what I did to her. She gave as good as she got, and there was something so fucking sexy about that smart mouth – even if it did drive me so crazy that I could hit her.

She was *nothing* like I had expected her to be. In the Greasy Spoon, she had looked sweet and innocent. And yet, I was happier with the Rachel I was given. She was fiery, and she was infuriating. She was sexy, and she was a mind-fuck. She intrigued me, and she drove me mad. I hated her, and yet I couldn't get enough of her.

I hated that she had an answer for everything. I hated that she always had to pick a fight. I hated that she wasn't scared and gave as good as she got.

I hated that I fucking loved all those things.

I hated that I no longer knew how I felt.

I wanted Rachel, because I figured she'd look after Bee and let me live my life as I pleased. She'd be too submissive to fight back. I didn't care if she was happy or cared about me in the slightest.

And now all I wanted was for her to smile. All I wanted was for the words to be on her lips, telling me how much she wanted me, how much she wanted to *be with* me.

I should have been patient. I should have done my research on her. I should have done a background check.

I should have done a lot of things differently.

Because now I was left with a woman who surprised me in all the best ways. A woman who challenged me. A woman who gets a rise out of me without even trying. A woman who I was struggling to see my life without.

And that gave her power over me.

And I was man enough to admit that scared the ever-loving shit out of me.

She drives me mad. She drives me to the point of destruction. And yet I can't stay away. She's all I think about. She's all I *want* to think about.

And I fucking hated that. I hated her. And yet I was obsessed with her.

So I ran away. I looked down at her, her eyes wide as she took my cock. The same eyes so full of passion and arousal, and my heart leapt in affection.

All the research and background checks in the world could not have prepared me for that.

Even when we were arguing, even when she was spitting poison and venom at me, I wanted her.

I'd spend every day annoying her, if only it meant I had her attention for five minutes.

I was in too deep, with a woman who couldn't stand to be near me unless I was fucking her.

I hated that, and I hated her.

But I didn't hate her. Not anymore. Not even a little.

I was obsessed. Enthralled. Enchanted.

I was fucked.

Chapter 38

Rachel

I woke up the next day and immediately sighed.

That's when you know it's going to be a shit day. If even opening your eyes depresses you, you may as well go back to bed and try again tomorrow.

But I knew hiding wouldn't solve anything. I had to find a common ground with Dante. How far would we both go if we were both playing games?

And whilst I knew that neither of us were the type to run off to the suburbs and play happy families, we also had to set some ground rules. We would always challenge each other, we would always argue, and go back and forth, but right now, we were doing nothing but humiliating the other in our attempt to be the victor.

And the prize we were trying to claim wasn't even worth it.

But if we both set aside our pride and stubbornness, we could form a new prize that we could share together.

I picked up my phone, noticing that Dante had messaged me:

I saved my card to your phone. Take any bike of your choosing and get what you need. There's a party tonight. I trust you, Rachel. I don't want you to feel like a prisoner.

I pulled up Google Wallet, seeing Dante's card saved, just like he said.

Grinning to myself, I pushed the covers off my body and hopped out of bed and straight to the bathroom, getting ready for the day. I wanted to stop playing games with him, but that didn't mean I couldn't deliver one last surprise.

It was time to say goodbye to the mask, the disguise, and the pretence. It was time to finally be Rachel.

Not selfish Rachel.

Not infuriating Rachel.

Not murderer Rachel.
Not hiding, on the run Rachel.
Just Rachel.
I liked the sound of that.

Dante

The whole club was here, ready and waiting to surprise Rachel at her initiation party. The whole thing had been Bee's idea, as a way to make Rachel feel more welcome in her new home.

These were not the type of people to hide behind the furniture, only to jump out screaming "surprise" when Rachel arrived, but I hoped she would enjoy the effort they all put in.

They had been anxious to meet the woman who I had declared as my own – especially as she would eventually be the woman standing at the side of their future leader. Which meant she had influence. Women were not members of the club, but any man would be a fool if they believed their woman didn't have a voice. She could help shape this club going forward, including memberships. We didn't tend to kick anyone out without good reason, but it had happened in the past when people weren't a good fit for us.

I checked my watch once more, noticing that the minutes were flying by, and Rachel was still not here. An anxious pit formed in my stomach, and I had to resist the urge to check the tracking on the bike she had taken. I had given her free rein to go and spend some money on herself, and if I was going to offer something, I had to respect that. I had to trust that she would make her way back to me.

Unless she wasn't back here by midnight, then I would be dragging Cinderella back in here kicking and screaming, and I'd never let her leave her room again.

The longer Rachel took, the more drunk these people got. And there was no controlling them when they were drunk. We had few rules when we were on our own territory, and often tempers soared beyond anything that could be contained. I didn't want Rachel walking into what would essentially be a wrestling match.

A smile twisted my lips as I pictured the look on her face. She'd probably tie her blonde hair high on her head and join in the fun, the psychotic bitch.

I heard the roaring of the engine and gave the signal to Vienna to turn the music down whilst Rachel came in.

I spied her through the window and gritted my teeth as I noticed she was wearing skintight leather pants that hugged every curve of her thighs and ass. She kept her helmet on as she walked closer to the door, her boots crunching the gravel under them.

She entered the door, and everyone went silent as she stood still, hands on her hips. Just as I was about to get up and go and greet her, she ripped the helmet off and tipped her head back, shaking her hair over her shoulders.

My mouth fell open as the blood left my brain and shot straight into my dick.

Gone was the long blonde hair and in its place was a fire red do that fell in layered waves halfway down her back, framing her face on the way down. She looked fucking ravishing. The slight tan she still held from her summer trip around Europe complimented her hair perfectly. This was also the first time I had seen her with makeup, and the smoky eye, the long lashes, plus the nude lip made her an absolute knockout. She had complimented all of her best features, her green eyes piercing me from the other end of the club, seeming brighter and more intense than ever. She was beautiful as a blonde, but she had an air about her as though she was pretending, as though she didn't belong. It's what had drawn me to her. I had mistaken it for innocence, whereas now I knew it was hiding in plain sight, terrified she'd be discovered. With her red hair, she was exuding confidence. She knew who she was, where she belonged, and she had come home.

It was the biggest fucking turn on I had ever known.

She locked eyes on me and shot me a small wink, pulling off her leather jacket to reveal a skintight top that cupped her tits and pushed them upward.

"Are we having a party, or what?" She asked everyone, beaming a smile that lit her entire face up.

She turned her head to Vienna, and he quickly shut his mouth, which had been hanging open just as mine was, and obeyed her command to get the party going, cranking the music back up to full volume. "Your wish is my command! Nice hair," he grinned at her.

"Nice beard," she smiled back.

"Thanks. I grew it myself."

"Likewise. We are two talented people, Vienna."

"Peas in a pod. Come see me when you've had enough of the boss man. I'll let you stroke my beard." She laughed at him, shaking her head.

"I'm afraid I don't share your love of a death wish."

"Shame. I like living on the edge."

"Dante will push you off if you keep talking like that to me," she grinned wider.

"Don't walk in here looking like that then," he raised his bottle at her, and went to mingle with the rest of the club.

Rachel swung her eyes back to me and made her way forward, her hips sashaying as she walked, filling my mind with all sorts of filthy thoughts.

Mainly of her riding me, her hips rotating as she brought us both to orgasm with that tight pussy of hers.

"Dante," she said as she approached where I was sitting on one of the bar stools. She automatically slotted between my legs, resting her ass on my inner thigh, taking the bottle out of my hand and throwing back a long swig.

"You look amazing," I whispered in her ear as my arm came around her waist, pulling her closer to my body. "But I hope you didn't do this for me?"

She shook her head, her eyes clouding slightly. "The blonde hair was my mother. It was me trying to be someone I'm not," she murmured and then looked up at me through those long lashes. "I'm ready to leave that girl behind now. I'm ready to finally start being me."

"Does that mean less of the smart mouth?" I joked.

"Oh no," she laughed, taking another drink of my beer. "You've been getting the watered down, friendly, Rebecca Brooks version of me. You think you can handle me stepping out of my mother's shadow and embrace the full Rachel Brooks?"

"No," I said honestly, causing a laugh to bubble up from her lips. I grabbed her wrist and brought the bottle to my mouth. "I think you'll eat me for breakfast and spit me back out again when you've had enough." She laughed even harder, tipping the liquid into my mouth. I placed a kiss on her inner wrist, my cock jumping in response when she gasped. "But I'll have my fucking fun with you all the same and gladly accept my punishment."

A spark of lust rushed to her eyes. And for the first time, I genuinely believed we might actually be okay.

I stayed where I was most of the night, watching Rachel as she enjoyed herself.

She took herself off dancing, stopping to speak to this person or that person as they all made their introductions and asked her about herself. I noticed once or twice the familiar blank look fell over her face, and I knew that she was struggling with all the attention she was receiving.

Every so often, she would shoot me a look, her eyes growing wild with panic. I would smile at her, wink at her, or just nod. She understood, and it was all she needed. She would take a deep breath, and she would continue the conversation, her smile as radiant as ever.

I also knew that she had fantastic fight-or-flight reactions, and since she hadn't fled, she was going to fight through it.

Only this time, she wasn't fighting with her words or with violence. She was using her other superpower. She was fighting with resilience. Instead of being resilient through training herself to be uncaring, she was pushing herself through, having the confidence that she was worthy and belonged. With grit and determination. Rachel could get through anything – she'd already been through the worst. She just had to believe in herself.

Which is why I hadn't intervened when she threw panicked looks my way – looks she probably hadn't even realised she gave me. She was searching for an anchor, without realising she was her own anchor, her own strength. I left her, letting her work out how to handle her emotions. She didn't need me to rescue her. I was not her saviour.

She could, and would, save herself.

And that's exactly what my girl did.

I watched as her spine straightened and she plastered a grin on her face, answering the questions from my club members, faking it until she made it.

As the night progressed, the spine relaxed. The smile became less forced. And she realised she had found her place. No-one here would harm her, no one here would make her feel less than. She was free to be herself.

And with that, she freed herself.

I was sat watching as she danced, her hips moving freely, her arms swaying. She laughed at something Shark said and gestured to the bar for another drink to be brought over. He tripped over himself to rush a drink to her, and I bit back my grin. Despite the difficult start, she had won over everyone here.

She had even flirted with a couple of the more boisterous men, throwing teasing looks my way. My teeth had gritted, my jaw tensing, but I stayed where I was. I hated to admit it, but I actually *liked* seeing her flirt with other people. I liked the tiny glimmer of hope in their eyes, thinking they might have a chance with her. It was a fucking turn on knowing she was going to be in my arms tonight. She belonged to me, despite how many other people might crave her.

The music slowed, and through the crowd, Rachel locked eyes with me. Her body swayed, her hips rotating, her eyes seducing me. She wasn't trying to be sexy; she wasn't calling to me; she was just moving her body in time to the music, effortlessly arousing.

I shuffled in my chair, my cock hurting as it strained against my trousers to be free, to sink inside her and return home.

But I waited.

Rachel could enjoy her party, and tonight, I would enjoy Rachel.

No games. No arguing. Just us.

Chapter 39

Rachel

I took a breather from the festivities, taking myself off to the bathroom so I could splash some water over my wrists.

Tonight had been a lot. And whilst I felt happier than I had felt in a long time, it was also overwhelming. The sea of faces had all blended into one, until I could barely recognise Dante in the crowd, never mind anyone else.

"Ooh, excuse me," a woman said as I went colliding into her.

"I am so sorry," I rushed out. "I was in a world of my own!"

"Don't worry about it." She gave me a kind smile. "Jenna."

"Of course. Sorry, it's just—"

"You don't need to apologise. I know what it's like when you first enter this place. I needed at least a week to recover after my first party. It will get easier. You won't always be the shiny new toy to fight over." She leaned against the wall as she spoke, stopping her from swaying.

"I hope that comes sooner rather than later. I don't like all of this attention."

"The trick is you need to play them at their own games. These men, they like to pretend they're the big, bad, and ugly. It's down to us to put them in their place." She pushed herself off the wall and linked arms with me. "Be worthy of the attention you command, Rachel. Don't let them make you feel nervous, intimidated, or any less than them. They'd be nothing without us. Come on," she said, pulling on my arm.

"Where are we going?"

"We are going to reserve one of those booths out there and have ourselves a breakaway party. Old ladies only. Let them sweat it out, wondering what we're talking about. I'll never tell if you don't."

I grinned at her, "lead the way, oh, wise one!"

She giggled, leading me through the doors, back out into the pub. Dante turned to look at me as I passed, giving me a smile of approval as he saw my arm linked with Jenna's. He caught Shark's eye, who looked at his old lady with such pride and admiration. A knot formed in my stomach, making me think this might have been planned. Some sort of conspiracy had gone off here. But did it really matter? If I could make a friend here, and not feel so lonely, did it really matter how the friendship started? Or who encouraged it?

Of course it didn't.

"Shark! Two of your finest. Make it snappy!" She called over to him as we took our seats.

"You're the one who fucking works here. Do it yourself!" He yelled back.

"You're the one who will be sleeping on the couch!"

"Was it two, you said?"

"Attaboy!" She leaned in and whispered to me, "See? Show them who is the boss. They soon fold."

"I think if I spoke to Dante that way, he'd pour the drinks over our heads."

"Yeah… you've got a point there. He's err… Well he's—"

"He's a bad-tempered cunt," I laughed. "You can say it. I know it, he knows it. 'Do as you're told, Rachel, don't answer back, Rachel'" I said, imitating his voice.

"We are *bikers*," she immediately joined in. "You must listen to bikers!"

"We are manly *men*. Hear us roar!"

We both laughed, stopping our performance as Shark brought our drinks over, shooting us nervous glances.

"I don't like this," he muttered, hurrying away from us.

"Pussy!" she shouted back. "I told you; they don't like it when we play them at their own games. They have church, we have… what would we call this?"

"Sin?" I offered after a moment's pause.

"Ooh, I like it. We're off to sin."

"Have fun at church, darling. It's time to sin!"

"I'll have to tell the other old ladies. They'll love this!"

"Are there many old ladies here?"

"A few," she said, bringing her drink to her lips. "Let me think, who here has an old lady? Oh, there's Trent – that's Zach's son. His old lady is lovely. She's called Imogen. Rooster and Chicken both have old ladies. We call them the birds. They're always together. Then there's Sasha. She's Sunshine's old lady. You know the guy who works at the garage? Sasha is an older woman, and she has a mean right hook, but she'll take care of you, so long as you get on her right side. Ant has an old lady, but I don't know her very well. She's called Gemma. She pretty much keeps to herself. And obviously you know big Mama. Everyone else is either single or has a girlfriend."

"What's the difference?" I asked, trying to process all the names she had just thrown at me.

"Girlfriends tend to stay away from the club for one reason or another. It might be that the guy just hasn't introduced them yet, or it might be that they don't want to be a part of it. Old ladies pitch in wherever they can. I work at the bar, as you know. Gemma does the valeting of the bikes. No-one asked her to. She says she enjoys it. Sasha walks the dogs – whenever Monster lets her, that is. Imogen helps Vienna with the bookkeeping. You should watch them one day. Vienna gets so mad when she starts demanding he justifies some of the expenditure. They'll kill each other one day, mark my words," she grinned at me. "The girlfriends probably couldn't tell you who anyone is outside of their boyfriend, or Dante. Everyone wants to know Dante."

"Why not Crash? He's the actual leader, isn't he?"

"He is. But Dante is the future, and everyone knows it. Crash has been stepping down more and more over the years. He's still the leader, but it's pretty much just a title for him now. He encourages Dante to take the reins. He's ready for retirement."

"I see."

"You have nothing to worry about. Dante has never shown an interest in any of them."

"I'm not worried. Dante will do what he wants, with or without my permission. I just have to trust that he'll have enough respect not to cheat."

"It's up to the two of you to set boundaries. I know Crash and Big Mama have a rule; 'what happens on the road, stays on the road.' It allows Crash to sleep with other people – usually the whores in the other branches – whenever they're away for days at a time."

"Why?"

"I don't know. It works for them, though. But then again, everyone knows the club whores sleep with everyone. Especially those in the higher ranks. See it like the Playboy mansion. None of them will be anything serious, but there are ranks amongst the whores, too."

"And they don't mind being called whores?"

"I never asked, to be honest. They've been called that for so long, I guess it's just default at this point. I personally couldn't give a shit who they slept with, how many men they've slept with, or anything else. If they're enjoying themselves, fill their boots as far as I'm concerned."

"What about Macbeth?" I asked, noticing him wandering around the room.

"What about him?"

"Does he have a girlfriend?"

"If he does, he's keeping her quiet. Ever since he was replaced by Dante, he's enjoyed his status in the club with none of the responsibilities. Son of the leader gives him a certain advantage over other members, and he knows it."

"Do you know the history there?"

"Nope," she said, popping the p. "I try to avoid Macbeth, to be honest with you. There's something about the man that has always given me the creeps. He always looks like he's sizing you up for his next meal."

"I get what you mean."

She leaned forward and lowered her tone. "Between you and me, everyone always says Dante is the scary one. And whilst that's true, there's something about Macbeth that's scary in an entirely different way. At least with Dante, he doesn't hide it. The man is dangerous, but you'll see him coming. Macbeth will hide in the shadows, and he'll strike when you least expect it. Stay friendly with him but do what you can to avoid him. You'll thank me in the future, I promise you."

Chapter 40

Rachel

I sat on the barstool, watching Dante as he did clean up duties. My eyes felt heavy, but I didn't want the night to end.

He had been so lovely tonight; I was scared to go to sleep and wake up tomorrow and have him be the moody, sullen man I had come to know.

I watched him throughout the night, noticing that he had never taken his eyes off me for long. He watched as I flirted with some of the crew, a dangerous spark in his eye – a spark that told me my punishment would be coming.

I had watched him as he danced with Bee, when he argued with Macbeth, and when he had been roped into playing limbo. He soon tapped out of that one when the frame went too low, and tagged me in. The other members had teased him, but he had grabbed my waist and pulled me in for a kiss, saying we were a team, and I was allowed to take over.

I had kept my eyes locked on him as I dropped to my knees and threw my back to the floor, slinking under the bar that two of the women had been holding. I cleared it easily, and when I got back up, I made sure to do so by rubbing up against his body. Bee had whooped her approval, and Dante had growled teasing threats in my ear.

I was conscious of the eyes on us, and so I pulled back first, earning a playful "coward" hissed into my neck.

And then, before I knew it, hours had passed, and people were slowly leaving. Some had to be carried out, some went singing down the street, and Vienna carried Shark on his back, with Shark pretending to be an airplane, saying I could ride him out of there anytime. I had just laughed and slapped his ass, telling Vienna to get him away from me.

Jenna had kissed my cheek as she left, telling me it was the best night she had had in a long time, and we needed to go and sin sometime soon. Dante had given us a weird look, but she had just winked at me and begun chasing Vienna down the street, telling him to put her man down. Vienna had called himself a ninja turtle, and Shark had started shooting pretend laser beams at Jenna.

I smiled as I watched them, feeling a sense of peace settle over me.

For once, I finally felt as though I was accepted – and not just because Dante said I belonged to him. I felt as though these people understood me. They didn't judge me. They didn't care what I had done in the past. The future was all that mattered.

"Are you going to stare at me all night, or are you planning on helping?" Dante teased, pulling me out of my thoughts.

I crossed one leg over the other and leant back against the bar. "I dunno. It's a pretty good view from where I'm sitting." I bit my lip as he bent low to pick up a broken glass. "Why would I want to give up this to help tidy? Doesn't seem enticing enough."

"No?" He said as he straightened. "What would be enticing enough?" He asked as he slowly prowled over to me.

"You're the one wanting me to move," I said, swallowing the lump as my mouth suddenly dried. My legs opened automatically, and Dante stood between them, looking down at me with an unreadable glint in his eyes. "You'd have to make me a pretty good offer."

"You don't want to move?" He breathed against my mouth.

"Uh-uh," I shook my head.

He grabbed the back of my thighs and pulled me down the stool until my ass was hanging off the edge. "How about now? Is this a better position for you?"

"Maybe."

"Just maybe?"

I nodded, and he grinned at me. "Seems pretty good from where I'm standing. It could be better, though."

"Oh?" I said, feeling suddenly breathless.

"Mmm." he reached into his back pocket and pulled out a pocketknife. He brought it between our bodies and flicked the blade out, causing me to gasp slightly. He gently ran the blade over my jaw and down my neck, pausing slightly at my frantically beating pulse.

"I think," he said, his voice heavy. "Removing this would make the view much, much better." And without waiting for approval, he ran the knife down my chest, letting the blade leave a red mark as he gently pressed it into my skin and hooked it under the straps of my top. With one flex of his arm, he sliced through the flimsy material. I spread my arms out along the bar to hold me in place, unable to take my eyes off the blade as he ran it down my stomach and inched it under the hem of my top. With a mischievous grin, he stabbed it through the top and sliced it up the middle.

I gasped again, the cool metal of the blade running along my stomach. The two pieces of material fell apart, leaving me bare for his hungry gaze. I wasn't wearing a bra, and my nipples instantly hardened. He brought the knife under my left breast and ran it along the curve of my body before circling my nipple with it and then delivered the same treatment to the other.

My chest began to heave as I watched, my throat becoming painfully dry. I swallowed heavily, unable to deny the throbbing between my legs as he continued to tease me with the knife.

He quickly glanced at me, locking eyes with my own, and seeing nothing but trust and arousal there, he shot me a smile that promised so much, and brought the knife to the middle of my chest and ran it down my stomach, digging in hard enough to have me wincing.

He ran it back up my stomach and my head rolled back as his other hand came up to squeeze one of my nipples, rolling it between his fingers.

I looked up when he stopped and saw the knife was now between his teeth, and his hands were sliding down my body. He popped open the button of my leather trousers and then slid his hands to my ass, lifting me off the seat. He pulled the trousers over the curve of my ass and then lifted my legs to his stomach, holding them high in the air as he pulled the trousers off me, leaving me in nothing but a red lacy thong.

He shuffled closer, leaving my legs over his shoulders. He looked down at me, his eyes half closed, his breathing heavy, and pulled the knife from his mouth.

I held my breath as he placed a kiss on my inner ankle, and then ran the knife down my bare leg, over my thigh, and up to my hip before bringing it back down again and repeating on the other side.

I squirmed in my seat, feeling the dampness pool between my legs, as he pressed the knife to my skin and ran it up the inside of my legs, coming dangerously to my pussy lips, making my clit throb in response.

He watched my face as he pressed the knife into my inner thigh, a feral look coming over him as I began to pant, the pain bringing an unexpected pleasure.

I brought my feet to his shoulders and let my knees fall apart, opening myself for him. He drew in a sharp breath as he saw my glistening pussy bare for his gaze.

"You're so wet for me," he said, running the knife up and down my inner thigh, leaving red welts as he did so. "Is this all for me, Rachel, or did flirting with my friends already get you going?"

I didn't say anything, but I tried to thrust my hips up at him, digging my feet into his shoulders. "I think you liked flirting with them. You liked watching me, to see me growing angry. You liked the thought that I'd deliver a punishment to you, didn't you?" He asked, and brought the knife to my pussy, scraping the tip of the blade along my pussy lips. My clit throbbed harder, aching to be touched.

The knife became slick with my arousal as he ran it around the outside of my pussy, pressing down gently to slightly spread my pussy lips before removing it again.

"Fuck, Dante," I whispered, my eyes rolling back as another wave of arousal rolled through me, forming into a knot at the pit of my stomach.

There was something so fucking sexy about this dangerous man brandishing a deadly weapon near me. Something that could bring about such pain, and he was using it to deliver a pleasure I hadn't experienced before.

I knew one wrong move, one smart comment, and he could use the knife to bring more pain, and a messed-up part of me wanted it. I wanted to see how far I could push him.

He laid the knife flat against my pussy, the sharp edge of the blade resting against one of my pussy lips, and pressed down, the cool of the metal hitting my clit. I hissed between my teeth, my back arching.

"You didn't answer me," he murmured, running the knife up my body again. I was bent in double as he leant forwards, capturing my lower lip between his teeth, the blade of the knife pressed into the smooth skin of my stomach. "Did you like flirting with my friends?"

"Yes," I whispered.

"Tell me what you were thinking."

He brought the knife up to my throat and ran it along my jaw at the same time as his other hand found its way between my legs, running up and down the length of my slit.

"I was thinking of you," I admitted. "I wanted you to be jealous." He pushed two fingers inside me and covered my mouth with his own, smothering the scream that had been ready to break free.

His fingers pumped in and out of me, the knife still resting against my jaw, digging further and further into my skin.

"I was jealous," he whispered against my lips. "I wanted to rip every man there apart. I wanted to grab hold of you and fuck you in front of everyone. I wanted my cock so deep inside you, to have you screaming my name in front of my entire club. I was jealous. I wanted to rip you apart."

I couldn't reply as his fingers picked up the pace, and a small drop of blood spilled from under the knife. I tensed, my pussy gripping his fingers as my own fingers dug into the wood of the bar. He removed the knife and laid it on my stomach as his mouth came to lick the tiny wound on my neck. He flattened his tongue and ran it along the cut, cleaning away the blood and licked his way up to my ear, swirling his tongue around it, taking the bottom of it into his ear and bit down, pulling it between his teeth.

"I saw you get more teasing, stroking Vienna's arm, or dancing with Monster, grinding your ass against him. You looked at me all the time, challenging me to do something about it. Did it make your pussy wet, thinking about all the ways I would punish you?" My hand left the bar and gripped onto his forearm as his fingers curled inside me, finding that one spot that drove me wild.

The pressure built, and all I could do was hold on as he fucked me with his fingers. "Do you know what held me back?" He whispered. "It was knowing that you would be in my arms tonight. That every man at the party wanted you, and yet it was me on your mind whenever you were near them. It's my name on your lips, it's me that has you coming and screaming. You belong to me, no matter who else wants you."

A guttural moan left my throat as the building orgasm climbed higher and higher. Dante brought a hand to my throat and squeezed, cutting off any air and all I could do was arch into him further, wanting more of what he offered.

"Say it, Rachel," he challenged, biting down on my lower lip.

I shook my head, and his fingers slowed, but his hold on my throat tightened. I tried to scream, but his hand prevented me. I gripped the bar harder as I tried to thrust against him, my legs bouncing against his chest as I tried to bring some movement back.

"Please, Dante," I breathed.

"Fuck," he whispered. "I love hearing you beg, but that's not what I asked."

"Dante…"

"Who do you belong to, Rachel?"

His fingers completely left me, and I almost cried with frustration, and then he slammed them back inside me, so deep his knuckle was resting against my entrance. I managed a scream then, my head flying back, my legs beginning to shake. He slammed his fingers in and out of me, making the stool shake with the force of it.

"Who?" He repeated, his jaw tense.

"You," I gasped. He gentled the hold on my throat, and I drew in grateful breaths. "I belong to you. Fuck me, Dante, oh God, fuck me."

His mouth came down on mine with an animalistic groan, his fingers curling inside me again. His tongue danced with mine and I screamed into his mouth as I sat on the edge of orgasm, waiting to tumble down into oblivion.

"Your greedy cunt is gripping my fingers so hard," he grunted against my lips. "You're so desperate to cum for me, aren't you, kitten?" I nodded frantically, unable to do anything else.

"I want you to cum for me, Rachel. I want to feel your cum on my fingers. I want your pussy soaking for when I slide my cock into you."

His filthy words sent me over the edge, and my head dropped back to lay against the bar as my release came. My legs shook so hard, Dante had to hold them with one arm as his other continued pumping his fingers in and out of me, wringing every last bit of pleasure from me that he could.

My chest heaved, and my mouth fell open in a silent scream as my entire body convulsed, my release dripping out of me and running down my ass to pool on the chair.

Dante pulled his fingers out of me and wrestled with the button on his trousers, his cock springing free the minute the button popped open. He grabbed me under my arms and hauled me up, my legs automatically wrapping around his waist.

He fisted the base of his cock and held it against my pussy, pushing the head past my lips. "I will never let you go," he warned as he thrust inside me in one smooth movement. His hands gripped my ass, pulling me into him. I locked my legs behind his back and whispered back; "fuck me, Dante. Fuck me so hard I'll never want to leave. Make me yours."

I gripped the back of his head as a roar left his throat, and his fingers tightened on my ass, lifting me up onto his cock and slamming me down with a force that both shocked and delighted me.

"More," I whispered, my pussy tensing around him. His hand left my ass to swipe at the table, knocking all the glass bottles to the floor as he laid me on it, grabbing my legs at the ankles and spread them wide. I rested them over his arm as he fucked me harder, his balls slapping against my pussy.

"You're so fucking tight," he groaned. "I will never get enough of feeling this pussy strangling my cock."

The table legs shook and creaked beneath us as he picked up the pace even further. I reached up to play with my tits, pulling on my nipples, knowing he was watching. His breathing increased as I lowered one hand between our bodies and spread open my pussy lips, circling my clit.

"Fuck, Dante," I breathed, squeezing my tit, my fingers digging in sharply. "Please, please, please," I whispered over and over. "I'm so close."

He pulled out of me and flipped me over, my tits resting against the table, and slammed back into me, fisting my hair and pulling my head back. "Cum for me," he growled down my ear. "Coat my cock in your pussy juice. I want to hear you scream my name as I pound into this tight pussy of yours."

He got his wish. My back arched, and I screamed until my throat was hoarse, my pussy contracting wildly as my orgasm flooded out of me, soaking his cock. "You're such a good girl," he grunted, placing his hand on my lower back, bending me back even further as he slammed his cock into me a few more times and then, with the sexiest moan I've ever heard, he released inside me. "Fuck, Rachel," he breathed, bending over to bite down on my shoulder.

My body spasmed beneath him, my legs shaking still.

"That was amazing," I breathed, and he laughed as he slapped my ass.

"That was only round one," he said, his cock hardening once more inside me.

I grinned to myself. *Maybe being punished wasn't so bad after all.*

Chapter 41

Rachel

The next two weeks flew by, with Dante and I settling down into a routine with an ease that took us both by surprise.

I would spend breakfast with his family, sometimes making small talk, sometimes not. His dad was easy to get along with, and I enjoyed the meals more when he was around. But most times, it was just me, Bee, his mother, and Macbeth.

I caught Macbeth throwing suspicious, almost nasty glances at me when he thought I wasn't looking, but I shrugged it off, deciding I'd deal with whatever his problem was if and when it became something serious.

He was probably still pissed that I had kicked off when he grabbed my arm, and I couldn't find it in me to be bothered about that. He needed to learn that he couldn't manhandle me. I put up with enough of that from Dante; I didn't need it from his brother too. Still... It made me uneasy when I saw the nasty glint in his eyes.

I didn't want to mention it to Dante and ruin the little bit of peace we had found. Jenna's words played in my ear, and I resolved to keep a closer eye on Macbeth. He might think he could sneak around, but I was smarter than that. I'd see him coming, no matter what the attack was.

I spent my days with Bee. In the morning, I would continue her homeschooling, going over the basics so I could assess her levels, strengths, and weaknesses. During the afternoon, we went around the village and volunteered at the numerous businesses that were around. It was important to me that Bee had social interaction outside of the clubhouse, and I wanted her to experience firsthand what hard work looked like.

Big Mama had more or less resigned herself to the fact that I was staying – at least for the time being. I hadn't thought about leaving since the night of the party. It was comfortable here, especially when Dante and I were getting along. So I stayed civil with her, and she stayed civil with me, and we settled into a truce of sorts. She had even given up homeschooling Bee and told me she was happy for me to completely take over. She had handed me all the schoolwork, and we had spent a rather pleasant evening with a bottle of wine, going over the plans for the rest of the school year. As much as I hated to praise anything Big Mama had done, she had been excellent with Bee's schooling. There were only one or two areas I wanted to work on, otherwise she was more or less where she should be for her age. Mama was strict, but she was thorough, and Bee wasn't being left behind. Mama had even tried to make the work more fun and had thrown me a nasty side eye when I told her I hadn't even realised she knew what that word meant. We laughed it off, and a line was drawn in the sand. It was an unstable truce, but for Bee's sake, and for her happiness, Mama and I kept things civil.

I had told Dante that I wanted more for Bee's future than to simply wind up as someone's old lady, and he agreed, saying that he wanted Bee to feel as though the world was hers to conquer, and there wasn't anything she couldn't do.

Dante would sometimes join us in the afternoon, his eyes always on me as he watched me work. On the days he wasn't there, I was always scanning for him, earning me more than a few teases from the local women.

I had spent a lot of time with Shark, Vienna, and Hacksaw these past two weeks as well. Dante had told me those men would be his right-hand men, and I was actually comforted by that. They were borderline insane, but they were always there whenever Dante needed them. They knew when it was business, and they knew when it was playtime.

Vienna was my favourite, and if Dante wasn't around, I found myself seeking him out. He made me feel safe. Even when he was acting the fool, you could see the sharpness in his eyes. He knew what was going off around him at all times. His senses were always heightened, and he was always aware. He just liked you to believe otherwise. Vienna made me relaxed, and Dante encouraged me to stay near him.

But then again, the entire club was always on high alert. I was suspicious about why they always seemed to think danger was on the horizon, but I didn't pry. I was enjoying myself too much to get drawn into the drama.

Oftentimes, the members of the club would have me laughing until my sides hurt. And Jenna had been right. It was particularly funny watching Vienna try to do the bookkeeping with Imogen. I had almost wet myself laughing when she grabbed every receipt from the office and tipped them over his head. He had flipped the desk up and laid down, making "receipt angels", as he had called them. Imogen had called him immature. He said she was a ball buster. She had dropped the box that had contained the receipts onto his dick and asked how that was for ball busting. They had both come flying out of the office, each speaking at the same time as they tried to recruit people onto their side.

Vienna had approached me and stroked his beard down my face, reminding me that we had hair growth in common. When I told him I was siding with Imogen, he had stormed off mumbling something about a power imbalance, and he was sick of the disrespect around these parts. Imogen had called him a bitch, and had stormed back to us, grabbed her around her waist and dragged her off, saying it was time the men took back the power, and we women were getting ahead of ourselves. Imogen took it in high spirits, and had laughed along with us, playfully threatening to chop off Vienna's beard whilst he slept.

Dante would join me in my bed every night. He sometimes arrived before dinner, enjoying his meal with his family. But oftentimes, he arrived in the wee hours of the morning. He always took a shower before joining me in bed, but not even that took away the metallic stench of blood that clung to him.

I refused to comment, preferring not to know what he got up to. I knew it would lead to an argument about putting himself in danger. He would accuse me of trying to control him. I knew exactly how it would go, and I couldn't find the energy to care enough to light the spark. He was a biker, through and through. I had come to accept that being part of this club had certain… responsibilities. I had already been told about the Rough Riders and the semi-war they were in. I preferred not to know the ins and outs by prying. Dante would tell me if it was important. Jenna had filled me in on the basics, but even she admitted she didn't know the ins and outs. If Jenna was unconcerned, then so was I. She had been here much longer than me, and she said the men would let us know if we were truly in danger, as the club would be placed in lockdown, and the women and children would be sent to church to keep safe. That hadn't happened, so Dante must not see an immediate threat coming.

In fact, Dante had been that relaxed, that for the first week, he tried to spend more time with me and Bee, taking us out for evening meals, or joining us at the park. His thoughts weren't on war or the Rough Riders. He made a true effort to put the club second, just long enough for me to settle in. I knew it wouldn't last forever, and that the club was always his priority, but I appreciated the effort.

He fucked me every night without fail, and I would often wake up in the night to find him reaching for me once more. I gave in every time. Sometimes I would put up a fight, loving the thrill of his threats and anger. He knew I would submit as much as I knew it, but he played along, reeling me back in as I ran.

But then I'd find him gone in the morning, and as the days went by, I found my curiosity growing.

By the end of the second week, there was an undeniable tension growing. Gone was the ease of the first week, and in its place was an atmosphere I couldn't quite decipher.

Macbeth was acting out. Dante was growing cold, with a furious anger simmering under the surface, and he started staying out later and later. He stopped spending time with me and Bee during the day, and he was often snappy whenever I tried to speak to him.

I laid in bed, glancing at the clock, seeing it was past two in the morning, and I couldn't hold back anymore. I was more than curious at this stage. I was growing angry with his secrecy, with his assumptions that I'd welcome him with open arms night after night when he left me alone the majority of the time. He was making me feel like a nagging housewife, and I didn't appreciate being thrust into that role.

So, with a determination that had me gritting my jaw, I kicked off the covers, threw on some clothes, and crept out of the house, determined to track him down.

He wasn't hard to find. He didn't like being away from club territory at night, not when Bee was at home sleeping soundly. He didn't trust his enemies not to strike in the dead of the night, and so he was always around, just in case.

Which made the process of elimination easy for me, and as soon as I saw lights under the garage, I knew that's where he was.

The rest of the community was dead, with only the odd light on in someone's home. Which was strange in itself, because there was always life after dark. These people were night owls, and yet it seemed as though there was a sort of mini lockdown taking place, just like Jenna had warned me about.

Feeling like a thief in the night, I stuck to the shadows as I moved towards the garage, my body growing tenser with every passing step.

As I walked up the pathway, I heard the undeniable sound of flesh hitting flesh. I paused, my heart in my throat.

There's no fucking way.

I felt sick as I imagined him in there with another woman. The sounds of wet flesh hitting wet flesh almost had me convinced until I heard the moan of another man. The moan was bordering on an anguished wail, followed by the laughter of other men.

What the actual fuck.

I clenched my fists and marched forward.

He left me alone to go play the bully with his stupid fucking friends?

I grabbed the bottom of the garage door and hauled it open, my eyes finding Dante straight away. I shot daggers at him, a spew of nasty words dying on my lips as I looked at the shocked, panicked look on his face. My eyes flew to Vienna, Shark and Hacksaw, all of whom looked as shocked and horrified as Dante did.

My heart skipped a beat at the look on Vienna's face in particular. Vienna was always chill and relaxed. If he was nervous, then something was seriously fucking wrong.

"What…" I began, only to be cut off as a pained moan had my head flying to the side, and my mouth fell open at what I saw. I stumbled backwards, the vomit rising up my throat.

"Ben?" I whispered, my entire body being overtaken by nervous shakes. He might be bloody, his face might be swollen, his body black and blue, but I recognised him. How could I not? That body had violated my own so many times. I would know him anywhere.

Ben turned his head and locked eyes with me, his own widening with surprise. "Please," he begged, blood bubbling from his mouth.

I froze for a split second before I turned on my heel and ran.

Chapter 42

Rachel

My chest heaved as I ran, determined to put as much distance between those monsters and myself as possible. I had dreamt many times of what I would do if I ever saw Ben again, and they always ended with me ending his life the same way I ended Alex's. But seeing him unexpectedly brought back my fight-or-flight instincts, and for the first time since I was a teenager, my instinct was to flight.

My training was gone. I couldn't even withdraw into myself and pretend I didn't care. Every hideous memory of what Alex and Ben had done to me came flooding back in an overwhelming wave. And with that came all the shame, humiliation and pain I had felt all those years ago.

I ran, because I didn't know what else to do. Ben wasn't supposed to be here. This was supposed to be my home. My safe place.

One look at that man had shattered that for me.

I heard the shouts of Dante and the men behind me, as they called for me to come back, and I pushed my legs, pumping them up and down as fast as I could, yet willing them to go faster still. I tried to hold my breath, not wanting my breathy pants to give my location away, but it served no use. It made me gasp in desperate, grateful gulps, my lungs burning with the effort.

I rounded a corner, forgetting which direction was the clubhouse, and hid in the shadows, clamping a hand over my mouth to smother the sobs threatening to erupt.

Heavy boots thundered past, and I shrank further back against the wall, seeing Vienna's face illuminated in the moonlight.

Don't find me, don't find me, don't find me.

It wasn't that I was scared of them. I was horrified at first, but that horror was soon turning to anger. They had no right to sneak behind my back. I couldn't give a fuck what happened to Ben. I cared about being kept in the dark.

Had I had a warning, I wouldn't have gone to the garage. I wouldn't have come face to face with a man who had haunted my dreams for so long. I prayed for the day Ben got his comeuppance, but I should have been warned so that I could prepare.

Seeing him unexpectedly brought back a rush of memories, and I just knew that sick bastard took pleasure in the fact that he was still able to reduce me to tears.

The look on Dante's face when I first opened that door also terrified me. He didn't look like himself – which I could sort of understand. He was hardly going to be smiling and high fiving a paedophile, but I also hadn't expected him to look so… vicious. There was almost a sadistic, perverse hunger on his face, as though the sight of Ben with his skin ripped off and broken bones turned him on.

I waited a few minutes, my ears straining for footsteps, and when I felt sure I was safe, I snuck back onto the street, looking for somewhere I recognised that would guide me back home.

There was only one place I was going when I got there, and I'd be locking the door behind me.

It didn't take me as long as I thought to reach the clubhouse, and I made the deliberate decision to use the back door, the one closest to the safe, and dialled in the combination.

Macbeth had given me the code during my first week here. He never explained why, other than to say, "you'll need it one day, you'll see." And the fucker was right.

I thought it would be because of the Rough Riders. But I was wrong. I needed protection from the man who was laying at my side night after night.

Dante was dangerous. I had always known it. But tonight solidified that in my mind. I had heard rumours of what he had done to people in the past – both men and women. And I had witnessed myself how cruel he could be when he didn't get his own way. But this was the first time I saw the level of violence with my own eyes, and I wasn't facing him again without protection.

I crept up to my room, looking behind me as I opened the door, and almost fainted as I turned back around, and my body collided with a mountain of sheer muscle.

"Dante," I breathed, taking a step backwards, swiping my hands behind my back so he couldn't see what I was holding.

"Were you expecting somebody else?"

"I wasn't expecting anybody," I said, gritting my teeth so the tremor did not come out of my mouth.

"Well… surprise," he said dryly, narrowing his eyes, and he looked down at me. "Why do you look fucking petrified?"

"I'm not," I said quickly, schooling my features back to the blank, neutral position I had hid behind for so long.

"Don't you fucking dare," he snarled, grabbing my arm and hauled me into the room, kicking the door shut behind him. "Don't you fucking dare hide behind expressionless robot mode. Aren't we past that?"

"Are we?"

"I thought we were."

"You thought wrong." Relief flooded my body as the familiar heat shot through me, my anger finally catching up with what had happened, and fought its way to the forefront of my mind. "You had a couple of dinners with me and shared my bed for a while. So have a lot of men. I trust them as much as I trust you."

"The difference between me and those other men," he said in a voice that made my blood run cold. "Was that I was in your bed because you wanted me. We shared something consensual. Don't fucking compare me to those bastards."

"Well…," I began, only to clamp my mouth shut at the vicious look on Dante's face.

"So help me God, if you finish that sentence."

"I'm not here by choice though, am I? You said it yourself. You're all I've got. It's you, or the streets. I made the best of bad options."

It almost didn't feel like me talking. My mouth had a mind of its own, and as much as I willed it to shut up, the need to lash out and hurt people was so ingrained in me, I couldn't stop it even if I tried.

I saw the relationship we had built the past two weeks crumble before my eyes, and there was nothing I could do to repair it. The foundation had been ripped out, and it didn't take long for the rest of it to come crashing down.

"Don't put me in the role of being your armed guard. You could have left at any time."

"With no money? No contacts? No family?"

"My card is saved on your phone. And don't act like you need anyone, Rachel. You made a life in America without knowing a soul. When will you start telling the truth? Lie to me all you want; I see right through you, anyway. But it's about time you stopped lying to yourself."

"What's that supposed to mean?"

"You're a survivor. You just like to play the victim. You won't admit you want to be here, that you *like* it here, so you thrust me into the role of the bastard kidnapper holding you hostage."

"You did kidnap me! And burnt my mother's house down when I tried to leave!"

"And have I not given you anything but freedom since? I have given you bikes, money, resources. You could have escaped. You chose not to!"

"That's not true." I shook my head, scowling at him.

"Oh, but it is. Even in bed, you prefer to fight me. I can smell your arousal the second I walk into the room. But you would prefer to fight me, to pretend that you're not gagging for it just as much as I am. You want to justify your surrender by saying you were forced into it, that I wore you down. The truth is, Rachel, this is how you get your kicks. It's a weird kink of yours. You want to be a victim so bad, that you'll make up this narrative in your head of a bad guy and the damsel in distress." He reached out to grab a lock of my hair, twisting it around his fingers. "I've indulged you because you play the role so well. That flicker of fear in your eyes makes my cock harder than I can ever remember. The tremors in your body as I bring my mouth to your skin and mark it as mine is enough to make me cum on the spot."

I closed my eyes as he spoke, the heat building in my stomach.

No! Do not give in like this.

I opened my eyes and saw the blood on his knuckles.

Ben's blood.

I pushed his hand away and brought my other hand out from behind his back and aimed the gun at him.

He let out a bark of laughter. "Are you fucking kidding me? What are you going to do, Rachel? Shoot me?"

I grasped the gun with both hands, my arms straight, aiming it at his chest. "Look at my hands, Dante. Do you see those precious tremors of yours now? Do you see your kinky fear in my eyes? You see nothing. I'm steady as a rock. I've killed before, and I'll happily do it again."

"So do it," he said, taking a step forward until the gun was pressed against his chest. "Pull the trigger, Rachel. Kill me. It won't solve anything."

"Stop talking!" I hissed at him, gripping the gun tighter.

"You'll run from here and settle back into the role as perfect Stepford wife material. But your body and soul will crave this. You will crave more than the quiet, drama free existence. You're not happy being boxed into a corner. You want to break the rules and to push boundaries. So you'll seek out another man. And he won't be able to handle you. You'll destroy him, and the next, and the next, because they're not me. The sooner you realise we're fucking perfect for each other, the sooner you stop fighting and understand we're both just the right amount of fucked up to make this work, the happier we'll both be."

My toes curled as the anger in me ramped up a notch. But I was beginning to realise, I was more angry about the fact that he was right. I had never met a man who had been able to keep up with me. A man who liked that I spat fire at him. Who encouraged me to reveal the worst I had to offer and loved it anyway.

"Fuck you," I hissed at him.

"Gladly," he grinned an evil grin, and then his hands shout out, grabbing my elbow and bending it backwards. I screamed, dropping the gun, my elbow feeling as though it was about to break in two. He bent low, one hand still gripping my skin in a vice and retrieved the gun from the floor, placing it against my temples.

I closed my eyes as the cool metal pressed into my skin, swallowing the lump of fear.

"Threaten me again, Rachel, and I won't hesitate."

"So do it."

He stroked the gun down my face and ran it over my lips. I opened my mouth to tell him he was sick, but the minute he saw the opening, he pushed the gun past my lips and cocked the trigger.

I froze, my entire body growing stiff. I looked at Dante, and at that moment, I hated myself more than ever.

Because despite being scared out of my wits, I liked it.

What the fuck did that say about me?

Why was I feeling my nipples harden? Why was I feeling heat between my legs, and a throbbing in all the places I shouldn't be throbbing?

What was wrong with me, that something like *this* would turn me on?

"Ahh, that's one way to shut you up," he smirked, his eyes raking up and down my body. He sucked in a sharp breath and stepped closer to me, his hardening cock pressing against my stomach.

"Jesus," he said in my ear with a breathy laugh. "Your nipples are rock hard. Do you like this, Rachel? Does it satisfy your victim's kink enough to get you going?"

I shook my head, clenching my thighs together as he ground his hips against me.

"You're a little liar. You're shaking. And once again, it's not because you're scared. It's the thrill of what's to come next. Admit it," he said, licking my lips before giving me a deep kiss. "Admit you're not angry because of what you saw in the garage. You're angry because you liked it. You ran, because the fucked-up part of your brain loved it. Admit that your pussy is fucking soaked right now. We all have kinks, Rachel, and you get off on being scared. If there's a note of fear, you're off like a bitch in heat."

To prove his point, he brought his hands to the front of my trousers and fingered the waistband. "Admit it, or do I have to prove it for myself?"

I said nothing, the stubborn streak in me refusing to give him the satisfaction.

He grinned and pushed his hand into my trousers and in between my legs. His fingers ran along my slit, instantly becoming slick and sliding against me with ease as they got coated in my arousal.

I closed my eyes, a wave of shame washing over me.

But that came second to the tsunami flood of arousal as Dante stroked along my pussy lips, the gun still deep in my mouth.

He pulled his fingers out of me at the same time he pulled the gun from my mouth. He tossed it onto the bed and brought his fingers to my mouth, covering my lips in my wetness.

I pulled my head back and scowled at him. "You're a cruel fucking bastard."

"For telling the truth?" he smirked.

"You know what for. You're cruel, you're vindictive, you're—"

"You're deluded," he interrupted, advancing on me, forcing me to back up until my body hit the wall behind us. He pinned me to the wall with his body, his hands coming up to rest on the wall on either side of my head as he lowered his voice to speak in a low, menacing voice. "You've been reading too many romances. I'm not the hero from those books, and you're certainly not the heroine. We don't belong on those pages. You and I belong in a world of our own. We're not bound by the rules of a chick flick. You're ashamed that you're turned on, without realising that you pointing that gun at me was the sexiest fucking thing I've ever seen. I have no problem admitting it. I don't give a fuck if the rest of the world doesn't understand. I'm not asking them to play with me. I want you to understand. I want you to play our game. Free yourself, Rachel, and stop being ashamed because the world has shamed you for your preferences."

"I don't want this," I told him, the words sounding hollow to us both.

"But you do. You're just too scared to admit it. You've had horrendous things happen to you, and now you're ashamed to admit an aspect of that horror has become a part of who you are. There's nothing to be ashamed of. You have taken control of something horrific and twisted it to become a positive part of your life. They tried to control you through fear and violence, and now you control the fear. You control the violence. They have no power anymore. Let go of the fairytales. It's not fair to you, and it's not fair to me. I will never be the hero, and if you try to put me on that pedestal, I'll fall immediately. A hero will always do the right thing. A hero would sacrifice everything, including his own happiness, for the greater good. I'm not that man. I'm selfish. I put myself first, and I won't ever pretend otherwise. I'm cruel and vindictive. But if you give me the chance, I will treat you as an equal. I will be selfish for you. I will be cruel and vindictive *for* you, instead of against you. Give yourself the chance to accept this life, and you'll see that I will happily set the world on fire and laugh as it burns, all for you. But also know that as the anti-romance hero, I wouldn't hesitate to throw you on the flames as a final sacrifice if ever you betrayed me."

"You're going to hell," I said, but I couldn't help the grin that played on my lips as his words echoed around my brain.

"Then I'll be following you there. Hell is where we belong, and when we get back to where we came from, we'll greet the devil as an old friend. Don't keep him waiting, Rachel. Embrace your dark side and stop letting someone else's rules dictate how you make yourself happy. We can make our own book. Fuck those trashy romances. We're made for so much more."

I looked at him through my lashes and was incapable of doing anything other than nodding.

He slipped his hands under my ass and hauled me into the air. My legs wrapped around him automatically, as they always did, our bodies fitting together perfectly.

He was right.

I was built differently.

I wasn't meant to be trapped in a perfect world, following someone else's guidelines.

I was meant to live by my own rules. I would never be controlled.

And it's about time I started accepting it.

Chapter 43

Rachel

The sun was beginning to creep through the clouds by the time Dante finally tired and closed his eyes.

My body was sore, and every part of me ached. He had fucked me in so many positions; I felt stretched and strained. I wanted nothing more than to sink down next to him and give myself to the pleasure of sleep he was experiencing.

But there was something I had to do. A final part I had to commit to in order to rid myself of the shackles confining me.

I placed a kiss on Dante's temples, and slid out of bed, creeping backwards, keeping my eyes on him. I opened the door, freezing as it creaked, but he didn't stir. He was lost in slumber.

I snuck out and pulled a hoodie over my head and pulled the hood up high.

I pulled open the garage doors and slipped beneath it. I kept my hands on the bottom and slowly lowered it, cringing at the noise it made as I removed my fingers and let it bang against the floor.

"Who's there?" Ben called, his voice strained and petrified.

I didn't answer. I just walked towards him, keeping the hood over my head as I inspected the damage Dante had inflicted.

His left eye was so swollen, he couldn't open it. His nose was bent at a grotesque angle, his lips swollen and split. As he panted through panic, I saw some of his teeth missing, and when his tongue came out to wet his lips, there were fleshy welts along it, letting me know he had bitten it more than once.

His arms were pinned above his head, the wrists bleeding and raw, with blood running down the length of his arms, some fresh, some dry. That let me know he had been here more than a few days. There were gashes along his biceps, and huge patches of skin removed in places.

His torso was black and blue, not an inch of him without a bruise. I grinned to myself, thinking he looked like a sheet of tie-dye. The marbled effect of all the bruises bleeding into each other had a sort of sickening beauty to them.

I could tell from his breathing that he had more than one cracked rib, and there was a huge slash across his stomach.

He was completely naked, and when I looked closer, I could see pins sticking out of his dick, and I cringed as I noticed one of the pins stabbed straight into the tip of him.

His legs were also black and blue, the knees bent at a weird angle, and three of his toes were missing.

"Who are you?" he spluttered.

"Oh, Ben," I said, pulling the hood down and revealing my face. "You know who I am. You knew from the minute you saw me earlier that I'd be back."

I pulled a stool and placed it in front of him and sat down, staring up at him.

"It's weird," I said with a small laugh. "You've been in so many of my nightmares over the years that it's strange to see you in person again. I built you up to be more than you are. You seemed larger than life as you haunted my dreams, as though you could reach out and crush me with your bare hands. And now… nothing." I said simply. "You're a regular man, made of flesh and blood, the same as me."

"Rachel… I'm s-sorry," he sobbed.

"Are you? Or are you sorry that Dante found you? You're sorry I managed to find someone to care for me, despite being your victim? Or are you sorry you didn't do more to ruin me? Sorry you didn't disfigure me enough?"

"Alex—"

"Oh, I know. It wasn't all you. Alex was the leader. Whatever you did to me, Alex was ten times worse. I know. I was there. But Alex has already paid for his crimes. He's dust in the ground by this point. But you," I looked up at him again. "You've been living free, benefiting from the sadistic little kingdom Alex created. You might not have been the worst abuser to *me*. Alex owns that title. But I bet you're the worst abuser to some other girl out there. I bet you've had your fair share of captives over the years."

"I sw-swear to you… I swear. We left all that b-behind when Alex—"

"Was murdered? Mm, I'm sure you did." I pushed myself up and approached him. "Except, I know that's not true. I might not have been around all these years, but I've kept an eye on you. I've looked at the news as girls went missing – and would you know it, so many of them were last seen near your haunting grounds. Isn't that strange?"

He didn't say anything. His one good eye went wide, almost pleading with me.

"Of course, I didn't know they were *your* haunting grounds. Oh, I knew you were still a part of it, but who would have thought little Ben had it in him to be a leader? And not just a leader, a pretty fucked up leader at that. How many girls have gone missing now?"

He shook his head once more.

"Once might have been a coincidence. Hell, even two. It's a bad part of town, after all. But last I counted, there were eight. Eight girls, Ben. Eight girls with families worried about them, who loved them. Eight girls who you stole from, whose future you ruined. Or did you extinguish their future completely? It doesn't matter," I said, my voice hardening.

My hand reached to the side and, with a quick look, I found the object I was searching for.

"It doesn't matter, because the eighth girl will be your last. You can't cause anyone else anymore pain." I stood on my tiptoes and brought my face close to his. "You're nothing, and you're done." I planted a hard peck to his lips and pulled back with a grin at the same time as I stabbed the knife into his stomach, into the wound Dante had already created for me, and twisted.

He screamed in agony as I twisted further, and then yanked it across his stomach, slicing him even deeper.

I pulled the knife out and pushed it back in with all the force I had in me and slashed his stomach once more.

I stepped back as his back arched in pain, widening the wound even more. He screamed until his throat was hoarse, and then his head flopped forward at the same time as his intestines spilled out of his stomach.

Dante was right.

I wasn't scared of what I had seen. I was scared that I liked it. I was scared that it made me think of all the things I could do that would be worse.

I'm not scared anymore.

I was no longer a victim. I was a protector. A protector of me, and all those other girls who had no one to protect them. I was a protector of the night, against these animals who preyed on the vulnerable.

And I fucking loved it.

Chapter 44

Rachel

Dante found me the next morning. When he woke up and found me missing, he knew where I would be.

I hadn't been able to move as Ben's life ebbed away. I curled up in the corner and watched the patch on the floor grow larger, darker, and thicker as Ben's blood pooled out.

The bigger the patch got, the harder my sobs came, until I was gasping for breath, unable to wipe my eyes quick enough as the thick blobs ran down my cheeks. My chest heaved with huge hiccupping wails until I thought the burning would never go away.

I wasn't crying because of what I had done.

I was crying as a release.

I was letting go of the girl I used to be. I had been clinging to the last strand of hope that I could go back to the innocent girl before Alex found me. But I accepted it now. She died the day I walked into the club with the recruiter and fell into Alex's trap.

I was crying for the shame I had held all these years, for actions I hadn't committed. I was crying for the other girls who weren't as lucky as me, who hadn't found their way out.

I was crying for my dad, rotting in a jail cell because evil ruled the world, and evil lived in his daughter.

I was crying for everything. I was letting it all go.

When Dante found me, I was all cried out. I just stayed on the floor, almost catatonic. He didn't say a word as he scooped me into his arms, cradling my head into his chest, blocking out Ben's lifeless body. I heard him say something, and Vienna's calm voice – the same calming voice he always had, no matter the situation. He said he would handle it, and that made me relax.

Dante and Vienna always handled it.

Weird how I could have such trust in two men I would have gutted mere weeks ago.

Dante carried me home and sat me on the bed. He dismissed Macbeth and his mother as they tried to speak to us.

He put me first.

He left me long enough to run me a bath, and then carried me to the bathroom, gently stripping me of my clothes.

He washed my hair for me, massaging shampoo and conditioner into the strands, and washed it out with such gentleness, careful to avoid my eyes. He carefully scrubbed the blood from my nails, kissing each fingertip as he did so.

He wrapped me in a fluffy towel and carried me back to bed, laying me atop the covers as he left to draw the curtains, blocking out the harsh light of day.

He kicked off his boots and climbed into bed with me, pulling me close. My head rested against his chest, hearing his steady heartbeat.

"Dante—"

"Not today, Rachel. Sleep. I'm not going anywhere." He kissed my temple and cuddled me closer, his arms tightening around me.

For once, I didn't fight. I surrendered to his commands and closed my eyes. I saw Ben behind my eyelids, lifeless and bloody. I saw Alex, laying on my parent's driveway, his neck almost severed.

I shivered, the sobs creeping up my throat again.

Dante stroked down my arms, grounding me, bringing me back to the present.

"Does it get easier?" I asked in a quiet voice.

"It's as easy as you let it be," he said calmly. "Do you actually feel guilty, or just think that's how you should feel? Are you sad because you regret it? Some people don't deserve the life they were given, and I have no guilt about taking it away from them. If you want to let guilt consume you, I can't stop you. But you didn't take another human life. You stopped a monster masquerading as a man. You ended so many people's sufferings by ridding two monsters from this earth. Don't feel guilty over an archaic law that claims every life is equal. People that prey on children deserve the darkest pits of hell, and you sent them there. Rejoice in that, and you'll find peace."

I nodded and closed my eyes, forcing Alex and Ben out of my visions. Instead, I thought of Bee. Would I feel guilty if I killed to protect her?

Absolutely not. I'd kill Dante if he ever harmed her.

So why should I feel guilty for protecting myself and the child I used to be?

"I don't know how to live with the past, Dante. Even knowing they're gone; I still feel so dirty. So unclean. The things they did to me—"

"Nothing can change the past, Rachel. And you hit the nail on the head. It was things *they* did to you. Things *they* inflicted. You didn't do a thing other than what it took to survive. You're not dirty, and you're not unclean. You are a survivor. You protected yourself, and countless other women."

"But—"

"No buts. You don't have to carry this alone. I'm here, ready to shoulder all the weight you can't handle. The past is a ghost that's been haunting you, but it doesn't define you."

"It feels so much more than a ghost, Dante. It's a sin that has marked my soul. My dad is in prison because of me. How do I just get past that?"

He tightened his arms around me. "You get past it with me. Let me share that mark on your soul. I've enough darkness in me to take it on. I've done things, Rachel, things that make your demons look like angels. Let me take all the darkness in your soul as my own. Let me take it so your light can shine through."

A peace settled within me, and I soon found myself slipping off into a settled, peaceful sleep. A sleep where I was not haunted by monstrous demons. Now I'm the demon haunting those that are remaining.

And I'd be coming for them.

And I'd have Dante by my side.

Chapter 45

Rachel

I tried.

I really tried to slip back into the routine with Dante. But there was an edge to all our interactions now.

I couldn't get over him hiding Ben here. Knowing he had been here for the past two weeks. I'd been in the office area of that garage. He'll have heard my voice, maybe even seen me as I passed by the doors leading to the workroom. I'd walked past numerous times. I had drawn hopscotch on the floor with Bee outside. And all the while, he was in there.

I understood he was trying to protect me, but I wasn't a child. He had never known the Rachel that was abused. He knew me as I was now, and I had never given him the impression that I wasn't more than capable of handling myself.

All our conversations were stilted now. We went from arguing all day, every day, to making polite chit-chat about the weather. Even Bee had commented saying we were acting weird, and she didn't want to be around us anymore discussing the miles of the wind speed.

Even our sex life had taken a nose-dive, to the point where in the week since I had killed Ben, Dante hadn't even bothered to come to my room.

He was holding back on me, just as much as I was holding back on him. But since neither of us spoke about it, nothing was getting resolved, and the distance between us was growing wider with every passing day.

"Penny for them?"

I looked up with a start and gave Macbeth a small smile as he sat down next to me. He had been friendlier since Ben-gate, which was something else I found suspicious.

I was living in a state of paranoia, constantly thinking the worst of people.

"Do people still carry pennies?" I asked Macbeth.

"If you find one on the floor, you should carry it with you all day."

"What?"

"You know the saying: Find a penny, pick it up…"

"With my luck, the penny will be covered in nuclear dust, and I'll die a painful death."

"The phrase is "All day long, you'll have good luck", not all life. Don't be greedy," he nudged me with his shoulder. "What's on your mind?"

"Do you actually care?"

"Mild curiosity at best," he said, grinning at me. I couldn't help but grin back.

"At least you're honest. Unlike your brother."

"If I had a hundred guesses, I would never have guessed it was Dante on your mind," he muttered sarcastically.

"Is it that obvious?"

"That the pair of you are miserable as sin? Yes. It's annoying, actually. I'm all for annoying Dante, but not in this mood. I don't have a death wish. So if you two could patch things up, I can resume my brotherly duties."

"Isn't it the younger brother that's supposed to be the annoying one?"

"You're telling me Dante isn't annoying?"

"Ha! Touche."

"Besides, he stole my role. I don't see why I can't steal his."

"Would you have liked to have been a leader?" I asked, narrowing my eyes at him as I considered his position in the club. It had never really occurred to me that he might be bothered by Dante taking over what should have been his. Macbeth just seemed to roll with the punches, nothing ever bothering him.

"It would have been nice to have been considered."

"Why did Dante come before you?"

"I guess Dante proved himself more than I did. But maybe they underestimated me. No-one ever really knows what someone is capable of."

"What do you mean?" I asked, a weird feeling shooting through me at the dark look that flashed in his eyes.

"Well, look at you, for example. Before you dyed your hair, I'd have pegged you for a dumb blonde that didn't know the difference between her left and right. Now, you're one more murder away from being a serial killer."

"Call me that again, and you'll be the third."

"Keep talking like that, Rachel. It's like nectar to my dick."

I burst out laughing. "You and your brother are more alike than you think."

"Hey," he scowled. "Don't compare me to him. I'd never betray the ones I'm supposed to love."

"Who has Dante betrayed?"

He looked at me like I was thick. "You."

"Me?!"

"Look, I didn't want to be the one to tell you this, but..." He bit down on his lower lip, looking nervous. He scanned the area and shuffled closer to me, lowering his voice as he spoke. "Why do you think Dante didn't kill Ben?"

"He said he was gathering info."

"But why do *you* think he didn't kill him? Ignore what Dante said. What do you think?"

"I... I don't know," I sighed. "A part of me wished he had."

"Ask yourself another question: How long does it take to gather info? Think about it, Rachel. You told Dante about Alex and Ben, and he managed to track down where the club was, infiltrate it, and kidnap Ben within a few days. We live in the age of technology. It doesn't take two weeks to get the names of Ben's friends."

"What are you saying?"

He sighed heavily, a pained look on his face. "I like you, Rachel, but you don't belong here. You might think you're tainted and corrupt, but you don't know the half of it. How do you think we got this village? An entire abandoned village waiting for us to move in to? Yeah, right. I know that's the story Dante likes to tell, but that's not what happened. A lot of blood was shed to take over here, and there are a lot of angry souls haunting these grounds. Dante is a clever man. If he wants something, he gets it, just like our grandad got these grounds. Dante learnt from the best. Maybe I'm wrong, though. Maybe Dante wanted to play the hero. Maybe he was waiting for the right time to show you what your big, strong hero had done for you."

I stayed silent, mulling over his words.

"Did you know Dante plans to expand?"

"Sorry?" I frowned, confused at the change of topic.

"He wants to expand."

"I assumed that was a possibility."

"You're not listening to me, Rachel."

"Well, stop speaking in fucking riddles, then!"

"What did I just say? Dante learnt from the best. There wasn't an abandoned village. There was a village that was stolen. And, flash forward to present day, now there's a club up for the taking, with a leadership vacuum taking place."

"You think Dante wants the club?"

"Are you kidding me? Having a branch of the Devil's Disciples being in the heart of Leeds? Why wouldn't he? Not every member is built for this type of communal living," he said, gesturing to the grounds ahead of us. "There are some nasty bastards in this club. Bastards that shouldn't be around families. And there's a nasty club in Leeds, ripe for the taking."

"You think that's why he didn't kill Ben?"

"Do you?"

"He beat him half to death. If he was hoping to befriend him, he went the wrong way about it."

"Or, he was torturing him to wear him down, forcing Ben to sign over everything to him."

My head shot up and scanned Macbeth's face. "Do you really believe that?"

He shrugged. "It sounds like Dante; I'm not going to lie. It also explains why he kept you in the dark about it."

"If he expanded to that club, he'd have to tell me, eventually."

"Ben doesn't have the same club Alex had. He took the contacts, the girls, the followers, and moved to a new location. Would you really have known if he covered his tracks well enough? Besides, even if you did, he could have easily twisted it to say he was making something good out of a place that held so much evil."

I opened my mouth and then paused. That did sound like Dante. He had said similar to me, about not letting the horrors of my past control me and turn it into something I enjoyed.

"What do I know?" Macbeth sighed, looking sadder than ever. "I'm just the discarded first-born. It's not like Dante confides in me."

He got up to leave, and I snatched at his elbow. "Do you really believe everything you've just said?"

"I gave you that gun for a reason, Rachel, and that was before I knew about Ben. I was just as much in the dark as you were, but I saw something like this coming. There's evil in Dante, and I didn't want you unprotected. So yes, I've never been more sure of anything. And if you've got any common sense, you'll take yourself far away from here, out of harm's way. There's a war coming, and with members like Ben's friends' part of the equation, do you want to be around when the first bomb goes off?"

He patted my hand, and I let go of him, feeling completely shellshocked.

Had I been completely idiotic?

I mentally ran through all the interactions I had ever had with Dante, seeing a different side of the story.

The man had kidnapped me, burnt my mother's house down, tied me up, starved me, slapped me, spat on me. He had beaten a man in front of me, abandoned me at the hospital, hidden my abuser just a few houses away from me… The more I thought of our time together, the more the rose-tinted glasses fell off, and the more I realised I might be in way more danger than I thought.

I tried to remember Jenna's conversation about not trusting Macbeth. But she had never given me a reason, other than Macbeth seemed calculating. Could he be calculating because he saw more than the club narrative? Could his position as the spare, whilst Dante reined as heir, give him a unique perspective? Jenna was an old lady. She only had Shark's perspective, and he was as close to Dante as Vienna and Hacksaw. He was going to push out Dante's version of events.

I had no idea what to fucking think anymore. I didn't trust Macbeth, but I didn't completely trust Dante, either. There were three sides to every story: your side, their side, and the truth. And I needed to find out what the fucking truth was.

Chapter 46

Rachel

"Rachel! How lovely to hear from you! We've been ever so worried about you."

"Thanks, Mrs Geller." Macbeth had inspired me. We lived in the age of technology. It was easy to find their home number with a quick Google search. I had actually got it from an ad they had posted for a new au pair.

I don't know why that had hurt, but it did.

"How have you been?"

Ahh, she's dropped the whole "call me Elizabeth", I see!

"Probably better than you've been thinking. I'm still here, aren't I?"

"Wonderful!"

Nothing about this was wonderful, you stupid old cow.

"How's Joseph?" I said, my heart pounding. I picked at the skin around my nails, having already chewed them beyond repair.

Just get through this small talk, and then you can ask the important questions.

"Oh, you know kids! They're resilient little things. He stopped crying for you after the first week, and seems well adjusted to his new au pair. Though I have to say," she said, lowering his voice as though we were old friends gossiping. "She's quite stern. She even told Mr Geller off. Can you believe?"

I could believe that.

"She's also much older. We thought it would be best. A young woman would remind Joseph of you too much. But they get along well enough."

What a complete joke that was. She didn't want her husband lusting after another young blonde, more like! She had never done anything for Joseph's best interests.

"Great!" I said, faking enthusiasm. "Hey, so I was just wondering, did you ever get around to sending my things to me?"

"Things?" Mrs Geller repeated, sounding a million miles away and bored with our conversation.

"My clothes, my documents... my passport?"

"But Rachel," she gave me a pitiful laugh, as though I was stupid. "How could we have sent your things without knowing where you are?"

"Macbeth gave you the address, didn't he?"

"He wrote down an address, but I'd rather not repeat it, thank you very much."

"Humour me."

"I shall not. But pass a message on to that young man for me, will you? Vulgar sex references like sixty-nine dine out street, dogging harbour, are not funny."

For fuck's sake, Macbeth.

"He's an idiot. Do you still have my things?" My tone was almost hysterical as my anxiety grew.

"Of course. Mr Geller suggested we post them to the diner, but Lord knows what state they'd end up in. You can give me your address now, if you like?"

"Actually... could you hold on to them a bit longer for me?"

"How much longer? We can't keep your belongings forever, Rachel. That man of yours made it clear you wouldn't be returning, and Joseph has just started bonding with Mrs—"

"I'm not asking you to keep them forever. I know I'm not coming back, that's not what I'm trying to say. I just don't know how long I'll be in this house for."

"You're moving?" She said, sounding suspicious.

"With Dante," I hurried to add. I don't know why. I guess I figured nothing was set in stone, so there was no point risking rumours getting back to Dante. "By the time you send my things, I might not be here, and then I'll be tracking them down all over again. Could you just hold on to them for a week, maximum?"

"I suppose so..."

"Hold on," I said, an idea coming to mind. "I could actually really use those documents – you know, for ID, for mortgage applications and such. If I give you the address of the post office, could you send them there?"

"I can't send your documents to you? Rachel...tell me the truth. Are you okay?"

"I am," I said, ridiculous tears springing to my eyes. "There are just dogs here. I don't want them getting to the post before me. Do you have a pen? I'll give you the address."

Clothes could be replaced. Hell, Dante had already bought me more than enough. But I'd feel much more secure knowing my documents were at least on the same continent as I was.

"Up," Dante demanded, kicking open my bedroom door, frightening me half to death.

"I beg your fucking pardon?" I scowled, remaining at the vanity table.

"Up. We have somewhere to be, and I'm sick of you moping in this room all the time."

I gestured ahead of me, drawing Dante's attention to the makeup I had been applying. "I had no intention of 'moping in this room all the time,'" I mimicked him. "As you can see, I was already getting prepared for plans of my own." Not that I had planned anything exciting. I just didn't want Dante coming in here and accusing me of exactly what he had just accused me of. I had to at least look like I had a life away from him, even if the most exciting plan I could think of was to walk far enough away to seem busy and then walk back.

"Cancel them."

I locked eyes with him in the mirror, pausing the lipstick halfway to my lips. "Well, that won't be happening."

"Did I make it sound like a request?"

"Did I make it sound like there was room for negotiation?"

"Rachel, you're coming with me. If I once again have to satisfy your victim complex by carrying you over my shoulder, I'll do it. I'd rather not. But those are your choices. Meet me downstairs in ten minutes, or I'll come collect you."

He walked back out of the room and shut the door calmly. I swirled around on the stool and threw the lipstick at the empty space where he had just been.

Arrogant bastard!

I knew just as well as he did that I'd be downstairs. Because I knew as well as he did that he didn't dish out threats. I'd been humiliated more than enough by him carrying me through this godforsaken village.

"Not a chance," I hissed, turning on my feet and going to leave. Dante blocked the door, my face smashing against his solid chest. He grabbed the top of my arms and spun me back around, pushing me forward.

"Yes, you are."

I dug my heels in, in a useless attempt to stop him from pushing me any further towards that fucking bed.

"I hardly think so."

"Everyone has one."

"I don't. Bee doesn't."

"Bee is a child, and you will in half an hour."

"I won't," I huffed, pushing my entire body backwards. He scooped me under my arms, forcing me to lean back into him, making me bend my legs, removing all the strength I had been using to dig in my heels.

Nice going, Rachel!

"Dante, I really, really don't want to do this." He pushed me forward, causing me to fall over the leather bed. I scrambled to push myself up, but he was quicker than I was. He grabbed hold of my ass and pushed it up onto the bed.

I quickly flopped over, but my hands were grabbed and pinned above my head.

"Of fucking course you're here!" I hissed at Vienna as he pinned my arms.

"Always happy to help, hair growth buddy!"

"I'll shave your fucking beard off, mark my words."

"That's an unnecessary escalation of threats, Rachel. I'm hurt."

"Fuck off!"

Dante grabbed hold of my ankles and, after a nod to Vienna, they flipped me over onto my stomach. I thrust my ass out, my back arching in an attempt to get away, but Dante just delivered a painful slap to my ass and laughed at me. "We've got a wild one, Ven."

"You're a beautiful girl, Rachel, but threesomes were for my twenties. Put your ass down."

"Fuck the pair of you," I spat at them, fighting to get out of their hold.

"I let you down gently. Please stop propositioning me. I'm just a man. I'm easily worn down."

They both laughed some more, and I silently cursed them both straight to hell and stilled my movements, knowing I was defeated.

That was, until the man came out of the backroom, carrying all sorts of scary looking tools, and I once again fought like a hellcat.

"Rachel!" Dante snapped, pinning the back of my knees with his elbows, leaning his torso on my legs. "You're being fucking ridiculous. It's just a tattoo!"

"A tattoo I don't want!"

"It's part of the initiation. Everyone has one!"

"Bee—"

"Don't you fucking dare say Bee doesn't have one. That's a ridiculous argument and you know it."

"Are you just going to allow this?" I hissed at the tattooist. "Don't you need written consent?"

"You going to revoke my license, sweetie?" He muttered sarcastically.

"I might have known you were another Dante lapdog."

"Is it wise to piss off the man who's about to permanently mark you?" He said, brandishing the tattoo gun in my face. "What we doing?" He said, directing the question to Dante.

"Club patch. Make it pretty, just like her." I spun around in time to see him wink at Vienna.

"Sweet talking me won't help!"

"You can decide where it goes," the tattooist said. "Since you're such a control freak."

"It's not fucking going anywhere!"

"I'm not familiar with that body part."

"Shoulder," Dante said firmly. "Nice and big."

"Like fuck!" I roared, straining harder than ever. I could feel my face growing red, but Vienna and Dante barely seemed to be breaking a sweat pinning me down. "Just a small one, please," I begged, realising this was happening, whether or not I liked it. "Somewhere on my neck or something. Or my wrist. I've heard wrists don't hurt."

"Rachel, you're not hiding the club patch on your wrist like you're ashamed of us. No old lady of mine is going to be ashamed of who she is and where she belongs. You can have it on your shoulder or plastered over your face. It's up to you."

"I'd go with the shoulder," Vienna said. "Don't want to ruin your pretty little face."

"So you admit that a tattoo would ruin me!"

"I'd imagine it would keep a permanent scowl on your face. I don't want to see that every day. It's depressing."

"Hey!" I snapped at the tattooist, seeing him dipping his needles in ink. "Don't you be getting things ready! I do not agree with this."

"I'm doing it, anyway. I suggest you stay still," he muttered, coming closer to me. "One wrong move and this will be ruined. It'll look as pretty as you allow me to let it look. Make your choice, Rachel."

I stilled, knowing I was defeated. I closed my eyes, hissing as soon as the needle touched my skin.

I'd kill Dante for this.

Chapter 47

Dante

"It turned out lovely, didn't it?" I said, leaning against the door frame as I watched Rachel twist in the mirror to inspect her tattoo.

She had taken herself straight home when the tattoo was finished and hadn't left her room all night.

At least, I thought she hadn't left her room. I went to bed and noticed she had slashed all my pillows to pieces, feathers covering my room. She had smashed the mirror, stomped on the clock face, and stabbed a helmet through the face guard, right where my eyes would have been.

I didn't even bother commenting on her temper tantrum. I had simply turned around, walked straight to her room, and climbed into bed next to her.

She tried to push me out to start with, and when she realised I wasn't budging, she shuffled away from me. I followed her; she shuffled some more. Eventually, she shuffled so far; she ended up falling off the edge of the bed. After slapping me in the face with her pillow, she had stormed to the bathroom and slept in the bath.

I had laughed so hard, I genuinely thought I was going to strain something or give myself a hernia. I had laughed even harder this morning when I had walked into the bathroom bright and early, flicked the light on, blinding her with the fluorescent bulb, and snapped a picture of her on my phone.

I went straight to the study and printed the picture out and pinned it to the toast I sent up with Bee to take to her.

"It looks awful," she said flatly.

"It's healing. If you hadn't thrown yourself around in bed last night, it wouldn't have rubbed so much."

"I'll fucking throw you around," she muttered under her breath.

"What was that?" I asked pleasantly.

"Do you know what? I'm sick of this. You're a fucking cunt, Dante."

"Tell me something I don't know."

"No, I don't think you do know. I don't think you understand how wrong this was."

"So kidnapping Ben and torturing him for you was perfectly okay, but a tattoo is too far?" I snapped, feeling my anger growing, the same as it always did when I was around her.

She threw a nasty glance at me. "Don't pretend you did that for me."

"Excuse me?"

"You heard."

"Who else would I have done it for?"

"The same reason you do anything. You do it for yourself. You said it yourself. You're a selfish bastard."

"I'm failing to see what interest I would have in beating a nobody like Ben, if not to protect you."

"Protect me from what?" She finally snapped. "Ben hadn't been near me in years. You didn't protect me from anything! It had already happened! You did it for yourself!"

"You've obviously decided to start another argument today. So go on," I said dryly. "Tell me what crime you think I've committed."

"As if you don't know."

"Clearly I don't."

"No, clearly you're a better liar than I thought."

"I really don't have time for this. Macbeth wants me to meet him in ten minutes. Can you just spit it out?"

"Answer me this: Do you, or do you not have plans to expand?"

"Eventually…" I said, eyeing her with suspicion. A light of anger flared in her eyes. But for the life of me, I couldn't figure out why.

"And do you, or do you not, plan on using Ben's club?"

"I can make use of it. Why are you asking this?"

"And what about the others?" She snapped, ignoring my question.

"What others?"

"You know what others. The other groomers, the other rapists, the other recruiters, the other abusers. The *others*!" She hissed at me.

"They'll be dealt with."

"You mean recruited?"

"Excuse me?" My head flew back in shock.

"And who else will you be sending there? Because I know damn well, the people here are not the only members of your club."

"They're not," I nodded. "I never said they were. I told you we had members up and down the country. Different branches, but they're all part of the Devil's Disciples."

"So, who will you be sending there? Don't answer, I can guess. You'll be sending like-minded people, am I right?"

"You think I would have rapists in my club?"

"You tell me, because you're sending them to a rapist's house. Everyone knows what goes on there, Dante. It's just no one talks about it. It's whispered about, and people know to avoid it. Now you're the one who is going to be whispered about."

"Nothing new there, then."

"Do you think this is fucking funny?"

"Am I laughing?" I growled at her.

"You're mocking me!" She shouted. "Do you seriously think I'm going to live with a man who lives like that? Who not only supports that place, but sends his men to live there. What is it, Dante? Are they going to be the new recruiters?"

That did it.

I marched forward and grabbed hold of her, shaking her small frame until her teeth rattled. "Is that what you really think—"

"Not think, *know*! I've heard all about it! Why didn't you kill Ben? Is it because you were hoping he'd give you everything if you pushed him enough? How convenient I came and finished the job for you. I made myself the perfect little scapegoat!"

Her words shouldn't hurt. I always knew she didn't have a high opinion of me. But for some reason, they cut me sharper than the knife she had stabbed me with our first night together.

"Is that really how little you think of me?"

"Have you ever given me a reason to think otherwise?"

"I only came up here to tell you your mother is downstairs. And believe it or not, I knew you were going to lash out. I knew you were going to be a brat because of the tattoo. But this? This is disgusting. Pack your shit and leave with your mother. I'm fucking done. Think what you want of me, but I won't be labelled a fucking rapist and child abuser."

"No, you would never be labelled that. You're just an enabler," she said coldly, her eyes full of hatred.

"Go see your mother, Rachel," I said, barely recognising my cold voice. "Go with her before I do something I fucking regret."

I walked away from her.

For good.

Chapter 48

Rachel

My stomach churned as I ran down the stairs. I couldn't shake the image of Dante's face. He looked... he looked fucking broken.

It's an act, Rachel. Remember what Macbeth said!

But was it an act? I didn't think anyone could fake a look like that. I didn't think I was even capable of hurting him like that.

I hadn't even meant what I said. It wasn't how I wanted to approach the topic at all. But, as always, I suffered from verbal diarrhoea. He hurt me, and I had to lash out and make him hurt, too. And now I might have fucked things up for good.

"Rachel!" my mother called as I walked into the bar, and I did a double take as I saw her stiffly sat in one of the booths, distracting me from all thoughts of Dante.

"Mother," I said cooly, shooting a glance over my shoulder at the empty staircase. I saw Macbeth come from the kitchen and make his way up the stairs, and hoped his meeting with Dante would calm him down. I'd have to deal with our problems later.

"You're looking well," my mother said as I sat opposite her.

"That's a lie."

"That's a lie," she admitted with a wry grin. "Your hair looks awful."

"Thank you. Are we done here?" I said, getting back to my feet.

"No! I'm sorry. Sit. Please," she said in a small voice.

"What do you want?" I said with a sigh. "I'm tired, mother." I could already feel myself slipping back into the blank, aloof personality I always portrayed around her.

"I wanted to see how you are."

"I'm fine, as you can see."

"Don't be difficult, Rachel."

Ahh… there it was. Don't be selfish, Rachel. Don't be difficult, Rachel. Don't be anything other than what I want you to be, Rachel.

"I never did thank you for saving me, Rachel. From the fire," she added when I didn't respond.

Of course it was the fucking fire. What else would I have saved her from?

Beige hell. That's what. But knowing my mother, she wouldn't have considered that saving.

"Mmm," I mumbled, because I had nothing else to say.

"Rachel… Please."

"What, mother? Yes, I saved you. But I wouldn't have had anything to save you from had I just stayed away. We both know it."

"It happened. We have to move on."

Well, well, well. Who are you and what have you done with Rebecca Brooks?

"I'm surprised you'd come here. Especially given what Dante did, and the things you said to me."

"Well," she said, twisting her lips. "Dante came to see me."

"He did?" I said, my mouth falling open.

"Mhmm. He said he would pay for all repairs on the house. Or pay for a new one entirely. He didn't apologise, though."

"No," I said with a bark of dry laughter. "I can't imagine he did."

"He also told me a few things, Rachel. Thing I wished I had heard from you."

"Like what?" I said, squirming uncomfortably. I sighed in relief as Vienna chose that moment to bring over two beers. "Thanks, Ven."

"Always happy to help," he said with a wink, repeating his words from the tattoo shop. "Looks nice." He grinned and then walked off.

"That beard is disgusting," my mother grimaced.

"He knows," I said with a small grin. "He says he keeps it to annoy his ex. He'll tell her it still smells of her. It pisses her off."

"Smells of her? How can it smell of her?" I raised my eyebrows and gave my mother a pointed look. "Oh," she gasped, shooting a look at Vienna. "Oh," she repeated, this time in disgust. "I've a mind to go shave it off him myself."

358

"He'll snap your arm off and beat you with it before he lets that happen."

"I can't tell if you're joking."

I didn't answer, I just picked my beer up and took a grateful sip, memories of mine and Dante's game playing in my mind. I put the beer back down. Alcohol was not my friend. The last person I wanted to loosen my tongue around was my mother.

"So…" she said, shuffling uncomfortably. "About Dante."

"I was hoping you might have forgotten," I said sheepishly.

"You should have told me, Rachel."

"What exactly did Dante say?"

"He told me about what really happened with Alex and the things you went through." Her hand reached over the table to cover my own. "Why didn't you tell us?"

"Dante had no right."

"I'm glad he did. It makes things… easier to understand."

"You mean easier to forgive?"

"That too," she admitted. "I know you weren't happy with us, but you also weren't the easiest person to live with. You said and did some pretty horrendous things to us. Your dad was on anti-depressants at the time. We were both in therapy – both for ourselves and seeing a child psychologist to try to understand you better."

"I had no idea," I mumbled, the guilt making my stomach flip.

"We didn't want you to know. We didn't want you to know the extent of how much you were hurting us. We were just trying to be there. We wanted to protect you – which, I think, is what you were trying to do as well by not telling us about Alex."

"I didn't want you to think it was my fault," I admitted in a small voice. Tears sprang to my mother's eyes, and she squeezed my hand tighter.

"It was *never* your fault. Anyway," she said, pulling back and flapping her eyes in front of her face to dry her tears. "It's not all bad news. At least I'll be able to bring your dad with me next time."

A crash from upstairs had us both jumping in fright. I looked at Vienna, who mumbled something to Shark.

"Nothing to worry about, folks. Dante and Mac," he said with a shrug, and the rest of the bar gave a whoop, knowing what the brothers were like. I noticed Shark slip out of the door, though, and make his way upstairs.

"Would you like that?" my mother said, pulling my attention back to her.

"Like what?"

"For me to bring your dad!" she said with a small laugh.

"What are you talking about?"

She huffed in frustration. "Do you and that man of yours not talk at all? He took the evidence to the police. Your dad is getting out on parole. Dante showed them Alex's crimes and made it look like self-defence."

"I beg your fucking pardon?"

"Don't swear, Rachel."

"I'm sorry. I beg your flaming pardon?"

"Wait," my mother said, her eyes growing wide. "Did you not know?"

"I had no fucking clue," I said, sweat beginning to break out over my entire body.

Oh god.

What the fuck had I done?

"Dante sorted the whole thing. He went to the police with written statements from other victims, photos, videos… you name it, he had it. I asked where it came from, and he said I would rather not know, but rest assured they paid with their blood. I don't condone violence, but in this instance…" she sniffed, her nose high in the air, letting the statement go unspoken.

Paid with their blood…

Ben's blood.

Oh, God…

Macbeth had fucking played me.

"Mother," I said, shooting to my feet. "I am so sorry. I've got to go." I needed to get upstairs. Macbeth was alone with him.

"What? But I've just arrived! I was hoping—"

"Another time. I promise! Please. Please, just trust me. Dante is in trouble."

"What?" she said in a horrified voice.

"I don't have time to explain! Vienna!" I shouted. "Dante's in danger."

He didn't hesitate. He saw the wild look on my face, the panic I was only barely keeping contained. He grabbed the shotgun off the wall behind the bar and ran up the stairs with me hot on his heals.

Fucking Macbeth. He knew what he was doing. He had planted the seeds of doubt in my mind. He had played on my weakness and vulnerability. He had lied straight to my face but sprinkled in enough facts to make it all believable.

And now Dante was the one paying the price.

Vienna took the stairs two at a time, and I raced after him like the devil himself was snapping at my feet.

We flew down the corridor, my heart beating in my ears. I could hear my blood rushing, making a roaring sound in my head.

And then Vienna kicked the door open, and the rushing disappeared.

There was nothing but silence.

Because Dante was not in the bedroom, and neither was Macbeth.

But there was blood.

And a lot of it.

A pained moan had our heads snapping to the side, seeing a stabbed Shark struggling to stand, using the wall as support.

"What happened?" Vienna demanded, shoving the shotgun in my hands as he raced to help his friend.

"They took him," he panted as Vienna hauled him to his feet. His face was twisted in pain, and he nearly snapped Vienna's hand as he pressed a t-shirt to his wound.

"Who took him?" I snapped.

"The Riders?" Vienna asked.

"I have no fucking idea. I didn't recognise any of them. They came through the window." I looked at the window, noticing the frame had been removed.

How long had they been planning this?

"Macbeth went with them," Shark panted. "Rachel," he said gravely, his eyes locking with mine, and said words that chilled me to the bone. "Dante wasn't in a good way. If we don't find him soon, they'll kill him."

Printed in Great Britain
by Amazon

47919094R10205